PRAISE FOR *INTERFERENCE*

"Readers will fully engage with the various characters as Parks convincingly reveals the science that buttresses the suspenseful plot. Michael Crichton fans won't want to miss this one."

—*Publishers Weekly* (starred review)

"Parks' suspenseful novel will beguile, entrance, and fool the sharpest readers."

—*Kirkus Reviews*

"To be pleasurably bamboozled, try this nifty scientific thriller by a onetime *Washington Post* reporter who writes prizewinning novels over breakfast at a Virginia Hardee's."

—*Washington Post*

"A cutting-edge stunner (that) reminded me of Michael Crichton in all the right ways . . . A book that checked all the technological boxes, while telling a great story."

—*Providence Journal*

"A smart, innovative thriller that evokes the best of Michael Crichton and Blake Crouch. Parks proposes the seemingly improbable, makes it plausible, and then weaves in twists and turns, taking the reader on a mind-bending ride."

—Robert Dugoni, *New York Times*, *Wall Street Journal*, and Amazon bestselling author of the Tracy Crosswhite series

"*Interference* brings all the right ingredients to a novel! Brad Parks has created a story with a fascinating plotline and great characters—an up-all-night page-turner. I loved it!"

—Heather Graham, *New York Times* bestselling author

"Utterly absorbing, relentlessly paced, and cunningly assembled. Brad Parks is the sort of master craftsman who makes everything look easy. I hate him a little bit."

—Marcus Sakey, *Wall Street Journal* bestselling author of *Afterlife*

UNTHINKABLE

OTHER TITLES BY BRAD PARKS

Stand-Alone Novels

The Carter Ross Series

UNTHINKABLE

BRAD
PARKS

 THOMAS & MERCER

Published by Thomas & Mercer, Seattle

www.apub.com

Amazon, the Amazon logo, and Thomas & Mercer are trademarks of Amazon.com, Inc., or its affiliates.

ISBN-13: 9781542024952 (hardcover)
ISBN-10: 1542024951 (hardcover)

ISBN-13: 9781542022606 (paperback)
ISBN-10: 1542022606 (paperback)

Cover design by Anna Laytham

Printed in the United States of America

First Edition

To Patricia S. Olson, the first author in my life and still one of my favorite people

CHAPTER 1

NATE

When I came to, breaching that little-understood divide between the murky depths of insentience and the bright conscious world, the first thing I became aware of was my tongue.

It was exploring the inner recesses of my gums, probing the soft tissue for damage, doing a census of my teeth, all in a kind of doped man's reflex.

What it found was a mouth that, while otherwise intact, had been flooded with an anesthetic funk—the faintly metallic aftertaste of whatever had been used to sedate me.

The next sensation to penetrate my still-fogged brain came via my nose. It reported a sharp, astringent smell. Like industrial-grade soap. It was coming from my right hand, which was slightly damp.

I flexed my fingers—all ten of them, still there—and wiggled my toes, also operational.

This strange softness surrounded me. A pillow-top mattress. And sheets. Really nice sheets. Either satin, or cotton with a seriously high thread count.

As the rest of my faculties slowly returned, I replayed what little I knew about my current circumstances. I had been puttering around the house, retightening the child locks on some cabinets, about to get started on fixing a leaky faucet, when a man I had never seen before appeared on our back porch and knocked on the door.

Solicitors, proselytizers, and other strangers usually came to the front. But he seemed harmless enough. Average in height, just past middling in age, unexceptional in dress, almost as if he was cultivating his blandness.

When I opened the door, he flashed me an apologetic smile, like he was sorry to bother me—one nice guy to another.

Then he shot me in the neck with a tranquilizer dart.

Whatever drug it carried hit hard and fast. As I fell to my knees, two more men, dressed in black tactical gear, came toward me through our back gate.

My scream never made it past my throat. And I remember recognizing there was no way, in my rapidly diminishing state, I could stop these men from doing whatever they wanted with me.

But what really alarmed me—more than having been randomly assaulted, more than my burgeoning loss of awareness—was that I had seen their faces.

Having once been a lawyer, I was at least mildly familiar with the felonious mindset. Criminals only allowed their faces to be seen when they knew they weren't going to be leaving behind any witnesses.

So this was it.

They were going to kill me.

What I didn't know—what I couldn't even begin to guess—was why.

If called on to testify about my existence in a court of law, I would raise my right hand and swear to Almighty God that I, Nate Lovejoy, was basically nobody: an ordinary stay-at-home dad whose existence was of little consequence to anyone but my wife, Jenny, and our two preschool-age daughters.

As a full-time caregiver, I spent my days changing diapers, cleaning messes, enforcing nap time, and chasing a pair of rambunctious little girls from room to room of our Richmond, Virginia, town house. It was thankless, monotonous, joyful work.

But, more to the point, it was completely innocuous.

I was innocuous.

To the best of my knowledge, I was not harboring any valuable secrets. I didn't do drugs, gamble, or frequent houses of ill repute. I had not crossed any international crime syndicates, witnessed any illicit activities, or participated in any unlawful ventures that might have brought me to the attention of dangerous people.

It seemed unlikely their motivation was ransom. Jenny was a partner at Richmond's largest law firm, so we were comfortable, but not especially wealthy; and neither of our families had money either.

The kidnappers also weren't interested in my kids. I had dropped off three-year-old Parker and eighteen-month-old Cate with my in-laws for the day so I could accomplish the aforementioned home-maintenance projects. These men had come for me during one of the rare times when I was alone.

So what, exactly, was this about?

I opened my eyes.

And everything got weirder.

It was like waking up in a museum. I was lying in a four-poster bed that, in and of itself, could have been the crowning life achievement of a virtuoso craftsperson.

But that was just the beginning. Elaborate hand-carved moldings ringed the ceiling. Magnificent wainscoting covered the lower portions of the walls. Queen Anne–style furniture—each piece an antique more priceless than the last—filled the floor.

Then I got to the room's real showpiece, hanging above the unlit fireplace in front of me. It was a Rembrandt. An honest-to-goodness, no-doubt-about-it Rembrandt.

To its left was a Vermeer. The works of other Dutch masters covered much of the remaining wall space. I was surrounded by art whose value was easily in the tens of millions.

Where was I? What was this place? And why hadn't I been hand-cuffed or restrained in some way when I had so clearly been brought here against my will?

I sat up in bed, propping myself on my elbows. To my left were two windows on either side of a door that led outside—perhaps to a balcony, except I couldn't say for sure. All three portals were sealed with this semiopaque vinyl covering that allowed light in but didn't let me see out.

All I could say for sure was that it was quiet outside. There were no sounds to indicate this was an urban area.

The quality of the sunlight coming through the shades suggested it was around lunchtime, which made sense because it had been mid-morning when I was taken. I just hoped it was still Monday.

Any further observation was cut short by a whirring noise to my right. A mechanical lock was releasing itself. The main door to the bedroom opened, and a man in black tactical gear came in behind it.

It was one of the men who'd abducted me. He was shorter than me—I'm six foot four, so most people are—but stockier, laden with gym muscles.

I immediately scrambled off the bed to the other side, bracing myself to fight or run or be murdered.

"Dude, you're cool, relax," he said, holding up his empty hands. "I was just coming to see if you wanted anything to eat. The chef here is amazing. He can do pretty much anything."

The chef.

Because of course a household like this had a chef.

Meaning Muscles here was . . . a waiter or something?

"I'm not hungry," I said warily.

"You sure? He could grill a rib eye for you in, like, no time. And I guarantee it'll be one of the ten best steaks you've ever had. Or he makes these duck-fat brussels sprouts. Amazing."

"No thanks."

"What about a drink? We've got fresh organic juices that are flown in from, like, Bolivia. Or maybe something a little stronger? Some wine? A cocktail? If you're a beer guy, we've got a dynamite local IPA."

I was a beer guy. But I didn't want to fuzzy my mind just as it was becoming unfuzzied.

"I'm fine, thanks."

The guy shrugged. "Okay. Rogers will be up in a second."

"Who's Rogers?" I asked.

But the man just turned and left.

Duck-fat brussels sprouts? What kind of kidnapping was this?

I walked to the door the man had just exited. It had a key-card reader, recessed into the doorframe. I depressed the handle and pulled, but nothing budged.

On the other side of the room, the door that led outside was also locked. The windows had thick muntin that, upon closer inspection, was actually reinforced with steel bars. I wasn't getting out that way.

The only other door led to a bathroom that had no windows or other apparent means of egress.

Meaning this suite was essentially an incredibly ornate prison cell.

I was still in the bathroom, exploring the last details of a ceiling exhaust fan, wondering if I could unscrew the grate, when I heard, "Hello, hello?"

It was a male voice. I returned to the bedroom to see the man who had shot me with the dart.

He was in his midsixties, with a slight build and side-parted gun-metal-gray hair. He wore khakis and a light-blue polo shirt, neatly tucked. But I already recognized him as that peculiarly creepy version of human being: the person who could look harmless while inflicting great harm.

"Nice to see you up and about, Nate," he said, like he hadn't been the one who tranquilized me.

And how did he know my name?

"Why don't you have a seat?" he said, gesturing toward a gilded, inlaid mahogany table ringed with Louis XVI chairs, any one of which probably cost more than what was currently in my bank account.

"I'll stand," I said as he sat. "Who are you?"

"I'm Rogers."

"Is that a first name or a last name?"

"Last. My first name is Lorton. But everyone calls me Rogers."

"Where am I?" I asked.

"You're in a safe place."

"Why does my hand smell like soap?"

"Don't worry about that," he said. "You really don't need to worry about anything."

His tone was neutral, patient, calm—so at odds with the panic tumbling through me.

"If there's nothing to worry about, can I leave?"

"No," he said simply.

"So I'm a prisoner."

"That seems like such a punitive word. I'd like you to think of me as a friend, and of yourself as our guest. My boss is a very hospitable man, and he wants you to enjoy yourself while you're here. Why don't you relax and let the drugs wear off a little more and then we can talk. Would you like something to eat or drink?"

"I've already been asked that and no. Let's talk now."

"Okay, if you'd rather do it that way," Rogers said. "I'd like to start with an ethical question, if I may."

"An ethical question."

"Yes. What if I told you that killing one person would save the lives of five other people. Would you do it, Nate?"

This was the classic trolley problem: you can either let a runaway trolley kill five people; or you can pull a switch, diverting it to a track where it will kill just one person—but making you directly responsible for the death.

It wasn't a game I felt like playing at the moment. But given that I was trapped in this room with no apparent way out, maybe it was better than the game that would come next if I didn't cooperate.

"Well, it would depend on who the person was," I said. "If it was killing one innocent kindergarten teacher to save five convicted murderers? No, I wouldn't do it."

"Ah, so for you it's a question of the perceived value of the human beings involved. Excellent. In that case, you would kill five murderers to save one kindergarten teacher. Do I have that right?"

"I mean, yeah, probably. But again it could depend on the circumstances. What if the murderers were all teenagers who might be rehabilitated or do some good for society someday and the kindergarten teacher was old and suffering from a fatal disease?"

"Okay, then let me simplify things. What if killing one person would save the lives of five average people, people who were the same mix of good and bad that we all are? Or ten average people? Or a hundred? Is there some number large enough that you wouldn't have to factor in the value of the life being sacrificed against the lives being saved?"

"I'm not sure. What does this have to do with anything?"

"It has to do with your framework for moral reasoning, Nate. I'm just trying to understand where you're coming from. Give me a ballpark figure. A thousand? Ten thousand?"

"This is ridiculous," I said. "I don't know who you are. I don't know where I am. I don't know why you're asking."

"So you won't answer my question?"

"No. Not until you at least tell me a little more about what's going on."

Rogers nodded. "Very well. Have a seat, though. I'm getting tired just looking at you standing there."

"Fine," I said, pulling out one of the chairs on the other side of the table and planting myself in it.

"That's better. Now, I guess I should start by telling you about our host. This house belongs to a man named Vanslow DeGange. It's one of his many houses, actually. Have you ever heard that name before?"

"No."

"Good. We work hard to make sure that's the case. Everything I'm about to tell you about Mr. DeGange is confidential. It must be kept secret."

"And why is that?"

"There are those who wouldn't approve of our ways," Rogers said.

"Because what you're doing is illegal?"

"Illegal, probably. Amoral, absolutely not. That's a big distinction around here, what's legally correct versus what's morally correct. We lean heavily on the latter."

"And what happens if I tell someone?"

He allowed himself a small smile. "We're just becoming acquainted with each other, Nate. I don't want to get into threats."

"Yet you just implied one."

"True. Though, to be honest, even if you did try to divulge what I'm about to share, no one would believe you. You would be ignored, dismissed as a lunatic."

"I'm sorry, I still don't know what you're talking about."

"Right. Of course you don't." Rogers paused, like he knew he was about to unpack a difficult concept and wanted to give me an extra moment to gather myself.

Then he said, "It may sound fantastical, but Mr. DeGange has the ability to understand how certain events will unfold with total and complete accuracy."

"He can see the future?" I said, duly incredulous.

"Something like that. He can't see everything in the future—just as no one can see everything in the present. But sometimes, especially when he really concentrates on a person or a subject, an idea about what will happen next arrives in his head. And he is able to recognize it as being valid."

"Ah. Right."

"You don't believe me."

He said it as a statement, not a question.

"Does it even matter? I've been drugged, kidnapped, and am being held against my will. What I believe doesn't seem to have a lot of bearing on my current circumstances."

"But you're skeptical."

"Of course I am," I said.

"You should be. I was just like you when I was first approached. It's part of my job to convince you everything you're about to hear is real. I know that's probably impossible right away, so for now please listen with an open mind. Or, better yet, look around. As you can tell, Mr. DeGange has used his gift to amass an incredible fortune. But he's also used it to help humanity, to save it from tragedy. And he has gathered around him a group of people who assist him in that endeavor. We've seen his predictions come true many times, enough that we know it couldn't be a fluke or explicable by any other means. And now we follow his orders. We call ourselves 'the Praesidium.' That's Latin for 'protector.'"

"The Praesidium," I repeated. "So you're the disciples, the true believers."

"I suppose so, though Mr. DeGange strongly discourages the use of sacred language. The Praesidium is not a cult. Mr. DeGange does not claim to be a god. His abilities are a manifestation of science and evolution, not divinity."

"Okay, sure," I said. "And what, exactly, does this nongod tell you to do?"

"We're getting to that. But please allow me to continue. It turns out that when a human being dies, there's a dip in what Mr. DeGange refers to as the currents of the universe. But if you can make the opposite happen—if you can save the life in question—there's a rise. When that occurs, when a dip is replaced with a rise, it creates a ripple in the currents. Most of us have no awareness of these ripples whatsoever. But Mr. DeGange can feel them. Do you follow me?"

"He has a sixth sense."

"Yes. Very good. And now we get back around to why I started with the ethical question that I did. The ripples are very powerful. And Mr. DeGange can not only sense them; he has developed a kind of instinct for understanding what will trigger them. In particular, Mr. DeGange is sometimes able to foresee when eliminating one person in the present can avert a much larger catastrophe in the future, thus saving many lives."

"Eliminating as in . . . killing them?"

"That's right," Rogers said. "Though, by most people's moral calculations, it's an act that is completely justified."

I looked at the Rembrandt above the fireplace. A seventeenth-century man with an agonized expression stared back at me.

"All right, Rogers. Let's just say for sake of argument I've bought in. Your boss saves lives by killing people. What does any of this have to do with me?"

"Actually," he said, "it has to do with your wife."

CHAPTER 2

JENNY

Jenny had not visited this exact house before. Just a lot like it.

It was shotgun-style, sided in yellow clapboard, with an asphalt roof many years past its sell-by date. The properties on either side contained familiar markers of urban decay: concrete front steps to nowhere, the dwellings they once led to having long ago been demolished.

A pair of basketball shoes with the laces tied together hung from a nearby power line. An advertisement of sorts. Not for sneakers.

Jenny had been out to this neighborhood often enough that she didn't pay much attention. Nor was she bothered by the two teenagers at the corner gawking at the white lady in the tailored navy-blue skirt suit who clearly didn't belong in this part of town.

When you're a six-foot-tall woman—and you reached your adult height in the eighth grade—you get used to the stares. And you either shrink your shoulders, put on flats, and pretend you really couldn't beat the boys at basketball; or you eventually learn to do what Jenny did.

Carry yourself with pride. Wear heels. And kick everyone's ass.

The other partners at Carter, Morgan & Ross hated that Jenny Welker came out here, to this derelict section of Richmond's East End. Why didn't she send an associate or a paralegal? Or outsource this part to some ham-and-egg attorney with what they delicately termed to be "local knowledge"—read: dark skin—who would sign up clients in exchange for a small bounty?

Better yet, why didn't she just drop this Hail Mary loser of a lawsuit to begin with?

But Jenny was generating enough revenue elsewhere that she could afford to take on a passion project. Plus, the potential dollar figures involved made this a long shot worth taking.

It had started two years earlier as a pro bono case by one of the associates Jenny supervised. The client was a woman with terminal lung cancer who was being given a hard time by her insurance company.

Then her pastor mentioned that this was his fifth parishioner to be diagnosed with lung cancer in the last two years. And, wasn't it strange, none of them smoked.

That one offhand comment had launched the associate, and then Jenny herself, into what was now a mass action tort claim with 279 clients—and growing.

And, sure, Jenny could have relied on underlings to sign up number 280. But she had never wanted to practice what she thought of as database law, where the plaintiffs existed as little more than names on a spreadsheet. She felt that getting to know her clients—and their families, and their suffering—would allow her to more passionately advocate on their behalf.

Plus, she liked the people here. At heart, she was still a farmer's daughter. And the folks in this neighborhood reminded her of her neighbors in Surry, the rural Virginia county where she grew up. They didn't necessarily have the polish or sophistication of an equity partner at Carter, Morgan & Ross. But they also didn't have the self-importance, the mindlessly unexamined privilege, or the unabashed pretentiousness.

They were real.

And so she climbed up to the front porch of the house on North Twenty-Second Street that belonged to Clyde and Danece Henderson. Ignoring the **POSTED: NO TRESPASSING** sign, she knocked on the door.

A rheumy-eyed man a few inches shorter than Jenny answered the door.

"Can I help you?" he asked.

"Mr. Henderson?" Jenny asked hopefully.

"Yeah."

"I'm Jenny Welker. I'm with Carter, Morgan, and Ross."

"Uh-huh."

"Did you get the letter I sent you and your wife?"

"You the lawyer?"

"Yes, sir."

"Yeah, I got your letter," he said, without allowing any indication as to what he might have thought about it.

She was, by now, accustomed to the guardedness. It was the same thing an outsider faced in Surry, where it was generally accepted that educated, well-dressed people only came around to take advantage of the locals.

"Do you mind if I come in so we can talk about it?" Jenny asked.

Henderson cast a glance over his shoulder. "Afraid my wife isn't feeling very well."

"I'm sorry about that. But that's why I'm here."

He nodded. "Okay. Hang on. Let me tell her we got company."

Henderson closed the door behind himself, leaving Jenny alone on the front porch. One of the kids from the corner, now on a bike, was riding past for another look.

She dipped her head toward him. He pedaled harder, leaving the gesture unacknowledged.

Perhaps two minutes later, the front door opened.

"Come on," Henderson said.

Jenny followed him inside and to the left, where a small living room was dominated by a bed. The room smelled of peppermint air freshener and terminal illness.

The woman sitting up in bed—propped on some pillows, trying to look dignified—was obviously Danece Henderson. According to public records, Danece was fifty-eight. She looked twenty years older. Her salt-and-pepper hair was thin enough that the light from a nearby lamp bounced off her scalp.

A clear tube fastened under her nose led to an oxygen tank next to the bed.

Jenny introduced herself again.

"How are you feeling?" she asked.

"Been better," Danece said. "Can't get up the stairs no more. That's why I'm down here."

"I understand you've been diagnosed with COPD?"

Danece nodded. Chronic obstructive pulmonary disease was an umbrella term covering a number of conditions that affected breathing. It was a fancy way of saying your lungs were slowly dying. None of the diseases associated with COPD had a true cure, just varying rates at which they killed you.

"And you never smoked, is that right?"

"That's right," Danece said.

Jenny turned toward Clyde. "And you never smoked either."

"Little bit when I was in the army, before we got together. But not in a long time."

"Then you're really perfect candidates to join our lawsuit," Jenny said. "Did you read that letter I sent?"

Clyde looked uncomfortably at his wife, then back to Jenny.

"We read it," he said. "Can't say a lot of it really sank in. I been getting a lot of letters lately. Most of them from people saying we owe them money. Gets so I don't want to go to the mailbox no more. Between the medical bills and Danece not being able to work . . . it's been tough.

We're four months behind on the rent too. Landlord keeps threatening us. If we get kicked out of here, I don't know where we gonna go."

"I understand," Jenny said. "Let me just start at the beginning. Commonwealth Power and Light has a coal-fired electricity plant not far from here, in Upper Shockoe Valley. It's an old plant, one of the oldest in the country, actually. Even with some of the modern scrubbers they've installed, the smoke that spews out of it is very dirty, filled with mercury, lead, all kinds of other heavy metals, and pollutants. We have experts who can prove that under prevailing wind patterns, a lot of that smoke falls right around where you live. We have other experts who will testify it's making people sick—with lung cancer, COPD, asthma, things like that—and that those illnesses are unusually concentrated in this area, to a degree that simply wouldn't happen if the Shockoe Generation Plant weren't where it is. Have you ever seen *Erin Brockovich*?"

"That's that movie with what's-her-name," Clyde said.

"Julia Roberts," Danece said.

"Exactly," Jenny said. "That was all about water making people sick. This lawsuit is similar, except it's with air."

Clyde's attention had been fixed on Jenny. Now he was looking at his wife.

"So her lungs, this is because of them. The power company."

"We believe so, yes."

"And what's this gonna cost us, joining your lawsuit?" Danece asked.

"Nothing. All the up-front expenses associated with the suit will be borne by my law firm. The firm will get one-third of whatever we recoup from CP and L, after expenses. If we lose, no one gets anything."

"And if we win?" Clyde asked.

"If we are able to determine CP and L is responsible, there will be a separate calculation done for each plaintiff to determine damages."

She went through some of the factors. Loss of income. Medical bills—past, present, and future. Pain and suffering. A life-care plan, so that as Danece's condition worsened, she could have someone come in to help care for her. Loss of consortium for Clyde.

Jenny stressed that this was all just an estimate, that nothing was in any way guaranteed, that even if they got a favorable judgment, they would have to fight for every dime as CP&L appealed.

But then she spit out the final number she had added up in her head.

$1.5 million.

Neither of the Hendersons immediately responded. The only sound in the room was Danece laboring to suck oxygen into her ruined lungs.

But Jenny had been doing this long enough. She could see the answer on their faces.

Clyde already had tears in his eyes.

CHAPTER 3

NATE

As soon as Rogers said the words *your wife*, an electric current ran through my spine. The hair on my arms stood up.

"What about her?" I asked.

"You are, of course, aware of the lawsuit she's working on."

"Which one? The one with the power company?"

"Yes. According to Mr. DeGange, it's going to be successful. Too successful."

"What does that mean?"

"In a few days' time—Saturday morning at eight twenty-eight a.m., to be exact—she is going to brainstorm a novel legal argument that has never before been applied to the Clean Air Act. It will not only result in her winning this lawsuit against Commonwealth Power and Light; it will bring a massive wave of tort claims against power companies all over America. Think of the asbestos lawsuits of the seventies and eighties, only on an even larger scale, because more people live near power plants and breathe the air. Hungry lawyers will race to sign up plaintiffs. Power companies will realize they can no longer afford to release coal pollutants into the atmosphere."

"Well, that's got to be a good thing, right?" I said. "How many Americans die as a result of pollution from coal-fired power plants? Jenny has shown me the numbers. It's something like thirteen thousand a year. She would be saving them. That's a lot of good ripples for your boss to feel, right?"

Rogers shook his head. "I'm afraid not."

"Why not?"

"Because of the law of unintended consequences."

I felt another electric shock when he said *unintended*.

"Coal is still responsible for about thirty percent of the electric energy generated in America," Rogers said. "It's an enormous amount of energy. People like to say, 'Oh, just stop burning coal,' but it's much harder to actually do. You can't expect power companies to tell their customers to stop using their air conditioners and refrigerators. What the power companies will do instead is come up with a powerful new scrubbing mechanism. It will be cheap, relatively easy to install, and will make it safe to burn coal."

"Again, this sounds like a positive development."

More headshaking. "This scrubbing mechanism will require sodium hexafluoride. Are you familiar with it?"

"Uhh, no."

"It's a highly effective insulator. It's also the most devastating greenhouse gas ever created—twenty-four thousand times more harmful than carbon dioxide. And it stays in the atmosphere for up to three thousand years."

Rogers stopped talking for a moment, allowing his words to accumulate weight.

I had nothing to say. The place in my neck where his tranquilizer dart had hit me was throbbing gently.

He continued: "According to Mr. DeGange, the greatly increased production and use of sodium hexafluoride will result in the earth's atmosphere reaching a tipping point in the year 2029, triggering several runaway feedback mechanisms. By 2040, the planet will be eight degrees Celsius warmer than preindustrialized levels. *Eight degrees Celsius*, Nate. That's fourteen degrees Fahrenheit. The results will be even more profoundly devastating than the worst doomsday scenarios being laid out by the climate change alarmists of today. The seas will rise not by the inches we worry about now, but by several hundred feet. Major cities, including New York and Boston, will be completely submerged. Florida will disappear. So will entire archipelagos in the Pacific. Storms of unimaginable intensity will become commonplace and weather patterns will become wildly unrecognizable.

"Crop yields will plummet. The global system of trade that we rely on for our way of life will cease almost overnight, in a way that will make the coronavirus shutdown look like a hiccup. There will be enormous flows of displaced people that will create a breakdown in civil order. Europe will be anarchy. Most of Asia will revert to feudalism. Hundreds of millions of people in India and China will starve to death. Africa will be even worse off. Roughly half of the people on the continent, about seven hundred million, will die from either famine or war. The breadbasket of the world will become Russia, as huge swaths of Siberia suddenly become arable. But Russia will be an even more despotic kleptocracy than it is now, and it will hold the world hostage through the use of food, pitting crumbling nation against crumbling nation—"

"Okay, okay, okay, stop," I finally said. "It'll be bad. I get it."

Rogers had rattled all this off in an easy monotone, like he was narrating a documentary.

"I'm sorry," he said. "I know it's a lot to take in."

"I still don't understand why you're telling me any of this."

"Because Jenny is the linchpin to all of this."

"And?"

"It's quite simple, really," he said. "We want you to kill her."

He delivered the line plainly, with no embellishment.

I expected a promulgation of this magnitude to be accompanied by something else. Lights flashing. Walls shaking. Some special effect or supernatural revelation.

That didn't happen.

Next I thought perhaps my mouth would go dry or my heart would start thrashing against my chest. The words would fully sink in, and panic would begin cascading through me.

That didn't happen either.

Instead, my first reaction was very measured. Judicial even. The former lawyer in me kicked in. At this moment, Rogers and I were just two people sitting on opposite sides of a table with very different ideas about how matters should proceed.

So this was a negotiation.

Something I could talk my way out of.

"Look, with all due respect to your boss, there's obviously been some kind of . . . miscalculation here," I said in a surprisingly reasonable tone. "There's just no way this one lawsuit brought by one woman could have that kind of impact. This isn't a thought experiment in chaos theory. In real life, the butterfly flapping its wings in the Amazon doesn't really cause a tornado."

"I'm sorry. I can see where you might think that," Rogers said patiently. "I realize this is all new to you. But it's not new to us. Mr. DeGange has been consumed by this for some time. He's ninety-five years old—the healthiest ninety-five going, by the way. His energy is still quite something. Ever since he became aware of your wife's lawsuit and its implications, he's been pouring himself into this, trying to find another solution. He's convinced this is the only way. Again, I'm sorry."

"Wait," I said. "Just wait. If this really is all about the lawsuit, I can convince her to drop it."

"You can certainly try. Mr. DeGange says it won't work. Your wife is very stubborn."

"Believe me, I know. But she's also very reasonable. We can bring her here, she can meet with Mr. DeGange. Maybe Mr. DeGange can demonstrate his ability and make her a believer—or whatever you want to call it."

Rogers was shaking his head again. "Your wife cannot know about any of this. Mr. DeGange was very clear on that. As he explained it, the most dangerous thing here is not truly your wife. It's *the idea*. Once your wife is told she's going to have this breakthrough, even without the details, the idea will soon formulate in her mind. When it does, it's a genie you can't put back in the bottle. It will exist. It will have life. It will find a way out."

"But we can tell her to—"

"Listen, Nate, I know you're desperate to stop this. I would be too. But even without meaning to be, your wife is literally the most destructive person to ever walk the earth. We're talking about a billion people. *A billion.* If I gave you a gun and sent you back to Germany in 1930, would you kill Hitler? Of course you would. Anyone would. I'm sorry to tell you this, but your wife is worse than a hundred Hitlers."

Rogers had grown animated, working his butt to the edge of the chair in his excitement. I, on the other hand, felt this continued calm.

I was no stranger to logic problems. In college and law school, I had blathered my way through philosophy classes and ethics seminars. I could imagine some trolley problem–like situation where I could pull the switch and be directly responsible for someone else's death.

I could imagine no scenario, even one as dire as this, where that person could be my wife.

It was totally unthinkable.

My head pivoted away from Rogers, back toward the painting. Was it *really* a Rembrandt? Just hanging there above the fireplace in one of Vanslow DeGange's many guest rooms?

Or . . .

Or it was just a very good forgery.

Like everything else I had just heard.

It had to be. This was a hoax. A scam. A fraud.

As with a piece of art, it would take a while to spot the fine imperfections and false brushstrokes that betrayed a counterfeit. But even if I hadn't spotted the flaws in this scheme yet, I still wasn't going to fall for it.

Rogers seemed to be waiting for me to say something, so I turned back toward him and said, "Look, I'm sorry. Even if I believed everything you just said—and, for the record, I don't—there's no way I can kill my wife. It's just not possible."

He dipped his head, seeming to accept my rejection placidly. "Mr. DeGange said you would respond as such. He then sketched out some alternatives, none of which I think you'll find acceptable."

"What does that mean?"

"You killing your wife is the quickest, most direct way to make this entire thing go away. It will be such a scandal—a former associate at the firm killing his wife, a current partner—that Carter, Morgan, and Ross will want to distance itself from everything your wife touched as quickly as possible. The partners will decide the lawsuit probably wasn't winnable anyway, and they will drop it. The plaintiffs, all of whom are poor, will chalk this up to being just another time sleazy lawyers made false promises. Problem solved.

"If, on the other hand, you don't do it, it means we will have to. We can't risk having your wife killed in a way that might make anyone think it had something to do with CP and L. If the partners at Carter, Morgan, and Ross think they're being bullied into dropping a lawsuit, they'll come out swinging. Therefore, our only option would be to pay someone to make it look like an accident. There could be collateral damage."

He fixed me with an icy stare: "You. Your daughters."

A primal anger surged inside me. Forget the calm, measured lawyer. No one threatens my girls.

I lunged across the table at him, reaching for his throat. My hand was almost to his neck when this incredible white-hot pain surged through me. Every muscle in my body seized up simultaneously, like a full-body cramp. I flopped, stomach first, on the table.

The pain was indescribable. An animalistic shriek, completely involuntary, came from somewhere deep within me. My only thought was the all-encompassing agony that seemed to inhabit my every cell. I thought for sure I was dying.

Then, just as suddenly as it came on, it stopped. Maybe five seconds had elapsed. It felt like eight years.

I could move again. I was just incredibly weak. Sweat had broken out all over me. It was an effort to lift my head.

Rogers had scooted away from the table and was eyeing me guardedly. He had this small, stubby gun-like device in his hand.

A Taser.

He must have had it hidden under the table.

"Please don't make me do that again," he said calmly. "I didn't enjoy it, and I guess you didn't either."

I swore at him.

"I don't take pleasure in threatening your family either. But look at it from any perspective but your own. Killing one person to save a billion isn't a very difficult decision. And killing a family to accomplish the same objective doesn't change the math much. This is the way it has to be. Why don't you take a seat?"

Another swear from me. I was endeavoring—with very limited success—to raise myself from the table. I didn't even know what I planned to do next, since I really didn't have any fight in me.

"Sit. Down," Rogers said firmly.

He was aiming the Taser at me again.

I wasn't sure I could survive another jolt. With effort, I slumped back down to my chair.

"Will you behave yourself?" he asked.

"Yes."

I really didn't have much choice.

"Good," he said, lowering the Taser. "Now let me lay out what Mr. DeGange says is the easiest path forward, and maybe once you have some time to think about it calmly, you'll agree. On Friday evening, at nine forty-five, you are going to walk into your bedroom. Your wife will have just fallen asleep. You will take two minutes to summon your courage. And then, at nine forty-seven, you will place a gun next to her temple and pull the trigger."

"Oh I will, will I?" I asked sardonically.

"Yes. Hold on a moment, please. Let me get the gun for you."

As he went to leave the room, he pulled from his pocket a magnetic key card, which he then pressed against that reader in the doorframe. The lock whirred softly, and he was gone.

I already knew there was no escaping this place—especially now, with my strength still all but sapped. I looked around to see if there was anything else I missed during my first inspection.

It was the same room, with the same magnificent bed and the same lack of viable options.

Soon I heard the lock again. He didn't bother closing the door behind him. He also didn't seem to have the Taser anymore. He had either left it outside the room or pocketed it.

What he had in his hand instead was an elegant-looking silver-plated pistol, which he held with a handkerchief.

"This is the gun you will use," he said, holding it up like it was something I should marvel at. "It is properly loaded. It is essential you use this gun and the bullet that is currently in the chamber. We've had the bullet modified in a way that other bullets fired from this gun won't match when the state crime lab does its ballistics testing. This is what our lawyers will use to create doubt. There will be two trials. The first will end in a mistrial, because of some procedural errors by the prosecution. The second will end in a hung jury. It will all be because of that bullet. After the second trial, the prosecution will decide not to move forward. You will have spent more than a year in jail, and it will not be pleasant. But after that, you will be able to move on with your life."

"Some life. My wife will be dead and everyone will know I killed her, no matter what the courts say. I'll be a pariah. I mean, will my daughters even talk to me?"

"In time, they will understand what you had to do and why you did it. In the meantime, your in-laws will look after them. And the Praesidium will see to it everyone is fully taken care of, financially."

Incredibly, he placed the gun on the table, within easy reach.

I snatched it, feeling its cool weight, its awesome power. There was nothing, beyond my own reluctance to take a human life, that stopped me from blowing his head off.

"How do you know I won't just shoot you right now?" I asked.

"I asked Mr. DeGange that same question. He said you wouldn't."

I aimed the barrel at Rogers' head. He didn't flinch.

"You have an awful lot of faith in your boss," I said.

"True. But it's not just that. From talking to you, I can tell you're sensible. I'm no one special to the Praesidium. Shooting me wouldn't change the situation you're in. It would just mean you're dealing with someone else."

He was probably right. I still ached to pull the trigger on this man who had so amicably threatened the three people in the world I loved most.

"I know you have more questions, and there's more I'd like to tell you about Mr. DeGange and the Praesidium. But we're running out of time," he said. "You still need to pick up your girls at their grandparents' house, am I right? And Jenny usually gets home by six thirty, yes? We don't want you to be late. Hold on a moment. I'll be right back."

He stood up—like I didn't have a gun trained on him—and went into the bathroom.

The main door to the room was still open. I could run out and then . . . well, I had no idea. My legs were jelly. I didn't know where I was. I didn't know who else was in this huge house. Could I shoot my way out? How many bullets did that gun hold? How many people would try to stop me?

It was probably hopeless but—

Then I spied the key card Rogers had used on the door. It was twice as thick as what you might get from a hotel, and it had been imprinted with a logo: two block letters—a *P* and an *R*—inscribed in a square.

He had been so preoccupied with the gun he had simply left the key card on the table. I had been focused on the gun, too, and hadn't noticed him doing so.

But now it struck me as a useful thing to have, even if I didn't know what exactly I'd do with it. I quickly snatched the card and stuffed it in my pocket.

When Rogers returned from the bathroom, he was carrying a syringe.

"Why don't you hop up on the bed and roll on your stomach," he said. "It hurts a lot less if I inject this in your backside."

I again aimed the gun at his forehead. He stopped and frowned at me.

"Are you really going to make me do this the hard way? I could tase you again and then shoot you with the tranquilizer gun if you want. But it's really a lot easier for both of us if you just cooperate."

I felt the smoothness of the trigger with my finger. I wasn't sure I could actually kill anyone. Even a stranger who had kidnapped me. But one squeeze, and—

And then what? I would have killed a man for no reason and not measurably improved my situation.

I lowered the gun, lifted myself from the chair, and shuffled over to the bed. Then I laid myself gingerly on my front.

"Thank you," he said. "I know we've been a little rushed today. I assure you, this will not be the last time we talk between now and nine forty-seven on Friday night. But for now we have to get you back."

"Right," I said.

I was clinging to the hope that this was a game, a scam, a prank of the worst kind—and that I wouldn't have to kill anyone.

Not Rogers.

Certainly not Jenny.

"Okay, here goes," he said.

I felt the pinch of the needle. Then I drifted off.

CHAPTER 4

JENNY

It never failed. Even on days when Jenny thought she'd be able to slip away easily from the glass stockade that was Carter, Morgan & Ross's sleek downtown headquarters, there would be some last-minute turmoil.

A judge would need something.

An associate would find themselves on the verge of self-inflicted destruction.

An urgent 5:30 p.m. conference call would mysteriously appear on her calendar.

Inevitably, it made her nightly escape feel like she was running out of a burning building, leaving her colleagues behind to fight the flames—and earning her their thinly veiled contempt.

But flee she did. As she hustled out to her car, she felt the familiar working-mom tug-of-war, the desire to be able to split herself in two so she could simultaneously slay dragons at the office *and* be with her children.

Typically, Nate got the girls fed, bathed, and into their pj's, and Jenny made her jailbreak-style dash away from work so she could get home by six thirty and play with them until it was time for bed.

And then—and it was safe to say this was everyone's favorite part of the day—she would sit them on her lap, with Parker on the right and Cate on the left, and read to them until it was time to tuck them in; though, really, it was as much snuggling as reading.

It was the only time she got to spend with them during the week. And Jenny's goal was to pack an entire day's worth of love, attention, and affection into those ninety minutes. To be fully present. To mother them relentlessly.

The drive home only took fifteen minutes, even with traffic. The Welker Lovejoys lived in the trendy Fan section of Richmond, in a three-bedroom, circa-1885-colonial-revival-style row house that Jenny just adored. They had bought it when Jenny was pregnant with Parker because it had a recently redone kitchen and—perhaps most importantly—two off-street parking spots, located just outside the fence that sectioned off their small backyard.

She parked and hurried inside to find Nate wearing this strange look, staring at her like he was almost afraid of her, a countenance she wasn't sure she had ever seen on her husband before. Then he gave her an extralong squeeze, which was also odd. Normally all they did was exchange a quick kiss so Jenny could get to the girls faster.

"Everything okay?" she asked when he finally released her.

"Yeah, fine," he replied, in a way she didn't quite believe.

"How's that faucet?"

"Oh. That. I had to go back to the hardware store three times for parts, so I didn't get it quite done. I may have to drop the girls with your parents again tomorrow if that's okay."

Jenny shot her husband a worried look, wondering if this actually had anything to do with plumbing. Nate had never complained of burnout. He always seemed perfectly happy with their domestic arrangement.

Yet she had enough friends who had decided to stay at home with their children, and they all talked about what a grind full-time caregiving could be. How fifteen minutes could sometimes feel like fifteen hours. How it eroded your sense of self, abrading you slowly, molecule by molecule, in a way you barely even noticed until one day you looked down and you were staring into this Grand Canyon of despair.

She had also listened to the men at the firm talking so dismissively about their stay-at-home wives. *How hard can it be? So she's with the kids all day? She doesn't face anything like the pressure I face.*

What clueless jerks. Like being solely responsible for the rearing of children five days a week wasn't its own crucible.

She looked at her husband's handsome face, always a little crooked in that charming way. She reached out and placed a hand on his chest.

"I doubt they'd mind more grandparent time, but are you sure you're okay?" she asked. "I know it's not easy with the girls. Maybe we could look into having someone come in a couple mornings a week, so you could—"

"I'm fine," he insisted, then kissed her forehead. "Go be with your daughters. They need their mom."

Jenny leaned into the next ninety minutes with her usual loving intensity until bedtime arrived. Cate surrendered to sleep quickly, her eyes closing shortly after her head came to a rest in the crib.

Parker was a different story. The little girl had climbed into bed without being asked and was now waiting patiently for her mother.

Jenny turned off the light as she entered, then sat on the edge of the bed. They had an evening ritual they both cherished. Parker would say, "Mommy, tell me about my day," and Jenny would proceed to narrate.

Except, really, it was Parker providing the details of all the things her mother had not been around for.

First, Daddy made you breakfast and . . . what did Daddy make for breakfast?

Oatmeal and bananas.

And so on.

But on this night Parker had something else in mind.

"Mommy, I have a secret," she said in a whisper.

"Oh, and what's that?" Jenny asked, expecting to hear about some intrigue involving dolls and stuffed animals.

Instead, she heard:

"Daddy has a gun."

Jenny's first instinct was to assume her daughter was mistaken. Nate was a city kid, born and raised in Manhattan. He hated guns. One of their earliest arguments when they began dating had been about guns. Jenny, who had grown up around firearms, saw them as little more than farm tools: worthy of respect, sure, but no more or less inherently evil than a chain saw or a shovel.

Nate mostly associated guns with tragedy. She couldn't imagine him wanting to be in the same room as one.

But there was something in Parker's eyes, glowing in the half light seeping in from the hallway, that made Jenny realize this was serious business for the little girl.

Not wanting to spook her daughter, Jenny remained calm and said, "Oh, really?"

"Guns are bad," Parker said earnestly.

"Sometimes they are. It depends who has them and what they're going to do with them. Grandpa has guns and he's not bad."

"Oh. Okay."

Parker said it like this perhaps settled matters. But Jenny still had questions.

"Did you actually see Daddy with this gun?"

Parker nodded.

"Where was it?"

"In the kitchen."

"When you got back from Grandma and Grandpa's house?"

Parker nodded again. "He thought I didn't see. But I saw."

"What, exactly, did you see?" Jenny asked, still uncertain if this was a figment of her little girl's creative mind.

"It was shiny."

"A shiny gun."

"Yeah."

Jenny was aware of Parker studying her carefully.

"I see," Jenny said, working hard to maintain her unworried, calming bedtime demeanor. "And how did that make you feel?"

"Scary," Parker said. "But if Daddy has the gun, it must be okay. Like Grandpa."

Jenny looked off into a dark corner of the room.

"Yes, honey, like Grandpa," she said.

Then she pulled the blanket up, closer to her daughter's chin, and smoothed it out. "We can talk more about this tomorrow if you want. Now it's night-night time. Love you, my big girl."

"Love you, Mommy."

She bent over and kissed Parker's forehead, then straightened and walked unsteadily out of the room.

It was one of the first pieces of advice Jenny Welker had ever received as a trial attorney: *Never ask a question in the courtroom to which you don't already know the answer.*

Which was easy enough when you had the opportunity to depose a witness, collect documents, and spend months preparing.

What was she supposed to do with this? Had the "leaky faucet" existed at all? Had he dropped the kids at her parents' house and then used his time away to . . . buy a gun?

Why would Nate feel like he needed a gun?

And why wouldn't he tell her about it?

For Jenny, the flint that created the spark of their relationship wasn't the immediate physical attraction she felt to Nate, a six-foot-four former college swimmer with a V-shaped torso and an easygoing charm.

It wasn't that he was secure enough in himself not to be intimidated by a powerful woman. It wasn't even the incredible passion and creativity he brought to their lovemaking.

It was that, unlike so many of the guys she had been with, Nate Lovejoy never tried to hide anything. He didn't play games.

He was the guy who, at the end of their first date—which wasn't really a date as much as an extended make-out session in the back of a bar—had come right out and said, "Jenny Welker, I think you're dazzling."

And he had never really budged from that way of being.

So what was she to make of this?

Did she ask him about this when she didn't know what his answer would be?

But how could she not? After all, this wasn't a courtroom. It was a marriage.

Their normal routine, once the girls were in bed, was to finish cleaning up, eat a quick dinner, then flop on the couch and either talk or cuddle while watching TV. Jenny lingered upstairs for a few more minutes, going into their bedroom, thinking about how she wanted to approach this.

Before long, the door to the bedroom was opening.

"Hey," Nate said as he came in behind it. "I made stir-fry. Are you going to come down and eat with me?"

"Yeah, I just . . . I need to ask you about something."

"Uh, okay," he said, shutting the door behind himself. "That sounds ominous."

Might as well come out with it: "Parker said she saw you with a gun earlier today."

"A gun?"

He laughed nervously.

"Yes," she said.

There was a pause. Then there was that look again. The same one he had been wearing when she first came in the door.

And then, again, the look went away.

"Well, you know what kind of imagination she has," Nate said.

"So she's imagining it."

"Well, of course she's . . . oh, I know."

"What?"

"I was watching a movie on my laptop this afternoon while the girls were playing. There was a man brandishing a gun at one point. Did she say it was a silver gun?"

"She said it was shiny, yes."

"Yeah, that's it then. There was a man with a silver gun. And she . . . she was just suddenly looking over my shoulder and she must have seen it."

"You were watching a violent movie in front of the girls?"

"It wasn't violent, it was just . . . but, you're right, I shouldn't have. I started it during nap time last week and I wanted to know how it ended. It was stupid. I won't do it again. Anyhow, are you hungry?"

Jenny noted the pivot, but decided to let him get away with it.

"Yeah," she said. "Let's eat."

CHAPTER 5

NATE

The gun.

That stupid silver gun.

When I'd regained consciousness after my chat with Lorton Rogers, I had been lying on our living room couch. The gun was digging into my back.

I hadn't known what to do with the damn thing. I barely had enough time to make the hour drive out to Surry to pick up the girls and get back before Jenny arrived home from work. In a panic, I had just tossed the gun in a drawer in the kitchen on my way out the door.

During the drive, as my brain finally started working again, it occurred to me that was an incredibly stupid place to store a deadly weapon.

When we got back home—with about fifteen minutes to spare—I had to make a snap decision about where to move it next and decided on the basement.

I thought I had been stealthy enough about sneaking the gun out of the drawer. But leave it to my precocious Parker to notice everything.

Before I stashed it—high up in a storage bin, between some sweaters, in a place Jenny would never have a reason to go and the girls couldn't reach—I took a quick moment to study it.

The silver plating made it feel like something that belonged to the Lone Ranger. The butt of the gun had an oval-shaped stamp on it that read **WHITE CHUCK NO. 8** along the top half and **BEDAL, WASHINGTON** along the bottom.

Whatever that meant.

I probably should have just thrown it in a dumpster, or tossed it into a reservoir, or turned it in to a police station. It's not like I was actually going to use it. There were things I simply wasn't capable of doing, and pulling the trigger of a gun placed next to Jenny's head was at a prominent spot at the top of that list.

In some ways it was just selfish. I didn't want to think of my life without her.

We had been together for thirteen years, having met when we were both twenty-five, on the first day of new-associate orientation at Carter, Morgan & Ross. The moment she walked into the conference room, an army of harpists began playing in my mind. She was absolutely striking, with wavy brown hair that fell perfectly about her shoulders and this powerful stride, like she knew exactly where she was going in the world.

In other words, she was way out of my league. But I summoned the nerve to walk up to her and say, "Hi, I'm Nate Lovejoy."

I've always been killer with the lines that way.

I soon learned she was Jenny Welker; that she had grown up on a small farm in rural Virginia and still liked to help her father fix broken fence posts on weekends; that she was the first in her family to go to college, much less law school; and that whereas everyone else was shyly nibbling at the spread of pastries and fresh-cut fruit the firm had put out for us, she loaded her plate, then went up for seconds. I was instantly smitten.

We ended that evening making out in the back of a dive bar, so I think it's fair to say I had made a positive first impression too. As we parted that first evening, I breathlessly said, "Jenny Welker, I think you're dazzling."

She loved that line.

Primarily because it wasn't a line.

Even still, it became a running joke with us—all the things that were dazzling.

But it really was the perfect word for her.

In the romance that ensued, the country girl introduced the boy from the Upper West Side of Manhattan to some of life's finer pleasures (pig roasts, sunsets on the porch, cheesy country music), and the city boy reciprocated (with foodie restaurants, sunsets on the rooftop, and indie rock).

It was a dizzying time. My childhood was something I worked hard to overcome—mostly by trying to act like it never happened. My parents had split when I was small. To further cement my disillusionment, my mother divorced twice more, fracturing whatever faith I'd had in relationships.

As a kid, I drowned all my resentment and frustration in the pool, becoming an accomplished junior swimmer. I had the kind of body— long arms, broad chest, size sixteen feet—that college coaches coveted, earning me a scholarship. I spent most of my youth and early adulthood swimming from my troubles.

But I never really recovered. At least until Jenny came along. Even when I told her my most horrible secrets, she only seemed to love me more.

Before I knew it, I believed in fairy tales again. Over the course of two years, we breezed through all the milestones, moving from dating exclusivity to cohabitation, then to engagement.

The only dilemma we faced was that Carter, Morgan & Ross had a nepotism policy. The firm could not hire or promote into partnership any family member of an existing partner.

So before we got married, Jenny and I made a deal. Whoever made partner first, their career would receive priority. The other would step aside.

This, I later came to realize, ran counter to advice my grandfather had once given me: *Never start a fight you can't win.*

Whereas I was a fine lawyer—methodical and workmanlike—Jenny was a rock star, a highly intuitive problem solver, gifted in both the conference room and the courthouse. She was always ten steps ahead, always anticipating her opponents' moves and then countering before they could even make them.

She made partner when she was thirty-two, one of the youngest in firm history. I hung on as an associate for another few years. But when she got pregnant and we decided it would be best for our family to have a parent stay home? That parent was clearly going to be me.

Our marriage wasn't perfect, inasmuch as I nagged her about spending less time at work, and she exasperated me by coming home and trying to tell me how to run the house.

And, at least lately, our love life had been nonexistent. There's nothing like a three-year-old and an eighteen-month-old to sap the libido. Between that and Jenny's work schedule, which had been particularly hectic, it had been two months since we'd done anything in bed that didn't involve reading or sleeping.

But that little dry spell was just a temporary problem. We were basically happy; and more importantly, we were fulfilled—with each other, with our girls, with the beautiful family we had created together.

So to think I might ever be able to harm her?

It wasn't just unthinkable. It was appalling—total anathema to who I believed I was as a human being.

Especially when Vanslow DeGange was so clearly a fraud to begin with. Could anyone actually see the future?

No. Of course not.

Vanslow DeGange wasn't some soothsaying guru. He was the Wizard of Oz, the supposedly all-powerful leader who turned out to be a con man.

Or maybe he was Keyser Söze: he had been summoned from the depths of Lorton Rogers' imagination and didn't actually exist at all.

Either way, I needed to figure out who was behind this, and, more importantly, where their hiding place with the fancy paintings was. Then I would report them to the police and get them charged with kidnapping—and whatever crime it was to scare a man into thinking he needed to kill his wife.

This was finally coming to me late that night, as I lay in bed sleeplessly, long after Jenny's breathing settled down. Really, it was the first time I had been able to calm my brain enough to let logic take back over.

Whoever these people really were, they wanted me to believe that my wife's lawsuit against Commonwealth Power & Light was the source of all evil and needed to be quashed.

Therefore, the simplest explanation for the Praesidium, Vanslow DeGange, and all this nonsense?

It was really CP&L.

The company's executives had come up with a wildly creative way to make this lawsuit go away and had hired Lorton Rogers and the Praesidium to work the scam.

There was no question CP&L had the money to pull it off. Part of what made it such an attractive target for a mass tort claim was its deep pockets: roughly $20 billion in annual revenues and $80 billion in assets.

CP&L also had the motivation. For all those riches, this lawsuit still posed an existential threat to the company. Jenny kept a tally of the total damages she had estimated for the 279 clients she had signed up thus far. The last number I saw was above $400 million.

That was manageable for something CP&L's size. But if she could actually establish a precedent? CP&L had at least ten other coal-fired plants around the state. The Shockoe Generation Plant wasn't even the largest. It would take time and legwork to sign up more clients, sure, but damages would easily run into the billions. Plus the endless legal fees.

If things went poorly, CP&L could become the East Coast version of PG&E, the huge California power company driven into bankruptcy by its culpability for a deadly wildfire.

And Lorton Rogers—if that was even his name—was absolutely right about one thing: if there was no Jenny, there would be no lawsuit.

She was the one partner at CMR who believed in this thing. The associate managing partner, Albert Dickel—a friend, mentor, and erst-while racquetball combatant of mine—was even starting to make noises about how the firm should drop it.

The rest of the partners on the executive committee seemed to be somewhere in between, willing to keep tossing money at it for a while. One-third of $400 million was sufficient motivation, and the firm could afford to bankroll what was essentially an expensive lottery ticket.

But without Jenny to spearhead it, no one else at CMR was going to risk their time or their reputation. If she lost faith or got scared away, the case would be over.

It wasn't a stretch to think CP&L had figured that out. Richmond may have appeared as a medium-size city on a map, but it was really a small town. Everyone knew everyone else's business, especially in the tight circle of people who actually ran stuff—the business, legal, and financial communities, all of which overlapped because we sent our kids to the same schools, socialized in the same places, gave money to the same charities, and so on.

Someone could have easily whispered into a CP&L executive's ear: *You know, the only thing keeping this lawsuit going is Jenny Welker.*

There was no finessing Jenny or talking her out of something once she got her mind set. CP&L's chief counsel would discover that quickly if he didn't know it already. Jenny was an uncrackable egg.

Me? I was a much softer target. The guy who had been a good lawyer but not a great one. The husband who had stepped aside so his wife's career could thrive. The affable pushover.

For $400 million, it was worth hiring Lorton Rogers and a band of brutes to grab and terrify me.

That mansion they'd taken me to, for all I knew, belonged to CP&L's CEO, a stuffed shirt named J. Hunter Matthews II. He was pulling down something like $20 million a year and could probably afford a Rembrandt or a Vermeer—or knockoffs good enough to fool an amateur like me.

Maybe they could convince me to scare my wife into dropping the lawsuit with their wild tale.

Maybe they could even get me to kill her.

Either way, problem solved.

Did they really think I was that dumb? Obviously, yes.

It all added up to CP&L being the man behind the curtain.

Now I just had to prove it.

The next morning, Jenny made her usual early escape. Once I got the girls fed and dressed for the day, I set them up with age-appropriate distractions.

I began with Cate, a squirming mass of energy and springy brown curls who looked like Jenny's mini-me. I placed her in her high chair in the kitchen, then dumped a fresh lump of purple Play-Doh in front of her. She immediately plunged her fingers into it, squishing it with delight.

Then I handed my phone to Parker, a precocious, highly verbal child who had the misfortune of looking more like her father, with straight brown hair and serious eyes. But she also had the virtue of being easily entertained. For her, I queued up the ultimate toddler intoxicant: the original *Baby Shark Dance* video, three billion YouTube views and counting.

When it got to Grandma Shark, and Parker was properly entranced, I got to work.

The first thing I did—because isn't it the first thing everyone does these days?—was turn to Google. I typed in *Lorton Rogers*.

The lead result was a Facebook account for Mary Rogers, who lived in Lorton, Virginia. Then there was a LinkedIn entry for a man named Lawrence Lorton from Rogers, Arkansas. Many pages of similarly irrelevant entries followed.

Next I googled *Vanslow DeGange*. The first match was a book about rangeland stewardship where one author had the last name Vanselow and another had the first name Degang. Nothing else was even remotely close.

Had these men really been that assiduous about obscuring their digital tracks?

Or were they simply fictions?

Next I turned to the only tangible piece of evidence I had: that key card I had swiped off the table while Rogers wasn't looking. The Praesidium was obviously . . . something. A private detective agency? Mercenaries for hire? Once I figured it out—and pointed the authorities in their direction—I was sure this scam would fall apart.

The key card had that PR logo, which I scanned into my laptop. Soon, I was uploading it onto a site that promised me the web's most expansive reverse image search.

I was expecting hundreds or thousands of results. What company didn't plaster its logo all over?

But there was just one. I clicked on it.

The link was dead. It was giving me a classic "404 not found" message.

I returned to the search results to make sure I hadn't imagined it. And, yes, there it was: the *P* and the *R* inscribed in a square. The search engine must have latched onto an archived version of the image floating somewhere out there on the web.

Then I looked at the URL of the website that—at some point in browsing history—had contained the image.

It was for something called the Cult InfoShare Network.

Was this not the first time the Praesidium had posed as a secret society, a.k.a. cult?

I went to the home page for cultinfoshare.org. According to the "about," the Cult InfoShare Network was a 501(c)(3) whose mission was to "inform and educate the public and people whose loved ones may be involved with potential cults and NRMs (new religious movements)."

Reading on, I learned the site essentially acted as an information clearinghouse for people whose children, spouses, relatives, or friends may have gotten wrapped up with one of these shady outfits.

It was all about lifting the veil of secrecy underneath which cults thrived. Details of each organization were shared, wiki-style, by people who operated under usernames—but gave their email addresses to the Cult InfoShare Network.

Users could then opt for different levels of privacy, everything from no contact, to messaging through the site, to permitting the Cult InfoShare Network to share their contact information with any member who asked. The ultimate point of the site was to connect people (mostly parents) who were trying to get their kids (mostly young adults just above the age of consent) away from these cults.

The founder and executive director was a man who freely shared his heartbreaking story in his bio. His daughter had been repeatedly sexually assaulted while in a cult, then killed herself. After he retired from a career as an IT executive, he created and ran this website. It wasn't difficult to infer this was his therapy.

There was a phone number listed on the contact page, so I called it. I reasoned that because it was barely after seven in the morning, I'd get some kind of voice mail.

But after two rings, a man answered. I introduced myself and soon learned I was talking with the aforementioned founder and executive director.

I talked him through how I found his site, then emailed him the image.

"Oh, yeah. Those guys," he said. "Maybe three years ago I added a page for them. As soon as I put it up, I got a cease and desist letter from a lawyer, telling me to take it down. This wasn't my first rodeo with this sort of thing. One of the things all cults have in common is that they don't like being called cults. They threaten to sue anyone who tries to out them. But the ultimate defense against libel is the truth. So if I can establish that the information on the page is reliable? I tell the cult to go pound sand. We don't let ourselves be bullied."

"But in this case you took the page down," I said.

"Yeah, I can't remember what happened. Hang on, let me pull up the file."

I heard him typing.

"That's right," he continued. "Everything I got on the Praesidium came from one user. That's not game over, but it is a red flag. So I reached out to the user. His email bounced but I had a snail mail address. I sent him a letter the same way I always do, with 'return service requested' on it. The letter got returned with a new address. Then I sent a certified letter to the new address. He definitely received it. But he never answered. At that point, I felt like I had no choice but to take the page down."

"Can you tell me who the user is?" I asked.

"Let me see what kind of permissions he gave us," he said, then typed some more. "All right, here we go. Full access. His real name is Robert McBride. Want his contact info?"

I said yes, and the man gave me both addresses. One was in Hudgins, Virginia. Wherever that was. But it didn't really matter, since he wasn't there anymore anyway.

The second address was in Williamsburg, Virginia, which was about an hour away.

"So this Robert McBride, all your information about the Praesidium came from him?"

"Correct."

"Can you tell me what the page said?" I asked.

"Not without potentially committing slander. Sorry, you seem like a nice guy. And I want to help you. But for all I know you're from the Praesidium, you're recording me, and you're trying to see if you can trap me. Some of these cults play dirty."

I told him I understood, and before long I was thanking him and wrapping up the call.

There was no chance I was going to send a letter to this Robert McBride. I didn't have that kind of time.

I needed to pay him a visit. I googled the second address so I could see where it was on the map.

Instead, I found myself staring at a litany of results for Dominion State Hospital.

Which was its modern, politically correct name. But that's not what it was called for the first hundred or so years of its existence.

It used to be known as Dominion State Lunatic Asylum.

CHAPTER 6

JENNY

If you had told fourteen-year-old Jenny Welker that one day she would go to work in one of the tallest buildings in Virginia, she never would have believed it.

After all, she was just a farmer's daughter who lived in a county where the tallest occupied structure topped out at three stories. Early on, her greatest aspiration was to be named a 4-H All Star.

Once she achieved that, she set her mind on something even more audacious: becoming valedictorian of her small high school class, a distinction that almost never went to a true local. It was usually the child of some Yankee doctor or businessperson—a "come here," as they were known, and they usually beat the "born here" kids for every significant award and honor.

Until, four years of A-pluses later, born-there Jenny was delivering the valedictory at graduation.

Her next ambition was to earn enough scholarships to be able to go to college. And, lo and behold, she did that too—graduated Phi Beta Kappa and everything.

Then it was law school, something no one in her family had ever even thought about aspiring to. After that came law review, and a prized summer internship with a federal judge, and on and on and on.

At every step she had to stare down the self-doubt, beat away the feelings of inadequacy, ignore that voice in her head that said a farm girl probably wasn't good enough.

And now here she was. Thirty-eight years old and going to work at the world headquarters of Carter, Morgan & Ross, a sleek tower encased in reflective glass, located just around the corner from the federal courthouse, near the state capitol, in the locus of all that mattered in Richmond, Virginia.

Jenny parked in a garage across the street, walked through a plaza dotted with fountains, then entered through a needlessly large atrium-style lobby with polished marble floors and a bronze statue of the firm's long-dead founders.

It was all meant to convey the power, wealth, and importance of the building's occupants—a thirteen-hundred-lawyer firm whose annual revenues topped $1 billion.

Jenny's small slice of this domain could be found on one of the lower floors. She spent the morning jumping between meetings and conference calls. The usual. Then, around 10:45, she received a text message: Short notice, I know, but can you do 11:30?

It came from a burner phone, a number she knew well, even though she had never programmed it into her phone. Every time she saw it flash up, a jangle of nervous excitement passed through her.

She wrote back one word: Yes.

The same word she almost always wrote back to this particular texter, who had become so important in her life.

Then she immediately erased the exchange. You could never be too careful.

Half an hour later, Jenny informed her assistant she was headed out to an early lunch. The assistant accepted the lie smoothly. Soon Jenny was crossing back through the marble atrium and past the fountains again.

But she didn't go to her car. She kept walking at a brisk pace—just another woman in high-heeled shoes, a leather document case under her arm, hurrying along the street in downtown Richmond, Virginia.

Her destination was The Commonwealth, a hotel within sight of the state capitol. She had kept a room booked there for the past two months. These meetings were difficult to schedule and often only came together at the last moment, when schedules meshed. It was easier to keep the room on standby, just in case it was needed.

She had arranged for the billing to go directly to Carter, Morgan & Ross, so it wouldn't show up on her credit card or in her expense report. CMR's coffers could handle it.

There were certainly grander hotels in downtown Richmond—the Jefferson, the Berkeley, the Omni. There was just too great a chance of running into someone she knew in the lobby.

She didn't want to have to answer any questions about what she was up to.

The Commonwealth, while not exactly a hot-sheet establishment, was simpler. Its lobby was small, and not noted for being a local hangout. Yet the hotel was still centrally located, which made it the best of both worlds.

The elevators were directly in line with the main entrance—no awkward nods at the reception desk staff needed—and Jenny was soon zooming up toward the top floor.

Once there, she turned left down the narrow hallway, and went to the room at the end, taking a key card out of her purse and letting herself in.

She was not the first to arrive.

There was already a man waiting for her there, his large frame sprawled across the bed. He was about Jenny's age. He had a square jaw and full-bodied hair that was the envy of all.

"Hey," she said as she entered, tossing her document case on the desk.

"We've really got to stop meeting like this," he said, grinning.

"We'd better not."

"The lady is so demanding," he said mock-seriously.

"So, what, is this not going to be worth my time today?"

"No, no. I promise it will be."

CHAPTER 7

NATE

Robert McBride wasn't a doctor.

Google could tell me that much.

Nor did he seem to be any other kind of staff member. A quick check of the Virginia public employee database on the *Richmond Times-Dispatch* website confirmed as much.

Which meant he had to be a . . . patient?

A man who had mental illness severe enough to be hospitalized and yet also knew something about the Praesidium.

Had Rogers kidnapped him too? Perhaps driven him to madness?

Whatever was going on, Robert McBride knew . . . something. More than I did, at any rate. I had to at least attempt to talk with him.

Without the girls, obviously. I needed to jettison them with their grandparents again. Dominion State Hospital was not quite on the way to Surry, but it was at least sort of in the same direction.

My in-laws, Sebastian and Deborah Welker—Seb and Deb, as everyone called them—lived on a farm that had been in the family for three generations. I called them and was soon overwhelmed by Deb's gushing about how she'd love to take the girls again.

Seb, who was beyond handy—and had a stash of spare parts that would make a prepper blush—offered to help me with the plumbing problem that I was, once again, using as cover for emergency childcare. I talked him into realizing he was really too busy with the farm and convinced him I had it covered.

I quickly threw on some business casual clothes—no shower for Daddy—then got the girls loaded in our SUV. We had a gray Range Rover that Jenny had picked out for us when she first got pregnant because she had read somewhere that it had advanced antirollover technology. Also, it looked like it could survive a cruise missile strike.

As I got underway, I kept checking my rearview mirror, seeing if I was being followed. I didn't want Rogers and/or the higher powers at CP&L to know what I was up to. I assumed I had been under some kind of surveillance for a while now. Rogers knew what time Jenny got home, and he knew that my girls had been with their grandparents the day before.

I didn't see any obvious tail as I left the city and got on the highway. The closer I got to Surry, the more I became confident I really was alone. At least for now.

After dropping the girls off, I made my way to Dominion State Hospital. The site that had once been the home of the lunatic asylum—and all the electroshock therapy, phrenology experiments, forced sterilizations, and other horrors of early-twentieth-century psychology—had been condemned long ago.

Dominion State Hospital was now housed in a sprawling complex of two-story buildings with wings extending in every direction. Numerous signs warned me I was under video surveillance.

I parked and went into the main entrance, where I found the admissions desk.

"Hi," I told the receptionist. "I'm Nate Lovejoy. I'm here to see a patient named Robert McBride."

She typed and stared at the screen.

"He's in our high-security unit. Are you law enforcement?"

High security. So, unsurprisingly, Robert McBride had done something criminal.

Like getting conned into killing his wife?

Thinking quickly, I said, "Oh, actually, I'm a lawyer."

Which was not untruthful—at one point, anyway.

If she asked for a business card, I was going to be out of luck. But she said, "Okay, Mr. Lovejoy. Can I please see a driver's license?"

I had one of those, no problem. And before I knew it, she was entering me into the computer, taking my picture on the small camera attached to the computer, and printing out a visitor's badge.

She informed me I couldn't take my phone into the high-security area, so I ran it back out to my car. When I returned, she asked me to wait "a moment" for my escort.

A moment turned out to be more like half an hour, but eventually a guard led me down a long series of hallways, through a pair of locked doors that we needed to be buzzed through, and into a small interior room. It had been divided in half by a thick Plexiglas partition, which had a circle of pea-size air holes drilled into it.

There was a chair in front of the glass. The guard told me to have a seat and left me alone.

Another wait ensued. Then, finally, the door on the other side of the divider was opened by a guard. A man entered. He was dressed in orange scrubs that had been tucked into an elastic waistband and wore black plastic slides on his feet. No belts or shoelaces in this part of the hospital.

He was anywhere between forty-five and sixty. What little hair he had was shaved down to an uneven stubble. His beard was gray and ill tended. His glasses were at least thirty years out of style.

I don't mean to say that having a bad haircut and unfashionable eyewear made him look like he belonged in a psychiatric hospital. But as social mammals, human beings have many millions of years of evolution that make us gifted readers of other human beings. We instantly judge a thousand small factors—everything from the way someone walks to, yes, what kind of glasses they wear—to make decisions about each other.

And based on nothing more (and nothing less) than all that, my first impression of Robert McBride was that it was entirely possible he was mentally unbalanced enough to belong here.

He sat down.

"Mr. McBride, I'm Nate Lovejoy. Thanks for coming to see me."

"Call me Buck," he said. "Everyone else does."

Buck McBride. He had a rural southern Virginia accent, not terribly different from my father-in-law's.

"And you can call me Nate."

"They say you want to be my lawyer or something?" he asked, appropriately mystified.

"Something like that," I said. "I got your name and address from the Cult InfoShare Network. I was hoping you could tell me more about these people."

I reached into my pocket and took out the key card. The moment he saw the logo, Buck leaped from his seat, knocking the chair over as he scrambled toward the back wall—because apparently that thick glass partition didn't give him enough separation from me.

"Where did you *get* that?" he hissed, glaring at it like it bore the devil's mark. "Vanslow DeGange sent you, didn't he? Don't lie."

"I assure you, he didn't. I've never met the man. Some of his people kidnapped me yesterday but I managed to get away. I stole this key card off one of them. But I don't know a thing about them."

"Prove it," Buck snarled. "Take off your shirt. Take it off, right now."

I had no idea how that would prove anything, but I did as he asked, unbuttoning my shirt and stripping it off.

"The T-shirt too," he said.

Again I complied, pulling it over my head so I was now sitting there bare chested.

"Lift up your arms," he ordered. "Hold them out."

I obliged him, hoping neither of the guards was looking in at what would have appeared to be one of the stranger attorney-client conferences in legal history.

"Look, Buck, I don't know what we're doing right now, but can I put my shirt back on?"

"You're really not with them?"

"I'm really not," I said, redonning my clothes. "I don't really even know who they are."

Suddenly, he was in the chair and had gotten as close to the air holes as he could get.

"Then run," he said in a fierce whisper. "If you're not mixed up with them yet, run away, right now, as fast as you can. Don't bother packing. Take anyone you love with you and go. Get far away and don't come back, do you hear me? Just run."

I watched with fascination as spittle flew from his mouth. He was either thoroughly terrified or completely unhinged. I honestly couldn't decide which.

"Okay, I hear you. But . . . who are these guys, really? Do you know where I can find them?"

Buck suddenly got this cagey look. He leaned away from the glass.

In a louder, stiffer voice, he said, "I'm sorry, sir. I can't help you. I don't know anything about them."

His eyes were casting about this way and that, but in a deliberate manner, like he was trying to tell me: *Look around.*

And then I got it. He thought the place was bugged.

"Oh," I said. "Look, don't worry about that. Just say I'm your lawyer. I'll represent you pro bono."

"Fine. My old lawyer quit on me anyway. You're my lawyer. How does that help?"

"Because now this conversation is protected under attorney-client privilege," I said. "They couldn't use what was said here against you. It would be illegal."

"Great. Illegal," he said derisively. "If you actually think that would stop them, then you belong in here with me."

"Buck, please, I need some help here. Just . . . give me the basics here. Like, where is the Praesidium located?"

He studied me again—in a way that did not feel tinged with insanity—then said, "You'll either take the advice I just gave you or you'll find out the hard way. Your choice."

"Is the reason you're in here . . . is it because of them?"

"Oh yeah," he said, adding a derisive snort. "You got that right."

"Why? What happened?"

He looked at me, grimaced, then shook his bristly, lumpy head.

"Nope," he said. "Sorry. I'm not going there. There's nothing to talk about."

"Please?" I said, aware I sounded pathetic. "Look, if someone could have helped you before you got to this point, wouldn't you have wanted them to? *Please.*"

I looked at him imploringly. Our eyes locked for a moment, and I thought for sure I was reaching him.

Then he looked away.

"I . . . I'd like to, okay? But . . . you have no idea what it's like in here," he said. "There are guys who'd finger-paint with their own crap all day if you let them. Then there are others, they're more like animals than people. The only way to keep control of them is to drug them so bad they don't even know which way to drool. And the staff, shoot, some of them are worse than the patients. They do these strip searches for quote-unquote 'contraband' and I swear they get off on it. I can't spend the rest of my life in here, and the only way I'm going to get out is . . ."

His voice trailed off. He closed his eyes, rubbed his temples.

"I'm sure it's horrible. I understand," I said. "Look, I'm just a guy trying to understand what's going on here. Maybe we can help each other. I'll be your lawyer. I'll help you get out of here. And in the meantime, if you can give me some idea what I'm up against . . ."

He opened his eyes and unleashed a large sigh.

"I have a storage unit behind the NAPA Auto Parts in Hudgins," he said. "It's called the Lok-N-Key. I'm number two fifty-seven. It's mostly just junk in there. But there's a box. It's in the well of an old piano. Take the lid off the box, dig under the sheet music, and you'll find . . . well, some reading material. If you're going to be my lawyer, you're going to need to see that stuff anyway."

"Right, do you have a key to the unit, or—"

"Maisy will help you out. Her number's on the sign. She runs the place. Just let her know that I said you're my lawyer and it was okay. Tell her . . . tell her it's probably a good thing we never went to homecoming together. That way she'll know we talked."

"Got it."

"Just read the stuff. That's everything I know anyway. And maybe when you come back we can talk a little more. But for now . . . sorry, friend. I should probably go."

He was already standing up. I had a thousand more questions for him. The first one that came to me was, "Wait, why did you ask me to take off my shirt?"

"Because I wanted to see if you had one of these."

His fingers went to the sleeve of his scrubs, which he lifted. The letters P and R, inscribed in a box—identical to the key card—had been seared into the flesh of his inner left arm.

He walked over to the door and tapped on it. As soon as the guard opened it, Buck announced in a loud voice, "So like I said, the Praesidium doesn't exist. I thought it did once. But I was wrong."

CHAPTER 8

NATE

The number to call for assistance on Lok-N-Key Self Storage's sign connected me directly to the one and only Maisy, to whom I explained my circumstances.

She sounded skeptical but was soon pulling into the parking lot in an ancient pickup truck. The woman who disembarked outside storage unit number 257 wore mud-stained boots, lived-in jeans, and a flannel shirt.

"So you really talked to ol' Buck, huh?" she asked.

"I did. He said to tell you that he's glad you never went to homecoming together."

Maisy chortled. "Yeah, me too."

"What was that about, if I may ask?"

"Our families figured out we were distantly related and put the kibosh on it. That happens around here."

She was already fumbling with a large key ring and muttering to herself about which one to choose. So obviously the homecoming line had been convincing.

"How's he doing, anyway?" she asked.

"About as well as you'd expect," I said honestly. "I don't think the company in there is very pleasant."

"Well, he should have thought of that before he went and killed someone."

So Buck was a murderer. That explained the high-security unit.

"Yeah, who did he kill, anyway?" I asked. "We sort of got interrupted before we could get to that."

"His neighbor," she said, inserting a key into a padlock and then frowning at it when it didn't work. "Don't get me wrong, everybody hated the guy. He was a real jerk-off. Buck probably did the world a favor. But he still shouldn't have done it."

"Why did he, then?"

"I dunno. The paper said it was something about a property dispute. You'd have to ask Buck. I don't think he's really crazy or anything, but maybe temporary insanity took hold of him. Here. This is it."

She removed the lock and rolled up the garage door to the unit. A wall of musty, stale air hit me. We both took a moment to survey what was inside. There wasn't much. An old lawn mower. Some hideous green couches. Empty bookshelves. A few floor lamps. Several stacked towers of boxes, some of which had gone marshmallow shaped from the humidity.

And a piano with a sheet covering it. I went over to it; lifted the sheet; and, sure enough, there was a banker's box in the well. Upon lifting the lid, I saw sheet music.

"I think this is what Buck sent me to find," I said.

"All right," she said. "Well, I don't have time to stay out here all day while you read whatever is in there. How about I just leave the lock with you? You can close up when you're done. I'll swing by later to check and make sure you did it right."

"Sounds like a plan."

Her pickup truck was soon rolling away. I found an old lawn chair to sit in, set the box on the ground in front of me, and dug into its contents.

After excavating a layer of sheet music, I found a disorganized pile of legal papers. I skimmed through them, picking out the pertinent facts and assembling the narrative of *Commonwealth v. Robert "Buck" McBride*.

The prosecution had exploited the property dispute between the two men to claim that Buck had committed murder to gain "a pecuniary benefit"—the precise language used in Virginia statutes to define a capital crime, which meant it was punishable by death.

This may have just been a negotiating ploy by the commonwealth. During law school, I'd worked at a free legal clinic that did some death penalty work, and my understanding was that "pecuniary benefit" meant murder for hire.

The discussions between the prosecution and Buck's lawyers were not in the documents. Was it possible that this was when Buck had started talking about the Praesidium? Had Buck started yammering about how this secret society had approached him and coaxed him into killing his neighbor to prevent some catastrophe?

I had no way of knowing just by looking at the paperwork. But at some point, Buck had been offered the option of pleading not guilty by reason of insanity, which he'd accepted.

NGRI, as it's known in legal circles, is not the Get Out of Jail Free card that it is sometimes portrayed to be. Once Buck pleaded NGRI, a judge would have mandated that he report to a mental hospital. And he wouldn't be able to get out until he convinced his doctors—who would then have to testify before a judge—that Buck was mentally competent.

Which explained why, after his initial shock at seeing that PR logo, Buck didn't want to say anything about the Praesidium.

I can't spend the rest of my life in here, and the only way I'm going to get out is . . .

. . . to keep his mouth shut and act like the Praesidium didn't exist.

This was all just a theory, of course. There was no mention of the Praesidium anywhere in the official documents—or, it seemed, anywhere else in the box.

At least not until I reached the very bottom of it. There, I found a tiny notebook. The first few pages were filled with small, neat handwriting.

Vanslow DeGange

b. 1925

Poor. Mother was seamstress. Father unknown.

Gypsy (not PC—called Romani now)

Grandmother, great aunt were fortune-tellers

Had many visions as boy/young man

Mother, grandmother called them his "special thoughts."

Warned him never to share outside community

US Army 1943-46

Assigned to Special Engineering Detachment (SED). Genius at fixing radios.

Promoted to Sergeant

Stationed at Los Alamos

Los Alamos as in . . . the Manhattan Project? I lowered the notebook for a moment and gazed into the trees in the distance. Vanslow DeGange had worked on the Manhattan Project?

Over a hundred thousand Americans did, of course. Almost none of them knew what they were actually making. It wasn't a stretch that a young man who had demonstrated a special aptitude for fixing radios would have been sent to Los Alamos. I continued.

First major vision, late June 45: the bomb wasn't necessary.

Had foreseen Japs would surrender Oct 45 b/c of pending US invasion of main island

Tried to convince SED colonel not to use the bomb

Colonel pretended to take it up chain of command. (Probably did not.)

Bomb goes off. DeGange devastated.

Vows never to rely on others again. Will recruit his "own Army."

Decides to found Praesidium

Has vision regarding White Chuck No. 8 silver mine, Bedal Wash

Buys stocks: IBM in 40s, Disney in 50s, McDonalds in 60s, etc.

So this was the Praesidium's alleged origin story: Vanslow DeGange found himself at Los Alamos and realized they were making a weapon of mass destruction that—according to his read on the future—didn't need to be deployed. But he couldn't get anyone to listen to him because, ultimately, he was just a poor gypsy boy who repaired radios.

This failure launched him on the quest to create his own future-fixing organization. The Praesidium. And he had no trouble funding the venture, because making money wouldn't be that difficult for a man who could see the future.

Even White Chuck No. 8, the stamp on the bottom of my gun, made sense. That was where he began to amass his fortune.

It actually sounded strangely plausible—if you forgot for a moment the whole thing was completely implausible.

Then I read on, and it took a turn toward the ridiculous, because the next entries were supposed case studies, times when the Praesidium had intervened in world affairs. Success stories, as it were.

And the first one was a whopper.

Case 1: John F. Kennedy

Killed because: Would have attempted to sneak nuclear missiles into Turkey, despite promising not to do so. Limited but devastating nuclear conflict with USSR would have resulted.

Lives saved: 2 million.

I sat there, blinking at the page a few times.

The Praesidium had killed Kennedy?

Really?

And yet . . . well, I had read a few biographies of Kennedy. All the Camelot stuff aside, he was a fairly belligerent guy. Some of his biographers suggested he exhibited classic sociopathic behavior, and that the only reason he went into politics instead of crime was that he had a rich father. There was the Bay of Pigs; his escalation of our presence in

Vietnam; the Cuban Missile Crisis, which was as close as the US and the Soviet Union had ever come to nuclear war.

Was it out of the realm of imagination to say that Kennedy would have eventually pushed too far?

Mr. DeGange is sometimes able to foresee when eliminating one person in the present can avert a much larger catastrophe in the future, thus saving many lives.

No, stop. This was absurd. And it only became more so with the next alleged intervention.

Case 2: Martin Luther King

Killed because: Would have succeeded in uniting Black Power movement in early 70s. Disturbance in Gary, Indiana, would have triggered unrest across nation. National Guard response would have led to small-scale civil war.

Lives saved: 8,000.

I was aghast. How could anyone claim killing a peace-loving humanitarian was good for the world? What would the Praesidium take credit for next? Gandhi?

And yet . . .

King had reached the nadir of his popularity by 1968. He was trying to organize something called the Poor People's Campaign, which smacked too much of socialism for mainstream America's tastes. If there was a time to kill him before he started becoming powerful again, that was it.

It wasn't inconceivable that once he returned to racial themes, he would have been able to use his celebrity and charisma to unify the heretofore-splintered African American political organizations. And, sure, King never would have condoned violence. But once he brought everyone under one banner, could it have created a group too unwieldy for King to control? Possibly.

Or I was possibly losing my mind. I read on all the same.

Case 3: Terry Nienhuis

Killed because: Would have recruited Norman Borlaug to work for DuPont, taking Borlaug away from work with Rockefeller Foundation in Mexico that triggered "Green Revolution"—dramatically raising plant yields and saving developing world from starvation.
Lives saved: 1 billion.

I had never heard of Terry Nienhuis. And a quick Google search suggested no one else had either. His death, whenever it happened, had gone unnoticed by the wider world.

Was this the kind of precedent Rogers would claim in asserting I needed to kill Jenny? That sometimes the person to be sacrificed wasn't a world leader but rather some relatively anonymous small cog who would unwittingly throw a much larger machine dangerously out of whack?

The notes ended there. I snapped photos of each page, in case I wanted to refer to them later. Then I closed up the storage unit as I had been instructed.

As I drove back to Surry to pick up the girls, I tried to make sense of everything.

This was only speculation, but I could imagine Buck's scribblings were notes he had taken while he was being indoctrinated into the Praesidium. Perhaps this was the rah-rah speech that preceded the branding with the PR logo.

Except if that was the case, I still wasn't buying it. That a secret society founded by a billionaire veteran of Los Alamos had killed Kennedy and King and God knows who else? Come on.

More likely: The notebook had been planted there by Lorton Rogers. Buck McBride was another Praesidium employee—or some kind of adjunct—who had been paid to perpetuate this whopper of a story. That brand on his arm was really stage makeup.

Perhaps he was simply a past associate of Rogers' who really had killed his neighbor and pleaded NGRI, and now Rogers was using him to bulwark this extravagant fiction.

But how could Rogers have anticipated I would even follow the digital bread crumbs that led to Buck in the first place?

Unless . . . well, I had once posted a comment about reverse image searches on a mommy blog I followed. Had Rogers scoured the web, found that, and known I would do the same with the key card logo, which would eventually lead me to Cult InfoShare—which was a fake website being run by the Praesidium—and then to Buck McBride?

Under this scenario, was I actually *supposed* to steal that key card? Had that, in fact, been a little too easy?

Or there was another possibility entirely:

Buck McBride had had a past encounter with Lorton Rogers and the Praesidium—who were working some entirely different scam than the one they were perpetrating now—and they had twisted him so thoroughly he'd wound up going insane. All these stories about Kennedy and King were merely instruments of that manipulation.

Making these notes little more than the ravings of a madman.

CHAPTER 9

JENNY

Once again, Jenny made her mad dash away from work so she could get some mommy time before the girls went to bed.

And, once again, Nate was acting aloof and strange. He had dumped the girls in Surry most of the day but was insisting this was not a sign he needed more help on the home front.

At least he'd managed to get the faucet fixed this time.

Jenny tried to put it out of her mind. Still, there was something gnawing at her all through the evening. And the next morning, right from the moment her alarm began its soft chirping at 5:30 a.m., she was gripped by this unplaceable dread.

Was it because of Nate and the gun? Surely she was being ridiculous. Nate would never hurt her.

Some things were just unthinkable.

And, really, what was more likely: That her very dependable, very agreeable, very loving husband—who had never lied to her and hated firearms—was suddenly trying to hide that he had bought a gun?

Or that her three-year-old daughter had conflated a gun she'd seen on a screen with a real-life gun?

That had to be it.

So she was mostly trying to put this odd feeling of apprehension out of her mind. But then it kicked up again as she parked in the garage across from her office and began weaving her way through the fountains.

Then, just as she was about to enter the front doors of CMR's glass tower, Jenny saw a woman loitering nearby.

She was older. Sixties. Seventies. She had hair whose orange coloring could have only come from a bottle. She had a solid build, larger on top than on bottom—the kind of woman whose sons, if she had any, would have become linebackers. She wore a plain red T-shirt that billowed on her, jeans, and bright-white sneakers.

The woman stood out because in this part of Richmond, at this time in the morning, there were really only two sorts of people on the street: those who were going to work, who walked with an unmistakable direction; and those who didn't have homes, who tended to move with less purpose.

This woman was neither. She was rooting through a grubby, floral-patterned bag that looked like a Vera Bradley knockoff and was too large to really be called a purse. More of an on-the-go bag.

But Jenny could have sworn that, a moment earlier, the woman had been staring at her and was now only pretending to look for something in her bag—all the while keeping Jenny in the corner of her eye.

Even stranger was that, as soon as Jenny saw the woman, that prickle of danger that had been with her all morning grew even stronger.

Jenny tried to tell herself she was being ridiculous. She was quite sure she had never seen this orange-haired woman before. There was no concrete reason to suspect her of anything.

She could have just been a little lost on her way to . . . somewhere. And maybe she was looking in her purse for her phone.

Nevertheless, when Jenny reached her office, she tapped out a quick email to Baraz "Barry" Khadem, a former high school football star, army intelligence officer, and Virginia State Trooper who was now CMR's director of security and investigations.

Barry's job, in football terms, involved both offense and defense. He coordinated the gathering of information for the many legal actions in which the firm was involved, dispensing both staff investigators (all of them, like Barry, former cops) and freelancers alike. That was the offense.

The defense involved making sure CMR's people and image—which, when combined, were what made the firm a billion-dollar-a-year business—were protected.

After requesting a meeting with Barry as soon as he had a moment, Jenny tried to put all the weirdness out of her mind and prepare for her first meeting of the day.

The man visiting her was a college professor who realized his sharpened pencil and similarly pointed mind could give him a lucrative side hustle as an expert witness in statistics. For $5,000 a day (his rate when testifying), or $2,000 a day (his rate when consulting), he could make math sing to juries and judges alike. He had been certified as an expert over a hundred times in both state and federal courts.

He arrived promptly at nine. Appropriately nebbish, the man set up his laptop and, one password later, had it communicating wirelessly with the conference room's smart board.

Jenny had barely introduced herself when he dived into his analysis, bringing up a map of the Richmond area with census divisions drawn on it.

Then he began what might as well have been a lecture to one of his advanced analytics classes. The rate of lung cancer diagnoses—both nationally and, by coincidence, in Virginia—was fifty-six per hundred thousand people per year. But that was not the case in the census tracts near the Shockoe Generation Plant, where all the 280 clients in Jenny's lawsuit resided.

There, the professor reported, the rate of lung cancer had consistently been four, six, or even ten times the average.

The chance of that happening randomly in one tract was small. The chance of that happening randomly in a cluster of tracts all packed together in one section of Richmond, Virginia, was astronomically miniscule.

One in 1.6 billion, to be exact.

"So not random," Jenny said.

"Decidedly not," the professor said. "I can walk you through the entire analysis and overwhelm you with numbers like I would in court, or I can just skip to the end: in my expert opinion, this is a cancer cluster. If this was water, and you were looking at one clear point source, the defendant would be begging to settle. The problem is, it's air. I'm unaware of anyone being able to successfully use this kind of analysis with air. Because how do you prove who tainted the air? What you have is not a statistical problem, but a legal problem."

Jenny didn't need to be told that the Clean Air Act was one of the more misnamed pieces of legislation ever passed. It was actually a license to release a certain amount of pollution. That it could claim to be cleaning the air was only because, prior to its existence, there was no limit to what a company's smokestacks could spew into the atmosphere.

"I'm aware," Jenny said. "Believe me, I'm aware. Though I may have a trick up my sleeve there. Now, let's go back to—"

Just then, from outside the glass window of the conference room, she saw the imposing shape and shaved head of Barry Khadem.

"Actually," Jenny said, "would you excuse me for a quick moment?"

Jenny retreated into the hallway.

"Sorry to bother you," Barry said. "But your email made it sound kind of urgent."

"It might be, or I might just be losing my mind," Jenny said. "But I think I'm being watched."

CHAPTER 10

NATE

All throughout Tuesday evening and into Wednesday morning, I felt like the only way to gain any clarity on the jumble of thoughts now muddling my mind was to return to Dominion State Hospital and see how much more Buck might be willing to say.

If I could convince him the doctors really couldn't use our confidential conversations against him in a court hearing, maybe he'd be more forthcoming.

Like, had he seen any actual evidence to back up these outrageous claims about historic assassinations? Or was it just mythology, the Praesidium equivalent of the Arthurian legends?

And, yes, if Buck really was being paid off by Lorton Rogers, I would just get more runaround. But if I kept pushing, I was sure his story would eventually crack. And then I'd know this was all just part of the ruse.

There were just two immediate problems with my plan to revisit Buck. And they were currently finishing up breakfast. I couldn't exactly take two toddlers into the high-security unit at the mental hospital.

I thought about dropping them at my in-laws' again, but I was out of excuses as to why I would do so. Besides, Jenny already thought I was losing my mind. I didn't want to give her more evidence of how true that was.

There were other options, though. And the first—and best—was my friend Kara Grichtmeier.

She was a fellow stay-at-home parent who lived two blocks over and also had two little girls who were about my girls' age. We had met at a Mommy & Me class (where I was the token daddy) and immediately hit it off.

Then it turned out we also frequented the same coffee shop. And the same playground. And the same grocery store. Our worlds—both small—almost perfectly overlapped. It was only natural we'd become friends.

When I first started, uh, seeing her, I worried about what Jenny would think. In addition to being smart, kind, and randomly irreverent, Kara was, quite inconveniently, a knockout: shimmering hair, flawless skin, nicely toned legs.

To diffuse any potential jealousy—and to make it clear I wasn't trying to hide anything—I had the genius idea of hiring a babysitter for all four kids and going out on a double date with our spouses.

Greg Grichtmeier turned out to be every bit as attractive as his wife. He was this big guy with a chiseled jaw and the kind of thick, wavy hair that belonged on a politician or a TV weatherman. He was also gregarious, charismatic, and, of all things, an accountant.

In a prime example of just how small a town Richmond was, he was a partner at the city's premier accounting firm. Its biggest client? Commonwealth Power & Light, of course.

I had never mentioned the lawsuit to Kara. CP&L buttered a lot of bread in the Grichtmeier family. If and when this thing exploded into something public, contentious, and nasty—something that required everyone even remotely involved to pick sides—it was entirely possible I'd lose my friend.

And that would be a shame. Because after that first double date turned out to be a smashing success—a lot of eating, drinking, and uproarious conversation—we had since made it a regular thing. Kara and Jenny became fast friends, as did Greg and I. Even Greg and Jenny clicked.

Kara and I had since established a kind of childcare cooperative. If either one of us had to ditch our kids for a few hours—for a doctor's appointment or some other engagement where dragging along the kids was either inconvenient or impossible—we knew we could rely on each other. It had worked out nicely that I had tended to need her about as often as she needed me, so no one felt like they were being abused.

It was now nine thirty. I called and found her amenable to taking the girls around noon. This would give me plenty of time to hustle out to Williamsburg, talk with Buck, and get back home. Jenny would never know I had been anywhere.

My plan was set. As I halfheartedly played with the girls that morning, I once again thought through the CP&L angle, feeling more certain the power company had to be involved somehow, and that the bed I had been strapped to was in J. Hunter Matthews' guest room.

With the Rembrandt. Which felt like something that was verifiable. You didn't just own a Rembrandt and have people not know about it. When your friends and guests came over, you showed it off, right?

That was still in the forefront of my mind as I pulled up to the Grichtmeiers' town house at noon. Once I got the girls settled, I turned to Kara and lobbed out what I hoped sounded like a casual inquiry.

"Hey, this is a random question, but have you ever been to Hunter Matthews' place?"

"Hunter Matthews," she said, wrinkling her brow. "You mean CP and L Hunter Matthews? *J.* Hunter Matthews?"

"Is there any other?"

"Right. Uhh, yeah, Greg and I were there at a fundraiser for a hospital maybe two years ago? The firm paid our way. It was one of those thousand-dollar-a-plate deals. His wife, Heather, is a big do-gooder. And I know because ever since that night we've been Facebook friends. She's one of those Facebook addicts who friends everyone she's ever met and then posts four status updates a day about how amazing she is. Why do you ask?"

"Oh, nothing really," I said. "I was just reading a piece about him in a magazine and was kind of daydreaming about what it must be like to have that much money. Did you know he owns a Rembrandt?"

"No kidding."

"Yeah. I think the article said it was in one of the bedrooms. Did you see it while you were there?"

"I might have. Honestly, I get all the dead European artists confused. I know it's impressionism if it's a bunch of dots, and it's early Renaissance if Jesus looks like a tiny bodybuilder. Otherwise it all kind of blends together."

"Yeah, I hear you," I said, like this was all nonchalant. "What was the house like?"

"Oh, you know. It was one of those boss places along the James River. You can actually see it from two eighty-eight. All I could think is how long it would take to clean it."

I laughed, because that's what I would have done if I was just being Kara's good ol' friend Nate.

But her description certainly fit my experience of the place I had been taken to. It had obviously been a grand home. It certainly could have been one of the historic plantations set up on a bluff above the James River.

"I think they have people for that," I said. "But was there, you know, a lot of art hanging on the walls, or . . ."

Kara scrunched her face. "I don't remember any more or less than normal for a house like that. I didn't know you were into that sort of thing."

"Oh, you know, grow up in New York City and it kind of happens by osmosis."

"Right," she said.

"Anyway, thanks for taking the girls. This appointment shouldn't last *too* long. It's just that it's an hour away. I'll see you after nap time?"

"You bet," she said.

And, after one more exchange of friendly smiles, I was off for Dominion State Hospital.

I felt like an old pro, pulling into the hospital's main entrance, driving past the signs telling me I was under video surveillance.

As I walked up to the admissions desk, I already had my license out. It was the same woman who had helped me the day before.

"Hi," I said, extending my ID. "Attorney Nate Lovejoy here to see my client Buck McBride."

She looked mildly horrified by this.

"Well, you know he's not *here* anymore, right?"

"What do you mean he's not here?"

"The medical examiner's office has him. They came and got him a few hours ago."

"The . . . medical examiner's office," I said.

And I must have looked as puzzled as I felt, because she asked, "Didn't anyone contact you?"

"Contact me about what?"

She sat up a little straighter.

"I'm sorry, I thought you would have known already. Mr. McBride hung himself early this morning."

CHAPTER 11

JENNY

The door to Jenny's office was about seven-eighths closed, a position intended to say: *Bother me if you have to.*

But don't bother me.

The professor had left Jenny a two-inch-thick binder stuffed with figures, maps, and regression analyses, all of which undergirded his expert conclusion that the section of Richmond downwind of the Shockoe Generation Plant was a cancer cluster.

As tedious as it was, Jenny knew the numbers might end up forming the backbone of her case, and so she had dedicated herself to plowing through it on the off chance that a judge actually read the whole thing and wanted to ask questions or—as was much more likely—the defense decided to get picayune with it.

She was just beginning to recall some sliver of the college statistics class she had once vowed to forget when there came a tiny knock at her door—with a large man soon entering behind it.

"Sorry, is this a bad time?" Barry Khadem asked.

"No, come on in," Jenny said.

He closed the door behind himself, then crossed her office and sat on the other side of her desk.

"So as I believe you're aware, one of the things my guys do is keep an eye on the outside of the building—the parking garage, the plaza. We've got cameras all around. We don't want anything to happen to one of our people out there."

"Sure," Jenny said.

In his presentations to the partners, Barry was always referring to what "my guys" were up to. He was often deliberately vague about who the "guys" were and what methodologies they used.

"That woman you told us about? We've started referring to her as 'Code Orange.' I don't know if it's you she's after or not. But she's definitely up to something. She's been out there all morning."

Barry held up an iPad so Jenny could see it and began swiping through pictures showing the woman in various poses and various places in and around the plaza. He was going quickly until he stopped on an image that was much sharper than the rest, a close-up of the woman as she smoked a cigarette.

"One of my guys snuck out and took this with a zoom lens," Barry said. "Does she look familiar?"

Barry slid the iPad across the desk. Jenny tilted it upward and studied the photo. Up close the woman's hair showed the ravages of the cheap orange dye she had been using for too long. Her cheeks evinced the fine creep of age. Her eyes were smaller than Jenny remembered, surrounded by skin that had long ago gone loose.

Just looking at the photo, Jenny had that awful sense of foreboding she had felt this morning all over again.

But recognize Code Orange?

"No," Jenny said. "I've never seen her before this morning."

"Well, she seems to be hanging around for some reason. She stays on the move for the most part, but she almost always keeps a line of sight on the front entrance. That T-shirt she's wearing is so loose, she could have anything under there. And we don't like that bag she's carrying either."

"Because it could have a weapon?" Jenny asked.

"A weapon or a detonator or, well, who knows," Barry said. "You know I did a couple tours in Iraq, right? If I was in Baghdad or Mosul right now, I'd be thinking suicide bomber, all the way."

"But you're in Richmond, so—"

"So it's pretty unlikely, but we still want to keep a careful eye on her. Earlier, when you said you thought you were being watched, was there anything specific that made you think this woman is targeting you?"

"No, just a hunch, I guess," Jenny said.

"Okay. Well, I don't want to take any chances. Were you planning to leave the building for any reason today? Other than when you go home?"

"No."

"Good. When you decide you want to get out of here for the day, give a call down. If Code Orange is still out there, I'll have one of my guys escort you to the parking garage. Sound like a plan?"

"You bet."

"And in the meantime, if you change your mind and decide you need to go out—even if it's just for a smoke break, or to run to the store, or whatever—just give a holler and I'll send someone with you."

"I don't smoke."

"But still. You'll let me know?"

"Of course."

Barry smiled at her. "It's probably nothing."

Jenny wasn't so sure.

CHAPTER 12

NATE

Before I departed Dominion State, I let it be known with the hospital's legal department that, as Mr. McBride's attorney, I planned to make a formal inquiry into his cause of death.

I just didn't believe—in some very firm spot in my gut—that Buck McBride had killed himself.

There were the logistical difficulties: he was confined to the high-security unit at a state hospital, where they took myriad precautions to prevent patients from harming themselves; he was searched regularly for contraband; he wasn't even allowed to have a belt or shoelaces.

But it was more than that.

If I took him at face value—an admittedly dicey proposition—he had clearly been looking forward to getting *out* of Dominion State Hospital someday. His reticence about the Praesidium was because he didn't want to jeopardize his chances at freedom.

Would a man with that kind of future focus really kill himself?

I doubted it. Somehow, Lorton Rogers and the Praesidium had murdered him and made it look like suicide.

For someone with essentially unlimited resources, it wouldn't really be all that difficult. The simplest way would be to pay someone on the inside to do it.

A guard. An orderly. Rogers had probably supplied one of them with the same anesthesia he'd used to zonk me. From there, it would be pretty simple. A staff member would know where the security cameras were—and, more importantly, where they *weren't*. Then it was just a matter of smuggling in a rope, drugging Buck in his sleep, and stringing up his inert body.

As to why?

Simple. Dead men tell no tales.

Assuming Buck was being paid to mislead me—as part of CP&L's grand scheme—he had now served his purpose. Rogers had him killed before I could come back for a follow-up conversation, at which point Buck might have screwed up and said something that made me realize this was all a scam.

My chest felt heavy. Even though I had never touched the rope, I felt like I was responsible for this death. I had fallen into the trap Rogers had set for me.

Except, well, how did Rogers know I had even gone out to see Buck in the first place? It's not like he could have followed me yesterday. I had gone out to Surry first. I would have easily noticed a tail. Unless . . .

Were they tracking me electronically? Like with a GPS device they had installed on my Range Rover?

I was still on Dominion State Hospital grounds as this was all coming to me. Just to get away from hospital security cameras—and so no one would see Mr. McBride's attorney crawling underneath his car—I drove out, then pulled off at a nearby condominium complex and began searching my vehicle.

The GPS itself could be incredibly small, but it would need some kind of transceiver, which would be roughly the size of a small cell phone. I scoured my car's cabin, the engine compartment, the wheel wells, the entire undercarriage.

And that's where I found it, attached to one of the struts. I pried the thing off and studied it for a moment. There were no markings on it, nothing that identified it as belonging to the Praesidium.

I thought about trying some clever counterintelligence measure—attaching it to an out-of-state truck, making them think I was heading down to South Carolina or wherever. But I really just wanted to be rid of the damn thing.

So I spiked it on the asphalt, stomped on it with my heel, then tossed the shattered remains in a nearby dumpster.

Two minutes later, I was back underway, pointed toward Richmond and the girls, when my phone rang. The number came up as *Unavailable*.

"Hello?" I said.

"Hello, Nate. I see you found our tracking device."

It was the smooth, FM-radio-deejay voice of Lorton Rogers.

"Yeah, I did," I said, the anger immediately rising in me. "Why did you kill Buck McBride? Hadn't you done enough to destroy his life already?"

"Buck McBride?" he said, like this astonished him. "You mean *our* Buck McBride? He's dead?"

"Don't play stupid. Yes he's dead. He supposedly killed himself early this morning, but I know you're responsible somehow. Did one of your henchmen manage to break into the hospital or did you just pay someone to do it?"

"We had nothing to do with Buck's death, I assure you," he said. "We haven't had any contact with Buck in years."

I swore at him.

"You don't believe me?"

"Of course I don't. You're nothing but a killer and a liar."

Rogers absorbed the insults silently. "I assure you, if we had wanted to kill Buck, we would have done so a long time ago. We considered him to be effectively neutralized. He couldn't talk about the Praesidium without risking his own chances of ever being released from the hospital. How can I convince you of that? I don't want this to be a distraction for you."

"A *distraction*? You don't want me distracted from killing my wife. Oh, that's very, very considerate of you. Thanks so much for that, Rogers."

"You like to use sarcasm, Nate. That's fine. I suppose I would, too, in your situation. And I know up to this point we've had to use . . . a certain amount of coercion. But that's not really how we like to go about things. I want us to have an open, honest relationship. Are you really that interested in Buck McBride? Ask me anything. I'll tell you whatever you want to know."

Open?

Honest?

This guy was too much.

"Fine," I said. "Just for grins, go ahead. Tell me your version of the Buck McBride story."

"Very well. Buck was one of us. I'm sure he told you as much. We approached him in the same way we approached you. We needed him to kill his neighbor."

"Yeah, why?"

"The man was a pyromaniac. Mr. DeGange had foreseen that he was days away from setting a devastating fire at a nightclub in Norfolk that would have killed something like two hundred people."

"Okay, great. But then why didn't the Praesidium just kill this neighbor? Why involve a third party like Buck McBride?"

"For the same reason we've involved you. Mr. DeGange doesn't just see *who* needs to die, he sees *how* they need to die—in the neatest, cleanest way possible."

"You mean neat and clean from the Praesidium's perspective," I said.

"Well, yes. I suppose that's true. But think about the bigger picture. Mr. DeGange uses his gift to save lives. Sometimes in the hundreds. Sometimes in the thousands or millions. That's important work. He can't risk the organization being compromised. We were sloppy with that early on—this was before my time, mind you—and have since refined our operations. We are now scrupulous about keeping the Praesidium away from *any* potential suspicion. We simply cannot lead the authorities to our own doorstep. Not even once. Any law enforcement attention we attracted would severely hamper our ability to do our work."

"So you goad Buck into doing the killing—to make it look like it's just a guy murdering his neighbor—and then you hang him out to dry and let him go off to a mental hospital? Charming. You should definitely put that one on the Praesidium membership brochure."

"I assure you, that was Buck's own fault," Rogers said. "We had planted evidence to assure Buck would be acquitted. We had hired the best lawyers for him. All he had to do was keep his mouth shut. And then when the prosecutors came up with that nonsense about this being a death penalty case, Buck panicked. His mother wasn't well, and he worried that the stress of such a case would be too much for her. When the prosecutor dangled 'not guilty by reason of insanity' in exchange for taking the death penalty off the table, Buck took the deal before we could talk him out of it. That's the truth. Why, what did Buck tell you?"

There was nothing in the paperwork Buck had left behind to refute Rogers' version of the events. There was also nothing to support it.

"Buck didn't say much, to be honest," I said. "Though I did find his notebook—or, I should say, the notebook you planted there."

"I don't know what you're talking about."

"Of course not. It was the Praesidium's greatest-hits album—JFK, MLK, Terry Borlaug, or whatever that guy's name was."

"Really? Buck wrote that all down?"

"Ah. Now you're going to tell me he broke the rules and that I never should have seen all that?"

"No, you would have learned about it eventually. We give all our members a . . . I guess you would call it a history lesson. We usually just save that for a little later. It can be pretty overwhelming for people if we start by upending so much of what they think they know."

"Well, here we are. And since we're being 'open' and 'honest,' what I want to know is: If your Mr. DeGange is so great, why has there still been so much bad stuff in the world over the last sixty years? Where was Mr. DeGange in Syria or Cambodia? Where was he when Hutus were slaughtering Tutsis in Rwanda? Where was he on 9/11? Why didn't he find a way to head off the novel coronavirus before it got out?"

"Mr. DeGange is not omniscient. The further something is from his thoughts, the less likely he is to have a vision regarding it. And the Praesidium is not omnipotent. The coronavirus sprang forth on the other side of the globe, where we have no real presence. Furthermore, some atrocities, like the Rwandan genocide, cannot be averted simply by removing one person or even a group of people. They have developed a historical momentum over a hundred years or more that make them essentially unstoppable. By the time Mr. DeGange felt those ripples, those deaths were already inevitable.

"There are also times when Mr. DeGange says even the worst catastrophe is ultimately, for lack of a better word, necessary," Rogers continued. "In the case of 9/11, it was terrible, of course. An absolute tragedy. But it also resulted in the downfall of Saddam Hussein, who had already killed fifty thousand of his own citizens and would have murdered many more. Would you save three thousand Americans if you knew it would result in the death of an additional fifty thousand Iraqis and another fifty thousand Kurds? Because that's the kind of math Mr. DeGange has to do all the time."

"Yes, that must be very hard on him," I said, still in full sarcasm mode.

"I realize you still don't believe me. It's okay. You will."

"He's foreseen that too?"

"As a matter of fact, yes."

"I'm sure," I said. "Look, if your Mr. DeGange is so clever, why doesn't he give me some lottery numbers. I saw on a billboard I just passed that the Mega Millions is up to a hundred and seventy-eight million."

"This is not a parlor game, Nate," Rogers lectured. "Mr. DeGange is not going to pull your card out of the deck or make a quarter appear from behind your ear either. His gift is not attuned to frivolous matters like the lottery."

"Because his gift doesn't exist."

"No, it's because there's nothing life and death about the lottery. Two million people lose a dollar so one person can make a million. The rest goes to the government, and then everyone moves on."

"Fine. Great. So why don't you tell me about a place where there *is* a ripple? You're asking me to believe Vanslow DeGange is this great death-seeing prophet and you have a bunch of stories about catastrophes you've supposedly prevented. How about your soothsayer actually says some sooth about something that hasn't already happened?"

"You want proof, am I hearing that right?" Rogers said.

"Yes. Proof. I want your guy to make a prediction—one prediction about the future that actually comes true, and that I can verify myself."

"Very well. Sit tight. I'll consult Mr. DeGange and call you back."

"Fantastic."

I continued driving, wondering what kind of machinations I had just set off within the halls of CP&L.

Were they right now ginning up some reason the great Vanslow DeGange would be unable to demonstrate his powers? Or were they, in fact, trying to arrange for him to make a "prediction" they would then make come "true"?

Like, say, that a citywide power outage would happen. Or a transformer would blow up. Or tonight at nine o'clock my lights would blink three times. Something CP&L could manipulate.

I had merged onto the interstate and traveled maybe a dozen miles when my phone rang again.

Unavailable, calling back.

"Yes?" I said.

"There is a man named Marcus Sakey," Rogers said.

"Okay, what about him?"

"He's a bum. Sorry, I know you're probably not supposed to call them that anymore. He's homeless. Transient. Whatever the right word is. What little money he is able to panhandle, he converts into alcohol. His primary occupation is staggering around the city and rummaging through garbage bins for food."

"Sounds like a winner. Why are you telling me all this?"

"At 11:16 this evening, he will be struck and killed by a hit-and-run driver."

I felt a jolt, almost like I was the one being hit. "Oh God. Where?"

"It will happen within a few blocks of your home. Mr. DeGange was explicit that I couldn't give you any more details. You might attempt to intercede."

"Well, of course I'm . . . why aren't *you* interceding? I thought you guys were all about saving lives. You're really just going to let this man die?"

"I realize you'll find this to be more cruel calculus, but Mr. DeGange decided a long time ago that he would essentially allow individual deaths so that the organization could focus its time and energy on mass-casualty events," Rogers said. "Besides, this is a quicker, more merciful end than Mr. Sakey probably deserves. He has spent most of his life abusing his body. He should have died years ago."

"That doesn't justify letting him get run over like a piece of roadkill."

"I'm sorry, Nate. You wanted proof. That's your proof. Maybe the next time we talk you'll be a little less cynical about Mr. DeGange."

"He's a human being, for God's sake," I yelled. "Don't let this happen. *Please.*"

But Rogers had already hung up.

CHAPTER 13

JENNY

One of the things Jenny had always prided herself on was her ability to ignore all distractions and focus on the task at hand.

She was doing a fine job of it, plowing into some work for one of her non-CP&L-related clients, billing hours, ignoring Code Orange, ignoring whatever was going on with Nate, when she got one of those texts she couldn't ignore.

It was the burner phone: Hey, can you do 2:30?

Again? So soon?

No. She really couldn't.

She absolutely didn't have the time.

And yet . . .

Her thumbs punched the usual three-letter reply: Yes.

Which opened up a new conundrum.

Code Orange might have still been outside. Lurking. With that bag. And that billowing red shirt with who knows what underneath. And those ill intentions that Jenny swore weren't just her imagination.

Then there was the other problem: Jenny had told Barry she would ask for an escort if she left the building, but she couldn't allow Barry to know about this particular errand, and she didn't want any of Barry's "guys" knowing about it either.

She didn't want *anyone* knowing about it. The risk of exposure was too great, and the consequences of exposure would be . . .

Well, disastrous.

And, yeah, she could just try to sneak out and make a run for it. But she knew Barry had those cameras. If he or one of his employees saw Jenny, how would she explain herself?

There was no good solution here.

That left her with only bad ones.

Like a disguise. It didn't have to be elaborate. Just something that would get her past the cameras.

Looking around her office, she spied a Richmond Flying Squirrels baseball cap hanging on the back of the door. She had bought it the previous summer, when CMR had sponsored an outing to a game. The flying squirrel logo looked more like an angry vampire bat.

She grabbed the hat and some sunglasses from her purse, then told her assistant, "I need some air. I'll be back in a bit."

In the lobby, she quickly braided her hair into two pigtails, then shoved the hat on her head and tugged it down low. She donned the sunglasses and looked at herself in the reflection of the glass.

She was still a six-foot-tall woman—not exactly inconspicuous—but there wasn't much she could do about that, except the one thing she had always tried not to do. Hunch over.

So that was Jenny as she made her departure from CMR headquarters: pigtails, hat, sunglasses, stooped gait.

She spun through the revolving doors, then cut at an angle across the plaza, through the fountains, with an elongated stride that had her covering ground even faster than usual.

All the while, she kept swiveling her eyes, looking for a flash of red shirt or a tuft of orange hair.

Nothing yet.

She didn't know where Barry's cameras were. Probably everywhere. So she just kept her head down and hoped the hat was doing its job.

Once she made it to the sidewalk, she turned toward The Commonwealth Hotel and kept her legs churning.

Lest she look suspicious or draw attention to herself, she didn't want to look behind herself, which was where Code Orange would likely be coming from. If Code Orange was anywhere at all.

But it didn't seem like she was. After two blocks—at which point she reasoned she was out of range of Barry's cameras—Jenny turned around.

She had the sidewalk to herself.

Heaving a sigh, she completed the trip to The Commonwealth without incident.

Had this really all been nothing? Why did she feel so spooked?

She rode the elevator up to the usual room, waved the key card at the door, and there he was as usual, lounging on the bed with his perfect hair and his movie star jaw, just grinning at her.

"Ohhh, are we doing cosplay today?" he asked, smiling. "You're the farmer's daughter, right? Whatever it is, I like it."

She fixed him with a mock-angry look. "You're a real pain in the ass, you know that, Grichtmeier?"

CHAPTER 14

NATE

After picking up the girls at the Grichtmeiers'—and thanking Kara profusely for watching them—I parked my car in a nearby garage.

Now that I had successfully untracked it, I wanted it to stay that way.

Jenny arrived home at half past six. She asked where the Range Rover was, and I made up a story about how it was in the shop.

She then tossed herself into being with the girls like she always did. And I tidied up and made us dinner like I always did. It was, at least outwardly, a normal Wednesday night in the Welker-Lovejoy household.

Yet the whole time, I was becoming increasingly overwhelmed by anxiety.

The first source of it was what would allegedly happen at 9:47 on Friday evening, a clock whose ticking was getting to be like drumbeats in my head.

The second part was more immediate, and that was what would supposedly transpire at 11:16 this evening.

After tucking in the girls, Jenny and I ate and chatted. I lied about what the girls and I had done all day, saying we went to the park in the morning, and then the girls took extralong naps in the afternoon.

She then told me about her day. There was a bizarre episode involving a woman with orange hair, which had been concerning enough that Barry Khadem—who I knew a bit from my days at CMR—had insisted she be escorted out of the building.

Even more ominously, she enthused at length about this terrific meeting she'd had with an expert witness on the CP&L case. It was enough to make me worried she really *was* on the verge of a legal breakthrough, until I reminded myself that was just what Lorton Rogers wanted me to think.

After dinner, Jenny announced she was exhausted and going to bed. I joined her, because that's what I normally would have done. But sleep was far from my mind. As Jenny's breathing slowed and she drifted off to sleep, I began thinking about my next move.

It was staggering, being charged with the knowledge of a stranger's imminent death. I truly didn't understand how Rogers could be so indifferent about it. This wasn't some hypothetical scenario, tossed out in Philosophy 101 to be pontificated upon by half-interested students.

This was real. Marcus Sakey was currently a living, breathing person. Maybe he wasn't much of a person—not someone I'd invite to dinner, not someone I'd leave alone with my children—but he still possessed some portion of the infinite possibility, as any other member of our species did.

What if he was about to sober up? Find true love? Write a brilliant novel?

It was unlikely, sure; but as long as he remained with us, his redemption was still possible.

There was also a part of this that wasn't about him. It was about me. If I was going to maintain any correspondence with my humanity—with my sense of decency—I had to at least try to keep him alive.

Rogers had said the "accident" would take place "within a few blocks" of here. How many was a few? More than two, I guessed. But three? Five?

Once I was sure Jenny was solidly down, I eased out of bed and grabbed shorts and jogging shoes from the closet. I wrote a sticky note saying I couldn't sleep and was going out for a run.

I left the note on Jenny's phone, which was plugged in over at the charging station on the other side of the room. She didn't so much as stir.

Soon, I was out the door, into the streets.

We lived on Grove Avenue, in the heart of the Fan. Imagining our house as the epicenter, my plan was to walk in ever-widening concentric circles so I would cover the entire area around where we lived. I'd find him soon enough.

I set off at a brisk walk, taking right turns, searching for someone who might fit the rough profile of Marcus Sakey.

Shambling. Dirty. Lost in a bottle.

As block after pointless block passed under my feet, it didn't take long for my optimism to wane. My concentric-circle plan was fine for a stationary target. Sakey was moving.

And I was already running out of time. According to my phone, it was now 10:13, a little more than an hour to go.

Giving up on my circles, I pointed myself east, walking toward the center of the city, looking for someone who might be more familiar with society's underbelly. I was near the Altria Theater when I saw a guy with a bulging garbage bag slung over his shoulder, wearing way too much clothing for this warm a night, shuffling along with a limp.

I hurried to catch up, and had soon overtaken him.

"Excuse me, sir," I said.

He seemed to startle and cower simultaneously. I became aware of my size, which was considerably greater than his.

"Sorry, I didn't mean to scare you," I continued, even as he eyed me. "I'm looking for a man named Marcus. Marcus Sakey. Do you know him by any chance?"

"Marcus?" he said.

By this point, I was close enough that I could make out the yeasty smell rolling off him.

"Yes. Marcus Sakey. I'm trying to help him. It's important."

The guy considered this a little longer. He was struggling either with the question or with locating his own senses.

Then he said, "Don't know no Marcus."

"Sorry to trouble you," I said, then hurried onward.

Over the next twenty minutes, I had similar interactions with an older woman who was slumped against a building with her dog, with a guy who then attempted to panhandle me, with a guy who was sleeping on a park bench until I nudged him awake, and with a younger man who was clearly strung out.

Finally, an older man with salt-and-pepper dreadlocks, who had been hanging out in the parking lot of a 7-Eleven, brightened when I mentioned the name.

"I know Marcus, yeah," he said. "Haven't seen him in a minute, but I know him."

"Do you know where I might find him?"

"He sometimes hangs out near Catholic Charities."

Of course he did. Why hadn't I thought of that? I thanked the man, then sped off, breaking into a jog. Soon, I was standing in front of Commonwealth Catholic Charities on Grace Street.

It was buttoned up tight. There was no one hanging out nearby.

I swore softly but continued running, covering the block around it, then two blocks. I was now asking anyone I saw—dog walkers, students, and local residents alike—if they knew Marcus Sakey.

No one did. It was nearing 11:00 p.m. I was up on Broad Street by that point, in a part of town that might be deemed "in transition" but had been improving fast, thanks to the presence of VCU. It was also more than a mile from our house, which didn't seem to fit the definition of "a few blocks."

I hailed a cab and asked the driver to get me back to our address on Grove Avenue as quickly as he could. When he came to our corner, I said, "This is close enough," flipped a twenty over the seat, and got out while the car was still moving.

It was now 11:05. There were—if this whole thing wasn't just another facet of a continuing deception—exactly eleven minutes left in Marcus Sakey's miserable life, and I was no closer to finding him than I had been two hours earlier.

Not knowing what else to do, I started my concentric circles again, this time making lefts, if only to try something different.

There was almost no one out on the street. The night had cooled somewhat. I was still perspiring heavily.

In desperation, I started yelling every block or so, "Marcus. Marcus Sakey? Does anyone know a Marcus Sakey?"

11:08.

11:11.

11:13.

As the minutes fell away, my cries became louder and more frequent, but no more effective. The Fan was now mostly asleep.

I was hurrying down West Main Street, passing an Exxon station that was two blocks from where we lived. The only person in sight was a man pumping gas.

"Excuse me, sir, do you know someone named Marcus Sakey?" I asked, approaching fast.

In the way he recoiled, I could almost see my own mania being reflected back at me. I'm sure I was disheveled. My voice sounded unhinged. I could feel my own heart hammering.

"Sorry, pal, can't help ya," he said, but only after I had stopped running toward him.

I looked down at my phone.

11:16, exactly.

I had failed. I stopped on the sidewalk, listening for . . . something. The shrieking of tires. An engine gunning. A man's anguished scream as steel crunched bone.

But all I heard were the sounds of the city. Cars rolling past. Music from a nearby bar. Nothing at all seemed out of sorts or different.

11:17.

Had a life just been snuffed out or not? If Lorton Rogers and Vanslow DeGange were, in fact, frauds, then there was no Marcus Sakey, and therefore there would be no accident. They would probably try to fabricate one later. Perhaps they would hack into Richmond.com and upload a fake story about a hit-and-run death of Marcus Sakey, with police allegedly asking for leads.

11:18.

I was just walking aimlessly now, without a plan, half-blind from exhaustion and also a weird, aimless sort of grief. I was mourning someone I had never met, whose passing I ordinarily never would have known about. Did that even make sense? Thousands of people die every day in the United States—like, one every twelve seconds, right?—which meant even if Marcus Sakey had been killed at 11:16, ten more Americans had expired since then. Could I really—

And then a police car ripped past me, lights flashing, sirens wailing, heading south.

I sprinted after it, not slowing or breaking stride as I crossed through the next intersection, earning an angry honk from a truck that I had dashed in front of.

At the end of the block, the cop turned left on Cary Street. I continued my chase, arms pumping, legs flying.

As soon as I rounded the corner, I saw the officer's destination. There were already two other police cars and an ambulance at the corner of Granby Street. I pressed forward, determined to continue until some-one stopped me, which a young male officer soon did.

"Sir, I'm going to have to ask you to step back to the other side of the street," he said.

"What happened?" I asked.

"A pedestrian was struck and killed by a hit-and-run."

"Was his name Marcus Sakey by any chance?"

The cop looked at me strangely. "Yes. How did you know?"

Before long I was being questioned by a detective. I concocted a story about how I bought Marcus Sakey a sandwich now and then but didn't know anything useful beyond that.

Eventually, I was permitted to leave. I trudged home and silently entered through the back door.

I crept softly up the stairs and dropped my damp clothing in the hamper we kept in the hallway, then paused at the entrance to our darkened bedroom.

Jenny's breathing was still slow and steady. I didn't even think she had changed position since I'd left. I went over to the charging station and removed the sticky note from her phone, then eased into bed.

As far as she would be concerned, I had never left.

CHAPTER 15

JENNY

Jenny woke up at 5:22, eight minutes before her alarm clock would have rung, and shut it off so it wouldn't rouse anyone else in the household.

She turned toward Nate, taking momentary stock of the man she shared her life with.

He was sleeping on his side, his hands tucked under his pillow in childlike repose. She found herself thinking of their thirteen years together. Sometimes, the time seemed like an eyeblink—had it really been that long? Other times, she couldn't even remember a life without Nate.

Or maybe she just didn't want to. So much of her life was this precarious act. Whether it was as a lawyer or as a mother, she felt like she was constantly faking it, flailing in midair, moments away from a humbling and painful crash.

Nate was her solid ground.

The place where she knew she could dependably land, no matter what. The part of her life where she never had to fake anything.

Her favorite country song—no, her favorite song, period—was "Bless the Broken Road." And not the poppy, Disney-fied cover by

Rascal Flatts. The original, soulful acoustic version by the Nitty Gritty Dirt Band.

It was about someone who set out to find true love. And while there had been loss and heartache on the way, God had blessed the broken road that allowed them to find it.

He played that song when he proposed to her. They danced to it at their wedding. She still played it—sometimes just in her mind—when she needed comforting.

She was thinking about it as she watched him slumber.

Then something changed. She was looking even more closely at him now. His eyeballs were darting about under his eyelids, looking around at whatever dream his subconscious had conjured up.

It made him seem almost shifty, like someone who couldn't make eye contact. And for just a moment, she had this feeling like he was keeping something from her.

Something important. Something she really needed to know.

Then she told herself she was just imagining it. Nate never kept anything important from her.

Having chased the adverse thoughts from her mind, she lifted herself out of bed and got on with Thursday morning: a shower, which she turned cold at the end to wake herself up; a quick blow-dry, just enough that her hair was only slightly damp; and a dive into the closet, where she came away with a light-gray skirt suit and white blouse.

As she finished in front of the mirror, she listened to the noises of the house, which had come alive a little earlier than usual.

Parker was singing to her oatmeal, the lyrics a delightful mish-mash of preschooler jabber. Nate was announcing the arrival of avocado chunks to Cate, who immediately cooed her approval with a spurt of nonsense words.

Jenny loved these sounds. She made it a point to try to memorize them. Even though infancy and toddlerhood seemed to be lasting forever, the girls wouldn't always be so little. Someday soon their monologues would shift to the inside, leaving their mother to wonder what was going on in their heads.

Nate had a cup of coffee waiting for Jenny when she arrived in the kitchen.

"Good morning," she said brightly.

"Morning."

"How'd you sleep?"

"Like a rock. How about you?"

He looked up from some strawberries he was cutting with a weary smile. She noted the bags under his eyes, the way his posture was just slightly stooped.

Apparently, rocks didn't sleep as well as they used to.

"Fine," she said.

Then, from the table, Parker piped up. "Daddy, are we going to Mia's house again today?"

"I don't think so, honey," Nate replied.

Jenny's head jerked from her eldest daughter to her husband.

"You were at the Grichtmeiers' yesterday?" she asked.

"Uhh, yeah," he said, his attention back to the strawberries.

"When?"

"The afternoon."

"Oh. You just didn't mention that last night."

He kept cutting the fruit.

She prodded, "Was it a playdate or one of your childcare swaps or . . ."

"Yeah," he said.

"Which one?"

"Huh?"

"I asked whether it was a playdate or a—"

"Yeah, I just dropped them off for a little while. Why are you making a big deal out of it?"

"I'm not making any kind of deal. You just didn't mention it last night. You said it was a normal afternoon, that the girls took an extralong nap," she said, feeling like she was cross-examining a difficult witness.

"Oh. It must have just slipped my mind."

"What were you doing?"

"So we *are* making a big deal out of this," he said.

"Well, maybe we should. You said the other day after you dumped them on my parents that you didn't need extra help. Do we need to revisit that? It's okay to ask for help, you know. You don't have to be such a guy about it."

"I'm not being a guy, I just . . . I had to drop the car off at the Range Rover dealership—I told you that. And I didn't want to drag the girls along, so I asked Kara to watch them for a little bit. I'm fine. I don't need help, okay?"

The last part was snappish, which wasn't like Nate at all. Jenny decided to back off.

"Okay," she said, then plastered a smile on her face, went on her tiptoes, and planted a kiss on his cheek. "I have to go."

"Yeah, have a good day. Love you."

"Love you too," she said.

She kissed both girls, but as she went out to the car, she was again asking herself whether Nate was hiding something.

CHAPTER 16

NATE

I had been so focused on getting away with my evening adventure I hadn't been expecting more inquiry about my afternoon.

But I felt like I recovered well. As long as Jenny didn't insist on seeing service records, the Range Rover story was going to hold up fine.

Still, the weight of the lies was accumulating fast, like a load of boulders floating somewhere above me. How long until one of them came loose and bashed my head?

More than that, I hated how it felt. And I wasn't sure I had the capacity in my brain to keep all my falsehoods straight. Especially after the Marcus Sakey incident.

I had been mulling the implications of Sakey's death all night and into the morning.

Had it convinced me beyond a doubt that Vanslow DeGange could peer into the future? Not really. There were a hundred ways the Praesidium could have manipulated his "accident" to fit a supposed prophecy.

Had it convinced me Lorton Rogers and his accomplices were a ruthless bunch, fully capable of killing Jenny or my entire family to get what they wanted?

Absolutely.

Even if the predictions weren't real, the threat was.

And, to a certain extent, it didn't matter whether they were a shadowy secret society or a bunch of CP&L henchmen. One way or another, they wanted this lawsuit to go away.

So did I, when I really thought about it. This wasn't my fight. I felt bad for the people who were sick, naturally; and I felt like they deserved justice, of course; but I wasn't willing to sacrifice my family for it.

Yet, without being able to tell Jenny what was really happening, there was no chance I could convince her to drop the suit. She had spent two years building the case. She believed in it. She was attached emotionally to the plaintiffs.

I would have to make an end run around her. And I knew where to start.

Albert Dickel, my onetime mentor, had never liked the CP&L suit, which he viewed as an expensive loser.

But he did like me. He always had, for whatever reason. Even these days—when I was no possible use to the man—I would see him when I sometimes made random visits to the office, with the girls in tow. Jenny and I jokingly called it "Your Daughters Show Up at Work Day."

We did it maybe once a month. It was just an easy way to kill time—which, with two toddlers, I had way too much of. As soon as we showed up, half the associates, paralegals, and secretaries on Jenny's floor immediately quit whatever they were doing so they could make a fuss over the girls. I might as well have been invisible.

Not to Dickel. He often went out of his way to talk to me, to see how I was doing. He seemed to think I needed the attention.

So maybe he would help me now.

Once I got breakfast cleaned up, I parked the girls in front of *Dinosaur Train*. Then I took my phone into the hallway and dialed Albert Dickel's number, knowing I could get him easily at this hour, before the meetings and conference calls began in earnest.

One ring and I heard: "Nathan, Nathan, Nathan!"

He always had called me Nathan. I have no idea why.

"Albert, always a pleasure."

"What are you up to with your bad self?" he asked exuberantly.

"Oh, the usual."

I bored him—and myself—with talk about the girls and my small life, following it up with questions about his children, all of whom were older. Then—because time was money, especially when you were billing at $800 an hour—he said, "Anyhow, what can I do for you today? If you're hitting me up for racquetball, the answer is yes."

"Actually, I need a favor."

"Shoot."

"First of all, this conversation isn't happening. Especially as far as my spouse is concerned."

"I understand. What's up?"

"It's this CP and L lawsuit Jenny is mixed up in."

"What about it?"

"She tries to hide it, but it's stressing her out," I said. "And I worry about where it's sending her, career-wise. She's in her late thirties, at the top of her game. She ought to be out hustling clients, building her book of business, not going down this rabbit hole. I've looked at this thing from a hundred different angles. As long as CP and L is in compliance with the Clean Air Act, there's no touching them. This is a waste of her time and talents."

"I agree a hundred percent," he said.

"The problem is, I can't get her to see it. I've tried talking sense into her, but you know how stubborn she is. I was wondering if you could work some magic with the executive committee. Convince them to pull the plug on this thing. She'll end up with a little egg on her face, but it's a lot less than the entire omelet she'll be wearing if she takes this to a big expensive trial and fails to win a judgment."

"Absolutely. I'm so glad you called me with this. I had been thinking the same thing for a while now—I just haven't acted on it. This is the kick in the tail I needed. I'll get right on it."

"Thank you, Albert. It means a lot."

"No problem. Oh, and Nathan? We should definitely play some racquetball soon. The firm has drop-in childcare, you know. The girls would have a ball. And I know a great place where we could get a massage afterward. It really feels amazing after a good hard game."

"Yeah, sure," I said.

"You free tomorrow?"

"Uhh, no can do. But soon, for sure."

"You got it," he said. "Talk to you later."

I hung up, feeling greasy. I hated going behind Jenny's back.

But under the circumstances, I felt it was entirely justified.

The dinosaur train was still chugging its way through the late Jurassic, leaving my daughters' eyes blank with wonder, so I grabbed my laptop from the kitchen and joined them on the couch.

Ever since I'd had that conversation with Kara Grichtmeier where she'd sort-of-but-not-really told me where J. Hunter Matthews lived, I had been wondering if I could pinpoint his exact location.

After all, if I could determine that it really was Matthews' house I had been taken to, I could put a quick end to this whole thing.

I logged into LexisNexis, that digital trove of public and legal documents, via Jenny's username and password. A quick search on *Matthews II, John Hunter* in the state of Virginia yielded me an address in Henrico.

When I typed it into Google Maps and zoomed in on satellite view, it nearly triggered an episode of PTSD.

It was a mansion. A Tudor-style mansion. The kind that surely had a Rembrandt hanging in it. There were three chimneys; a gracious, wide covered back porch; a kidney-shaped swimming pool off to the right; and a broad lawn edged with well-trimmed lollipops for trees.

Zooming out just slightly, I could tell the property had significant elevation, with stunning views of the James River and the countryside beyond it. And it could be seen from Route 288, the divided highway that ran nearby.

This had to be the place.

My only remaining challenge was how to get inside and see if I recognized the room where I had been held. Then I could call the authorities, report that I had been kidnapped, and show them where I had been taken. Hunter Matthews wouldn't admit to a thing, but he would have to answer a lot of questions. Even if the cops couldn't ultimately press charges due to a lack of evidence, the law enforcement attention would make CP&L think twice about further threatening Jenny or my family.

I had the key card, which I slipped into my pocket. That would unlock doors for me. But it would only be of so much use if there were people there.

It was safe to assume Rogers and the Praesidium would not be there. They had already used the residence for their one purpose and would have no additional need to hang around.

But that still left the rest of the Matthews family, and/or any domestic help they surely had. I needed to either elude detection or come up with some kind of ruse.

There were two scenarios that came to mind. One would involve the cover of night, black clothing, and a whole lot of skills I didn't really possess.

The other involved me playing a much more natural role.

Committing the address to memory, I closed the laptop. The girls were still riveted to the television. They didn't even notice me leaving the room.

From the closet under the stairs, I grabbed my largest diaper bag and the Pack 'n Play, the portable playpen that could double as a crib for Cate. From the kitchen, I rummaged up some snacks.

Returning to the living room, I plucked the girls from in front of the television one by one and got them buckled in their car seats, chirping all the while about how Daddy had an errand to run.

Then I pointed us toward the home of J. Hunter Matthews II.

CHAPTER 17

JENNY

There was no sign of the woman with orange hair anywhere around the parking garage or in the plaza with the fountains.

Jenny walked briskly all the same. But when she made it into the CMR building and still didn't see the woman lurking anywhere near the entrance, Jenny decided to put Code Orange out of her mind.

It was probably nothing to begin with. She was already feeling sheepish for having wasted Barry Khadem's time with it.

Once at her desk, Jenny started working through the emails that had come in overnight and earlier that morning from clients, associates, and other partners, all of them eager to demonstrate how little work-life balance mattered to them.

Jenny was deep in that slog, lost enough in the flow that she didn't notice the man standing in her doorway until he coughed lightly into his hand.

Albert Dickel. Technically, he was CMR's associate managing partner. Jenny always thought of him as the firm's unofficial switchblade: he came out of nowhere, struck fast, and left behind pools of blood.

In the history of Carter, Morgan & Ross, most of the associate managing partners either moved up to managing partner or passed the title on to someone else after a few years, when the burden of constantly doing the wet work became tiresome.

Dickel hadn't. He seemed to enjoy it.

Short and nearly bald, save for a five-o'clock shadow of hair ringing the sides and back of his head, he remained trim thanks to a regimen of racquetball and balefulness.

There was talk he was gay. But in the fashion of southern gentlemen of a certain age and social standing, being gay meant having a wife, three children, and a few weekends of unexplained travel a year.

He was always dressed expensively, with monogrammed cuffs and a rotating assortment of designer eyeglasses to match whatever he was wearing.

On this day, his outfit's theme was blue. Navy-blue suit. Light-blue tie. Dark-blue framed glasses.

"Good morning," he said in a way that suggested he found nothing pleasant about it.

"Hi," Jenny said, returning his flat affect.

"May I come in for a moment?"

"Be my guest," she said, gesturing toward the chairs on the other side of her desk.

He sat and, without further preamble, said, "I've been asked to inform you that the executive committee will be holding a vote on whether to discontinue the CP and L case tomorrow afternoon."

Dickel had delivered the line with no apparent malice. But Jenny knew what Dickel was really up to here. He was the kind of man who clung to the belief that women were too emotional to make reliable decisions. What he really wanted was for her to blow up at him, hopefully loudly enough for someone else to hear it, thus justifying his prejudice.

Jenny wasn't going to give him the pleasure.

"And why is that?" she said evenly.

"Because it has little chance of generating revenue and it's way over budget."

"Three-quarters of the projects at this firm are over budget. Are those being voted on as well?"

"No, because they *are* generating revenue," he said. "They have this thing called hours that we get to bill to a client."

"Yeah, I've heard of those. I out-billed you last year, remember?" She added a sweet smile.

"This isn't personal," Dickel said.

"Of course not. It's all business. Which is why I'd like to remind you that we now have two hundred and eighty clients with estimated damages of—"

"I'm aware of your estimates," he said. "But you'll only start to see those numbers if you can prove liability, and you've yet to make a convincing argument for how you're going to do that. We need a cogent legal strategy, not pie in the sky."

"I'm working on it."

"I know you are. But there's a reason you haven't gotten anywhere: it doesn't exist. You've been wasting your time. A promising young partner like you ought to be out hustling clients, building your book, not going down a legal rabbit hole. We're doing you a favor by cutting this thing loose. I just talked to Lawrence. He agrees with me."

Jenny tried not to let Dickel see her suck in a breath. Lawrence Coates was the firm's managing partner.

"I see," Jenny said. "Will I have the opportunity to make a presentation to the executive committee before it votes?"

"If you'd like, yes."

"Terrific. Then please put me on the agenda," Jenny said. She smiled again, though this time it was a lot tighter.

"Your wish is my command," Dickel said smarmily. He rose from the chair and said, "See you then."

As soon as he was out of sight, she sagged.

She would be going into this meeting at a serious deficit. True, Dickel and Coates were only two votes on the nine-member executive committee. Still, they were two very influential voices. At least two other members of the committee were basically sheep. There were some independent thinkers among the remaining five, but Jenny would have to convince all of them to go her way.

Jenny could feel that old sense of inadequacy beginning to well up. This wasn't 4-H Club. She was out of her depth, trying to push a new legal precedent out of a piece of legislation that other lawyers had been squeezing for more than five decades now. Maybe Dickel was right to—

Then she thought about Danece Henderson, battling for breath; and Clyde, struggling to pay the rent; and all the other people out there relying on her.

She had to be strong. For them.

Before long, she was again sitting upright.

CHAPTER 18

NATE

I probably should have been fearful, driving myself and my young daughters toward a house where I had been chained and their lives had been threatened.

Instead, I felt strangely emboldened.

This time, I was visiting on my own terms—not drugged, not bound.

I had my phone on me and could call 911 if anything went sideways. And Lorton Rogers and his thugs wouldn't know I was coming, because I had removed that tracking device.

Still mindful of the potential of being followed—if someone had been watching the house and then picked us up coming out of the parking garage—I drove with one eye on the road and one on my rearview mirror.

Once we hit Chippenham Parkway, I began countering maneuvers, slowing to as little as forty, then accelerating to eighty. I pulled off at random exits and turned circles. I ducked into parking lots. All the while, I stayed alert to any cars that may have been repeating themselves.

There was nothing. I was clean.

I was soon entering J. Hunter Matthews' neighborhood, which was riddled with multimillion-dollar homes, each more magnificent than the last, with their circular driveways, tennis courts, and topiary shrubs.

I could feel my jaw growing a little more slack with each bend in the road. It's not that I grew up in poverty. Far from it. Still, we'd lived in a two-bedroom co-op on the Upper West Side, back when that wasn't necessarily considered anything worth bragging about.

The Matthews abode—gleaming white with the signature brown half timbering of the Tudor style—was all the way at the end, perched out on the bluff that overlooked the James. As I had already seen in satellite view, there were no gates to stop me.

I kept an eye out for security cameras but was relieved not to see any. A neighborhood like this—so insulated from the real world—probably made them feel unnecessary.

There was an enlarged section of driveway directly across from the front entrance of the house that seemed to have been designed for vehicles to pull into, so that's what I did.

Importantly, I didn't see any other cars. Or vans. Another sign that Rogers and his people weren't here.

I cut the Range Rover's engine, slung the diaper bag and the Pack 'n Play over one shoulder, then unbuckled the girls. Cate had fallen asleep during the drive. She stirred for a moment but settled right back down when I rested her head on my free shoulder.

The house was large enough that there were two potential front entrances. One was less formal. I went for the more formal one. It had a slate path lined by gumdrop-shaped shrubs, leading to a set of semi-circular stone steps.

Without a free hand for Parker, I asked her to stay close to me. As we walked toward the house, I was alert to any sign of hostility coming from inside, ready to dash back to the car if need be.

Reaching the double doors that served as the main entrance, I rang the doorbell. A woman in a light-blue maid's outfit answered. She had a wide, Mesoamerican face; caramel-colored skin; and *Elena* stitched into the pocket.

I put on my best smile, hoping I looked like the very picture of harried fatherhood: Two bulky bags on one shoulder, a sleeping child on the other, a toddler clinging nervously to my knee.

"Hey!" I said. "We're here!"

Before she could react, I pushed past her into the house.

"Don't tell your boss I said this, but he gives lousy directions," I continued. "I barely found the place. Is he here?"

Elena gave me this blank stare.

"He no here," she said, in an accent that hailed from somewhere in Central America.

The door was already closed behind me. We were in.

Now I just needed to create a little more chaos. But toddlers are nothing if not good for that. I felt terrible about what I did next, but I think if Cate had fully understood the circumstances, she would have forgiven me.

So: I took a small piece of my daughter's tender little thigh and pinched it. Hard.

Like she had been scalded with hot water, Cate came roaring awake, going from peaceful slumber to full-throated cry in less than two seconds.

"Sorry," I said to Elena. "It's still nap time. He told me to just pick a room upstairs and throw the girls in it. Hopefully they'll settle back down. Come on, Parker."

I don't know how Parker could even hear me over her sister's caterwauling. But she moved obediently with me as I went toward the opulent wooden staircase, which had heavy carved spindles supporting a squared-off handrail, all of it stained a dark cherry.

Though certainly different in style from the woodwork of the room I had been held in, it was nevertheless beautiful craftsmanship, the product of a skilled artisan. Did that mean this was the same house? It was hard to know. I had only seen that one room during my first visit. Until I saw that room again, I felt like I couldn't be totally sure.

But that's why I was now tromping up the stairs. Elena was clearly nervous about the propriety of this intrusion. But I was moving with impunity, and she was too uncertain to stop me.

"I'll be right back," I called over my shoulder.

I reached the top of the stairs, which opened into a long, straight, reasonably wide hallway with a parquet floor. The furniture was different from what I had seen in my one room. It wasn't the curvy grace of Queen Anne. It was more Gothic: sturdier, darker, less whimsical.

A golden chandelier hung above me. The walls were sectioned off with more of that half timbering. To the right were several doors. To the left, there was one door; then the hallway bent around a corner.

Snap judgment time. I went left.

If Elena rejoined me, my pretense was that I was looking for a bedroom suitable for my daughters to nap in. I came to the first door and opened it.

It was not the room I had been in. Not even close. I quickly closed the door and continued my search.

Around the corner, there was less hallway remaining than I thought there would be. Just one more room, then another staircase.

I checked the room, and it was also not the one.

Now my choices were to go up to the third floor, or to double back and complete my tour of the second.

I stayed on the second, mainly because I was pretty sure the rooms on the third floor would have dormers and slanted roofs, and the space I had been held in did not have those features.

Cate was still making noise, but it was more halfhearted moaning. Parker was, bless her, following Daddy without objection.

Retracing my steps back down the hallway, I had just reached the main staircase again when I was confronted by a less-than-optimal scenario.

Elena was back. And she had been joined by a middle-aged white woman with impeccably cut, expensively treated red hair. Her chin was up. Her carriage was rigid. Her clothing was casually exorbitant.

The lady of the house.

"Hello, I don't think we've met," she said coolly. "I'm Heather Matthews."

"Hi," I said, smiling. "I'm Tim. And this is Cate, and this is Parker. Say hello, girls."

Cate looked at the woman warily through red, tear-rimmed eyes. Parker was back to crowding my legs. Neither said a word.

"Are you here to see Hunter?" Heather Matthews asked.

"Hunter? No, actually, I'm here to see the Rembrandt," I said.

"Excuse me?"

"The Rembrandt. Your husband said it was in one of the bedrooms. I thought he was going to be here to show it to me."

If she pressed, I was going to be an art appraiser, here to look at the Rembrandt—I was hoping they only had one—so I could use it as a comp for another painting.

Or something like that.

"He's at work," Heather said.

"Ah, well," I said, like I was mildly put out by this. "I guess if you can just point me in the right direction, I'll have a quick look and take a few pictures—no flash, of course. And then I'll be on my way before Mount Vesuvius here blows up again."

I jerked my head toward Cate, bouncing her on my hip slightly. With exquisite timing, she started struggling against my grasp.

"Down, down," she said.

"No, Cate-Cate, not right now. Daddy just has to visit a painting, okay, baby?"

I looked at Heather.

"Sorry. I wasn't supposed to have the girls with me today. But then my wife suddenly had an appointment and I didn't want to have to reschedule. Your husband was so kind to agree to let me see the paint-ing in the first place."

"The painting," she said. "The Rembrandt."

"Yes, of course."

"And I'm sorry, what did you say your name was again?"

"Tim. Tim Robertson."

I slurred it a little, such that it could have easily been Roberson, Robinson, or Richardson.

Heather Matthews was now frowning. "If you don't mind, I'm going to call my husband. He didn't mention anything about a visitor today."

Her voice had gone from questioning to circumspect.

"Sure, sure," I said, trying to keep my tone even so as not to betray my rising panic.

She pulled out her phone and was already swiping at it. I couldn't lose my cool. Hunter Matthews clearly wasn't going to know any Tim Robertson—or Richardson, or whatever. I hoped he wouldn't answer his phone and I could continue to obfuscate my way through this.

That hope was short lived.

"Hey, honey, it's me," she said. "Sorry to bother you."

I was, officially, screwed. My bluff had been called. I wasn't going to get any further with my self-guided tour without turning it into criminal trespass. It was time to abort before police were called or any more was done to alert the powers at CP&L that Nate Lovejoy had gone on the offensive.

"Tell Mr. Cabell I said thank you again," I said loudly.

"Hang on," Heather said into the phone, then turned toward me. "What did you say?"

"Just tell Mr. Cabell I said thank you."

Cabell was a Richmond name, one that dripped with old money. There were enough of them still running around that it was a plausible choice for a mistaken identity.

Heather Matthews had tilted her head. "Whose house do you think you're in right now?"

"The . . . Cabell residence . . . your husband is Robert Cabell, isn't he?"

"Ah," she said. Into the phone, she said, "False alarm. I'll call you later."

She ended the call. "You're at the wrong house. This is the *Matthews* residence."

I looked at her like I was embarrassed. "You know, I thought maybe those directions were off. I just . . . confidentially, Mr. Cabell is not as sharp as he used to be and . . . I'm so sorry to have troubled you."

The set of her mouth indicated she wasn't totally buying my balderdash. I was ready to give Cate another surreptitious pinch.

"No trouble at all," Heather said. "I'll show you out."

Thank goodness. I readjusted Cate on my arm and allowed myself to take a full breath for the first time since I'd seen Heather at the top of that staircase.

Then, for half a second, she brought her phone back up to eye level and quickly jabbed at it.

Almost like she was snapping a picture of us.

CHAPTER 19

NATE

My greatest frustration, as I drove away from the Matthews mansion, was that for all the trouble I had just gone through—and all the trouble I might be in—I hadn't really ruled out anything.

The portion of the Matthews house I had seen looked nothing like the room I had been held in.

At the same time, the place was large enough, and expensive enough, that perhaps they had part of it done in a different decorating style. Something not so Tudor and Gothic. Maybe one of those doors down the right side of the hallway opened into an entirely new motif; say, a room that had been specifically designed to showcase the Rembrandt.

Likewise, Heather Matthews had not explicitly confirmed or denied the existence of the painting. She'd never said *Rembrandt? We don't own a Rembrandt.* Or *Rembrandt? No, I won't show you our Rembrandt.*

When I had asked to see it, she had called her husband. Then I'd made my ignominious retreat.

As I drove back home, I was sorely tempted to call Jenny and spill the whole ridiculous story.

After all, when you want cockroaches to scatter, you turn on the light.

Still, there was this gnawing tatter of doubt: I was 98 percent sure Vanslow DeGange didn't exist and Lorton Rogers and the Praesidium were frauds.

But there remained that 2 percent chance they weren't. In which case, telling Jenny would trigger a cascade of events that would be a death sentence for my family.

Once we arrived back home, I parked back in front of the house. I couldn't keep up the lie that the Range Rover was in the shop forever.

If Rogers put another tracking device on my car, so be it. He surely had me under some other form of surveillance anyway. I was kidding myself to think I would be able to do much without Rogers being aware of it.

The girls were irritable from having spent most of the morning in the car. I felt that pang of guilt from treating them like such an afterthought— behavior I easily recognized, because it was exactly how my own mother used to treat me.

I was constantly striving to give my girls something better than what I'd had.

My childhood had been, to put a word on it, craptastic. I didn't really know my father, who'd taken off when I was still a baby—basically, the moment my mother had given him an out from their marriage. His idea of fatherhood was remembering to send a birthday card. Most years.

That left me to be raised by my manic mother. To her credit, she got the basics covered. I was always fed, clothed, and pointed in the general direction of school 180 mornings a year.

Otherwise, the organizing principle for my early years was benign neglect. I was roughly her fifth priority, somewhere behind her diet and exercise obsessions, just (barely) ahead of appointment television.

Her first priority was always whoever she was dating and/or married to at the time. She poured her energy into their relationship and into crafting this mythology about the perfection each guy possessed until—surprise!—he either tired of her or cheated on her, or she realized he was actually an asshole.

And, let me tell you, she brought home some certifiable ones. I gave them all nicknames, always with the prefix "Mister," because I was a respectful boy. The names weren't, looking back on it, terribly creative. They were always based on something superficial. There was Mr. Onions, because he was a chef who always seemed to smell like them; or Mr. Met, because he had a big, round head, just like the baseball team's mascot; or Mr. Belly, because his stomach hung over his belt.

A few of them were decent guys. Most weren't. There are parts of my childhood I don't talk about much.

Somehow—and this is the power of compartmentalization—I still turned out fine. Maybe even better for it. Jenny tells people the reason I'm a good husband is because I got a master's degree in the worst of male behavior and just had to do the opposite. The same was essentially true with parenting.

And so, after getting the girls back into the house, I did exactly what my mother never did when she was facing a personal crisis: I leaned into my job of being a dad, determined to give my girls extra attention and affection.

I busted out an old assortment of clothes I had collected from various sources—thrift stores, their grandmothers' closets, and so on—and began playing dress-up, much to the girls' delight.

It was going great. For about fifteen minutes. I had just put on a wide-brimmed gardening hat and a fake British accent when my phone rang.

Unavailable was calling again.

I thought about ignoring it but knew I couldn't. With regret, I slid out into the hallway and took the call.

"Hello," I said.

"Good morning," Rogers said. "How was your evening?"

"Busy. Tragic. Except I'm not fooled by the Marcus Sakey thing."

"Fooled?" he asked.

"Yeah. How do I know your people didn't just grab a street person, liquor him up, and then push him into traffic? How do I know you weren't driving the vehicle that mowed that poor guy down?"

Rogers sighed. "You remind me of the stories I've heard about Stanislav Petrov."

"And who is that?"

"Google him sometime. He's another part of Praesidium lore. On September twenty-sixth, 1983, with Ronald Reagan in the White House and the Cold War very much raging, Petrov was the duty officer at a Soviet nuclear early-warning station when he received six reports that the United States had launched missiles toward Russia. He knew they were false alarms, so he went against protocol by not alerting his superiors about what otherwise appeared to be an imminent attack. In fact, he was right. One of the Soviet satellites had malfunctioned. To this day, people celebrate him for having prevented an almost certain nuclear Armageddon. How do you think he knew to do that?"

"I'm guessing you're going to say it was because of you guys."

"Indeed. Our people had been working on him for a month. He was incredibly skeptical, convinced we were CIA operatives there to trick him into allowing the United States to obliterate the USSR without fear of reprisal."

"Yet another fascinating story," I said.

"Earning me more sarcasm. What can I do to satisfy your skepticism?"

I doubted he could. But I said, "How about Mr. DeGange makes some kind of prediction that couldn't possibly be under your control. Like, tell me about something that's going to happen on Mars."

"Very well. He's just waking up and it always takes him a little time to get going in the morning. Can I call you in an hour or two?"

"Sounds great," I said. "I can't wait."

I ended the call, then went back into the room, where more child-like joy was experienced as Parker put on a fashion show for us.

A short time later, my phone rang again.

But it wasn't Unavailable.

It was Kara Grichtmeier.

"Hey, how are you?" I asked.

"Fine. I have to ask you about something," she said, her voice sounding distant and cold.

"Shoot."

"Why on earth did you go to Heather Matthews' house this morning?"

There was this immediate lurch to my stomach. Obviously, Heather Matthews really had taken a photo of me.

"I . . . I wanted to see if she had that Rembrandt," I said. Which was also true.

"Couldn't you have tried to call her first or something? Or sent her an email asking if you could see it? I would have made an introduction for you. I can't believe you just crashed her house."

"It was," I began, groping for the right words, "sort of an impulse thing. How did this . . . how did you even find out about that?"

"She posted a picture of you on Facebook just now. It was you and the girls, standing in her house. The message that went with it asked if anyone could identify you. She wants to report you to the police."

"Ah," I said, because that was about the most cogent thing I could come up with.

"You should read the comments. Everyone thinks you're a criminal who was there to case her house to see if there was anything worth stealing."

I closed my eyes. So much for CP&L not knowing I was onto them.

The line hissed quietly. She was waiting for me to respond, so I said, "Well, obviously I'm not."

"I know that, but . . . I almost feel like you made me an accessory to a crime or something, just by telling you where her house was," Kara said. "She's seriously scared. And I don't blame her."

"Did you tell her who I was?"

"No. I don't want to have anything to do with this. If this backs up on Greg in any way, he would be livid, and I wouldn't blame him. The CP and L account is a huge deal at his firm."

"Of course it is," I said, just to sound reasonable.

"I think you should just reach out to her. I told you, she's a Facebook maniac. She has like three thousand friends. Someone is bound to see that picture and recognize you."

"Right," I said. "I'll do that."

"And please—*please*—don't mention that you even know me."

CHAPTER 20

JENNY

The call came in around ten fifteen, and it created its share of confusion in the glass-encased headquarters of Carter, Morgan & Ross as it bounced from one phone to the next.

The attorney on the other end of the line was in-house counsel for Dominion State Hospital.

She was looking for Nate Lovejoy, who, according to FindLaw. com, was an associate at CMR. Yet no one could seem to pinpoint Nate Lovejoy's extension.

The attorney insisted it was an important matter, and she really needed to speak with Mr. Lovejoy as soon as possible.

Finally, a helpful secretary in Lovejoy's former practice group forwarded the call to the one person who would absolutely know how to track Nate down.

His wife.

"And, I'm sorry, why are you looking for Nate?" Jenny asked, after the woman explained who she was.

"He was inquiring about a client who is a patient of ours—sorry, was a patient of ours—but he didn't leave any contact information," the attorney said. "And now I'm a little confused. Does Nate Lovejoy work for Carter, Morgan, and Ross or not?"

Jenny was even more baffled than the woman. When he'd quit CMR to stay home with the girls, Nate had switched his state bar membership to associate status. He was not currently allowed to practice. Why would he claim to be representing any client, much less one who was a patient at Dominion State Hospital?

Now deeply curious, Jenny came up with: "He's an emeritus associate"—which wasn't even a thing at CMR. "We still work on some projects together. Perhaps I can help you?"

"That would be great," the attorney said. "I'm just trying to prevent a molehill from turning into a mountain. Has he mentioned Robert McBride to you?"

"The name sounds vaguely familiar, but I'm afraid you're going to have to get me up to speed."

"Of course. Mr. McBride is an NGRI who has been a patient here for four years. Unfortunately, he committed suicide yesterday."

"Oh my. I'm so sorry."

"Yes, it's terrible. I was speaking with one of the doctors about it this morning. Mr. McBride had been doing quite well, but two days ago he had a setback in his treatment. A guard heard him talking about some things he apparently shouldn't have been talking about. The doctor was made aware of it and spoke with Mr. McBride yesterday. He didn't indicate any intent to self-harm, but sometimes a slip like this can be devastating for an NGRI who has been working hard to convince everyone that he's ready to rejoin society."

"Of course."

"My guess is that your husband has been in contact with some of Mr. McBride's family members. It's often the case that families who are upset and in shock start to question whether their loved one really committed suicide. Sometimes we can't provide the answers these families are looking for. But in this case we have a video that should give them the closure they need."

"A video?" Jenny asked.

"Security camera footage, yes. If you can give me your email address, I'll share the file with you. I should warn you, it's . . . well, it's pretty upsetting to watch, of course. It would probably be prudent for your husband not to let the family see it. But maybe he could just view it himself and then talk the family down? It would probably save everyone a lot of anguish and heartache."

"I understand. Thank you."

The call quickly wound down after that. But all the while, Jenny was wondering:

A mental hospital patient? A suicide? How had Nate gotten involved in something like this?

She was just beginning to ponder that question when her assistant poked her head through the office door.

"Hey," she said tentatively. "I'm sorry to bother you, but there's a police officer here to see you."

CHAPTER 21

NATE

I was still thinking about how to handle Heather Matthews when my phone rang again.

Unavailable was getting back to me.

Vanslow DeGange—and the wild imagination of the people who worked for him—must have finally woken up.

"Hi," I said.

"Do you think we can control the weather?" Rogers asked.

It seemed like it must have been a trick question, but I couldn't figure out what the ruse was. At least not yet. So I said, "I suppose not, no."

"Good. Early this afternoon a tornado will touch down outside Enid, Oklahoma, near the Cornerstone Assembly of God. It won't damage the sanctuary, but it will steamroll the church's gymnasium during the middle of the Women's Outreach Ministry's annual luncheon."

I gripped the phone harder.

Marcus Sakey was one thing. I had barely begun to touch all the ways that prophecy was just manipulation.

I couldn't imagine how they were going to fake this one. Was there any precedent of people being able to predict tornadoes? Or spawn them? I didn't think so, but . . . this couldn't possibly come true, could it?

"Please tell me you're making this up."

"I wish I were."

"Oh God," I said. "How many people will die?"

"None. We're going to see to it that there's going to be a sewage backup in the gym. It will result in a terrible odor and will force the ladies to reschedule their luncheon. The gym will be empty when the tornado hits. Mr. DeGange said there are a lot of ripples—a lot of lives saved. The story will quickly go viral, as you can imagine. People of faith all over the world will see it as divine intervention. And we're going to let them. You will be one of the very few who knows the truth."

I blinked once, twice, three times before my senses came back online.

This man wasn't actually capable of forecasting a tornado. There was going to be some kind of sleight of hand. I just had to be watchful for it.

"Okay, to make sure I've got this straight: a tornado will destroy the gymnasium at the Cornerstone Assembly of God this afternoon, but there will be no injuries because someone—"

"The Praesidium," he interjected.

"Yeah, you guys, whatever, will make sure the building is empty."

"That's right. By late afternoon, it should be on all the cable news stations. Pick a channel. It's a slow news day. It ought to play big."

"Sure," I said. "We'll see."

"I'll call you after it happens. In my experience, you'll need to talk."

"Right. Whatever."

I hung up.

There was this tightness in my face and chest. What kind of crap was Rogers going to pull now? I took a few deep breaths, trying to relax myself.

The whole time, I had been keeping one eye on the girls. They were still playing dress-up, though now Parker was using a patterned maxi skirt to play peekaboo with Cate, repeatedly tossing it over Cate's head, waiting until the tension built to nearly unbearable levels, and then—surprise!—ripping it away.

"Where's Cate-Cate? Where's Cate-Cate . . . there she is!"

Every time Parker made the big reveal, it absolutely busted Cate up. My younger daughter had the best laugh, this deep-in-the-gut chuckle that was both slightly devious and totally delightful. And pure. And joyful.

Ordinarily, this was the kind of thing that made stay-at-home parenting worth the struggle. Yet there I was, feeling like I was going to throw up.

If this tornado actually happened, it would mean Vanslow DeGange was the real deal, and . . .

No. That was a blank I couldn't fill in.

And, in any event, I wouldn't have to. Because there was no way this was going to unfurl exactly the way Rogers said. I just had to stay on my game to spot the deception.

With the girls still happily diverted, I pulled out my phone and did a quick search on tornado tracking.

The first story was "Why it's impossible to predict where a tornado will strike."

It confirmed my general understanding of twisters: that while meteorologists know certain conditions are likely to lead to tornadoes, even the most powerful computer models are helpless at forecasting the specifics of where or when one will touch down.

So, obviously, Rogers was planning some kind of artifice here. Could the Praesidium use some special effects or Hollywood backstage to make it seem like a church gym had been wrecked? Hire some actors to pretend to be pious women who had been spared God's wrath?

It was time to start fact-checking this thing from every angle. To start, I went to a weather site on my phone and typed in *Enid, Oklahoma.*

If it was a clear day, I would know right away something funny was going on.

But no. A line of powerful thunderstorms was already being forecast to roll through early in the afternoon, with the potential to spin off . . . Tornadoes.

I stared at my phone for a moment or two, blinking some more.

Okay, obviously Rogers had done his homework. He wouldn't be so careless as to fake a tornado where none had been forecast.

Next, I searched for the Cornerstone Assembly of God in Enid. I was soon on a website whose home page was a photo of parishioners, their arms in the air, smiling rapturously.

In a copperplate script, it said, *Cornerstone Assembly of God: It's Church. But Better.*

Above the photo were headings: *About Us|Our Mission|Our People|Events Calendar|Contact*

I clicked a few of them. Either this was a real site or someone had gone through *a lot* of trouble to make an excellent forgery, right down to the picture of and greeting from the Reverend Kenneth L. Neathery Jr. He had a glorious dome of a bald head, grandfatherly rimless glasses, and an understanding smile.

My final stop was the events calendar. The lone item in the block for today was *12 noon. Women's Outreach Ministry Annual Luncheon and Awards. Location: CAOG Gymnasium.*

Right. So, again, Rogers was making sure all his t's were crossed.

I left the website, trying to think of some aspect of this "church" the Praesidium wouldn't be able to counterfeit. I went back to the main Google search. In addition to the website I had just been on, there was a Facebook page, an Instagram page, a Yelp listing, a YellowPages.com listing. All had seemingly legitimate followers and customer reviews. There were also local news reports about church happenings, obituaries of dearly departed parishioners, and so on.

This was a real church.

I looked up the address on Google Maps, switching to satellite view. It was on the outskirts of town, in an area that appeared mostly agricultural, save for a convenience store just up the road.

Set down in the middle of all those fields, the Cornerstone Assembly of God was a large rectangular structure, surrounded by a semicircle of asphalt. Behind it, connected to the main sanctuary by a narrow walkway, was a second building. It was smaller, and square, and looked from above like it could be a gymnasium.

Something about this had to be fraudulent, though. I decided to call the church, but I didn't trust the number listed on the website. Rogers could have hacked in and planted a number that one of his people was now answering.

I went to the local paper, the *Enid News and Eagle*, and typed in a search for Cornerstone Assembly of God. I scrolled down until I found a listing for a food drive the church had organized three years earlier, which had a phone number in it.

That seemed like something I could trust. Jenny's lawsuit hadn't even existed three years ago. There was no way Rogers could have been planting newspaper listings that far back.

I dialed the number. After two rings, I heard a sweet-as-pie voice say, "Cornerstone Assembly of God, this is Connie, may I help you?"

"Yes, hi," I said. "My wife was wondering if there was still room at the Women's Outreach luncheon today."

"Oh, there's plenty of room, honey. You tell her to just come on down. We'd love to have her."

"And does she need a ticket, or . . ."

"Oh, heavens no."

"Is she supposed to bring something? A casserole—"

"Just herself. It's a buffet, so the food is already taken care of."

"It starts at noon, yes?"

"That's right."

"Wonderful," I said. "Thank you."

"You're welcome. Have a blessed day."

I assured her I would, then ended the call and stared at my phone some more. The church and the event seemed to check out. Where was the chink in the armor here?

Whatever my next step was going to be, I never got there. Someone was knocking on my front door.

Through the window I could see a tall man wearing sunglasses, an off-the-rack suit, and a tie that didn't quite make it all the way down to his belt.

I was no Vanslow DeGange. But I could make my own prediction: Heather Matthews had found me. The police had arrived.

CHAPTER 22

NATE

My mind was working quickly even as I slow-walked to the door.

Was there some way I could finesse my strange performance from earlier this morning?

No, I would just have to stick with my existing fib: I was an art enthusiast there to see a Rembrandt; I'd just gotten the wrong house.

I was at least reasonably certain I hadn't broken any laws. The housekeeper had let me in. I had walked around without breaking anything or taking anything. And then I had left when asked.

So, okay, let the cop lecture me, scare me, whatever he had to do to satisfy Mrs. Matthews.

I opened the door. The guy was maybe half a decade younger than me, about two or three inches taller, and had a well-tended beard.

"Hi, can I help you?"

"Are you Nathan Lovejoy?"

"Yes."

"I'm Detective Ishmael Khalilu. I'm with the Youth and Family Unit of the Richmond Police. May I come in?"

"Of course," I said.

Youth and Family? What did this have to do with either of those things? Was it because my girls had been with me? Was this guy going to report me to Social Services or something?

He walked in past me, and I closed the door behind him. He was doing that cop thing where his eyes were going all over the place, greedily collecting information—to be used against me later, no doubt. He wasn't even trying to be that surreptitious about it.

I suddenly wished I hadn't invited him in. It wasn't too late to ask him to leave. The Fourth Amendment was squarely on my side with this one. The guy didn't have a search warrant, and therefore he had no right to be inside my house.

But if I started getting pushy with him, he might return the favor. And that wasn't a fight I needed.

"Are your kids around?" he asked.

"Yes, my daughters are in the living room," I said. "As a matter of fact, if you'll just let me slide by you, I need to check on them."

I dipped my head as I passed, a small gesture of deference as one large man invaded the personal space of another.

The girls were still tangled in a mess of clothing, though now it was more parallel play, with each lost in their own imaginary realm.

I wanted to get this over with. Maybe if I took the initiative, I could spare myself the lecture. *Look, I know why you're here. Let me explain . . .*

"It would be better if we could talk somewhere they couldn't hear us," he said.

"Well, then I'm afraid you're just going to have to keep your voice down, Detective Khalilu, because I have to keep at least half an eye on them," I said, ever the good dad. "Our youngest is only eighteen months. They get into trouble fast at that age."

"Okay," he said. "Let's keep this chill, then. I just wanted to have a little talk about the argument you and your wife had this morning."

"What?" I said, unsure of what he was even talking about.

Then I remembered our minor spat—could you even call it that?—about me not telling her the girls had spent the previous afternoon with Kara Grichtmeier.

"Things get a little out of hand?" he pressed. "Hey, I get it, man. Me and my lady, sometimes we go at it and it's like, whoo, bombs going off."

"There were no bombs. We had a . . . a short conversation, and that was it."

"Uh-huh. Look, I know how it is, man. Especially when you marry a strong, intelligent woman. Because they start twisting things, and twisting things, and suddenly you don't even know which way is up, you know what I'm saying?"

"Actually, no, I—"

"And sometimes it's like, man, you just want to remind them who's boss, you know? Like, you're not going to hit her, because that's not right. But you want it to stop so you—"

He made a guttural noise. Then he reached out with both hands and pantomimed strangling something.

"Something like that, am I right?" he continued. "What were you guys fighting about? Money? I don't know about you, but my lady, man, she spends it as fast as I can make it."

"No. We weren't . . . I swear, we didn't have any kind of argument."

He raised both eyebrows. "You sure? Okay, maybe not an argument. Just a discussion that got a little hot?"

"No, nothing like that. We talked briefly while the girls were eating their breakfast, but I was just . . . answering a question she had. I think the only time we touched at all was when she kissed me on the cheek at the end of it. That was it."

"Really?"

"Yeah."

And then he floored me with: "Because we received a call that you choked your wife this morning."

"You . . . that's . . . that's not true. Who told you that?"

I could hear my own voice climbing through the octaves on its way to shrill.

"So you deny that you choked her?"

"No. I mean, yes, I'm denying it. I didn't do it. I would never hurt her."

"Uh-huh. So you're saying you didn't put your hands on her. Maybe just a little—"

And, again, he made his hands into a circle, then gave them a shake for emphasis.

"No. Nothing like that."

"Because you should know, we take this sort of thing very seriously," Detective Khalilu said. "Attempted strangulation is a significant predictor of future violence. They've done studies. People who have been choked by their partner are ten times more likely to be murdered by that person later."

I had been keeping eye contact with the detective the entire time, but as soon as he mentioned murder, I lost it. There's a legal concept called *mens rea*. It's an essential part of most prosecutions: proving criminals know their actions are wrong—a classic example being the bank robber who wears a mask.

Mens rea literally translates as "guilty mind." And even though I hadn't done anything to my wife, I had mens rea all the same, because of what Rogers had told me I needed to do.

And on some level I must have been contemplating actually doing it.

Detective Khalilu seemed to be able to smell the guilt on me.

"Look, I didn't do anything like that," I said. "Who made this call? It wasn't Jenny."

It couldn't have been, right? Why would Jenny invent something like this?

"I can't tell you. And, frankly, it's beside the point. The point is not how we know; it's that we know."

He was looming over me, closing the gap between us in a way that made me feel like I was wearing his deodorant.

"But it's not true," I said. "Ask my wife."

"I did."

"What did she say?"

"That's between me and your wife."

"Well, I'm sure she told you I didn't touch her. I mean, did you look at her? There were no marks or bruises."

"There often aren't with strangulation. A lot of perpetrators choose it for that exact reason, because it doesn't necessarily leave marks."

"But I'm not a perpetrator of anything. I would never hurt her."

"Right, right, of course," he said. "Then here's what you need to know at this point. We've opened a case file on you. Whether we decide to charge you or not, there's now a record of this, you understand? And if something else happens, we're not going to look at it like some one-time thing. It would be part of a pattern."

The words were landing like punches. *Case file . . . record . . . pattern.*

"And we've told your wife that if she has any concerns about your behavior—*any* concerns whatsoever—she can reach out to us."

He then turned back to good-cop mode and described the "resources" with which he could connect me. Anger management. Domestic violence counseling. All voluntary. No admission of wrongdoing.

I didn't bother interrupting him with more denials. He wasn't going to believe me anyway.

"And in the meantime," he finished, "I'm going to be keeping my eye on you, you understand?"

"Yes, sir," I said, chastened. "I assure you, you have nothing to worry about."

I had succeeded in shunting him back toward the front door. He was on his way out.

But before he left, he fixed me with a meaningful glare.

"All right, then. You have a good day."

CHAPTER 23

JENNY

After the strangeness of that video—followed by an even stranger visit from a police officer—Jenny had been trying to get Nate on the phone.

She couldn't concentrate on anything else until they spoke.

But Nate wasn't answering. Which wasn't like him. He was usually so starved for adult conversation he picked up by the second ring.

What was he doing, anyway? Was this because of Robert McBride? Was he busily continuing to make inquiries on behalf of McBride's aggrieved family, involved in a case he shouldn't have been anywhere near—for reasons Jenny could not begin to guess?

Was *that* what he had been doing when he dumped the girls on her parents the other day? And yesterday, when he dropped the girls off with Kara Grichtmeier?

She kept calling him, getting no answer, trying to focus on her work, failing, then calling him again.

Finally, on her fourth attempt, he answered with a terse "Hi."

"Hey, do you have a second? I really need to ask you about something."

"That's funny," he said, in a way that sounded like nothing was funny at all. "I really need to ask you about something."

"Okay, but I think I need to go first. Why did you tell Dominion State Hospital you're representing someone named Robert McBride?"

There was a hiss of silence on the other end. Then:

"How do you know about that?" he asked.

"Their in-house counsel called here looking for you. Nate, what's going on?"

"I . . . I'm just doing a favor for someone."

"Who?"

"A college buddy of mine. I don't think you ever met him. He called me up out of the blue this week. He knew I was in Virginia and that I was a lawyer, so he asked me to help him out with his brother."

"His brother. The one who committed suicide in a mental hospital."

"Yeah," Nate said. "I mean, how was I supposed to say no?"

"Oh, I don't know, maybe because you're not currently licensed to practice law in the Commonwealth of Virginia?"

"No one checks for that sort of thing. All he wanted was for me to make a phone call or two. If it got any more serious than that, I was going to refer him to someone else."

"Nate, that doesn't matter. This isn't giving random legal advice over cocktails. This is calling a state agency and claiming to represent someone. You could get disbarred for that. Why didn't you just ask me to make the call?"

"You're busy. I didn't want to get you involved."

"Well, I'm involved now. I just talked to their in-house counsel. She said this guy had some kind of a setback in his treatment where a guard overheard him talking about some things he shouldn't have, and then the doctors were informed. It sounds like it pushed him over the edge. She sent me this video. I'm supposed to forward it to you."

"All right, then forward it to me," Nate said.

Jenny paused and turned it over in her mind for a moment. Favor or no, it was foolish of Nate to have involved himself in something like this. It could jeopardize his chance to ever practice law again, something she assumed he would want to do in a few years, when the girls reached school age.

But forwarding the email was now the quickest way out of this potential mess. Once Nate saw the video, he'd tell his college buddy, and that would be the end of it.

"Fine. I'll send it," she said. "But you have to promise me it's over after this. You could get in real trouble for this. Heck, *I* could get in trouble for playing along. Promise me it's over."

"I promise. And I'm sorry you got involved. But to be honest, that feels like the lesser of our problems right now."

"And what does that mean?"

"I just got a visit from a detective asking me about why I choked you this morning," he said.

Jenny gave the phone a hard squeeze. It had been mortifying to have the detective show up at her workplace. White-shoe law firms like Carter, Morgan & Ross didn't get visited by police officers very often. Jenny was sure she was currently the talk of the entire floor, if not the entire firm.

But she could deal with idle office gossip. To have the detective also visiting her home was far more troubling. She was already worried about Nate feeling overburdened with his home duties. What if he snapped around the girls?

"Hang on, let me close the door," she said. She quickly crossed the room before returning to the phone. "Okay, I'm back."

"What did you tell the guy?" Nate asked.

"I didn't tell him anything."

"What does that mean?"

"Exactly what it sounds like. I told him I had nothing to say and then I asked him to leave."

"Nothing to say?" Nate burst.

"I have the right to remain silent."

"I'm not talking about your . . . your legal rights," Nate sputtered. "I'm talking about the truth. I didn't choke you. Couldn't you have just told him that?"

"I didn't want to give him anything. I just always remember this criminal defense attorney I did a symposium with when I was a two-L. He had this whole bit about, 'You give them nothing and what do they have . . . ?' He made the whole class say, 'Nothing.' And then he made us repeat it like five times."

"Well, sure, but—"

"Honey, there's no telling what this cop's real angle is. The really clever ones never come at you straight. They can lie to you, mislead you, do anything they want. We don't even know what he's actually investigating. The whole choking thing struck me as a front for . . . something else."

"Like what?"

"I don't know. That's the point. It just struck me that the safest, smartest thing to do was keep my mouth shut—at least until I had a chance to talk with you. That's why I've been trying to call you. This guy was from the Youth and Family Unit. Maybe you were at the park and something happened with the girls—"

"Nothing happened with the girls."

"But I didn't know that," Jenny said. "All I knew was this cop was suddenly asking questions. Point is, I didn't want to give him something on the record that I'd later regret saying for some reason I couldn't even imagine. You give them nothing and what do they have? Nothing."

"I . . . I guess."

"Honestly, I was hoping he wasn't even going to bother you. I thought once he got stonewalled by me that would be the end of it."

"I'm not so sure that's the end of anything," Nate said. "He pretty clearly didn't believe me when I denied it. He probably thinks you're a battered woman, too scared of me to say anything, and that's why you clammed up."

"Well, let him think what he wants. It doesn't really matter."

"Do you have any idea where this accusation even came from?" Nate asked. "He wouldn't tell me."

"He wouldn't tell me either."

Neither of them spoke for a short while.

Then she volunteered, "I'm sure it was an anonymous tip or something. The police are probably required by law to follow up. But really it was just some crackpot calling, inventing a few details, then hanging up."

"Why would someone do that?"

"Oh, who knows," she said. "It's kind of creepy. Someone just deciding to make a call and inventing something like this."

"Very creepy."

"Maybe it was one of the neighbors or something."

"We don't even *have* neighbors," Nate pointed out. Which was true, at least in the immediate sense. The town house to their left was currently for sale and unoccupied. The town house to the right was owned by a man who kept saying he was going to move down from New York and never did.

"Well, not that we share a wall with. But this is a city. Maybe someone walked by, heard one of the kids crying, and thought it was something else. Maybe someone forgot to put on their tinfoil hat and is getting signals from beyond. I have no idea. But I know it didn't happen, and you know it didn't happen. That's all that matters."

"Well, yeah, except now this Khalilu guy has opened a file on me. He said they might charge me."

"He's just trying to scare you. There's no evidence. You can't charge someone based on one anonymous phone call."

"Still, just the accusation is—"

"Unsettling," she said, finishing the sentence for him.

"More than unsettling. It feels like a violation."

"I know, I know," she said. "And maybe I'm just saying this because I've had a little more time to process this, but put it out of your head, okay? It's nothing."

"It doesn't feel like nothing."

"I'm sure it doesn't. And we can talk more about it tonight if you want. But right now I really have to get back to work. Sorry, I just haven't gotten nearly enough done today with all these distractions. If I'm going to have any chance of getting home at a decent time—"

"Sure. Just get back to work. I love you, okay?"

"I love you too. Give the girls a kiss from Mommy. I'll see you tonight."

CHAPTER 24

NATE

My heart was pounding so hard by the time I hung up the phone with Jenny I had to sit down.

The combination of lying to her about Buck McBride and at the same time being falsely accused of choking her was triggering some kind of panic attack in me.

I was worried I was going to pass out. Which is not exactly an option for someone who is the sole caregiver to two preschoolers.

After a few minutes of deep breathing, the feeling began to subside, enough that I was able to stagger back into the living room and join the end of the girls' dress-up play. I made all the right noises of engagement—oohing and aahing and whatnot—but the whole time my mind was elsewhere.

I honestly didn't know what to make of this sudden and incredibly ill-timed accusation of domestic violence.

It was possible Jenny was right, that some random crank had, for reasons known only to him or her, decided to toss this spiteful incendiary bomb into the middle of my life.

But really? It didn't feel all that random. This was part of the bigger something that was happening to me. I was just too small to be able to see it.

It was, of course, possible this was the work of Lorton Rogers and the Praesidium. Sure, Rogers *said* he wanted me to get away with killing my wife. But, come on, did he really?

Assuming Rogers represented CP&L—and not some secret society—he wouldn't care if I rotted in prison for the rest of my life. He'd probably even prefer it, because it would keep me out of the way. Planting a domestic violence report would help assure that.

Then again, what if it wasn't Rogers? What if there was yet another actor, still unknown to me?

It honestly troubled me that Jenny hadn't just straight up told the cop I didn't choke her. Yes, I understood her logic. And, yes, it wasn't unusual for my brilliant wife—with that ten-steps-ahead genius—to reach an unorthodox conclusion about the best course of action.

But at a certain point, why not just tell the detective the truth? We didn't have anything to hide.

Did we?

I felt like a housefly batting itself against a window, thinking I would soon reach the wider world, totally unaware I was never going to get there.

Once I got the girls down for a nap, I was going to return to monitoring the weather in Oklahoma.

But first I checked my email.

There was a forward from Jenny, which contained a link to a video that had been posted to a file-sharing service.

In short order, I was looking at a man lying on a bed, propped on one elbow, facing the far wall in what I assumed was a patient room at Dominion State Hospital.

It was dark in the room except for some ambient light coming in from the parking lot. The camera must have had an infrared day/night filter, because Buck—if this was, in fact, Buck—appeared to be a lighter shade of gray than his surroundings.

On the bottom right of the screen was a time-and-date stamp, which told me this video had been taken at 1:41 a.m. Wednesday morning.

At first, very little was happening. The man seemed to be working on something that his body was keeping shielded from the camera. His hands and forearms were busy. Now and then an elbow would flare. But mostly he was just lying there.

Then he swung his legs around so he was facing the camera and setting his feet on the floor. And, yes, it was Buck. Even in black and gray, his features were quite clear.

He was clenching something in his fist, though it was difficult to tell what it was. And, in any event, he was already on the move, grabbing a chair from the corner of the room and placing it in the middle.

Then he stood on the chair, and it suddenly became very obvious what he had been holding in his hand.

An extension cord.

That had been tied into a noose.

What happened next seemed to move almost too fast. He reached up toward an exposed fire sprinkler head in the ceiling. The plug on the free end of the extension cord had been sheared off, such that it was thin enough that he could thread it through the supporting brace of the sprinkler head. He tied three quick granny knots and tugged hard on the cord, to make sure it was secure.

Then, without any hesitation, he slipped his head into the middle of the loop and kicked away the chair.

He dropped, his feet stopping maybe a foot above the floor. His legs flailed, furiously trying to find firm ground. His hands clawed at his neck. His body was reflexively fighting the terrible thing that was happening to it.

The battle didn't last long. There were a few spasms and jerks toward the end. But soon he was just hanging there, completely still.

The video ran for another two minutes. Nothing changed. Then it ended.

If I believed what my eyes had just shown me, Buck McBride hadn't been murdered by CP&L or anyone else. He really had committed suicide. In which case . . .

No. Couldn't be. This had to be some kind of incredibly well-done deepfake. A powerful computer, applying the latest in machine learning, could easily create footage convincing enough to fool an amateur like me. CP&L could have then hacked Dominion State Hospital's security camera system—I was sure that wouldn't be hard—and planted the video.

That was clearly it. I watched the video several more times, pausing it and zooming in on the screen, looking carefully for signs of fakery. There was nothing obvious.

Next I googled *how can you tell a deepfake* and confirmed my basic understanding that, actually, if it was well done enough, you couldn't. That's what made them so pernicious.

Once the girls woke up from their nap, I tried to put it out of my mind. The video was really just more evidence that CP&L and Lorton Rogers were sophisticated operators with a lot of resources at their disposal—something I knew already.

Besides, it was snack time. Then game time. Then I acknowledged we were basically out of food and badly in need of a trip to the grocery store.

By the time we returned, it was approaching four thirty. I put Cate in the corner of the living room, where there were some of her favorite toys, and some plastic barriers to keep her from getting free and hurting herself. I turned on *Dora the Explorer* for Parker so I could put the groceries away in relative peace.

As I did so, I powered up the small TV we had in the kitchen and tuned it to CNN, which was reporting on the latest ridiculousness from Washington. I kept half an eye on it as I stored the cold stuff.

Then I stopped cold myself.

The bottom of the screen read, **BREAKING: CHURCH SPARED TORNADO'S WRATH.**

I increased the volume in time to hear the anchor toss the story out to a local correspondent in Oklahoma, and to footage shot from the air—from a helicopter, it appeared—that looked a lot like the Cornerstone Assembly of God I had seen in that satellite photo earlier in the day. It was a closer view, but there were fields on all sides, and I recognized that semicircular parking lot.

The sanctuary was the same rectangle.

But the square building that had been behind it was gone.

The walkway that had led to the building was now like a trailer link with no trailer—just a thin extension that led to nothing.

It was easy to make out the path the tornado had taken on its way toward the church property. It was this jagged gray line in the earth, the shape of a lightning strike, standing out vividly against the green around it.

The area where the gymnasium had once stood was scattered with debris. Pieces of siding. Parts of trees. Piles of junk you couldn't even identify from that high up.

Total devastation.

I realized I was holding my breath. As I slowly let it go, a voice-over intoned: "The National Weather Service has estimated it was a category F-four tornado, with winds above two hundred miles an hour. It touched down about a mile from a nondenominational Christian church, the Cornerstone Assembly of God, at approximately one fifteen central time."

The screen switched to footage that had been shot from the ground. A tractor, its cab planted on the ground, its wheels pointed toward the sky. Mature trees uprooted and lying on their sides. Cornstalks parted like a biblical Red Sea.

And then a building—had it once been a gymnasium?—which was now just a concrete pad with a few steel ribs jutting up from it at strange angles. There was no roof, no hint the building ever even had one.

The view changed again. It was now a pleasant-looking older woman with a round face and glasses. Beneath her was CONNIE BILSON, CHURCH SECRETARY.

I actually gasped. It was the Connie I had talked to earlier, the Connie who had answered that not-fake phone number from the three-year-old church listing.

"Our ladies' luncheon was scheduled to start at noon," she said, in that sweet-as-pie voice. "But we had an issue in one of the bathrooms. One of the ladies came to us and said, 'We have to cancel the luncheon.' I really think it was an angel at work."

From Connie, it went to a CNN reporter standing in front of the wreckage. "A hundred and fifty women would have been inside this building when the tornado hit. Instead, it was empty."

Gesturing to the main building, the reporter said, "The sanctuary was completely untouched. The tornado continued for another half mile, damaging a grain silo and several other farm-related structures before dissipating. Authorities have so far reported only minor injuries, and no fatalities."

The screen was now filled with a close-up of a man I recognized as the Reverend Kenneth L. Neathery Jr., standing outside the church. He had the same beautifully rounded bald head as he did in the website photo, though his eyes were now full of awe.

"We pray," he said. "We ask God for his protection. We ask him to watch over us and he has blessed us this day. All we can do is give our thanks. No one was hurt. All this damage and no one was hurt. It's truly a miracle."

The reporter signed off, and the screen went back to the anchor in Atlanta.

I just stood, rooted, the remote control still in my hand. Had CP&L somehow managed to fool CNN? Gaslight an entire network? I didn't know how that was even possible.

Plus, when I switched over to Fox News, the story was there, too, with the breaking-news graphic and **DID GOD CALL A PLUMBER?**

Fox's overhead footage had been shot by a drone, though it looked very much the same as CNN's: the tornado's barbed path, the devastation of the former gymnasium, the haphazard debris.

I began googling *Enid, OK tornado*, and sure enough, it was on every local website and television station. There were also numerous social media posts—each with thousands of likes and shares—from women who were supposed to have been at the luncheon and were now attesting to God's grace.

It was straining credulity to think anyone could have orchestrated all this. With enough resources, could you make a real church gym look like it had been flattened by a tornado? Then hire actors to play Connie Bilson, who had somehow also answered the phone when I called earlier; and Kenneth L. Neathery Jr., who had been featured on the hacked website? Then plant some fishy Facebook posts, Russia-style?

I didn't think so. And yet I still wanted some kind of third-party source that Rogers wouldn't think to manipulate.

Then I remembered the convenience store I had seen on the satellite footage, the one that was just up the road from the church.

I called it, and a man answered.

"Hi," I said. "This may sound like a strange question, but did a tornado pass your way a few hours ago?"

"Oh, yeah!" the guy replied enthusiastically. "Saw it coming about a mile off—"

I hung up.

This had to be a dream, or a hallucination, or some kind of psychotic break. And yet I could look down at my hand, move it, and it responded. And I could feel the coolness of our granite countertops as I leaned against them for support.

One of the major weaknesses of many conspiracy theories—from Area 51 to 9/11 as an inside job—is that they require omnicompetence from the people carrying them out, a perfection that simply doesn't exist when you have large groups of inherently infallible humans trying to work in concert.

Rogers had asked me if I thought they could control the weather at nine thirty in the morning. To have created all this—hacking dozens of websites, hiring actors, staging a massive disaster, creating a scene legitimate enough to fool a dozen news outlets, thinking down to a level of detail that you would even remember to get a convenience store clerk in on the act? All without a single blemish? And doing it in just seven hours?

It wasn't possible.

This had really happened. There were too many layers—too many real people; too many angles from which I had approached this, trying to prove the falsehood of it, only to be confronted with one long, consistent line of truth.

I looked outside the window, where a gentle breeze stirred a nearby tree, the meteorological opposite of the tornado that had apparently ripped through Enid, Oklahoma.

Just like Vanslow DeGange had predicted.

As if I were some lumbering prehistoric beast, straining for branches only barely within my reach, my brain grasped at this new reality.

I started with Buck McBride and the improbable series of steps I had taken: that I would swipe that key card; do a reverse image search;

find a dead link on a website; talk to the website operator, who'd happened to send a letter with return service requested and then still have the address several years later; and that all of that would lead me to Buck, sequestered in the high-security unit at a mental hospital.

Then I thought about Buck's terror when he'd first seen that Praesidium logo. His whispered warnings for me to take my family and run. That neatly written notebook, hidden deep in a storage unit that smelled like it hadn't been opened for years, beneath a box of sheet music in Hudgins, Virginia.

Yes, perhaps I could reasonably explain any one of those things as Rogers' manipulations or Buck's good acting . . . but *all* of that? Really?

Then I remembered what Jenny had said shortly before she'd told me about the video. That Buck had had a "setback" in his treatment. The setback was me. I had gotten him talking about the Praesidium. And once the doctors heard about that from the guard and confronted Buck, he would have known any chance he had of being declared mentally fit to rejoin society was gone—at least for another decade or two.

He couldn't handle that. So he committed suicide. He really had been a member of the Praesidium, which wasn't just a front for CP&L—because him killing his neighbor had nothing to do with CP&L and had happened years before Jenny had ever dreamed of suing the power company.

Which meant that video wasn't a deepfake at all. It was the result of a series of events that I had tragically set into motion.

And if Buck McBride had killed himself . . .

And Vanslow DeGange had actually predicted a tornado . . .

And the Praesidium wasn't a front for CP&L . . .

Did that mean . . . was Jenny really about to have a brainstorm that would radically alter the future of the planet? And if that was true, then the only way to save a billion people, including my own daughters, was to—

The thought was interrupted by my cell phone.

Unavailable was calling.

I managed to answer it with a dry, "Yes."

"Are you near a TV?"

"It's already on."

"And?" Rogers asked. "Do you believe me now?"

There was no other answer to give him.

"Yes," I said, just above a whisper.

"I know this is hard."

"No," I replied. "You have no idea."

CHAPTER 25

NATE

Rogers was right. I needed to talk.

This was too big a mouthful for me to digest on my own.

He volunteered to come over in an hour. It gave me time to get an early dinner in the girls and then park them back in front of the television.

I had just succeeded in doing that—turning up the volume so they wouldn't hear us talking in the kitchen—when I heard a soft knock coming from the back door.

It felt strange to invite into my home a man who, upon our first meeting, had forcibly kidnapped me. But at this point, my need to understand what I had just witnessed—what I was up against, really—overwhelmed everything else.

"You're going to have to keep your voice down," I said. "The girls are just down the hall."

Rogers acknowledged the request. I pointed him toward the kitchen table, then sat across from him.

"You know, for a while, I didn't even think DeGange was real," I said. "I thought maybe he was your version of Keyser Söze, this boogeyman you were just making up."

"No, he's real," Rogers said, pulling out his phone, tapping it a few times, and turning it toward me so I could study it for a few seconds.

The man in the picture had a mound of curly white hair and a serious visage, one that seemed to suggest not only intelligence but wisdom. His nose was hooked and large for his face, though his most prominent feature was a puffy mole above his right eyebrow.

"So how does he do it?" I asked after Rogers restowed his phone. "How does he see the future, or whatever you want to call it?"

"I've been watching it for twenty years and I'm still not sure I can describe it," Rogers said.

"Please try."

"We've come to think of Mr. DeGange almost as a different species, one that has evolved a new form of consciousness, or a new sense. Think back hundreds of millions of years to the first organism that, through whatever mutation, had developed the ability to sense light. Even if that organism had been able to talk, would it have been able to describe to other organisms what light was like? In terms they could understand? Of course not. His friends would have had no experience of light. That's the challenge for Mr. DeGange and people like him."

"People like him," I said. "You mean there are others?"

"Well, not as powerful as Mr. DeGange. At least not that we're aware of. But the Praesidium has studied this subject at some length. We have come to believe that, throughout history, there have been human beings who have possessed this mutation, which has been passed to them just like any other genetic trait. We believe that most of the carriers are actually unaware of exactly what they have. They deny it, or assume that little tickle they sometimes feel is something to be ignored. But a few of them have attempted to cultivate it. They were our soothsayers, our oracles, our seers. Depending on their position in society, they have either been embraced or repelled. It tends to be if you were a male of the dominant culture, you were revered as a prophet or you founded a religion. If you were a woman or part of a disenfranchised group, you were persecuted."

"The witches of Salem," I said.

"Exactly. In Mr. DeGange's case, he is Romani—a gypsy, as they are sometimes incorrectly called. A marginalized group. There is a strong tradition of what might be called fortune-telling or clairvoyance among the Romani. A lot of that was fraudulent, carnival sideshows and the like. But we believe there were a few people who genuinely had this ability, and because the Romani have been so tightly knit throughout the centuries, they have passed the gene or genes to others within their community, and then been able to recognize it when the gift reveals itself in one of their offspring."

"Is that what made Vanslow DeGange more powerful—or however you want to describe it?"

"That may be part of it," Rogers said. "Though we have come to believe it's a combination of factors. Part of it is intelligence. Mr. DeGange has an IQ of a hundred and sixty. As a boy, he could pick up any piece of electronics and almost immediately understand how it worked, and then be able to fix it. He had almost no formal schooling, and yet he taught himself algebra and calculus, mostly by working things out on scrap paper. The Praesidium believes having that kind of intellect amplified his gift."

"In other words, a dullard could have these genes and not know what to do with them."

"Exactly. The other part is that Mr. DeGange had the occasion to be near some of the world's brightest scientists as a young man."

"At the Manhattan Project."

"Yes. He was around people who were pondering the very nature of time and openly speculating about how it might function. One of them was Richard Feynman, who was then bandying about the belief that antimatter is actually just ordinary matter traveling backward through time. Feynman showed that a positron could actually be an electron in reverse. No one has ever proven that experimentally. But no one has disproven it either. It made Mr. DeGange realize that being aware of so-called future events wasn't actually impossible. In fact, there's nothing in the laws of physics that forbids it."

"So there's scientific grounding for this."

"Absolutely. How are you with physics?"

"We've met," I said. "Barely."

"Okay. In that case, a brief history of the human understanding of time. According to the ancients, from Copernicus to Newton, time was absolute, and it only flowed in one direction. It never occurred to them the cosmos might behave otherwise. Then Einstein came along and said, no, time is relative, and the universe shows no particular preference for which direction it goes. The fact that we only perceive time moving in one direction seems to be an accident of the human senses. It may be peculiar to our species or to life on Earth generally. Another revelation Einstein had was that space and time are actually the same thing. They're both part of a four-dimensional continuum he referred to as space-time. Everything in the universe exists somewhere in space-time. Are you with me so far?"

"Sort of."

"I know, it gets difficult. Think of it like this: Omaha, Nebraska, is a place, right? Even if you can't see it right now, even if you're not there, you know it exists. There are people there, having the experience of Omaha. You can believe that, right?"

"Sure."

"Okay. In that same way, next Tuesday is a place that exists. You can't see it or touch it. But it's still out there, being experienced, much in the same way Omaha is out there."

"So next Tuesday already exists."

"Exactly."

I stopped and juggled this in my mind for a moment or two. "But if next Tuesday already exists, then there's no free will."

"Not for you, my friend. You can't change next Tuesday any more than you can change last Tuesday."

I shook my head as I struggled with the concept. "So we're basically these little monkeys hurtling through the universe, thinking we're in charge, when we're actually just . . . ants marching to some predestined plan?"

"Free will is another accident of the human senses."

"But how can that be? I make a thousand decisions every day. Whether to go left or right. Whether to feed my daughters oatmeal or pancakes. Whether to offer you a drink or smash the glass on the floor. And I could change my mind at the last second. It's all very much in my control."

"That's what you believe, yes. It might even be what you *need* to believe to stay sane. It's really just an illusion, in the same way that you need to have the illusion time only moves in one direction, because the alternative is too much for your limited human brain to handle. In reality, whether you go left or right—even if you change your mind at the very last moment and do the opposite of what you thought you were going to do—it was all preordained."

I took a deep breath.

"Okay, but wait," I said. "If free will doesn't exist, then what's the point of the Praesidium? Why do you guys go through all this effort when everything—good and bad—is basically inevitable anyway?"

"This is perhaps the greatest aspect of Vanslow DeGange's gift. Because he is aware of next Tuesday—he can visit it, in a manner of speaking—he can change it. He understands how to manipulate the future. Remember, he's the one organism who sees the light. Everyone else is bumbling around in the dark."

"So Vanslow DeGange has free will, and the rest of us do not."

"That's oversimplifying it a bit. But, yes, that's essentially correct. Remember how I told you about the currents? They're flowing around us all the time, moving both forward and backward. Mr. DeGange can sense them. And the more he concentrates on a subject, the more he's able to get in touch with them. And the more he understands and anticipates how certain actions will divert the currents and change the outcome."

"Like how killing Kennedy will stop a nuclear conflict."

"Exactly."

"Which brings us to me killing my wife," I said.

Rogers looked down at the table, where there was truly nothing to see. He held his gaze there for a moment, then brought his eyes back to mine.

"I'm sorry," he said, like he really meant it. "I know it's difficult for you to accept, but this is all predestined. This conversation. Everything I'm doing. Everything you're doing. I'm telling you, as sure as I'm sitting here, it's all leading up to nine forty-seven on Friday evening, when you will do what you were always meant to do."

"And I'm telling you, as sure as I'm sitting here, that's not happening."

"I know you believe that right now. You're going to keep believing it right up until the final minute. But in the end, you're going to do it."

"There has to be *some* other way, some other intervention that will work," I said. "Tell Mr. DeGange to get back in touch with the currents and shift them in some other direction."

Rogers started shaking his head before I was even finished.

"Remember when I was telling you about the genocide in Rwanda? How it had a certain momentum to it that couldn't be stopped? That's the case with a lot of future events. They have this broad impetus to them. But every now and then, everything squeezes down to a particular choke point.

"I know you think I just popped into your life with this idea on a random day, but Mr. DeGange began focusing on climate change many years ago. It had a ton of momentum already, obviously. Humanity has been using fossil fuels for energy for a long, long time now. That's a lot of smokestacks and exhaust pipes. But Mr. DeGange kept focusing on it, and reading everything he could about it, and getting in touch with the currents, and he eventually realized there *was* a choke point. And the choke point is your wife."

"No. There's another one," I said. "The problem here isn't truly Jenny. It's this dangerous gas, this sodium hexafluoride. What if instead of killing Jenny, the Praesidium used its money and influence to stop the power companies from using sodium hexafluoride?"

He let out a chortle.

"What?" I asked.

"Think about that. A secret society that has deliberately avoided the spotlight for more than half a century attempting to emerge from the shadows to fight a regulatory war against every utility company in America and an army of lobbyists who make it their life's work to wrap politicians tightly around their fingers? Especially when half those politicians see global warming as a sham to begin with? You don't need Mr. DeGange's gift to know that would never get off the ground. Hang on."

He had gotten a text. As he pulled his phone out of his pocket to look at it, I stared at him, his bland face, his gray hair. It sounded strange to say, but I really felt like he didn't have animosity toward me. Or Jenny. He was just very patiently, matter-of-factly explaining why it was she had to die by my hand.

To me, it was this equilibrium-shattering suggestion. To him it was the logical conclusion of years of careful study.

But not *his* study.

He was just the messenger.

"I want to meet Mr. DeGange," I said. "There has to be something he's missed here. I want to talk to him directly."

Again, Rogers' head was moving back and forth before I could finish. "That's not going to happen."

"Why not? I won't hurt him. You can search me for weapons or tie me up or stick me behind bulletproof glass or whatever you have to do. But there's no way I'm going to be able to kill my wife until I feel like I've exhausted every other conceivable possibility. And, no offense, I won't get that from talking to you. The only way to do that is talk to Mr. DeGange."

"You're not the first to make that request. The Praesidium has developed rules over the years, rules that have been put in place for very good reasons. Even if I felt like breaking them, there would be dozens of other members who would stop me before I got more than two steps down that road. One of the rules is that Mr. DeGange never interacts with anyone who isn't one of us."

"Then how do I become one of you?"

Rogers fixed me with a steely look. "You really want to know?"

"Yes."

"First, you kill your wife."

Now it was my turn to look down at the table.

"Every single member of the Praesidium has killed at least one person on Mr. DeGange's orders," Rogers continued. "Many of us have killed multiple times. Believe me, we don't relish what we've done or enjoy the task. We're not a consortium of psychopaths. We're ordinary people who have been brought together by this man's abilities, people who—like you—didn't know if we were capable of taking a human life. But we have all proven to ourselves and to each other that we will do what it takes to help Mr. DeGange make the world a better place. Even at great personal cost. It's ultimately what bonds us. Once we take the oath and are accepted, each one of us gets this. This is the mark of the Praesidium."

He raised the sleeve of his shirt and showed me a brand identical to Buck McBride's, with the *P* and the *R* inscribed in a square.

"That must have hurt," I said.

"It hurts less than what we've done already by that point."

I looked from his *PR* brand back to his eyes, and it occurred to me Rogers was no ordinary messenger. He may have looked like a high-end butler, but at some point in the past, his actions had belied that.

"Who did you kill?" I asked.

Rogers lowered his sleeve and looked down at his watch.

"We don't have time for that story right now," he said.

"Why not?"

He tapped his watch.

"Doesn't your wife usually get home around this time?" he asked.

"Oh," I said. "Right."

"I'll come by tomorrow morning," he said. "We need to start getting certain things in place. Try to get some rest tonight. Tomorrow is going to be a big day."

CHAPTER 26

JENNY

The late-afternoon sunshine seemed overbright as Jenny pushed through the glass revolving doors of CMR's headquarters and out into the plaza beyond.

She was, more than anything, simply fatigued. By Albert Dickel's noxious incursion. By that strange phone call from the hospital lawyer. By the visit from the police officer.

And especially by the niggling worry that it wasn't even over yet—that there was another shoe, somewhere out there, still waiting to drop.

Squinting, she pointed herself toward the parking garage across the street, more or less on autopilot as she made the familiar walk, not really noticing her surroundings.

As such, she didn't really see what was coming in fast, at a sharp angle, roughly from the northwest.

The woman with the orange hair. With a red T-shirt. And bright-white sneakers.

Jenny stopped short, her path to the parking lot having been blocked.

"Jenny Welker?" the woman said.

"Yes?" Jenny replied.

The woman was reaching into that grubby floral-patterned handbag of hers.

"I'm tired," the woman said. "This has to end."

With an unsteady hand, she brought up a pistol and held it level with Jenny's nose.

"I'm sorry," the woman said.

For some sliver of a second, Jenny didn't react at all. It took her that long to register that, yes, this was a gun. And, yes, the gun was being pointed at her by this woman. And, furthermore, this woman was probably going to squeeze the gun's trigger very soon.

Jenny was, for all intents and purposes, frozen in place. Her surprised brain simply couldn't make the correct sequence of neurons fire to make her enervated body wince, recoil, duck, or produce any other reaction suitable to the situation.

She was still standing there, statue-like, when the sound of a gunshot echoed across the plaza.

But it didn't come from in front of Jenny.

It came from behind. And above.

By the time Jenny registered the noise, a bullet had already pierced the top of the woman's head and exited out the base of her skull. A spray of bone shards, blood, and soft tissue followed the projectile like a gory exhaust stream. A small portion of it spattered across Jenny's white blouse and light-gray jacket.

The force of the impact knocked the woman backward and caused her to throw her hands in the air. She released her hold on the weapon—or, perhaps more accurately, was no longer capable of gripping it—sending the gun hurtling in a short arc through the air. It came to the ground, harmlessly, roughly twenty feet from the woman's body.

Altogether too late, Jenny finally unfroze, screaming and diving to the ground, taking skin off her right knee and both palms. As soon as she skidded to a stop, she covered her head with both arms, as if that would help.

She was still prone, and still shrieking nonsensically, when she felt a hand on her back and a large shape looming over her.

"It's over, it's over. You're all right, you're all right."

The voice belonged to Barry Khadem.

She looked up. CMR's director of security and investigations had placed himself between Jenny and the dead woman and was using his bulk to spare Jenny any further view of the carnage.

"You okay?" Barry asked.

Jenny looked at her knee, which already had a trickle of blood coming from it, and her palms, which were lined with thin red scrape marks, punctuated by embedded pieces of sidewalk grit.

"I'm fine," Jenny said.

She was a farm kid, no stranger to a skinned knee.

And it could have been much, much worse.

"What . . . what happened?" she asked.

"Code Orange showed back up this afternoon," Barry said. "One of my guys noticed her around four o'clock, loitering near the entrance again. She kept sticking her hand in that bag of hers and at one point we were pretty sure we caught a glimpse of a gun. That's when I called a former state police colleague of mine who also happens to have been the best man at my wedding. He now supervises the Tactical Operations Team for the Richmond area. His team didn't have anything else going on, and we agreed if nothing else it was a hell of a live training drill. They had the whole plaza covered."

He pointed to the top of the CMR building, where the shot had come from; then vaguely to his left; then to the parking garage across the street.

Jenny didn't see anything in the first two spots. But there was no missing the man in green military-style clothing who was still standing five stories up on the garage's top deck, his long rifle now in a resting position.

She looked down at her wounded hands, shaking from adrenaline, shock, and fear. She didn't know if she was going to cry, laugh, or vomit.

Never had her life felt so fragile. Or come so close to ending.

If Barry Khadem's people weren't quite as vigilant . . . if Code Orange had realized she was being watched and disguised herself somehow . . . if she had used a rifle from a distance instead of a handgun up close.

There were too many ways this scenario could have ended with Jenny being the one whose brain matter was sprayed across the concrete.

Members of the Tactical Operations Team now seemed to be pouring in from all over. Jenny hadn't noticed any of them.

And, more to the point, neither had the woman.

Barry remained in a spot where he was blocking Jenny's view of her assailant. Jenny tried to look around him, wanting to get another glimpse of the person who had nearly ended her life.

"So who is she?" Jenny asked.

"I don't know," Barry said. "But we're going to find out."

CHAPTER 27

NATE

Rogers departed, leaving me and the girls alone to wait for Jenny's imminent arrival.

Although apparently it wasn't so imminent.

Around six thirty, Jenny sent a text saying she had been held up at work. She suggested I get the girls ready for bed, and she would try to be home in time to tuck them in.

I was actually grateful for the delay. It gave me more time to think through what had happened that afternoon.

Vanslow DeGange had, quite incredibly, predicted a tornado. I kept the television in the kitchen on as I fed the girls dinner, and every time CNN cut back to Enid, Oklahoma, there was more footage to serve as confirmation.

This was no hoax. The man's abilities were real.

But that still didn't mean I was going to kill my wife for him.

Whatever Rogers said my destiny was, there had to be some other way this could end.

There didn't seem to be any reasoning with Rogers, Vanslow DeGange, or the rest of the Praesidium. Their minds were made up, and, if anything, what I had learned this afternoon had only reinforced that they would not negotiate.

I had to come up with another plan, one that didn't involve the Praesidium; one that took Jenny, the kids, and me far out of Vanslow DeGange's reach—and far out of harm's way.

And there was only one thing, it now struck me, that could accomplish that. I would do exactly what Buck McBride had told me to do days ago.

Take the family.

And run.

I would have to find a way to slip past Rogers and his people, who would be watching us, probably following us. I could do a sweep of the car for a tracking device again. Better yet, we could just drive to a rental-car place.

Either way, we would elude them. Somehow.

Where would we go? And how, exactly, do you run from a man who can see the future—or sense the currents, or however Rogers described it? Was there any place on the planet that Vanslow DeGange wouldn't be aware of us if he concentrated hard enough?

I had no idea. But Rogers had said DeGange wasn't omniscient. There had to be a way.

The ripples. DeGange's gift was tied to them, right? We just had to be careful we didn't make any. We could run, get set up somewhere completely off the grid, where we didn't have to interact with anyone. There, we could lie low, live quietly. And frugally. We had enough savings to last a long time. Especially if we sold the house.

If death and the lack of death were the things that DeGange sensed most easily, we'd simply have to stay alive.

Without Jenny, CMR would drop the CP&L lawsuit. We could let some time pass, to make sure it was good and gone. And maybe then it would be safe to resurface, because Vanslow DeGange would no longer perceive her as a threat, and the Praesidium would have moved on to preventing other cataclysms that had nothing to do with us.

This, of course, was assuming I could convince Jenny to come with me.

A daunting task. Think about the proposition from her perspective: your husband, who has already been acting squirrelly, is now proposing you hastily pack up your young family and run off in the dead of night with no plan of where you're going and little thought of when you might return.

Yeah, no chance.

Could I drug her? Roofie my own wife and haul her off?

It was a short-term solution, at best. At least it would get her out of the house and away from the Praesidium's immediate grasp.

Eventually, the drugs would wear off. I couldn't keep her hostage forever.

At that point, I would have to somehow get her to buy in without explaining why. According to Rogers, merely the knowledge she was going to have this brainstorm might trigger the idea. Once that happened, she became the most dangerous person in history, and the Praesidium would stop at nothing to eliminate her.

Unless, of course, she shared the idea broadly? Once it was out in the world, ranging free, it would quickly gather its own momentum, and Jenny's existence would become incidental. She would no longer be the choke point. The Praesidium would just have to find another way to avert this crisis.

I flirted with that course of action. It certainly solved my immediate problem.

But what would happen after that? What if the cascade of consequences set off by Jenny's big idea truly was inevitable and unstoppable, as Vanslow DeGange had prophesied?

Morally, I couldn't make my win come at the expense of more than a billion people's loss.

Even being strictly selfish about it, I would be dooming myself—and, more importantly, my daughters—to live in a world past its boiling point, as members of a civilization in collapse.

No, I had to stop this here and now.

So. Run. And keep Jenny clueless.

It seemed to be the best among my very bad options.

That was about as far as my thoughts had made it by seven thirty. Having given the girls their bath and read them a book, I had just put Cate in her crib and was pulling the blankets up to Parker's chin when I heard noise coming from downstairs.

Jenny was home.

But she hadn't come alone.

There were two men standing in our kitchen, having been escorted inside by Jenny. One of them had a bushy white mustache. The other had a gray flattop.

Jenny introduced them, but I missed their names. I was still confused as to why they were even in our house.

Then Jenny explained how a few hours earlier, someone—she had no idea who or why—had tried to kill her, muttering about how something had to end, and about how sorry she was.

Jenny delivered this news without hysteria, in a low voice so the girls couldn't hear it. It wasn't difficult for me to summon all the shocked-husband sounds that should have accompanied this news, because I really was stunned by it.

Given how close this person had come to success—and that no one knew if the assailant was acting alone—CMR had hired two body-guards, both ex-cops, to watch over her for the evening.

And, perhaps, longer.

One man would be stationed in front of the house. The other would be behind. Both had concealed carry permits and bulges in their jackets.

And I was of two minds about it. If I decided to let 9:47 p.m. Friday come and go without acting, having this detail assigned to us might—might—protect us from whatever attempts the Praesidium would make to eliminate the entire family.

But having two bodyguards also made it harder to flee. Perhaps even impossible, if they were instructed to keep us in the city.

Was this my destiny, reminding me of its presence? Was this the reason future me was unable to take the family and run?

Unaware of my inner turmoil, and having briefed me on everything she knew at the moment, Jenny announced she was going upstairs to say good night to the girls.

I let her go. Frick and Frack—or whatever their names were—then took their leave, assuming their stations outside. And I was left to ponder: Who *else* wanted to kill my wife?

It couldn't be the Praesidium. Rogers and his buddies were waiting on me to do the killing, weren't they?

So was it actually CP&L? Jenny had said her would-be killer was a grandmotherly-looking woman with orange hair—not exactly the profile of a for-hire assassin.

I had made no further progress on this problem when, maybe fifteen minutes later, there was a knock on our front door. I went into the foyer to see Barry Khadem standing on the porch.

"Hey," I said, opening the door for him. "Thanks for"—I faltered momentarily—"thanks for saving Jenny's life today."

"It wasn't me," he said. "You should be offering your thanks to the Virginia State Police."

"I'll think about that the next time I'm paying state income tax. Come on in."

He followed me into the kitchen just as Jenny was descending the stairs. I invited him to sit on a stool at the kitchen peninsula and stood on the other side. From under his beefy arm, he produced a folder, which he placed on the counter.

"The police got an ID on the woman who tried to attack you and we did some background on her as well," he said. "I volunteered to run it over to see if any of it was meaningful to you."

"Okay," Jenny said, pulling up a stool next to him.

He opened the folder, producing a blown-up driver's license photo of a middle-age woman with shoulder-length brown hair.

"Meet Candice Carter Bresnahan," Barry said. "Born January tenth, 1955. Her most recent driver's license lists her address as a post office box in White Stone, Virginia. Does she look familiar?"

Jenny didn't hesitate. "No. And I've never heard the name Candice Carter Bresnahan either."

"She went by Candy, apparently."

"That doesn't help. Should I know her?"

"Probably not. She grew up in Warren, Indiana, a small town halfway between Indianapolis and Fort Wayne. Most of what we learned about her came from stories written about her in the Fort Wayne *Journal Gazette*. She was described as an all-American girl with a happy childhood—a cheerleader, that sort of thing—when she abruptly dropped out of school and married her high school sweetheart."

"Sounds like someone got pregnant," Jenny said.

"This was 1972, pre–Roe v. Wade, so that's not a bad guess," Barry said. "In any event, she settled in her hometown and had two more kids. In ninety-three she was working the parts desk at a local auto dealership when she allegedly poisoned her husband, Jerome Bresnahan, with ethylene glycol. Killed him."

"Ethylene glycol?" I asked.

"That's the active ingredient in antifreeze," Barry said. "At the trial, the prosecution made sure the jury knew that Candy had plenty of access to it because of her job. Jerome was a long-haul trucker. He worked for Dynamic Waste Disposal, one of the largest toxic-waste haulers in the country. He was gone a lot, and the prosecution's theory was that he had cheated on Candy on the road, and she punished him for it."

"Ouch," Jenny said.

"The defense countered that Jerome was an alcoholic and may have guzzled antifreeze in a drunken stupor. Her lawyer also managed to hint that when Jerome drank, he got heavy handed with Candy and the kids. The defense attorney's closing argument was basically a version of, 'She didn't kill him, but even if she did, he had it coming.' The jury deliberated for five days before telling the judge it couldn't reach a verdict. The prosecution decided not to retry it—a tacit acknowledgment they just didn't have enough evidence to get a conviction. At the end of it all, Candy was a free woman.

"But that's actually not the strange part," Barry continued. "After the trial, everyone expected she'd return to Warren. What else did she know? Instead, she disappeared. To White Stone, Virginia, of all places. The Fort Wayne *Journal Gazette* did a story on the ten-year anniversary of Jerome Bresnahan's death. Candy Bresnahan could not be reached for comment. She hadn't even come back to town for the birth of her grandchildren."

"Maybe she just didn't want to live in a place where everyone looked at her like she was a murderer," I said, wondering if I was simultaneously talking about Candy's past and my future.

"It's possible," Barry said. "All I can say is she doesn't seem to have done much in White Stone other than get a driver's license. She didn't buy a house. She didn't start a business or register a corporation. She didn't even register to vote. Then she resurfaced to try and kill you. Thank God we got her first so she ended up like this instead."

With that, he casually flipped another picture of Candy Bresnahan on our kitchen island. It was a postmortem shot of her entire body, in situ.

When I saw it, I had to stifle a gasp.

In the photo, her left arm was raised. The sleeve of her T-shirt had slipped up, revealing a distinctive scar.

It was a square with a *P* and an *R* inscribed inside.

CHAPTER 28

NATE

Barry continued to share what the state police knew—or didn't know, since the gun had no serial number, and the body yielded no clues about what Candy Bresnahan had been up to for the last quarter century.

I knew.

Or at least I could assemble a pretty good guess.

Sometime in 1993 she had been approached by Lorton Rogers, or some other member of the Praesidium, and jolted out of her otherwise ordinary mother-of-three-in-small-town-Indiana life. She was told she needed to kill her husband because . . .

Well, because Jerome Bresnahan was a man with a drinking problem who chauffeured toxic waste for a living. You didn't need to be one with the currents to know it was destined to end poorly.

Maybe Jerome was going to drive a truckload of nasty goo into a school bus, or spill a deadly mess across a busy interstate, or inadvertently taint an entire city's water supply with his boozy recklessness.

Whatever it was, it was bad enough that Jerome had to go. And the Praesidium decided he needed to die in its preferred manner: at the hand of his own spouse.

Everyone knows Jerome is a drunk, Candy was told. *We'll just say he guzzled some Prestone thinking it was a mojito. The jury will deliberate for five days and then you'll be free.*

Had Candy fought the inevitable, like me? Did she need to be convinced by a demonstration of DeGange's power? Or had she accepted her fated future at face value, eager to be rid of her drunken, abusive husband?

Whatever it was, she had gone through with it. And then she decided she wanted no part of the reception she'd get if she returned to Warren. She couldn't face the withering stares at church or the under-the-breath mutterings at the grocery store.

Or perhaps it was that working for Vanslow DeGange, a billionaire who helped the world dodge punches before they were ever thrown, was more interesting than selling auto parts in Indiana.

Whatever the case was, she got her brand and she joined the Praesidium, at which point she did . . . what exactly? Procured replacement mufflers for the Praesidium's fleet of cars?

Or was she more like Rogers, jumping from crisis to crisis, never knowing who she'd have to conspire to kill next?

And then, one day, that someone became my wife.

Except it made no sense Praesidium would dispatch her on that errand. Why send her to do on a Thursday afternoon what I was going to do on a Friday evening? Rogers said the Praesidium had a rule about not doing its own dirty work.

And why, for that matter, was she so bad at it? The Praesidium surely had more capable people. Why send a woman in a bright-red shirt to fumble around the plaza in front of Jenny's workplace for an hour, slipping her hand in and out of her bag, being so obvious with her ill intentions? Why not plant a sharpshooter on the top of the parking garage, much like the state police had done? Or simply kill her as she walked out to her car in the morning?

None of it made sense.

I actually wished I could talk to Rogers. He surely had some explanation. Perhaps this was part of the effort to exonerate me. The jury would hear that the day before Jenny's death, this other woman had tried to kill her. And therefore it was reasonable to believe that someone else—some associate of Candy's, perhaps—had shown up and finished the job.

Was Candy really willing to sacrifice herself for the Praesidium like that? Or perhaps DeGange had already sensed that her death was imminent, but it would be slow and painful. So she was willing to sacrifice herself for the greater good.

Whatever the answers were, Barry Khadem didn't have them. And neither did Jenny, who kept insisting in different fashions that she had no knowledge of Candy Bresnahan and no inkling of her motives.

Once they had hashed that through a few more times, Barry announced he was headed home for the evening after one last check of Jenny's protective detachment.

That left Jenny and me alone in the kitchen, but not alone in any broader sense. Between Rogers and the bodyguards, we had plenty of people around us who would constrain any move I was contemplating.

"So," I said, trying to sound like a concerned husband. "How you doing?"

"I'm fine," she said.

Except the way she said *fine* made it sound a lot more like some other four-letter words.

"No, seriously. Barry's gone. You don't have to keep up a brave front anymore. How are you? You must be—"

"Fine," she insisted. "It happened so fast. And then it was over. Even now it feels like something I saw in a movie, not something that actually happened."

There was again silence in the kitchen. And in that moment, I was again tempted to blurt out everything. Just tell her the whole story; ask her to run off with me and the kids; beg her to not just drop the lawsuit, but never think about the lawsuit for another second, lest she have the brainstorm that would change everything.

But before I could even think of how to form the words, she yawned and stretched.

"I'm beat," she said. "I think the adrenaline has finally worn off. Let's go to bed."

"Actually, can we talk?" I said. "There's something I really need to discuss with you."

She shot me a look I had seen before. I called it her brick-wall look—because I would have better luck talking to one of those. She was worn out. She had been through hell. She wasn't going to be able to hear anything I said.

But shouldn't I try anyway? Nothing could have been more important.

And yet, in the Rogers-inevitable version of my life, maybe *this* was exactly why I had failed to convince her to run away with me. I had pushed it, instead of waiting until the right moment.

So. Exercise some free will. Think you're going to do one thing? Decide to do the opposite.

"Actually, never mind," I said. "It can wait until the morning."

"Great, thanks," she said, sliding off the chair.

She kissed me on the cheek, then left the kitchen.

I stayed behind to turn off the lights and do the last of the dishes, worried I had actually made the wrong decision, wondering if this was what I had been fated to do all along.

CHAPTER 29

JENNY

There was no sleeping. Not for a long time. Jenny's brain kept replaying images of Candy Bresnahan.

Then, at a certain point, the fatigue became its own self-perpetuating problem. Every time she was about to drift off, her body would spasm, waking her back up.

At some point after 2:00 a.m., she finally dozed off. When her alarm clock bleated out its 5:30 a.m. call, she shut it off and rolled back over, intending to doze for another few minutes.

Two and a half hours passed.

When she awoke again, daylight was streaming into the room from the sides of the curtain. Still a little dazed, she propped herself up to look at the clock, unable to believe she had overslept by so much.

And then, like he had been listening for the sound of her blankets rustling, Nate eased into the room.

"Oh, hey," he said. "I didn't realize you were awake."

"Yeah," Jenny croaked.

"I was just coming in to get my slippers."

"Oh," she said, then stared emptily at his socked feet as he walked across the room toward the closet.

He retrieved the slippers, put them on, and then came over to the bed.

"Can we have that talk now?" he asked.

"Sure."

He sat on the side of the bed. She scooched herself up into a sitting position.

"I need a favor," he said. "Actually, calling it a favor makes it sound small. It's not small. But it's something I need all the same, more than I can possibly explain. As a matter of fact, I won't be able to explain it. But it's still something I really, really need."

"Okay. Are you going to start making sense anytime soon?"

"Yeah. Sorry. So here it is: I want you to drop the CP and L lawsuit."

Jenny was suddenly wide awake. She crossed her arms. "I see. And why is that?"

"Like I said, I can't explain it."

"Well, you're going to have to try. Because 'Hey, throw away two years of work because I need a favor' isn't really going to cut it."

"Okay. I just . . . I have this really awful feeling about where this is heading. That woman who tried to kill you yesterday, doesn't that *have* to be related to CP and L somehow?"

"What makes you think that?"

"Nothing else you're working on is that huge. I mean, four hundred million dollars can make people do desperate things."

"So CP and L sent a deranged grandma from Indiana to try and kill me? That doesn't wash."

"No, I'm not saying that. I'm saying an action like this, it's going to make you a lot of nasty enemies. *A lot* of them. CP and L is just the start. We don't know what drove this lady or who she was working for. There will also be other power companies, not to mention the entire coal industry. Those coal barons are no sweethearts. They play for keeps."

She was already grimacing. "I don't know about that. Face it, the woman was mentally ill and decided to target me for some reason that only she understands. Maybe she has a thing against female lawyers. Maybe I represent some client who did her wrong. We'll probably never know why."

"You can just dismiss it that easily?"

"I'm not dismissing anything," she said. "Barry is still looking into it. If he wants to keep me under protection while he sorts it out, fine. If he is able to figure out this woman had some connection to CP and L or some other entity we need to worry about, we'll deal with that. But if he doesn't come up with anything substantive, I'm not going to let it paralyze me."

"Okay, so forget what happened yesterday. This thing, it's a very different kind of law than what you signed up to practice, a very different kind of law than what CMR is really set up for. How many other partners are pursuing huge mass-tort claims? None that I'm aware of. You've gotten this far in your career by playing the game the right way. This is a completely different kind of game. You're at a stage of your career where you ought to be out hustling clients, building your book, not going down this rabbit hole with CP and L."

She shot him a look that could have cut glass. What was Nate really up to? Where did this fit in with all the other unexplained and unusual behaviors? With the gun that wasn't a gun. With the off-the-books lawyering. And now, here he was, acting conspiratorial, using some suspiciously familiar language.

"Have you been talking with Dickel?"

"What? No," Nate said hastily.

"Because that's practically word for word what Dickel said to me. *Word* for *word*."

"Well, because it's true. The man has a point."

"I don't care if he does or not. Did you go behind my back with Dickel?"

"No."

Jenny watched Nate's gaze shift to the floor like some middle school truant. He had never really tried to lie to her, at least not that she was aware of. And now she understood why: he was terrible at it. His body language screamed *deception*.

"When's the last time you talked to him?" she pressed.

"I don't know. Probably one of the times I visited with the girls."

"Have you been playing racquetball with him?"

"Not in a while."

"Are you lying to me right now?"

"About racquetball?"

"No. About having talked to Dickel about this."

"Why would I talk to Dickel about this? And what makes you think Dickel would care even if I did?"

"Oh, please," Jenny said with an eye roll. "He's had a crush on you since the first day of orientation. He'd do anything for you just to have the chance to ogle your ass while he's doing it."

"Don't be silly. I don't even know what you're talking about."

Nate was at least again making eye contact. Did he actually think he was getting away with this? Pulling one over on her? Jenny took in a deep breath and prepared to dismantle that misapprehension.

"Yesterday Dickel came to my office and, without citing any particularly compelling reason, said the executive committee was going to have a vote this afternoon on whether to continue the CP and L case. When he was talking about why, he used almost the exact phrase you just did, with the rabbit hole and everything. And you're saying you *didn't* talk to him about this?"

"No. Definitely not. It's just a coincidence. Saying someone is going down the rabbit hole, I mean, that's a pretty common saying."

Jenny sat there for a moment, staring at him, trying to peer into his soul. Nate, the non-game-player, was playing some kind of game. Jenny just couldn't figure out what it was.

She understood Dickel's motivation for wanting to submarine the CP&L case: he was a generally miserable human being who was tormented about not being able to live authentically and therefore enjoyed the suffering of others.

But what was Nate's angle?

"Okay, forget Dickel for a second," she said. "Forget everyone else. Why do *you* want me to drop this lawsuit? Don't tell me you're worried about my career. That's nonsense. We both know my career will be fine."

"Look, I'm afraid, okay?" Nate said. "I'm afraid of what this suit will do to you, to our family. I feel like this Candy Bresnahan lady is just the start. There will be other stuff. And it's not worth it. Say you win everything you're asking for and it doesn't get knocked down one penny on appeal. Great. The partners at Carter, Morgan, and Ross will have another hundred-whatever million to divvy up at the end of the year. Everyone will have a great Christmas. And your year-end bonus will certainly be healthy, but so what? Do we really need the money? It's not like we're hurting here."

"It's not about the money," Jenny said. "It's about the Hendersons. And the Griffins. And the Russells. I've looked into their eyes. I've seen their suffering. They didn't do anything wrong. All they did was breathe, for God's sake. Power companies like CP and L have known for a long time that coal kills, but they keep burning it anyway. Why? Because it's too expensive to build new plants that don't burn coal. Well, okay. If that's how they're going to play it, then the only way to get their attention is with a huge settlement like this."

"That's all well and good, and I don't disagree with you. But it's still too big a risk for you. For us. I'm not talking about your career. I'm talking about your *life*, Jenny. No offense to them, but the Hendersons, the Griffins, and the Russells are not my greatest concern. The Lovejoys are. Parker and Cate. And they'd rather have you alive."

"Really? Keeping me alive. *That's* your concern."

"Yes. Of course."

Jenny studied him, sitting on the edge of the bed. For perhaps the first time in this conversation, he wasn't lying.

But she was now detecting something else. Exhaustion. His face was lined in ways it usually wasn't. It wasn't merely crooked. It was like it was an extra degree or two out of joint. Lopsided.

Nate's presence had always been a calming one in her life. He had this insouciance about him—this air that, yes, the girls were hard work, draining in ways not even their early years as associates had been, but he was still basically content with his life, safe in the knowledge that everything was somehow going to work out okay.

That was gone. This was a man under strain.

"Has someone tried to threaten you?" Jenny asked quietly.

Nate seemed to have something stuck in his throat.

"No," he finally choked out. "It's just . . . I worry, that's all. I worry you're getting involved with people who have no moral compass and no conscience, and they'll stop at nothing to win."

"And therefore you want me to drop this case."

"Right. Exactly. Look, you say there's a vote today? Let's just agree on this: If the members of the executive committee vote this thing down, don't fight it, okay? Accept their wisdom and move on. Is that a fair request? Can we make that the favor I'm asking for?"

"It makes no sense for them to drop this. We've already made a huge investment in time and resources—"

"But if they do, you'll respect the decision. Is that fair?"

"Sure. Fair deal."

"Okay," he said, then practically bounced off the bed. "I'm going to check on the girls."

"Wait a second," she said quickly.

He paused in the doorway. Jenny felt like there were still too many unanswered questions. And she—a woman who had taught herself not to back down from anything—found herself in the strangest of mindsets:

She was afraid to ask them.

Because she truly didn't know how he'd react. And that was scarier than having him lie to her, scarier than all his erratic behavior of late. For the first time in their thirteen years, she wasn't entirely sure of Nate Lovejoy—solid, dependable, calm Nate. And it terrified her.

But rather than confront him, rather than do anything that might push him further away, she instead felt this desperate urge to bring him closer.

"I love you," she said. "I hear what you're saying about this case, and . . . just remember, no matter what happens, I love you. Keep that first and foremost in your heart, okay?"

CHAPTER 30

NATE

I shouldn't have been surprised that Jenny—ever-intuitive Jenny—had been able to sniff out my conversation with Dickel, or that she was circling around the truth of why I wanted her to drop the lawsuit.

Still, her revelation about the executive committee vote gave me hope. There were nine of them, all partners who were more senior than Jenny.

Dickel was the only one I knew well. The rest were high in other regions of the CMR atmosphere, places I hadn't interacted with much, if at all. It would be weird for me to call and lobby any of them to vote against my wife.

Dickel would just have to be persuasive on his own. He probably had either leverage or plain dirt on at least four other committee members. If he was willing to twist arms, he might just be able to—

I didn't dare get too optimistic about it. But maybe this was my out, the wrinkle in the currents that Vanslow DeGange had overlooked. This executive committee was effectively my Supreme Court. All I needed was five votes and my problems were over.

Not long after Jenny left for work, taking her protection detail with her, Rogers appeared on our back porch.

He was attired in his usual manner—as the older guy in the dentist's office who felt like his semiannual cleaning was worth putting on a crisply ironed dress shirt.

I let him into the kitchen and pointed toward the living room, where I was once again letting a screen watch my children.

"Just keep your voice down," I said. "You want some coffee?"

"That'd be great," he said.

As I asked him for his cream-and-sugar preferences, he sat on a stool at the peninsula. I couldn't believe I was being hospitable to a man who had kidnapped me, threatened my children, and wanted me to kill my wife. At the same time—and this must have been some bizarre form of Stockholm syndrome—I felt like I needed him.

He was the one person in my life who actually seemed to know what was going on.

I slid a coffee mug toward him, and soon he was unspooling his version of Candy Bresnahan's story.

She had been a longtime member of the Praesidium, predating Rogers' arrival by a year. He told me things I already knew or had guessed about her husband, whose drunken spilling of toxic waste was, in fact, going to poison hundreds of people had he not been stopped.

The environment had since become an important issue to Candy. Although, lately, Rogers had been worried about her mental state. She was showing signs of dementia—not just the forgetfulness but also the irritation and agitation known to accompany it.

In her lucid moments, she had been hyperfocused on Jenny's case, demanding that the Praesidium move to take her out. Not trusting in me to get the job done, she had decided to do it herself.

"So, basically, she went rogue," I said.

"Exactly."

"The last thing she said to Jenny was something like, 'This has to end.'"

"That's what she thought she was doing. Ending the looming global warming crisis."

"Why wasn't Vanslow DeGange able to see this coming and stop her?"

"We've had this problem a few times in the past," Rogers said. "The Praesidium is kind of Mr. DeGange's blind spot. He's concentrating so hard on things outside the group, he doesn't really focus on us. He assumes our past loyalties—and the way we're bonded to him and each other—will keep us in line. And most of the time he's right. Except, every now and then, a Candy Bresnahan slips through the cracks.

"Candy wasn't . . . well, it's not like we have ranks in the Praesidium. You're either with us or you're not. But in the unofficial pecking order, she had been slipping for some time. She definitely wasn't being trusted with bigger assignments anymore. I think it bothered her. I can't pretend to be in her head, but it's possible she saw this as a way to reestablish herself as a useful contributor and bring up her stock."

Which meant the Praesidium—as unusual as its mission and methods may have been—was just like every other human organization: prone to politicking and infighting.

"Where are you in the pecking order?" I asked.

"Me? Oh, I don't know. Somewhere in the middle, I'd say. Maybe a little higher. I'm viewed as reliable. Mr. DeGange trusts me. Though I'm perhaps not as talented as others. I'm certainly not seen as anyone special. When I told you killing me wouldn't help you, that's accurate. I'm replaceable."

He took another sip of his coffee.

"You never did tell me who you killed to become part of the Praesidium."

I saw a brief flash of an expression I couldn't entirely diagnose. Maybe sadness. Or regret. Or anger. Rogers' personality was as buttoned down as his shirts, so it was hard to get a read on him.

He took a long sip of his coffee, set it down, then reset his face.

"My younger brother," he said.

"I'm sorry."

He made an ambiguous gesture with his right shoulder. "He was a good kid. He really was. He just got . . . mixed up with the wrong people at a time in his life when he was really impressionable. My parents didn't know what to do and I wasn't paying as much attention as I should have. Maybe I couldn't have stopped it, but .. ."

"What was it? Drugs?"

"Well, partly. But mostly it was ideology. You'd never guess it, looking at me, but my brother was this latter-day hippie. Free love. Peace on Earth. Everything was a conspiracy between the government and the corporations. It was like he came along too late for the sixties and was trying to make up for it. He actually did join a commune out west. Then he drifted for a while. By the time he came back home he had been . . . radicalized, I guess you could say. He was convinced that capitalism was the root of all evil and that our government was a corrupt handmaiden of capitalism that needed to be overthrown by violent insurrection. This was early nineties, so there wasn't really an internet as we know it now. But there were these bulletin board systems that people could log into and anonymously post all sorts of crazy stuff. Including how to make bombs."

Rogers was sharing this story like he had told it before. Was this the way members of the Praesidium got to know each other? Sit around and talk about who they had killed?

"I was approached by a man who told me my kid brother was going to bomb the Mall of America the weekend before Christmastime. It would have killed close to two hundred people, according to Mr. DeGange. I had doubts about Mr. DeGange—it's crazy, right? But ultimately I wasn't as difficult to convince as you are. I knew my brother had been hanging around with people who had twisted his mind and that he had way more fertilizer socked away than my mother's vegetable garden needed."

"Why you?"

"Pardon?"

"Why were you the one who had to kill him?" I asked.

"Oh. My brother didn't have a lot of friends. He had turned pretty paranoid about outsiders. He was living in this man cave my parents had built for him—a detached garage with living quarters over it. It wasn't easy for anyone else to get close. By the time Mr. DeGange sensed the ripple of what was going to happen at the Mall of America, there wasn't a lot of time. I was the only one who could get access. So I did what I had to do."

"Did you . . . end up going to jail, or—"

He shook his head. "I was given a device to plant in the garage. When it detonated, it set off all the other bomb-making material my brother had, blew the place sky-high. The authorities pretty quickly concluded he had accidentally killed himself with one of his own bombs."

"And then you ran off and joined the Praesidium," I said.

"I wouldn't say I ran off. You have to keep it secret, sure. My mother is still alive. As far as she's concerned, I have a job with an educational consulting firm that involves a lot of travel. It's not like being part of the Praesidium means you have to sever all ties with the world. Some, like Candy, decide to do it that way. But that's their choice. Basically, I was given the same talk that you'll be given once this is over."

"Which was?"

"A combination debriefing and job offer, I guess you'd call it. It was explained to me that I was not to share anything I had learned about the Praesidium—certainly not about Mr. DeGange's abilities, not even that the group existed—and there would be consequences if I did."

"Consequences like . . ."

"What do you think?"

"They'd kill you if you talked."

"Actually, it's more interesting than that," he said. "It was explained to me that I'd likely be silenced *before* I talked, because Mr. DeGange would know it was coming."

"Punished for a crime you hadn't even committed yet."

He made another ambiguous move with his shoulder.

"And then the job offer?" I asked.

"That I was eligible to join them if I wished."

"And obviously you did."

"I was a high school English teacher, divorced, no kids. I liked my job fine, but it wasn't anything special. What the Praesidium was proposing just seemed more interesting, more fulfilling."

"And what, exactly, was the proposition?"

"You mean what would the offer be for you?" he asked, smiling slightly.

"No, I—"

"Just relax. It's not something we can talk about yet anyway. The time will come. Suffice it to say, the Praesidium takes good care of each other and we'll take good care of you."

He reached out and patted my arm.

"I actually can't stay," he said. "If you need to talk more later, just call this number."

He slid over a piece of paper where he had written ten digits.

"Is this your number?"

"It's . . . I guess you'd call it an answering service. If you need to leave a message for a member of the Praesidium, they always know where to find us. But maybe I shouldn't call it an answering service, because believe me, you won't get any answers out of them."

He stopped to smile at his own thin attempt at a joke.

"And now, if you'll excuse me," he said, "I have some business to attend to."

"Can you tell me what it is?"

He smiled again. "Not yet. But I suspect you'll learn about it soon enough."

It was the weirdest sensation, this feeling of near normalcy that descended over the house after Rogers left.

I was alone with the girls. Just like I would be on any other Friday.

Except if Vanslow DeGange was to be believed—and I was having an increasingly hard time doubting him—this would be a Friday unlike any other.

I'm always aware of the time, especially on Fridays, because it means we're so close to the weekend—two days when I don't have to be as much of a single parent as I am the other five.

On this Friday, I found myself even more aware of the clock, especially when forty-seven minutes past the hour rolled around.

Because at 10:47 I was eleven hours away.

And at 12:47 I was nine hours away.

And so on. I spent most of nap time pondering free will—or the lack of it—dreading what the future had in store for me, asking myself whether it was already preordained.

Was I, in fact, a man in full control of his actions? Or was I just another leaf being blown along by the breezes of fortune?

I found myself thinking about the lessons of big data when it came to this question. Trying to use data to predict when one person will be involved in a traffic accident is a hopeless exercise. The chances are so small each time the person gets behind the wheel it's impossible to say with any certainty that, yes, *this* is when it will happen.

Furthermore, when you look at any one accident, you can usually pinpoint the cause. A person made a decision to text while driving, or drive too fast, or have that extra drink, or run that red light.

It looks a lot like free will in action. Haphazard. Chaotic. Unpredictable. The human animal in all its quirky glory.

But when the frame of reference is pulled back far enough, the picture changes. The data shows a certain number of people absolutely *will* be involved in accidents each year. And a certain percentage will be caused by texting, or speeding, or drinking, or failure to obey signals. The results are remarkably predictable, with a high degree of confidence, and they only vary by so much year-in, year-out.

From that perspective, we don't seem to have free will at all. We look like a bunch of mindless electrons, slavishly fulfilling the needs of the data set. Oh, sure, you can't necessarily say what any one electron will do. But the entire system behaves very neatly, according to equations that are relatively easy to calculate. Insurance companies do it all the time.

It makes you question whether the individual has any say in it at all.

Then again, according to that classic statistician's joke, the average American has one ovary and one testicle.

Once the girls woke up, I was yanked out of these meditations and back into fatherhood, all while continuing to eye the clock.

At Parker's insistence, we were having a tea party. We all got dolled up—me in a top hat and a clip-on bow tie, the girls in hats and old costume jewelry—and huddled on the floor around the tiny tea set that my mother got Parker for her last birthday.

Cate wasn't quite all in on drinking nonexistent tea and eating air scones. She mostly fussed with her jewelry over Parker's objections ("No, Cate-Cate, that's not a toy!"), until—inevitably—she destroyed the necklace she had been yanking on, sending little plastic pearls bouncing all over the floor.

Parker immediately began howling about the broken necklace. Once we collected all the parts of it, I saw it was actually an easy fix. I just had to get a tool from Jenny's jewelry box.

That's how I ended up in our bedroom, rooting through Jenny's stuff, where I found something that definitely didn't belong among all the baubles and trinkets.

It was a thumb drive, artfully camouflaged behind Jenny's charm bracelet.

What was a thumb drive doing there?

I pulled it out of her jewelry box, holding its string between my thumb and pointer finger, letting it dangle in front of my eyes.

According to the clock by her bedside, it was exactly 2:47 p.m. Seven hours to go.

It gave me an involuntary chill. Had I been fated to find the thumb drive at this exact moment? Was the broken necklace not a random accident but, rather, another move in a prechoreographed dance?

Stuffing the thumb drive in my pocket, I went back downstairs. I fixed the necklace, which calmed a teary Parker. I put Cate behind the plastic barriers in the corner—over her vociferous protests—and told the girls Daddy needed to go potty.

I took my computer into the bathroom and set it on my lap, using the toilet as a seat. The thumb drive had just one file on it—a video.

It was called *Lovejoy Trip*.

My screen was soon displaying an image of a gray Range Rover—my Range Rover—shot from high altitude. It was driving down a suburban road I didn't immediately recognize, even though I presumed I was the one driving.

The camera seemed to be following along. It must have been attached to a drone.

There was a time-and-date stamp on the bottom right of the screen, which told me this was Thursday morning. Suddenly, I recognized exactly where I was, and I knew where I was going.

This was my drive to the Matthews residence.

I thought back to all those wrong turns and double backs I had performed. I had been looking in my rearview mirror the whole time. I never thought to look up in the sky.

Why did Jenny have this video? Was she having me followed?

I watched as I turned into the Matthews' neighborhood, now seeing all the same in-ground pools and tennis courts from above, as opposed to street level.

There was no sound. Just the picture. The Range Rover pulled into that parking area across from the Matthews mansion. As soon as I stopped, the drone's camera zoomed in. The angle was off to the side enough that I could see my own face as I got out of the car.

I watched myself going around to Parker's side, feeling a pang as the tiny brown head of my eldest daughter emerged. Then I went around to Cate's side. Before long, there was Cate's head, with its mass of curls.

Soon, I was making that unwieldy walk—with one child on my hip, one at my hand, and a Pack 'n Play on my shoulder—up the path toward the mansion. I rang the doorbell, and then disappeared inside, almost like I had been invited.

Then the screen went dark.

There was no footage of my burned-ass retreat, nor of my drive back. Just this one five-minute snippet of my life, with no explanation.

I was stumped. Utterly. Jenny had put this in her jewelry box, a place I ordinarily never would have waded into. Not her drawer, which I might have gone into while putting away her laundry; not the bathroom, which I shared with her; not under the mattress, where I might have unearthed it while changing the sheets. Her jewelry box.

So she must have wanted to hide it from me.

At the same time, she obviously wanted to be able to watch it again sometime, or have it for some future reference. Otherwise she would have just thrown it out.

Had she hired someone to produce this video for her? Or had someone given it to her? I was pretty sure she hadn't made it herself. My wife's talents, while myriad, did not include drone piloting.

I was baffled. And I wouldn't have believed it, except the evidence was right in front of my eyes:

Someone besides Rogers and the Praesidium had been following me.

CHAPTER 31

JENNY

From the moment she arrived at work—more than two hours late, escorted by a pair of armed guards—Jenny was aware that pretty much everyone at Carter, Morgan & Ross was tiptoeing around her.

They had, of course, heard about the attempt on her life. Some of them had still been in the building when it happened and heard the gunshot. Others had seen the woman with the orange hair lingering near the entrance and were eagerly tossing what details they could into the office rumor mill.

Jenny had the sense it was probably all anyone was talking about. She didn't know if it had made her an object of fascination, revulsion, pity—or some combination of all three.

Whatever it was, she wished it would go away. She had things to accomplish and an all-important 5:00 p.m. executive committee looming.

Then she checked her voice mail and had one more problem added to the pile. It was Clyde Henderson, Danece's husband. And he sounded distraught.

Jenny had two other voice mails as well, but she called Clyde first.

"Hello?" he answered.

"Mr. Henderson, it's Jenny Welker from Carter, Morgan, and Ross."

Jenny could hear Danece coughing in the background.

"Sorry to bother you, Ms. Welker, but I didn't know who else to call. Landlord came by this morning. He's fixing to evict us. He says we got to get out by the thirtieth or the sheriff is going to throw us out. Don't know what we're going to do. I already called the shelter and they can't take us on account of Danece's oxygen tank. I talked to one of those extended-stay hotels they got by the highway, but—"

"Slow down, slow down," Jenny said. "First of all, have you been served an unlawful detainer notice and given a court date?"

"An unlawful what?"

"An unlawful detainer notice. Unless your landlord has filed one, and unless a judge has ruled in your landlord's favor, the sheriff's office isn't going to throw you anywhere. Eviction is a legal process, not a blanket excuse for your landlord to bully you. And shame on this guy for lying to you and making you think you have to go anywhere when he hasn't even started the proper court proceedings. So the first thing you're going to do is give me your landlord's name and number because I'm going to tear the guy a new one."

Clyde gave Jenny the man's information.

"Good," Jenny said. "Now, how much do you owe this guy?"

"It's more than three thousand dollars."

"That's not a problem. My firm has a fund for clients who are struggling with their bills and whatnot. Basically, it's an interest-free line of credit, using your future judgment in the CP and L suit as collateral. Once the CP and L money comes in, you pay off the loan. Is that something you might be interested in?"

"What if we don't win the lawsuit?"

"Then the loan is forgiven. You really have nothing to worry about. I'll arrange for the fund to pay your landlord the back rent you owe. I can send some paperwork next week. In the meantime, all I need is your verbal okay to proceed."

"Oh, you got my okay. You got my okay, my thank-you, and my thank-the-lord too."

"You and Danece are going to be just fine, Mr. Henderson," Jenny assured him before she hung up. "The fund is going to take care of you."

The fund would do no such thing.

The fund didn't actually exist. The loan was really going to come from Jenny.

But she knew Clyde Henderson would have a much easier time accepting the money if he didn't know that.

CHAPTER 32

NATE

Feeling like someone else was operating my body, I called the number Rogers had given me.

I told the woman who answered I wanted Lorton Rogers to contact me and left my number.

Fifteen minutes later, he showed up on my back porch.

"Come on in," I said, opening the door for him. "Check this out. This was on a thumb drive Jenny had."

My laptop was waiting on the kitchen peninsula with the video already queued up. I hit play, then went into the living room to check on the girls, both of whom were showing signs of impending meltdown from having been ignored by Daddy so much.

I returned to the kitchen as the video finished. Rogers was staring pensively at the screen.

"Where did you find this?" he asked.

"Her jewelry box."

"Did she say anything about it to you, or—"

"Why would she say anything about it? She's clearly trying to hide it from me."

"Right, right, of course," he said, letting out an oversize breath. "Well, that explains that. It's all coming together. It always does."

He had this look of wonderment, joined by a small smile—like a clergyman who had seen miracles before, but still took the time to be moved by them.

"What's coming together?"

"Mr. DeGange's prediction. It's making more sense, that's all."

"How so?"

"We had seen a drone in the sky over your house now and then. We thought maybe it was unrelated. Now I get it."

"Get what?"

"You're not going to like it."

"What's new? I don't like any of this."

"I realize that, but . . . well, I had hoped this wouldn't come out, to be honest. I wasn't going to tell you about it because . . . I know you think I don't care about your feelings and I don't, in some ways. But I also didn't want to cause you unnecessary pain, and—"

"Would you just spit it out?"

He bowed his head for a moment before bringing it back up.

"I'm sorry," he said. "Jenny is cheating on you."

I had heard some unbelievable things tumble out of Rogers' mouth. And not that this was the strangest—not by far—but my first reaction was still doubt.

"No she's not," I said. "When would she even have the time?" *Or the energy? Or the desire?*

"I'm sorry. It's why she's having you followed. You know how you and the girls sometimes visit her in the office?"

"Yeah. We call it 'Your Daughters Show Up at Work Day.'"

"She was worried about you coming into work unannounced, not finding her there, then asking questions about where she was. Whoever she hired, they were good. We never saw them. But we would see that drone. It went into the air whenever you left the house."

Was that true? How had I not noticed?

Then I thought about the trips I made most of the time—to the grocery store, to the doctor's office, to Parker's tumbling class. It was all routine stuff. And I was always wrestling two little girls in and out of the car, worrying about their snacks, their toys.

I probably wouldn't have noticed an F-18 following me, much less one little drone.

"There's got to be another explanation," I said. "I just can't believe she would . . ."

I couldn't complete the sentence.

Rogers pulled out his phone and swiped at it, like it pained him to do even that much. Then he held out the screen for me.

It was Jenny, dressed as she had been on Tuesday, leaving the headquarters of Carter, Morgan & Ross. She had a leather document case under her arm and was walking with her head down, almost like she was embarrassed by what she was doing and didn't want to be seen.

"You've been following her?" I asked, as if it wasn't already obvious.

"Of course we have. We leave nothing to chance. You must know that by now. We followed her to a hotel called The Commonwealth."

He showed me another picture of her walking past a bellman. I knew The Commonwealth. It was just down from the state capitol.

"Okay, so she walked into a hotel—that doesn't mean she's having an . . . an affair."

I could barely spit out the words.

"Well, except this is who walked out twenty-five minutes later," Rogers said, then held up his phone again, showing me a picture of a man in a suit.

The gasp got stuck in my throat. He was a big guy, with a chiseled jaw and TV-weatherman hair.

Greg Grichtmeier. Kara's husband.

I felt like I had been stabbed.

"Your wife walked out about three minutes later," Rogers said, showing me that picture.

"But that's . . . that's got to be a coincidence. I'm sure he just had a meeting there, or—"

"It's not the first time. They've been doing this a lot. I could get you other pictures if you like. Here, hang on."

He tapped at his phone, then brought it up to his ear.

"Could you text me some of the other photos of Welker and Grichtmeier at The Commonwealth?" he asked. He listened for the response, then said, "Yeah, that'd be fine. Thank you."

Nausea was welling up in me. I seriously thought I was going to vomit. I glanced toward the sink, feeling like I might need to make a dash that way.

Rogers wasn't looking at me, and I didn't blame him. I'm sure it was difficult to watch a man sinking slowly from shame, horror, and disgust.

His phone pinged. He looked down at it.

"Yeah, here we go," he said. "This was the first time. Or at least we think it was."

There were two pictures in the same text message. One showed Jenny, with the same document folder, this time with her winter jacket on. The other was Greg, dressed in a different-colored suit. Both photos were shot from the same angle, at the same time of day, showing them walking into The Commonwealth.

"They're good," Rogers said. "You never actually see them together. Usually they spend anywhere from twenty minutes to an hour in there."

The phone went off again. Two more photos. Different day. Same hotel.

Then there was another text. This time it was Jenny from Wednesday, wearing some thin attempt at a disguise. A Richmond Flying Squirrels baseball cap and sunglasses. But it was still very clearly her.

"How . . . how long has this been going on?" I asked, after he had shown me the third set of pictures.

"Two months."

Another stab. This time with an ice pick.

We hadn't had sex in two months. That was also when her hours at "work" had begun to noticeably pick up.

I had written it all off. The lack of sex and the longer hours were because she had this demanding case on top of all her other work.

Really, was it all because she had been having nooners with goddamn Greg Grichtmeier?

I buried my face in my hands.

Jenny? My Jenny? For the entire time we had been together, our faithfulness to each other had been a given, an immutable part of our equation. All the other variables had changed—what words we used to define our relationship (dating, engaged, married), where we lived, how many people were in our family—except for that one. Jenny and I were monogamous. Period. I couldn't believe she would even think about cheating.

But I had obviously been a fool to believe that. And I would only compound my foolishness if I ignored the evidence in front of me.

Shouldn't I have known? Didn't all relationships turn toxic eventually? I'd learned that from watching my mother. How many times had the latest Mr. Onions or Mr. Belly cheated on her?

Any notion that Jenny wasn't like that had just been wishful thinking. The only difference was that it had taken her longer to get there.

Without wanting to, I thought about Jenny and Greg together, in that hotel: about her giving her body to another man; about that bond I cherished being so freely shared with another; about the duplicity, the betrayal.

And I couldn't hold it in any longer.

I walked over to the sink, turned on the tap, and puked.

Then I hurled again.

Rogers walked up behind me and put a hand on my back. I brushed it away.

"Just give me a second," I said.

"Sorry," he said. "I'm really, really sorry."

It took longer than a second.

I kept taking in large mouthfuls of water and swishing it around, trying to rinse away the acid. But it was still burning my throat, coating my teeth.

At one point, Parker wandered into the kitchen. She must have heard the strange noises.

Her little eyes went wide as she took in the sight of her indomitable daddy leaning on the sink, defeated, tears leaking down the side of his face. I didn't want to know what her three-year-old brain made of it.

"Daddy's tummy is just upset," I said. "It's okay. My friend here is going to help me feel better."

She glanced suspiciously at Rogers. "Okay, Daddy."

"Go look after Cate-Cate. Maybe play peekaboo with her."

Again: "Okay, Daddy."

She practically ran out of the room. I grabbed a kitchen towel and mopped my sloppy face, embarrassed she had seen me like that.

I had myriad memories of my own mother in similar poses. She would then descend into these long blue periods during which there would be no joy (or cooking or cleaning) in the household. Until she recovered—usually because she had met the next Mr. Whatever—it would be all I could do to get her to order me takeout from the pizzeria on the corner. By the time I was ten or so, I learned to make the call myself.

One thing I had already resolved: I was *not* going to let my children suffer the same way. As far as they would be concerned, nothing had happened.

Daddy was fine.

Even if Daddy was actually furious. I could feel the rage bouncing around inside of me, making me want to tear my own face off—and someone else's too. I swear, if Greg Grichtmeier had walked into the kitchen, I would have punched that perfect jaw of his.

And as for Jenny . . .

I spit into the sink, trying to get more of the rancid taste out of my mouth. I could already imagine confronting her. Would she deny it? Or try to explain herself? Or say it was my fault in some way, that Greg was giving her something—emotionally or physically—that I hadn't?

Would she beg for my forgiveness? Or—and this seemed more like Jenny—would she simply hold up her chin with that stainless steel confidence of hers and essentially tell me to deal with it? As I thought about the possibilities, my fury only grew.

I looked up and saw Rogers studying me.

"Is this why I end up killing her?" I asked grimly.

"I don't know if anything is ever that simple. I think it's probably the totality of the situation, knowing you ultimately didn't have any other choice. Though I couldn't say for sure. Not even Mr. DeGange could say. He only knows the what, not the why."

"I still can't believe it," I said. "I mean, I'm . . . livid. Beyond livid. But even as angry as I am right now, I'm not sure I could . . . you know."

"In some ways, it's not really your decision," he said.

"Because there's no free will. Because next Tuesday has already happened."

"That's right."

"Yeah, I still don't know if I buy that."

"I thought you were finally convinced about Mr. DeGange's gift."

"Sure, it's just"—I released a large sigh—"I don't know. Even now, talking about future me, it feels like I'm talking about someone else."

"That's because you *are* talking about someone else," Rogers said, with surprising passion. "The things that will happen to you, even if you're actually the passive receiver of them, they don't feel like they're inevitable. Your brain is trained to believe it has free will, and therefore the events of your life impact you as if you chose them. Does that make sense?"

"I guess so," I said.

"It's not all bad, by the way."

"What do you mean?"

"It's hard to describe, even though I've seen it dozens of times. You're about to have a series of life-shaping experiences that you'll always remember and refer back to. It's a powerful thing, going through the trial, becoming part of the Praesidium. As I told you, Mr. DeGange discourages religious language, but it really is like an awakening. Or call it a personal transformation. But, yes, you'll be a different person by the time it's all over."

He paused, then gave me this paternal smile. "Mr. DeGange says the two of you are actually going to become close. I wouldn't say he'll become a father figure, because he's a generation beyond that. Maybe a grandfather figure. You'll come to see him as a mentor, a confidant."

I felt my sarcasm returning.

"Yeah, sure. I'm going to become best pals with the guy who is forcing me to murder my wife. Absolutely."

"I know it seems hard to believe, but it's true. You even told him about—"

Rogers stopped himself abruptly.

"About what?" I asked.

"Nothing."

"No, what?"

"Forget it. I shouldn't have said anything. It wasn't . . . it's nothing."

"At this point, nothing is nothing. What does Mr. DeGange, my future best friend, supposedly know about me?"

Rogers wore another one of his inscrutable looks.

Then, softly, he said, "He knows about Mr. White."

At the mere mention of the name, my mouth went dry. If there were anything left in my stomach, I probably would have vomited again.

Mr. White, named for his hair color, was the prime exemplar of my mother's terrible taste in men. He was wealthy, suave, and about fifteen years older than my mother—which was strange, because she usually went for younger men. I was aware, even back then, that the relationship was not so much romantic as transactional. He constantly found ways to use his money to ingratiate himself to us: toys for me, jewelry for her, a little help with the rent check now and then, even a new refrigerator when ours went on the fritz.

What he got out of the deal?

Me.

Mr. White was a pedophile. He would "look after" me while my mother was off for another one of her hour-and-a-half self-torture sessions at the gym. He played these games that were essentially an excuse to molest me.

I was eight.

Even after my mother dumped him—because, truly, he wasn't into her—he kept finding excuses to hang around for the next four years or so, until I started going through puberty and he lost interest.

By the time it finally clicked in that what he had been doing to me was wrong—very, very wrong—he was already long gone. He had found a new desperate single mother with a young son to prey on.

I'd done my best to forget about it and move on, though I always knew it shaped me. It was around that time that I found competitive swimming, and, looking back, there's no question in my mind why I took to it the way that I did. Practicing hard, pushing myself for new personal bests, it was a way of taking control of the body that someone else was trying to usurp.

When #MeToo first hit, I felt emboldened to finally do something about Mr. White. Even though he would have been getting up there in years, I had to make sure he wasn't still on the prowl. I did an internet search for him, looking to see if he had finally turned up on the sex offender registry. It turned out he had been shot and killed a few years after he'd left us. According to a *Daily News* article, police said it was a robbery gone wrong.

I doubted that then and still do. It was probably a family who'd discovered what Mr. White really was and decided to enact their own justice.

Or maybe that's just what I wanted to believe.

I'd never told my mother about Mr. White. I knew—even at age fourteen, or sixteen, or whenever it was that I fully realized what had happened—that it would have sent her spiraling into one of her depressions. And I didn't want to have to deal with another one of those.

The only person I had ever told was Jenny.

And now, apparently, at some point in the future, Mr. DeGange.

Which was a lot to wrap my head around at the moment.

"Sorry," Rogers said. "I know I'm probably not supposed to know about that. As you'll discover, we don't have a lot of secrets in the Praesidium."

"Don't worry about it," I said casually. "Maybe it would have been more traumatic for someone else. For me, it was just another weird part of my childhood. I got over it. It really wasn't that big a deal. I mean, look at how normal I am now."

I grinned, aware that my lame attempt at humor was just a defense mechanism.

Just then, from the next room, Cate let out a cry. It wasn't a real cry. Just the mournful, I-need-attention cry she used when I had been ignoring her for too long. But it would continue to ramp up until she got what she wanted.

"Now *that* sounds like a big deal," I said. "I think I have to go."

"That's okay. So do I," Rogers said, glancing at his watch.

"I guess I'll, what, see you later?"

"Yes," he said, and then with all the gravity it was due, added: "Afterward."

Just the one word was enough to trigger a spurt of anxiety in me. Predictably, Cate started making more noise.

I kept talking over her. "It might not happen, you know. There's still the possibility Jenny's firm is going to pull the plug on the CP and L lawsuit. She's meeting with the executive committee this afternoon, and—"

Rogers was shaking his head.

"I'm sorry, that vote is not going to help you," Rogers said quietly.

"Okay," I said. "I just . . . well, if it doesn't, what do I . . . what exactly am I supposed to do?"

"You still have the gun I gave you, right?"

"Yeah."

"Good. First of all you might need this," he said, reaching into his pocket and pulling out a piece of black cylindrical metal.

"What's that?"

"It's a silencer for the pistol I gave you. Jenny will have a protective detail outside. They'll come running if they hear a gunshot. With this thing on, it won't be much louder than a book dropping. There are grooves in the barrel of the pistol. All you have to do is screw it on."

"Okay," I said, feeling enormous culpability just by accepting it.

"Wait until your wife goes to sleep. Then put on gloves, long pants, and a long-sleeve shirt. Make sure you cover as much of your exposed skin as you can. That's to protect it from both blood spatter and gunshot residue. Got it?"

"Got it."

"At nine forty-five, you enter the room. You make sure she's sleeping. You summon your courage. And then, at nine forty-seven, you put the gun next to her head, and—"

He dipped his head. I was glad he didn't actually articulate what my action would be.

"Then, we'll come in and help with cleanup," he finished.

"Don't I have to call you?"

"We'll hear the gunshot."

"But if it's as soft as a book dropping—"

"We'll hear it," he said more firmly.

He accompanied this with direct eye contact, which I then broke. Of course they'd hear the gunshot.

It wasn't just that Rogers probably had some kind of listening device turned toward the house. The Praesidium seemed to hear—and know—everything.

"Right," I said softly.

"Don't start doing anything on your own," he warned. "Let us handle it. Promise me that. I don't want you turning into another Buck McBride. You have to trust us."

"Okay," I said.

Cate redoubled her efforts.

"Daddy, Cate-Cate is crying," Parker called out.

"I'll be right there," I hollered back.

"That's okay," Rogers said as he moved toward the door. "I really do have to go. Good luck."

He held out his hand. I shook it.

"I'll see you on the other side," he said. "I know you might not believe this, but just remember: a billion lives are at stake. You really are doing the right thing."

CHAPTER 33

JENNY

The meeting was scheduled for 5:00 p.m.

Jenny knew that was likely the only time on Friday that all nine members of the executive committee were free.

Still, it felt like it had been scheduled specifically so she could be given bad news and then sent home for the weekend to mope, moan, and recover from the disappointment, such that she could then be firmly back in the saddle come Monday morning, generating revenue for Carter, Morgan & Ross.

That's if she lost the vote.

But Jenny had no intention of losing.

She checked herself in the mirror on the back of her office door, making sure her red power suit was hanging just right. Then she double-checked it in the elevator mirror on the ride up to the conference room on the top floor.

It was part of CMR culture that meetings began precisely on time—it was an if-you're-not-five-minutes-early-you're-late kind of firm—but Jenny didn't want to be forced to make a bunch of idle small talk.

So she waited until 4:59, then made what she hoped was a commanding entrance.

The firm's chairman, Lawrence Coates—he of the shaved head, bushy eyebrows, and head-of-the-table seat—was the first to greet her.

"Ah, there she is," Coates said. "Shall we get underway? I know the weekend awaits."

There were murmurs of consent around the room.

"Before I turn this over to you, Jenny, I'd like to say, on behalf of the entire partnership, that we're glad you're in one piece after yesterday's incident. My latest report from Barry Khadem said he hadn't been able to shed any more light on it. Is that still true?"

"As far as I know, yes," Jenny said.

"Well, I hope that changes. In the meantime, we're going to continue to have Barry's people keep an eye on you. I know it's a little intrusive but hopefully it's just temporary."

"Thank you."

"Okay then," Coates said. "I think you're aware of the agenda for this meeting, so why don't you just take it away?"

Jenny smiled at all of them as if they were all best friends—even Albert Dickel, who sat on Coates' right.

"Thank you, Lawrence. I'm going to keep this as brief as I can, because I know some of you are looking forward to getting home to your families and the rest of you are looking forward to getting home to the bar."

There were chuckles around the room, and Jenny smiled again. Jokes about booze seldom missed in a room full of lawyers.

"But I also have some other people on my mind every time I think about this lawsuit, and those are the plaintiffs, some of whom won't be going to the bar *or* to their families tonight. There are two hundred and eighty of them altogether. I have met with each and every one of them—either the plaintiff themselves or their surviving family members. I have sat in their living rooms and heard them take labored breaths. I have watched them slowly suffocating. I have even attended their funerals."

The room was now silent. Every eye was on Jenny.

"Now, being strictly calculating about this for a moment, I think about how this will play in front of a jury. And, PS, it'll play great. These are ordinary folks who were just trying to live their lives when this terrible thing happened to them. And their suffering is the kind that anyone—*anyone*—can easily imagine. Who among us hasn't, at some point, been grateful just to be able to take a nice, deep breath?"

She stopped, inhaled deeply, and let it out slowly.

"But can we actually *not* be calculating about this for a moment?" she said. "Can we forget about the money and, for a second, talk about justice? This case is really about the most basic right I can think of: the right to breathe air that doesn't make you sick. It's a right that's been denied to these people, most of whom are poor, disenfranchised, and don't have a lot of people looking out for them. And if you think back to why you became lawyers—"

"Jenny, I'm sorry to interrupt," came a voice from near the head of the table.

Dickel.

And he wasn't sorry.

"You're making a lovely speech, and justice is nice. But this case has already pulled more than a million dollars out of our collective pockets. And that only includes what we've paid our people and other expenses we can directly tabulate—the experts and the doctors and whatnot. It doesn't take into account the opportunity cost that while you and other members of your practice group are focused on this, you're not generating revenue on other, more immediately remunerative projects.

"When this group deliberates, we do so as fiduciaries for every partner in this firm," Dickel continued. "We have a responsibility to make decisions for *their* benefit, not the benefit of two hundred and eighty strangers. I realize we sometimes take on matters pro bono that we feel will serve the community, but I don't think you're arguing this case belongs in that category. So unless you can make a convincing argument as to why continuing this suit benefits the partnership as a whole, I don't see where we really have a lot to talk about here. Can you win this thing or not?"

Jenny smiled at him with both warmth and confidence.

"Thank you, Albert. You're actually giving me a perfect segue, because the second thing I wanted to talk about is the viability of this case. This is something I have not mentioned or put in writing—not even in our internal discussions about this case. No one else in the practice group knows about it. I haven't even told my husband. I'd ask that you keep the following in the strictest of confidence. This *cannot* leave the room."

Any momentum she had lost from Dickel's interruption was now gained back. The partners were again riveted as she continued.

"I have been working with an anonymous source who has been providing me documents that CP and L conveniently left out of discovery. They are damning, to say the least. They show that CP and L was aware its Shockoe Generation Plant was beyond obsolete and failing in any number of areas, including its air-pollution controls. It is also clear from documents that *were* included in discovery that CP and L couldn't take the plant off-line and keep the grid fully supplied and that replacing the plant would be prohibitively expensive. In other words, CP and L was stuck between a rock and a hard place. I have a memo from the head of the generation division to the lead supervisor at Shockoe where he acknowledges the plant's overwhelming pollution problems but advises what he calls a 'Band-Aid approach' to keeping the plant in operation."

Jenny paused to make sure that jaws around the room were dropping to the appropriate degree before she finished.

"I'm asking for your absolute discretion here, because I promised my source I would protect his identity at all costs. But this is the right lawsuit, we're in it for the right reasons, and with these documents, it's one we absolutely can win. Any questions?"

The room went silent until Lawrence Coates let out a low whistle.

"Hot damn," he said. "That's something."

Another one of the executive committee members raised his hand.

"I have a question," he said. "Can all those who are in favor of continuing full speed ahead on the CP and L lawsuit raise their hand?"

Every hand in the room went in the air.

Even Dickel's.

CHAPTER 34

NATE

I didn't need to ask Jenny how the vote had gone.

One glance at her as she came through the door—with a burst of buoyant energy—and I already knew.

But, really, hadn't I known before then? Everything Rogers told me had turned out to be true. Why should this have been any different?

Jenny wasn't going to drop the lawsuit of her own volition.

And her firm wasn't going to drop it either.

My last best chance of being spared this terrible choice—if I'd ever really had a choice—had come and gone.

I went through the motions of inquiry all the same, though I couldn't much look at her beyond that. I just pretended to be busy with dishes.

When she came over and kissed me on the cheek, I tried not to think about where else her mouth had been.

She didn't seem to notice that I practically recoiled from her touch. She was too distracted by her own triumph, not realizing how much she had actually lost.

We had all lost.

Brushing past me, she commenced her usual evening routine with the girls, and I once again retreated into replaying my final interaction with Rogers.

Hearing him talk about Mr. White had been a bizarreness I can't describe. It was like this stranger—and, really, that's what Rogers still was—using a can opener on my skull, reaching inside, pulling out the most sensitive thing he could find.

What I had told Rogers about Mr. White was at least somewhat true. It really hadn't traumatized me—mainly because I'd buried it so deep I'd never even given it the chance. That was why I hadn't told my mother or anyone else. It was all about making sure it could never climb out of the pit I had stuffed it down into, rather than allowing it to roam free and become some defining part of my childhood.

So why would I have told Vanslow DeGange? I couldn't imagine a universe where I had shared that strange chapter of my life with some random ninety-something-year-old guy—or with anyone other than my most intimate partner.

But I had obviously done it at some time that hadn't happened yet (at least not to me) but also *had* happened—in the cosmic, next-Tuesday place that only Vanslow DeGange could detect.

For me, still bound here in the present, it was like receiving a message from my future self:

You trust this man.

You share everything with him.

Even your deepest secrets.

And if that was true . . .

Good God.

But, really, what more evidence did I need? If I were on a jury right now, I would be forced to rule—beyond a reasonable doubt—that Vanslow DeGange was both a prophet and a savant.

He had risen from humble beginnings to become one of the richest men in the world, and he had—even more remarkably—done it almost entirely unnoticed. He knew which silver mines still contained hidden treasure, which stocks to pick, and which leaders to kill. He'd known the exact moment that Marcus Sakey's pointless life was going to end. He had accurately forecast a tornado, the most unpredictable force in nature.

Now this most extraordinary man had called on me for assistance. It wasn't something that would benefit him. It was—and, admittedly, this was the pill I had the hardest time swallowing—something that would rescue humanity from a sweltering Armageddon.

If I didn't do it, Jenny would wind up dead anyway, taken by the Praesidium. As would I. My daughters would be either collateral damage—as Rogers had so chillingly put it—or orphans.

This was exactly what had been explained to me four days earlier. I just hadn't believed it then.

I was out of reasons I shouldn't believe it now.

Whether it was the tug of destiny or the most brutal exercise in existential math—that there were three people who mattered most to me and there was only one way to keep at least two of them alive—I could no longer fight it:

I was going to do this.

This was really happening.

Heedless of my torment, the Welker-Lovejoy household slipped toward its final bedtime.

As the girls played upstairs, I continued mindlessly tidying the house, like it would really matter whether the toys were put away and the couch cushions were straight when the police came.

With no desire to make dinner—much less the stomach to eat it—I called Jenny's favorite Indian place and arranged for delivery. Her last supper would consist of vegetable samosa, palak paneer, and naan.

I could already feel myself starting to mourn her. She was, truly, the love of my life and always would be; the woman who dazzled me like no other; the one with whom I had shared sunsets, and music, and food, and love, and life.

The very best parts of life. I thought of all the different phases our relationship had been through, and found myself paging through scenes from every different chapter.

Climbing the ladder together as young associates, measuring our lives in six-minute increments, gleefully calculating how much it had cost the firm when we took time out to have sex.

Pitching in and helping her dad put a new roof on a shed, being astonished at how hard I had to work just to keep up with her.

Picking out an engagement ring only to have her make me return it, because she'd rather use the money for a down payment on a house that we would share, not a trinket that she alone would wear.

Having her fall asleep with her head in my lap early during her first pregnancy, looking down at the way her curls cascaded across my jeans, feeling astonished by what was growing inside her.

And a hundred other images, all of them running into each other, invoking different parts of our journey together.

With every new transition, the one thing that remained constant was that being with her—hearing her stories, seeing her smile, feeling her touch—was the best part of my day.

And, yes, I should have been livid with her, repulsed by what she had been doing with Greg Grichtmeier. And I was. Truly. It was a betrayal of the worst sort, a shattering of our vow and of the trust we had placed in each other.

But I already felt myself putting that in a box along with all the other recent and soon-to-happen things that I would try not to think about anymore.

I would never know why she'd cheated on me—what had been so bad about us that she felt she had to stray. And maybe that was okay.

The accusations, the explanations, the recriminations, the drawn-out and teary *how-could-yous*—those were only things that you needed to endure if you were somehow still trying to find a way forward with someone.

That was no longer happening. It had been ripped away from us. So what was the point of dragging us through that terrible, wrenching conversation?

Or maybe I just didn't want that to be my penultimate moment with her.

Nor did I need it anywhere near my heart as I killed her.

Because, truly, this was not an act of anger. Or of vengeance.

It was purely desperation.

I was doing it because I had no other choice.

Once I was out of things to fuss with downstairs, I crept upstairs, eavesdropping silently from just outside the door to the nursery, overcome with emotion—more for the girls than for myself.

This was the last time they would ever hear their mother read them a book. And they probably wouldn't even remember it. Cate certainly wouldn't. Parker? She might—*might*—be able to summon an image of her mother in her head someday. It would likely be an ethereal thing, a fuzzy face looming over her, some mix of an actual memory and the pictures of her mother I would show her. She wouldn't be able to place it in any sort of narrative. Three-year-old brains simply weren't that good at creating memories.

I peeked around the corner. As usual, Parker was planted on Jenny's right leg, Cate on the left side, the snuggle-read in full bloom.

Seeing Jenny just hurt. She didn't look like a cheater. And she didn't look like a hundred Hitlers about to unleash mass death on the earth.

She was just my Jenny, as beautiful as ever.

It was easier to focus on the girls. I would be doing this for them, after all.

Taking their mother but giving them their lives.

I stayed there, listening for as long as I could bear it. When I became aware I couldn't really breathe without sobbing, and that there were tears dripping down my face, I backed away and crept slowly back downstairs.

Jenny just continued with the book, either unaware of my presence or choosing to ignore it.

And wasn't it wild.

I still loved my cheating wife.

I still blessed the broken road that led me to her.

And I knew that when I pulled the trigger at 9:47 p.m., I would also be murdering some huge piece of my own heart.

CHAPTER 35

NATE

My girls were asleep. All of them.

I was sitting in the living room in my long pants and long shirt, as per Rogers' orders. I was wearing socks instead of shoes, reasoning that they would be easier to clean—and also quieter as I crept around the house.

Had Jenny walked in on me, she would have seen her husband listening to music with his earbuds in, never realizing he was only doing it so he didn't have to hear himself think.

Except Jenny hadn't come back downstairs after putting the girls to bed. She hadn't even eaten the Indian food I had procured for her. She had just gone to sleep.

Leaving me by myself to eye the clock.

The guards that had come home with Jenny had settled in outside. It was the same two as the night before. The guy with the bushy white mustache was out front. The one with the gray flattop was in back.

Every now and then I'd become aware of their presence because one of them scraped a chair across the porch, or checked his phone, or cleared his throat.

Just having them out there made me feel like a prisoner in my own house.

But I guess I was going to have to get used to that.

Being a prisoner.

Would this magic, ballistics-test-distorting gun Rogers had given me actually make that big a difference at my trial?

There was already a strong circumstantial case against me. I could easily imagine Detective Ishmael Khalilu on the witness stand, describing the anonymous complaint that had led to a file being opened on me, offering expert testimony regarding the high incidence of people who choked their partners who then went on to become murderers. There were two guards outside my house, making it extremely difficult for anyone else to get inside to shoot her.

Plus, there was that innate bias: wife dead, husband accused of murder. Three-quarters of the jurors out there would be ready to convict before they heard a word of testimony.

With Jenny dead, would I even care?

Maybe I'd feel different later, when I thought about the girls being raised without their father. Some sense of parental self-preservation would kick in, and the nihilism that currently consumed me would ease away.

For the time being, I felt like nothing I did mattered anyway.

Learning there's no free will can have that effect.

At nine thirty, I pulled out the earbuds and crept down into the basement, keeping the door to the upstairs open but the lights off. My first move was to put on a pair of thick leather work gloves. I had decided I might as well give myself the option of being able to establish a defense.

I had stashed the silencer in the same plastic bin as the gun. After delicately lowering the bin to the floor, I removed both pieces. The pistol felt even heavier than it had when I'd first hid it three days earlier.

Placing them both on the workbench, I studied them in what little illumination poured down the basement stairs from above. Jenny and I had a long-standing debate about whether a gun was a versatile tool with multiple uses or a specialized instrument of death.

Right now, I think even she'd have to agree with me. This gun had only one purpose, and it was lethal.

With the grip of the pistol still resting on the table, I tilted up the barrel, then picked up the silencer. After a few tries, I managed to get it properly threaded. A few rotations later, it was on securely, its dull blackness standing in stark contrast to the silver of the gun.

This was the part where a seasoned hunter or marksman—someone who actually knew what they were doing with a firearm—would double-check the weapon to make sure there was a round in the chamber. I had no idea where to even start with that. I also worried I'd never get the thing back together if I started pulling it apart.

That would have to be a detail I trusted to the Praesidium.

I picked up the gun. I wanted to be able to hide it somewhere—the waistband of my pants, my pocket, something like that—except now that the silencer was affixed, it didn't fit anywhere. I would just have to keep it in my gloved hand.

As I moved back toward the stairs, I felt like destiny really had taken over. It was not merely guiding me or making suggestions. It was fully in control of my central nervous system, making my thighs lift, my feet fall, my calves thrust. Nothing I did felt fully voluntary.

Including what happened when I reached the top of the staircase, where I froze in place for a moment.

The guy with the bushy mustache was sitting in the middle of the porch. If he happened to turn around—because he heard me or sensed my presence somehow—he would see me, standing at the top of the stairs, a gun clutched menacingly in my hand.

But it was fated to be that his head didn't move.

Such an irony that he was looking to safeguard Jenny from outward dangers when the greatest threat was actually coming from within.

I quickly pivoted, turning my back to him, keeping the pistol tight against my chest, so that if he did happen to turn, he wouldn't see that I had a weapon. Just the man of the house, going up to bed.

Once I hit the landing of the stairs leading to the second floor, I took two steps up quickly, putting myself out of his sight. I paused there for a moment, collecting myself, catching my breath.

Then I continued upward. Every creak of the stairs sounded like branches snapping. Every breath was a minor typhoon. I had to remind myself that though these noises seemed amplified to me, they were either routine—or inaudible—to everyone else in the house.

I knew I wasn't going to wake up Jenny.

Rogers wouldn't know about Mr. White if I had.

Two steps away from the second-floor landing, I paused again. I was now within sight of our bedroom door, which was ajar by perhaps six inches. Neither light nor noise came from within.

The doors to the girls' bedrooms were closed. This was the same scene that would have confronted me hundreds of other evenings, except this time, my heart was pounding so fiercely—the Telltale Heart, Poe might have called it—I swore it was nearly knocking me off balance.

I placed my foot on the second-to-last step. It groaned under my weight.

So did the next step. It was like the house itself was registering its protest to what I was about to do.

Finally I was on the second floor.

I shuffled silently toward our bedroom. I hadn't touched the door yet, but I could peek around it and see the lump of Jenny's body on the bed. She was on her side, turned away from me.

That must have been why I was able to do this. I don't think I could have pulled the trigger if I had to look at her, peacefully sleeping. That face I loved so much.

The digital clock on her nightstand read 9:44.

Then I watched as it turned to 9:45.

Exactly as Rogers had said it would. Exactly as DeGange had foretold.

That gave me two minutes to . . . what had he said? Summon my courage? What a terrible choice of phrasing. Like there was something courageous about shooting your wife in cold blood while she slept.

I pushed through the door, determined to finish this, reminding myself I had to do this for the girls, for the planet, telling myself that Jenny would forgive me if she understood my motivations.

My socked feet made no sound as they brushed against the hardwood floor of our bedroom. I took one step, two steps, walking in a line toward Jenny.

I was maybe eight feet away. I drew in a deep breath and—

Jenny whirled around into a sitting position, the sheet and blanket flying off almost like they had been thrown.

"Stop right there," she said. "Don't shoot."

She had her own silver-plated pistol.

And it was pointed at my head.

CHAPTER 36

JENNY

Up until the last moment, Jenny didn't think Nate was going to do this.

Not her Nate. No chance.

He was the man who had loved her, wildly and unconditionally—in a way she hadn't thought a man could love a woman—since the moment they'd met. He was a model husband who seemed almost devoid of ego, willingly stepping aside to make way for his wife's career. He was a selfless father, utterly devoted to his daughters. He was a gentle soul, the kind who captured wasps under a glass, then set them free.

Yes, he had lied about visiting J. Hunter Matthews' house. She had seen the footage on that thumb drive. And he had also lied about collaborating with Dickel to get the lawsuit dropped. She'd known the moment the words *rabbit hole* had left his mouth.

But he was as far from being a murderer as it was possible to be.

Which is why she never believed a thing about this deluded prophecy she had been given.

That her husband would enter her room at 9:45 on Friday evening with a gun.

That at 9:47 he would fire it at her head.

That the only way to stop him would be to shoot first.

And no.

No, no, and no.

Yet here was Nate, right on time. Just as Lorton Rogers had said he would be. Just as Vanslow DeGange had predicted.

"Put the gun down, Nate," she said. "Or I swear I *will* pull this trigger. And I don't want to pull the trigger, Nate, I really don't."

He had this terrifying blank look on his face, like Nate Lovejoy wasn't even there, having been taken over by some mind-controlling parasite.

"I'm sorry," he said. "I don't really have a choice."

"Of course you have a choice. Nate, look at me. It's me, Jenny. Your wife. I love you. That's what matters. Nothing else. Whatever they're paying you, it's not worth it. Now put the gun down."

"No," he said. "We only think we have choices. Everything is . . . it's already set. It's done. I'm sorry, Jenny. I really, really am. But I have to do this. At nine forty-seven. It's the only way to save the girls."

He edged a little closer. The gun was still level with her face.

"Save the girls?" she said. "What the hell are you talking about? How will shooting me save the girls?"

"You wouldn't believe me if I told you."

"Try me."

"I . . . I have to shoot you or else this man, this group, they'll come and take out the entire family. They'll blow up the house or—"

"You're talking about Lorton Rogers? Of the Praesidium?"

Jenny felt like she didn't even need to wait for Nate to answer. Of course it was Rogers. Manipulative, cunning Rogers. The only question remaining was how much of Nate's oddities over the past few days were directly attributable to the man.

The blank look had left Nate's face. He was now just startled. "You know him?"

"Oh my God, Nate. I have no idea what's going on right now, but please put the gun down. Yes, I know Rogers. He's been lying to both of us. He's trying to get me to kill you, and—"

"*You're* supposed to kill *me?*" Nate said, now plainly astonished. "He told me *I* had to kill *you*. And I did kill you. I must have, because he . . . he knew about Mr. White. How else would he know about Mr. White unless—"

"I told him about Mr. White," Jenny said. "I'm sorry. He was trying to spin this whole story about how you were going to . . . look, it was a lie. Probably everything he's told both of us is a lie. He said Commonwealth Power and Light was paying you twenty million dollars to either convince me to drop the lawsuit or to kill me if I wouldn't cooperate. The deadline was supposedly Friday at midnight."

"That's not true. I swear, I—"

"I know, I know. I believe you, okay? Just, seriously, put the gun down."

Jenny kept her grip firm and her sights level until Nate finally lowered his weapon. But even as he did, there was no sense of relief in her. They were both still in danger. Rogers was out there somewhere, listening, expecting to hear a gunshot any moment. She laid her gun on the pillow next to her and started talking quickly.

"Rogers has been manipulating everything. He said that once you failed to persuade me to drop the CP and L suit, you were going to enter our room tonight at nine forty-five with a gun and murder me. He said if I confronted you about the twenty-million-dollar payoff at any time before nine forty-five on Friday night, you would fly into a rage and kill both me and the girls. I said that was impossible, that you would *never* do something like that. That's when I told him about Mr. White. I said you could never hurt a child because you had been abused as a child yourself and . . . I'm sorry, that part just slipped out.

"But at the same time, DeGange had supposedly foreseen that you were going to do this awful thing. And I couldn't just dismiss it completely, because I had already seen some of DeGange's other predictions come true. I thought if there was even a chance this was real—"

"It was too great a risk to take with the girls," Nate said. "I understand completely. Believe me. But . . . are you sure he was trying to get *you* to kill *me*? Because all this time he's been pretty insistent that I need to kill you."

The clock had already turned to 9:47. Jenny knew Rogers might wait a few minutes before closing in, but he wouldn't hold off forever. She willed her mouth to go faster.

"No, trust me," she said. "You know that domestic violence complaint? I'll bet you anything that was Rogers. He was trying to create my defense. That cop who came and talked to you, that was all about establishing that you had been physically abusive toward me. That way, when you came after me with a gun, I could say I legitimately feared for my life and had no choice but to kill you."

"Okay, I grant you that, but why would Rogers want me dead? My understanding of the Praesidium is that it exists to save humanity from impending catastrophes. I can't imagine how killing me would accomplish that."

"It's not about you. It's about me," Jenny said. "Look, I don't know what Rogers has and hasn't told you. So I'm just going to start at the beginning. There's a man named Vanslow DeGange who can see the future."

"I'm aware. He predicted a tornado for me."

"Okay, so you've seen it demonstrated too. It's wild, right? And you've been told the stories about Kennedy and King and all that?"

"Yeah."

"Okay, so about two months ago, Rogers approached me with the whole spiel," Jenny said. "He wanted me to leave CMR, leave Richmond, leave you, and join the Praesidium. I said no way. I told him I had a great life, with a perfect husband and a perfect family, and

I had no desire to join some secret society, or to raise my girls in some weird cult, or go around doing . . . whatever it is they do.

"I wouldn't say he accepted my decision, but eventually he realized he wasn't going to change my mind, so he went away. I thought that was the end of it—that he was really going to drop it and move on to someone else—until earlier this week when he approached me again with this wild story about how you were going to kill me. He said it didn't have anything to do with me joining or not joining the Praesidium, but that Vanslow DeGange had foreseen it and now they wanted to protect me. I told him I didn't believe him, but he insisted I take this gun, because you were going to show up in the bedroom ready to kill me on Friday night. So the question is, what kind of crap has he been telling you to get you to actually do it?"

As she spoke, Jenny could almost see the Nate she knew and loved returning to her—the way his eyes searched out hers, the way his face was softening. He was looking more like the man she shared her life with, less like the stranger who had been inhabiting the house with her for the last few days.

"The better question is what kind of crap hasn't he told me?" Nate said. "Basically, it was that you were the most dangerous person in world history, because this CP and L lawsuit was going to establish this precedent that would lead to the elimination of coal-fired power plants, which would have the unintended consequence of triggering a global warming catastrophe. He said Mr. DeGange had foreseen more than a billion people dying as a result and that if I didn't take you out, the Praesidium would have to step in. And that because it had to look like an accident, the girls and I would probably be killed too. So it was basically: kill my wife, or the entire family dies."

"Oh God, Nate."

"I know."

"I think that's all . . . first of all, there will be no precedent established with the CP and L case, since it's based on one faulty plant that is clearly exceeding its Clean Air Act limits. The rest of that stuff, I'm pretty sure DeGange never predicted anything like that. Rogers is just making it up. You're the real target here."

"Yeah, and why is that?"

"I think I'm supposed to be incredibly grateful toward Rogers and the Praesidium for saving my life. And with you dead, and me having killed you, I wouldn't have that perfect life I bragged about anymore. Between those two things, Rogers was hoping it would make me feel compelled to run off and join the Praesidium."

"I still don't understand. Why does the Praesidium want you so badly?"

Jenny took in a deep breath and looked up at the ceiling before returning her gaze to Nate.

"This is going to be a little hard to believe," she said.

"I've seen a lot of things this week that fit that category."

"I know, but this one is . . ."

She faltered for a moment, then resumed with renewed purpose: "Vanslow DeGange isn't the only one who has this mutation, this thing that allows him to sense future events. I have the gift too."

CHAPTER 37

NATE

For a long moment, I just stood there like a big, dumb six-foot-four mannequin, neither moving, nor speaking, nor comprehending what my wife had just said.

It was like three days of almost nonstop turmoil and confusion had left me unable to parse even the most basic words. Everything she'd said after "mutation" had come in too fast or too loud—or too, I don't know, mind blowing—for me to handle.

"What do you mean, you have the gift?" I asked, stupidly.

"It's hard to describe if you don't have it yourself. Has Rogers told you about the currents and the ripples?"

"Yes."

"Well, basically, I can sense them too," Jenny said. "I can't do it nearly as well as Vanslow DeGange does. He's had a lifetime of practice and I'm . . . I'm just starting to open my eyes. That's why Rogers is so hot to have me join the Praesidium. I'm supposed to come and be trained by DeGange so that when he dies, I can take over and the Praesidium can continue its mission."

Finally, the electrical currents in my brain started moving again. Was this really so unbelievable? In some ways, I had known this for a long time now. Jenny always did have that incredible intuition. That ten-steps-ahead sense of anticipation. That talent that took her from that small farm in Surry County to the heights of corporate law.

She had always been like a slightly different organism than everyone else around her.

So dazzling.

"Basically, the Praesidium wants you, and I'm just the guy in the way," I said, shaking my head. "The thing I still don't understand is . . . I thought there was no such thing as free will. I thought that was an accident of the senses. But this, what we're doing right now, what we just did . . . it all feels a lot like we're actually in control."

"That's because we are," Jenny insisted. "I don't know what Rogers has told you, but the main problem the Praesidium faces isn't that there's no free will. It's that there's too damn much of it. That's why the Praesidium is constantly interceding in things, trying to change the course of human events."

"Rogers said that next Tuesday is a place that exists in space-time, much like Omaha, Nebraska, is a place that exists in space-time," I said. "And if next Tuesday already exists, then in a manner of speaking it's already happened, and there is no free will."

Jenny was shaking her head before I even finished the thought.

"Next Tuesday exists just like Omaha exists. That's true. But you can still alter next Tuesday in the same way that you can alter Omaha. You can knock down a building or build a new road or divert a river or do a million other things that change Omaha. The future isn't some stone monolith. It's like desert sands, constantly shifting in a windstorm. Every action you take is like another gust. If Rogers told you there was no free will, it's just because that's what he wanted you to believe, so he could twist your mind even more."

"He definitely succeeded at that," I said.

Jenny actually smiled. "I know. Look, I'm sure this is all a little bit of a shock. I've had two months to think about it and I still can't always get my head around it. And I promise I'll explain everything later—at least as much as I can. But for right now, Rogers is out there somewhere. And he's going to expect to hear a gunshot very soon."

"Okay. And what happens after that? I'm lying dead, he shows up, and . . . what exactly?"

"I don't know. As I understand it, my killing you is the first step. That's what allows me to take their oath, get their brand, join the order."

"It's what bonds them. He explained that to me."

"After that, I have no idea," she said. "I never let Rogers get that far, because I never believed you would try to hurt me. Every time he tried to talk about what we were going to do after I killed you, I shut him down."

"Well, we need a plan, and fast," I said.

My mind was a blank. Jenny's face was squeezed in concentration.

"I just don't know if we have any good options here," she said. "Rogers has made it very clear with me from the beginning that there's only one way with the Praesidium. Once you are made aware of them, you either do as they say and kill whoever needs to be killed or they kill you. There's no in-between. How do you think they've been able to exist this long without the wider world becoming aware of them? They leave nothing to chance."

"So that's it? Join them or die? Some choice."

"They see themselves as ultimately virtuous, making these sacrifices for the good of humanity. It's all about the math with them. Did they save more people than they killed? If they did, it's a win. They don't get that the ends don't always justify the means. But, look, forget about that. We need to focus."

"Can't you get in touch with the currents—or whatever—and come up with a plan?"

Jenny got her frustrated look, the one she wore during the rare times in her life when she wasn't able to bend the world to her will. "I wish I could. I'm still so new at this. And if it doesn't involve death or dying, I'm hopeless. Besides, apparently even Vanslow DeGange needs perfect conditions to be able to focus on the currents—quiet, calm, a period of uninterrupted—"

"Okay, okay. I get it. That's not now."

We lapsed into silence again.

A bad idea started coming into my head, one that had more flaws than I could even begin to enumerate. I began voicing it anyway, blurting it out before I could really think it through.

"What if we just pretend you've shot me?" I asked. "It's what Rogers is expecting so let's give it to him. We fire a gun. He comes running. You pretend to be completely distraught and say you just want to get out of here. I'll stay up here in the bedroom and pretend to be dead."

"So, what, I just take the girls and go wherever he leads me?"

"Yeah, basically. It's not like they're going to harm you. You're the prophet-in-training, the future leader."

"But what happens when the Praesidium figures out you're not actually dead? I have to imagine Vanslow DeGange will become aware of you at some point. And then I would have taken a false vow. I can't imagine they'll look too fondly on that."

"It's not a great plan," I admitted. "It's not even a good one. But Rogers has to think one of us is dead, and he'll be a lot happier if it's me. You and the girls will be fine for the time being. This at least gets everyone out of tonight alive. Then we'll worry about tomorrow."

"All right. There are like a thousand ways this could go wrong. But all right."

"Go get the girls. Take them downstairs. I have a death to stage."

Jenny climbed out of bed, tossed a fleece on over her pajamas, stuffed her feet into jogging shoes, and grabbed me on the shoulders.

"I love you so much," she said.

She was approaching like she was going to kiss me. I actually half turned away.

"What's the matter?" she asked.

"I realize this isn't the time, but . . . I know about Greg Grichtmeier."

"What about him?"

"That you've been having an affair with him."

Jenny was looking at me like I had fourteen heads. "No I'm not. I swear."

"Look, it doesn't matter right now, okay? Rogers showed me the pictures of the two of you going in and out of that hotel, The Commonwealth—"

I stopped myself. As soon as I said "Rogers showed me," I was realizing I had probably been played.

"Greg Grichtmeier is the one who has been secretly feeding me documents for the CP and L lawsuit," Jenny said. "You know he works on the CP and L account at his firm, right? During an audit, he became aware of massive problems with the Shockoe Generation Plant. I've been having us meet at the hotel because I didn't trust his email server or ours and it was the only place we could—"

"I get it. I get it," I said, feeling both a little stupid and enormously relieved. "Sorry. Rogers is just—"

She grabbed me and kissed me hard on the mouth.

"It's okay," she said.

"Thanks for not killing me."

"Likewise. Now be careful."

"I will."

And before I could tell her to be even more careful, she was out of the room.

I looked down at my gun, which had never left my gloved hand.

First order of business: Rogers was out there somewhere and needed to hear a gunshot. One that would sound like a book dropping. I aimed the gun at the ceiling, because I needed to point it somewhere, and the floor seemed like a poor choice.

"Okay," I called out softly to Jenny. "Fire in the hole."

I squeezed the trigger, flinching involuntarily as I did so. Even with the silencer, the noise was louder than I expected.

Good. Rogers needed to be convinced.

I looked up at where I had aimed, expecting to see a big chunk of missing Sheetrock.

Instead, the ceiling was totally smooth.

There were no holes. Not even one as tiny as a bullet.

I looked down at the gun again. I had definitely fired it. I had heard it. I could smell it.

So where had the bullet gone?

Not wanting to waste more time, I grabbed a glass of water and spilled it. That would have to be my stand-in for the volume of blood that should have spilled out of my body before my heart stopped pumping.

I lowered myself to the floor and lay facedown. I placed my arms and legs at awkward, deathlike angles and turned my head away from the door. My hope was that if anyone from the Praesidium came upstairs to investigate, they would see my prone body in the dark, lying in a pool of liquid whose color they wouldn't be able to see, and decide just to leave me undisturbed for the police to find.

As I lay there, I was still thinking about the bullet, and what happened to it, and why there was no hole in the ceiling.

And then I got it.

There was no bullet.

The gun had been loaded with blanks. Rogers had sold me that whole story about a bullet with magic, ballistics-test-defying properties simply so I wouldn't tamper with the weapon.

That's why he had so cavalierly handed the gun to me that night he had kidnapped me, then didn't flinch when I pointed it at him. It didn't have anything to do with any prophecy of Vanslow DeGange's. He knew I couldn't have hurt anyone with it if I wanted to.

Most of all, I wasn't going to be able to hurt Jenny, the chosen one, the next prophet. Even if I had pulled the trigger first during our confrontation, it wouldn't have mattered.

The whole time, this weapon—whose lethality I'd so feared—had been about as dangerous as a paperweight.

CHAPTER 38

JENNY

Jenny scurried into Parker's bedroom, then sat down and rubbed her daughter's back in one gesture.

"Parker, honey, you have to wake up. Mommy needs you to be a big girl and come with me very quickly."

Jenny could see Parker's eyes open and reflect back what little light there was in the room.

"Mommy," she said groggily.

"Yes, honey. Come on. We have to be quick like little bunnies. Fast, fast, fast."

Jenny was about to lift the little girl out of bed when she heard Nate's warning about the impending gunshot.

"There's going to be a noise. Don't be scared," Jenny said, covering Parker's ears.

The gun sounded its muted report.

Which meant the Praesidium was now on its way. Rogers had told Jenny he'd be listening for the sound of a gunshot.

She scurried to the other side of the room, grabbed a pair of pink sneakers, then shoved them on her daughter's feet.

"You're coming with Mommy now, all right?" Jenny said. "We're leaving Daddy here. He's fine. We're just going on a little adventure. You, me, and Cate-Cate. Got it?"

Parker just nodded. She dutifully followed Jenny toward Cate's room.

Halfway there, Jenny heard two thumps coming from the back porch.

Then, from the front porch, came two more thumps.

Each one sounded like a book dropping.

Jenny felt a sickening dread in her stomach from the knowledge of what those thumps might have been, even as she clung to the hope she was mistaken.

She kept moving all the same. Creating separation between Rogers and Nate was now her primary objective. She bent over the crib and scooped up Cate, who didn't stir as she was transferred gently to her mother's shoulder.

"Okay," Jenny whispered to a still-disoriented Parker. "We're going to the car now."

As they descended the stairs, the front door opened. A man dressed in black tactical gear appeared, straining to walk backward over the doorstep. He was dragging something bulky, something heavy.

A body.

The man with the bushy white mustache. Only now he had two neat holes in his forehead. The back of his head was mostly missing. It was slowly leaking a dark fluid—almost like motor oil—onto the black pants of the man in tactical gear.

Jenny had a strong stomach. She had helped her father process chickens on the farm. She wasn't going to allow herself to stop and think about how very different this was.

It was Parker she worried about. Jenny stopped halfway down the steps, blocking Parker's path, hoping the little girl either hadn't seen it, or hadn't been able to understand what she saw.

"Isn't it nice of him to help that man inside," Jenny said a little too loudly, hoping that would sate a three-year-old's curiosity.

The man in tactical gear, now breathing heavily, finished dragging the body inside, then laid it out in the entryway.

"Don't leave that there," Jenny said sharply, then jerked her head to the left. "Dining room."

"Yes, ma'am," the man said.

Almost like they had been talking about a piece of furniture.

"And tell Rogers to put the other one in the dining room too."

"Yes, ma'am."

Jenny waited until the man had dragged the body away, then continued downstairs, herding Parker to one side of the entryway so she wouldn't traipse through the blood slick.

They rounded the corner. As they neared the kitchen, which now had lights on, Jenny could see another gory trail.

And Rogers.

He was seated at the kitchen peninsula, calmly swiping at his phone, his clothes unwrinkled. Likewise, it seemed, was his conscience.

Jenny stopped for just a moment, feeling her insides go subzero at the sight of him. It was one thing to read Machiavelli. It was something else altogether to have him sitting in your kitchen.

Then she suppressed her revulsion, and with Cate still on her shoulder and Parker crowding her legs, Jenny walked through the kitchen with her chin high as always, summoning her best impersonation of supreme motherly command.

"I'm going to put the girls in the car," she said, as if she was marshaling a grand effort to keep her composure. "I have to get them out of here."

"I understand," Rogers said, looking up for a moment before returning his attention to his phone.

On the porch, Jenny passed a man in tactical gear. She ignored him, going straight to the Range Rover. She buckled in Cate, who stirred for just a moment before settling into her car seat. Parker remained wide eyed as she was snapped in.

"Mommy will be right back, okay?" she said, keeping a forced confidence in her voice that she hoped would be reassuring. "And then we'll take a drive."

To where, she didn't know.

That would be Rogers' call.

She shut the door to the car, then walked back into the house, again passing the man in black tactical gear, who was still keeping watch, though on what might be called low alert. He was slouched in the same chair that had, until recently, been occupied by Jenny's other guard, the man with the gray flattop. It was probably still warm from his body heat.

Behind the chair, splattered against the siding, was a dark stain. The man in tactical gear appeared unbothered by it. The general mien of Rogers' team seemed to be that the difficult part of the operation was now over. They had neutralized all the threats and were just waiting to be given the order to move out.

Jenny again entered the kitchen. She sat at the table, slumping as if enervated. Rogers joined her.

"How are you doing?" he asked.

"How do you think?" she shot back.

She rested her forehead on her hands, as if the weight of her head was too much for her neck to support, and stared down at the table.

Rogers seemed to be waiting for more, so she obliged him: "He came into the room at nine forty-five, just like you said he would. I still didn't believe it. Even when I saw the gun in his hand with the silencer, I still thought I could, I don't know, talk him out of it."

"And did you try?"

"I did, yes. I told him not to do it, that it wasn't worth it. Not for twenty million. Not for any amount of money. He denied it had anything to do with money, just said he *had* to do this. It was kind of mixed up, but he was saying in some ways he had already done it, and there was no free will, and . . . something about Omaha, Nebraska, and next Tuesday? I couldn't really follow it, to be honest. He was . . . basically delirious."

Rogers bobbed his head up and down. "I know this is hard to believe, but I really think that twenty million dollars almost induced a kind of insanity in him. Money can be an incredibly corrupting influence on the mind."

"I still didn't think he was going to go through with it. He seemed to be willing to talk at first. But then he started rambling about nine forty-seven, how he had to pull the trigger at nine forty-seven. I have no idea what was so magical about nine forty-seven. I just kept trying to stall him. And then nine forty-seven came and went, and I thought I was going to be able to talk him out of it. He even lowered the gun at one point. And then he brought it back up and I realized he was going to use it . . . and . . ."

Jenny covered her face with her hands, hoping her act was convincing. She put extra effort into breathing heavily. "I just . . . I shot him. I actually shot him."

"I'm sorry. I'm really sorry," Rogers cooed. "I wish Mr. DeGange were wrong sometimes. I really do. But—and I don't know if this will make you feel better—I'm not sure we could have left him alive anyway. The membership would never accept someone who hadn't been properly initiated."

Jenny rubbed her eyes so they would be red when she took her hands down.

"Well, thanks for not saying 'I told you so,'" she said, expelling a long breath.

"I know this is going to be difficult," Rogers said. "And there is probably a lot you're going to have to work through in the coming weeks and months. But this chapter in your life is over now. You're just going to have to put it out of your head as best you can. You have a lot to learn in order to develop your abilities. It's vitally important you focus on that. The Praesidium needs you to continue its work. The *world* needs you."

"I understand," Jenny said.

She breathed out again.

"However," she said, "we need to talk about what happened after I shot my husband."

"Which part?" Rogers asked.

It wasn't difficult for Jenny to summon anger. "Those two men. Why did you kill them?"

"You really think your rent-a-cops were going to let you walk away with a bunch of strangers in the night? They either would have refused to let you go, or they would have insisted they come with us. Either way, it was a problem. It had to be taken care of."

He said this as if it was the same as unplugging a drain in the bathroom, or some other nettlesome domestic chore.

"You can't just go killing people because they're in your way or they're inconvenient," Jenny said. "Maybe that's the way the Praesidium used to do things, but it's not going to be that way anymore."

"We can discuss that, yes," Rogers allowed.

"It's also reckless. What are we going to tell the police? I can explain that I shot my physically abusive husband in self-defense. How am I going to explain two dead bodyguards?"

"Your husband killed them when they tried to protect you. It will actually bolster your self-defense claim, because he was clearly in a murderous rage already. You had every reason to fear for your life."

"He killed them with a very professional, very expert double tap to the forehead?" she said, incredulously. "My husband. The man who's never even handled a gun before. You think the police are going to buy that?"

"We have a cleanup plan that will take care of that."

"And what's that?"

"There's going to be an explosion in a short little while," Rogers said, evenly. "We'll do it in a way that the authorities will think it was a gas leak. Don't worry. We're very good at this sort of thing. We've done it many times."

"You're going to blow up my house?" Jenny said. It didn't take much acting skill to sound panicked.

"Yes. We can blame that on Nate too. His plan was a murder-suicide. He turned on the stove. After he killed you, he was going to blow the place sky-high, taking him and the girls with him. You, who were just trying to flee the house with your daughters, didn't realize that part of his plan. The explosion and the ensuing fire will either destroy or badly confuse the evidence. The fire department will find three bodies, as expected—one you will have admitted to killing in self-defense, the other two killed by your husband. For as messy as it will be, it will actually put a rather tidy bow on the whole thing. And don't worry about anyone else getting hurt. The row houses on either side of you will be damaged, but as you're aware, they're unoccupied. The fire department will be able to respond in time to put out the fire before it spreads beyond that."

Jenny sat very still, trying to think of how to respond.

She couldn't exactly say, *That sounds good. Do you mind if I just go upstairs and tell my dead husband about it first?*

"There . . . there has to be some other way," she stammered.

"There might be. But this way really is best."

"No," she said. "I can't have you blowing up my house."

"Jenny," he said softly. "I know this is a lot to process, but this isn't going to be your house anymore. You're with the Praesidium now. And, trust me, your housing situation will improve dramatically. Mr. DeGange spares no expense. And lord knows he has the money. We've got a suite prepared for you and the girls at the main house. You'll be just down the hall from Mr. DeGange. When we travel, we go first class. He's never once balked at what we spend. We literally have a blank check. You'll be treated like royalty. No more cooking. No more cleaning. You'll want for nothing. It's a great life. You won't need this place anymore. Why would you even want it?"

Jenny sagged, like she was allowing herself to be convinced.

"I'm not in this for the perks," she said sulkily.

"I know. But, trust me, the perks are really something."

Her mind was still racing as to how she was going to get Nate out of here. The obstacles were formidable: there was Rogers in the house, a man out front, a man in back, and undoubtedly more men somewhere out there in the night, a mere block or two away.

As soon as Jenny was clear, those men were going to move in and stage their explosion. Could Nate slip out unnoticed while they worked? Would he even have the opportunity?

It seemed hopeless.

She had to get him out of here. Somehow.

"Okay," she said, sighing heavily. "Let me just go up and pack a few things before you blow it all up."

"There's no need. The Praesidium will provide everything for you."

"I know. I just want to grab a few sentimental things. Some pictures and whatnot."

Jenny stood up.

So did Rogers. Like he was going to help her.

Jenny put a hand on his arm.

"No. Please," she said. "I want to do this alone, okay? Let me . . . I just need to say goodbye, okay? To him. To everything. I'll be quick, I promise."

Rogers studied her for a moment that, to Jenny, felt like a week.

Then he said, "All right. But don't take too many things. There has to be a lot of rubble for the fire department to sift through. It can't look like you cleaned the place out first."

"Got it," she said. "I'll be right back."

"I'll be here," Rogers replied.

I know, Jenny thought. *That's the problem.*

CHAPTER 39

NATE

The right side of my face had gone numb from being pressed against the hardwood floor.

My joints had started to ache as well from being held in that awkward position—arms akimbo, legs splayed.

If this was what fake death was like, I didn't want to know how real death felt.

It was difficult to estimate how long I had been locked in that position. I tried to tell myself this was just like one of the countless times I had played hide-and-seek with the girls.

That's all this was. Just a game.

One with deadly consequences if I lost.

Still, I didn't dare move. I didn't even shift my weight. This house was too old. I didn't trust the floorboards not to squeak.

The only comfort I had was that the girls were safe. All of them. I had heard Jenny take Cate and Parker out of the house, out of harm's way. And Jenny herself would also be protected.

The Praesidium wouldn't dare let harm come to someone with the gift, would they?

From downstairs, I could hear voices—Rogers and Jenny, I assumed, because it was a man and a woman. They seemed to be having a casual conversation, but I couldn't really make out what they were saying.

Then I heard someone coming up the stairs. This set my heart to pounding, which was inconvenient, because it also made me want to quicken my breathing, which was something dead men weren't supposed to do.

My ears told me it was just one person, moving fast. The door to the bedroom was ajar, so whoever it was would be able to see me soon enough. All I could do was remain as inert and lifeless as possible and hope my spilled-water blood pool looked at least a little convincing.

I had my eyes open—dead people did that, right?—but still couldn't see much, because it was dark, and because I was turned in the wrong direction. The door opened. I slowly, soundlessly took in a breath and held it so my body wouldn't be moving at all.

It didn't seem to be working. The person walked straight toward me, bent down over me, and I thought for sure I was going to be killed for real.

And then I smelled Jenny, and heard her whisper, "You have to get out of here. Rogers is going to blow up the house."

"How am I going to do that?" I whispered back.

"I don't know. Rogers thinks I'm up here packing a bag. That will buy us a little time, but not much."

She raised herself back up, turned on a light, and then went into the closet.

Slowly, I lifted myself off the floor. I was still being cautious, but I didn't need to worry quite so much about making noise with Jenny shuffling around. She had grabbed a bag and walked back toward her dresser, where she was now sifting through her jewelry box, taking out some items, leaving others behind.

Softly, I padded over toward her.

"Where are the girls?" I whispered.

"Buckled into the Range Rover. They're okay."

"Where is Rogers taking you? Do you know yet?"

"No clue. I'll be fine. Worry about yourself. Can you jump out of the window or something?"

"I guess I'll have to," I said.

It was either that or the stairs. And the stairs would never work. Not with Rogers in the kitchen and other men coming in and out of the house while they set about blowing it up.

I thought about the logistics of a jump. The drop was higher than a typical two-story house, on account of the first floor's twelve-foot ceilings. And while it wasn't so high as to be deadly, there was still a chance of injury—a broken leg, a twisted ankle, something like that—that would make it difficult to flee.

Even more worrying: that someone would either hear or see me. Two hundred pounds wouldn't exactly fall like a feather.

Then there was the question of where I jumped from. Each of the girls' rooms had one window that opened to the front. Our bedroom had a window, as did our bathroom. Both of those were on the back side of the house.

There were no windows to the side. Not in a row house.

In the front, I'd land on some bushes that decorated either side of our entrance. The crash would be noisy. And I'd have to extricate myself from the bush before I could run, potentially making me an easy target.

Out back, I'd hit either the porch, if I jumped from our bedroom, or a small patch of grass, if I jumped from the bathroom. The bathroom struck me as the best option.

"Who else is here besides Rogers?" I asked.

"There's men on both porches. They both look like they mean business."

I grimaced. "That's not good."

"They won't be expecting someone to fall from the sky. You might have a few seconds to run away."

"But then the Praesidium would know I'm alive."

"True. I guess we'll have to hope they don't notice you."

"Hope hardly seems like a plan."

"Sometimes," she said, "hope is the only plan."

It was a thoroughly Jenny Welker thing to say, a decidedly Jenny Welker attitude to take. My can-do wife, can-doing.

Our faces were a few inches apart. All I wanted to do was grab her, kiss her, fall into bed with her. But that luxury seemed like a long, long way off.

"I love you," I said.

"Don't start with that," she replied. "Escape first, then love me."

It was when she said the word *escape* that I suddenly realized the best way out of this. For each of the girls' rooms, the nervous new father in me had purchased a three-story fire escape ladder—lightweight, fire retardant, guaranteed not to tangle, free shipping with Amazon Prime. It suddenly seemed like the smartest $49.99 I had ever spent.

I could climb down, hidden by the shadows, then vault over our fence and disappear into the night.

"Come with me into Parker's room," I whispered.

She nodded, then led the way. I crossed the hallway quickly, staying directly behind Jenny so our footfalls would sound like they belonged to only one person.

As soon as we entered the room, Jenny stopped and looked at me expectantly. I didn't break stride on my way to Parker's bed, just lowered myself onto my belly and lifted the bed skirt.

The fire escape ladder was exactly where I'd left it, packed in its neat little bag. As soon as I pulled it out, Jenny's face registered comprehension. She gave me an enthusiastic thumbs-up.

With the ladder under my arm, I walked across the hallway again. This time, Jenny followed close behind me.

"Okay. Just stall for me a little more, and I'll be out of here," I said when we reentered the bedroom.

"Got it," she said.

She poked her head out of the door. "Just a few more things," she called out. "Give me another minute or two."

"Okay," Rogers said from downstairs.

Jenny went to my dresser, which had some wedding photos and pictures of the girls as babies, and started scooping frames into her bag indiscriminately. I took one last look at her and tried to tamp down the thought that this might be the last time I'd ever see her.

Then I pushed forward. On my way back through the bedroom, I spied the gun that had come so close to being the instrument of my death. It was still lying on the pillow, exactly where Jenny had left it.

I thought about grabbing it and stuffing it in the waistband of my pants. It might come in handy. And I was pretty darn sure it wouldn't be loaded with blanks like the other one had been.

But somehow I just didn't. Really, what was I going to do, shoot it out with Rogers' goons?

No, the only thing I took from the bedroom was the PR key card I had stolen from Rogers, which I slipped into my pocket—because it struck me as something I just might need.

I continued into the bathroom, then raised the blinds, which were wooden, plantation-style, and, most importantly, silent. Next I eased open the window, thankful that, unlike the front window frames—which we couldn't change, because we were in a historic district—the ones in back had been replaced by sleek, modern, quiet vinyl.

The screen was already up, so there was now nothing between me and my getaway but a few feet of cool night air. I unzipped the bag and pulled out the ladder.

Then I triggered the release latch. The ladder's steps unfurled like they had something more than gravity propelling them, falling straight to the ground with a soft thud.

I couldn't see the man on the back porch. Did he hear the noise as well? Would he come to investigate? I listened for a moment, my breath held.

But there didn't seem to be any change below me. It was just our little patch of fenced-in grass, same as ever.

I didn't dare wait any longer. Rogers would be expecting Jenny any moment. I eased one leg over the windowsill, my foot groping around for a ladder step, which it soon found. I squeezed my body out next, ducking under the window. My other leg followed me through.

My body was now completely out of the window, thoroughly exposed. If anyone looked up, they would see my bulk dangling against the side of the house.

I turned my head toward the porch. Sure enough, there was a man sitting there. He was staring straight ahead, and he seemed relaxed, with his legs stretched out in front of him and his ankles crossed. I was perhaps two dozen feet over and another dozen feet up.

All he had to do was glance up and to his right, and I would be busted. I was relying on his obliviousness, my stealth, and all the luck I could scrape together.

Gingerly, I began climbing down, moving one foot, then the next. I was a little concerned about falling. I was more concerned with noise: the ladder steps were metal, and I was sure they'd clang against the brick of the house if I went too fast.

When I dared, I snuck occasional glances to the side, toward the man on the porch. Though mostly I kept my focus forward, pouring my concentration into making each movement as smooth and noiseless as possible.

It was all going well. Except, about halfway down, I felt this weird wiggling, almost like someone was trying to shake me off.

Then I looked up and saw what was actually happening.

Jenny was coming down the ladder too.

What the hell is she doing?

That was the only thought in my head for a good three seconds, which was longer than I really had to spend pondering anything at the moment.

Was she abandoning the plan and trying to flee with me, or . . .

Really, I had no idea. But this wasn't the time to ask. I put my head down and continued my descent, which had only become more difficult now that the ladder was jiggling so much.

And that, I think, was my undoing as I entered the final six feet. I didn't want to just drop—that would make too much noise—but, at the same time, I was no longer as smooth. What had once been a fairly compact motion was now a herky-jerky, knee-and-elbow-flailing exercise. This, just as I was entering into the peripheral vision of the guy on the porch.

The first indication that I had been made was when he stood up.

Then he shouted.

"Hey . . . hey!"

I let go of the ladder, shoving myself away from the wall as I did so. There was no longer any need for furtiveness.

The guy ran toward the edge of the porch and stopped at the railing. I landed maybe ten feet from him, my legs bending from the impact after a short fall, such that I was sort of crouching. His hand was going for something on his belt.

Like a gun? I couldn't see for sure, but I also wasn't going to gawk at him while I figured it out.

"Nate! Get out of the way!" Jenny shouted from somewhere higher on the ladder.

I started running across the yard, in the direction of the back gate.

"Hey!" the man said again.

Then, from above me, there were two gunshots.

Jenny, who'd obviously had fewer misgivings about the pistol on the pillow than I did, was firing at the man on the porch.

He was now scrambling for cover. Forget action movies, where the bad guys bravely return fire, heedless of their own safety. This was reality. I heard him crashing against my barbecue grill on his way over the side of the porch.

"Go to your car," Jenny shouted.

I was already headed that way. Now on the ground, she fired off another shot. I didn't know if she was really trying to hit the guy, or if she was just trying to keep him pinned down. I was now at the gate, which I threw open.

The Range Rover was just a few steps away. I had the keys in my pocket.

Then I heard another gunshot, this time not from Jenny's direction. The guy was returning fire from behind the porch.

Could he see what he was aiming at? Or was he just firing wildly too?

I yanked open the driver's side door to the Range Rover and got in the seat, starting it as I slammed my door shut. From the back seat, Parker said, "Daddy, what's—"

"Shh," I said. "Everything is fine, honey."

Just then, Jenny appeared at the gate. She fired off another round in the direction of the house, though she was shooting behind herself without even looking. It was as I expected: she was just trying to keep that guy from feeling like he could expose himself.

She slammed the gate closed and dashed to the passenger side of the Range Rover.

"Go, go, go," she said as she got in.

I didn't need further encouragement. I already had the car in reverse and was mashing down the gas as she shut her door. Then I shifted into drive and sent us hurtling down the narrow back alley behind our house.

When I reached the street, I turned right, because that was the easier way to go, and accelerated, putting distance between us and the house as quickly as possible.

"Okay, what now?" I asked.

"I don't know," she admitted.

There was a siren in the distance. Neighbors must have heard the gunplay and called the police. I wondered if they'd be able to figure out it had been coming from our house. What would they make of the scene—two bodies in the dining room—if they did?

Jenny obviously heard it too.

"Just keep driving," she said, then twisted in her seat to look behind us. "Is anyone following us?"

I glanced in the rearview mirror. There didn't seem to be anything unusual behind us.

"Not that I can see," I said.

"I'm sure that will change."

"I don't know," I said. "I removed a tracking device from my car earlier this week. I don't think they bothered to put on another one. We might have—"

And then I remembered the drone footage. The one allegedly shot by Jenny's so-called private investigator.

"What?" Jenny asked.

"That drone. That wasn't really you, was it?"

"What drone?" she asked.

"The one that shot that footage of me driving to Hunter Matthews' house."

"Yeah, that was Rogers," she confirmed. "That was part of how he convinced me you were really in bed with CP and L. Why *did* you go out there, anyway?"

I briefly explained to her how I'd come to believe that Rogers was an agent for CP&L. I was just getting to the end when Jenny's phone rang.

She swore softly.

"What?" I asked.

"It's Rogers."

CHAPTER 40

JENNY

Jenny looked down at the phone. It rang a second time, then a third.

Just before the call went to voice mail, she answered with a calm "Hello."

"Where are you going, Jenny?" Rogers asked.

Jenny didn't actually know. They seemed to be out of immediate danger, so Nate had slowed to where he was driving only a little over the speed limit. He kept checking the rearview mirror but didn't seem to see anything that alarmed him. They were pointed east, toward the dodgy side of Richmond she had learned so well during her many trips to sign up plaintiffs. It was as good a place as any to attempt to disappear.

"You really think I'm going to tell you?" she asked.

Rogers sighed. The background noise on his phone made it sound like he was on the move. In a car, perhaps. Was he already coming after them? Was his drone already shadowing them overhead?

Almost certainly yes.

"I'm disappointed in you, Jenny," he said. "You lied to me about Nate."

"Yeah? Well, you lied first. Nate wasn't offered any kind of twenty million dollars by CP and L."

"I suppose not. But at least I lied for a good reason."

"What, so I would kill my husband?"

"To be honest, yes. You have to see the big picture here, Jenny. The Praesidium's work is not the idle hobby of some wealthy man. It is incredibly vital. We save hundreds, thousands, even millions of lives."

"Yes, but at what cost? How many people have you killed in the process?"

"I know our methods make you uncomfortable. But anyone who has ever studied ethics for half a second would tell you we're on the side of right here. It's why I always start with the same question: Would you kill one person to save five? The answer is always yes. Our work has to continue. And you have to join us."

"Look, I'm just not interested in your math."

"You'll change your mind. This is your destiny. Mr. DeGange has foreseen it."

"Mr. DeGange can bite me."

Rogers sighed again. "I understand that you love your husband. Maybe we can come to some kind of arrangement here."

"How? You've been very clear that the Praesidium has its rules and it always follows them. Neither Nate nor I could take the Praesidium's oath, because we haven't killed anyone."

"These are exceptional circumstances. You'll eventually be the new leader. The rules will be different for you. I'll convince the members that you don't have to go through the same process."

"Really," Jenny said, the incredulity plain in her voice.

"Yes, really. Let's just slow down for a moment. Why don't we go somewhere that's neutral ground? A nice hotel, perhaps. Paid for by Mr. DeGange, of course. We can relax, discuss this all in a more leisurely fashion, and come to some kind of arrangement. Hang on a moment."

In the background, someone asked Rogers a question. Jenny couldn't hear what it was, but he told them, "Yes, go ahead."

"What was that about?" Jenny asked.

"Nothing. I just wouldn't think of running to the police if I were you."

"What does that mean?"

"Those men in your dining room? The police will easily be able to find the guns used to kill them. And those guns will have your husband's fingerprints all over them."

"How did you get my husband's fingerprints?"

"Oh, I have my ways," he said. "Let's just focus on the issue at hand. There's a resort I just adore in Martinique. You and Nate will love it. So will the girls. The weather is . . ."

He continued talking. Jenny had tuned him out.

Shortly after he had said "Martinique," a thought had appeared in Jenny's head. It came on suddenly: one moment it wasn't there; the next moment, it was.

It might not have seemed all that different from how anyone else got an idea—where *did* those things come from anyway?—except this one was about the future. She had been getting these kinds of thoughts since she was a little girl, and she had always ignored them to a certain extent, even when they turned out to be unerringly true. She thought everyone had occasional premonitions.

She really hadn't thought she was anything special.

But now, ever since Rogers had approached her two months ago and explained to her that she had this strange gift, she had started to pay more attention to her thoughts.

Especially this one.

She was at a luxury hotel. Was it Martinique? She didn't know. She had never been there.

It certainly could have been the Caribbean. Through a window, she could see a palm tree leaning over a pristine white-sand beach, with the azure ocean stretching beyond. It was beautiful.

And yet the overwhelming emotion of this thought was shock and disbelief. Rogers was there. He had just explained how Nate had died in an accident. A diving boat had capsized. Nate had drowned.

She knew instantly—both in the vision, and in the present moment—that it wasn't an accident. Diving boats didn't go any great distance from land. Nate was far too good a swimmer. He had attended college on a swimming scholarship and still swam four, five times a week.

This wasn't part of the vision. But Jenny could guess it all the same: Rogers would tell the other members of the Praesidium that Jenny had secretly arranged the accident. They shouldn't mention this fact—it was too painful for her—but she was now eligible to take the oath and—

"You're lying," Jenny said, interrupting whatever Rogers was in the midst of saying. "You're lying again."

"No, I'm not, Jenny. I'll float this idea past some of the members and they'll—"

"Stop lying," she shouted. "I'm not going to Martinique with you."

The moment she said it, the strangest sensation came over her. The thoughts that had been so powerful mere moments before—the images of that tropical island, the raw pain of Nate's death, the devastation of Rogers' duplicity—began to fade, almost like they had never happened. Jenny could still access the information, as though it were a memory. Except it now struck her as more like a daydream, not as the hard reality it had been moments earlier.

"Now, Jenny, be reasonable about it. All I'm proposing is—"

She ended the call. She had heard enough.

Because she knew—and this was not a thought appearing suddenly in her head, just cold logic—that Rogers was never going to let Nate live.

Even though she'd shut down the Martinique proposal, Rogers was going to continue scheming, conniving, and manipulating. Nate would never be truly safe.

She reached out and grabbed his thigh, just to feel his body heat, his very undrowned vitality. Even as a daydream, the memory of his death was still traumatic.

"What's going on?" he asked. "What's Rogers lying about now?"

"Everything. As usual. Did you give him a set of your fingerprints by any chance?"

"No, but . . . oh, man."

"What?"

"When I first woke up after he had kidnapped me, my hand had this astringent smell, like very powerful soap. He could have made a cast of it while I was asleep."

"And then he used that to make a glove or something?"

"Yeah. I've seen it on YouTube. People do it to hack into phones with fingerprint protection."

"Oh that's just perfect," she said.

Jenny balled her fist, then released it. She was the one who could supposedly see the future, yet Rogers always seemed to be a step ahead of her.

"Okay, we'll worry about that later," Jenny said. "Let's figure out where we're going first."

"I was thinking we'd find a hotel or something."

"And then what?" she asked. "I have six bullets left in this gun. That won't last very long once Rogers finds us with his drone."

"What did you have in mind, then?"

Jenny gazed out the windshield, willing herself to think rationally. Who could she really trust? Where did she turn when she was in trouble? Who had her back no matter what? It was suddenly obvious.

"My parents' house," she said.

"Isn't that exactly where they'll expect us to go?"

"Maybe. But think about the setup there. The house is up on that little knoll. It has a hundred acres of open land around it. There'd be no surprising us. Plus, Dad has half a million guns, probably some dynamite left over from blowing up stumps, and who knows what else."

"I don't know, I just—"

Jenny watched as Nate's eyes again flicked toward the rearview mirror.

"Oh crap," he said. "I think we've got company."

CHAPTER 41

NATE

The headlights were bright and high, like they belonged to a van or light truck; and they were perhaps a hundred yards behind us.

But they were coming on fast, closing the distance at a determined clip.

I pressed down the gas. I didn't know what they were driving, but it looked boxy and slow. I felt good about the Range Rover's V8. It had enough power to outrun anything that was as large as whatever went with those headlights.

That's if we were on a track, or a straightaway. The problem was, we were winding through neighborhoods with lights, traffic, and a smattering of late-night pedestrians.

The other problem was my back-seat cargo. It was a lot more precious—and a lot more vulnerable—than the Praesidium operatives now chasing us down. I couldn't dare be as reckless as Rogers.

I also didn't know where we were. All throughout Jenny's conversation, I had been making arbitrary turns, winding through the east end of Richmond at random—almost like I was trying to implement my free will strategy from earlier.

That had seemed like a fine idea when I thought getting lost was my goal. Now it struck me as another liability.

Jenny had twisted around in her seat again.

"Is it them?" I asked.

"I don't know. But who else could it be?"

I was barreling down an avenue that had two lanes going in each direction. It was a thirty-five-miles-per-hour zone, and I had accelerated to at least sixty. I swerved around a white sedan that was clogging the left lane, then weaved back to avoid running into the back of a pickup that was puttering along in the right.

From behind me, the headlights easily matched my moves and were still gaining on us. They were probably now fifty yards off.

The streetlights had all been green so far, but the one up ahead was turning yellow. I pressed the gas pedal all the way to the floor, making it through the intersection just as the light turned red, then looked behind me.

The vehicle blatantly ran the red, earning an angry honk from a car that had been waiting there. Any thought that this was just some traveler in a hurry now seemed unlikely.

This was the Praesidium. It had to be.

As if to confirm my suspicion, Jenny's phone rang again. She ignored it. She was still focused behind us. The headlights were now thirty yards away. I could now see they were attached to a Ford Econoline.

I passed another car. So did the Econoline, whose engine was revving hot, hard, and angry.

Then I heard this popping noise.

Gunshots. Two of them.

I risked a glance in the rearview mirror and saw someone leaning out the passenger-side window, holding on with one hand, firing with the other.

"Why are they doing that?" I asked. "Rogers needs you to stay alive, doesn't he? I thought it was only me he wanted dead."

"They're probably aiming for our tires," Jenny said.

"And then what? He's going to kidnap you and force you into cooperating? How would that work, exactly? The Praesidium's prophet-in-training working under duress?"

More gunfire.

"No idea," Jenny said. "Rogers keeps acting like he's going to talk me into this, given enough time. Maybe he knows if he has you and the girls I'll do whatever he wants? I don't get it entirely myself. He just keeps hammering that the Praesidium is now my home. It's like as long as he possesses me, that's enough."

I started zigzagging. Not enough to cost us too much speed, I hoped, but enough to make us a more difficult target. Between that and our speed—we were both traveling near seventy—I couldn't imagine the shooter would be able to take any kind of decent aim.

Up ahead, there were now two cars, traveling at roughly the same (slow) rate of speed, one in each lane. The avenue had a double yellow line down the middle, but there was nothing coming the other way—at least not until the next block—so I veered into the oncoming lane for a heart-stopping second or two to make the pass.

"Nice move," Jenny said. "He's caught . . . no, now he's around them."

We had slightly widened the gap behind us. Still, this didn't feel sustainable. We were going to hit something, or come up on something we couldn't get around, or run out of road.

Another series of loud pops.

"This isn't working," I said. "Do you actually know where we are?"

"Yeah."

"Is there a highway anywhere around here? Maybe we could outrun them once we got on some open road?"

"Not really. There's 295, but that's—*look out!*"

We were coming up on a red light. Two cars were entering the intersection perpendicular to us. I had no choice but to jam the brakes and let them pass. Then I had to make sure nothing else was coming.

The Econoline took advantage, roaring up to within a few feet of our bumper. I thought maybe it was going to ram us; then I saw a hole in the oncoming traffic that we could just fit through.

I stomped on the gas and threaded the needle between two cars, both of which slammed on their brakes, horns blaring.

The van clipped one of them with its front bumper, sending the car into a spin. The van continued more or less straight. It had lost some momentum, but its driver seemed undaunted. And although we had gained back a twenty-yard lead, it didn't feel like it was going to last.

Then Jenny said, "There's a train coming."

"Where?" I asked.

As far as I could tell, there was no train anywhere. I didn't see any tracks. I couldn't even hear one.

"No, not yet. But there will be," Jenny said, with utter certainty. "Just do exactly as I say. Go right. *Right!*"

We were very nearly to the next intersection—and still traveling about seventy—when she made the order. I braked hard and tugged the wheel right, suddenly thankful for whatever technology it was that made the Range Rover unlikely to roll over. Our tires squealed, but we made the turn.

So did the van, whose driver had used that extra twenty yards to his advantage, being able to see where we were headed.

This new street had just one lane going in our direction and parked cars on both sides, all of which struck me as potentially disastrous. There was just less room for everything. The van, which was again making up ground, would be able to push us into something, or pull even with us and sideswipe us into one of the parked cars, or use some other looming impingement to box us in.

I zoomed down one block, blowing through a stop sign. Midway down the next block, Jenny said, "Turn left here."

Without really looking to see what else might be coming—and, again, without stopping—I followed her directions.

And I was glad I did. We had left whatever neighborhood we were in. This road was wider, with no parked cars, and it was lined with industrial buildings. I felt like I had more room to maneuver. The van wouldn't be able to pin us in here.

Still, our pursuers were again right behind us, no more than ten feet off our bumper.

Then I heard it.

The train.

The one Jenny had predicted.

It let out three long blasts of its horn. The sound was coming from somewhere to my right. I still couldn't see it, or—

And then, four blocks down, I glimpsed the train tracks. There were lights flashing. The gates were dropping.

"Gun it," Jenny said.

I pressed down the accelerator. It was a straight shot from where we were to the tracks.

"You want us to, what, take out the gates?"

"Yes. You *have* to listen to me. Faster."

"I'm already flooring it," I yelled.

From the back seat, Parker started crying.

We had slowed to perhaps twenty-five to make the turn, but the speedometer needle was now sweeping rapidly to the right. Forty. Fifty-five. Seventy-five. The van was matching our speed, its headlights still filling my rearview mirror.

The gates had now fully dropped. The train let out three more horn blasts. I couldn't yet see the engine, but the sound was definitely close.

"Jenny, I don't think we're going to make it."

"Just keep going. Trust me."

She said this with fierce determination, like it was her gift talking.

I was doing ninety. Three of the four blocks had already melted away. I didn't need to look in the rearview mirror to know the van was still on top of us. It might as well have been in the back seat.

Then, to my right, I saw the lights of the train. It was not moving terribly fast. But it also wasn't stopping either. We were tracking toward the same place at the same moment—the same place in space-time, as Einstein would say. There was no way we'd survive the collision at this speed.

"We're not going to make it!" I screamed.

"Drive faster!" she screamed back.

Both girls were now crying.

In my peripheral vision, I could see this look on Jenny's face that was almost maniacal. I honestly didn't know why I listened to her. Maybe it was her certainty. Maybe it was my newly developing belief in her ability. Maybe it was just conditioning after thirteen years of being with someone who was stronger willed than me.

Whatever it was, I kept hurtling toward that train.

Its prow was now visible. We were on a direct path toward it. Did Jenny have a death wish? Was this how she wanted us to go? Family suicide by train?

The engineer must have seen me coming, because the train's horn blasted again. The space being illuminated by my headlights was all train. We were going to be crushed.

And then Jenny grabbed the steering wheel and yelled, *"Brake hard!"*

My foot went to the brake. She tugged down on the wheel so sharply she practically broke my wrist.

For a moment we turned toward the right. I could feel the antilock brakes engage. We went sideways into a skid.

It seemed to last forever. Our tires were getting no traction, just leaving rubber on the road surface and smoke behind them. We were drifting inexorably toward the train. Except instead of hitting it straight on, where maybe the bulk of our motor and our airbags would save us, we were going to sideswipe it.

I was dimly aware I was screaming. From the back seat, the girls' little voices added to the din.

Only Jenny was quiet.

The train loomed closer, ever closer, growing so large in my vision it was all I could see. My side of the car was going to strike first. It would be like a Matchbox car slamming into a tank. They would probably find small pieces of everything—the Range Rover, my family—for miles.

We had maybe six feet to spare when the tires bit the road, giving us a violent jolt. We rocked hard to the left, the suspension taking on the full brunt of the force, and I thought we might pitch over, the Range Rover's antiroll capabilities be damned.

Somehow, the vehicle stayed upright, bouncing off the railroad crossing gate. We were now pointed at a ninety-degree angle from the direction we had just been traveling. I was still nowhere near in control of the thing. We were going to hit something. It just might not be as unforgiving as the train.

We plunged off the asphalt. But as I braced myself for a collision, the steering wheel still not responding to my command, I finally saw the method to Jenny's madness: there was a gravel road that paralleled the train tracks. We were now traveling down it, quite safely.

Miraculously, we were going to emerge from this without a scratch.

The same could not be said for the Econoline, which didn't have nearly the braking or turning capacity of the Range Rover, yet had still tried to make the same semi-impossible maneuver.

And failed.

Badly.

I didn't watch the impact. I was too focused on trying to steady the bucking Range Rover.

What I heard made me glad I hadn't seen it. It was the gruesome crunch of metallic objects meeting, one far less yielding than the other.

CHAPTER 42

JENNY

It took some time before Jenny stopped shaking.

All the while, she kept replaying the train incident in her head. And praying to whatever god might be listening for forgiveness.

The thought—about where the train was going to be, about how they would be able to use it to escape—had been another one of those ideas that seemed to appear out of nowhere. What it hadn't included were the catastrophic implications for the van.

Was the gift always this ruthless? Was it actually Praesidium-like in its moral calculations, factoring that a family of four was inherently more worthy of survival than a van full of henchmen? Or was it simply that she would be able to see certain things but always be somewhat blind to the full picture?

It was like when she'd seen the woman with the orange hair, lurking outside CMR headquarters. Jenny had recognized instantly there was *something*—call it danger—surrounding the woman. Yet at no point had Jenny realized the woman was less than two days away from being gunned down. The specifics were absent.

Then again, when Rogers had said the word *Martinique*, she'd had a much clearer vision of the consequences. Was it just because she was getting better at recognizing the sensation? Or was it that the victim, her husband, was someone so close to her, whereas the victims in the other cases were strangers?

She still felt so new at this. So essentially clueless. It was like being given some fabulous new next-generation device—but no instruction manual.

Surely, it hadn't helped that she had been so resistant to the mere idea of the gift. When Rogers had first approached her two months ago, she'd assumed he was a scam artist. Even after he proved otherwise—DeGange perfectly predicted a deadly volcanic eruption in Alaska—she was still mostly interested in making him go away.

As such, she hadn't ever really quizzed him in greater detail about how, exactly, the gift worked. He had explained the basics, that she would feel the ripples from death—and the opposite of death, a life being saved—more strongly than anything else. But they had never really gotten around to talking about the more subtle aspects of the currents that were flowing by her all the time.

Maybe it didn't matter, because he didn't know.

Maybe only DeGange himself would be able to explain that.

And, at least according to the rules Rogers had explained, she wouldn't be able to meet DeGange until she was a full-fledged, oath-taking member of the Praesidium.

That was never going to happen. Which made the gift like so many other things in her life, whether it was playing the college-admissions game or acing the LSATs: she would just have to figure it out on her own.

They were now rolling through the countryside, closing in on Seb and Deb's. Jenny had convinced Nate that was the only safe place to go. Or maybe it wasn't so much that she'd convinced him as that he didn't have any other ideas.

After that, she had called to let her parents know they were coming. Deb, the light sleeper who answered the phone, had quickly turned matters over to Seb, who'd absorbed the details in typically analytical, unemotional fashion.

Otherwise, there had been no conversation in the car. The girls had both fallen back to sleep—after the excitement and the yelling—and the grown-ups hadn't wanted to wake them.

The stars were bright and in their billions. The moon was nowhere around. And there wasn't a streetlight within twenty miles to pollute the sky or spoil the show.

Under nearly any other circumstance, she would have found comfort in the soft luminosity of light that had started its journey toward Earth millions of years earlier, before she, her cares—or her species, for that matter—had even existed.

But Jenny was in no condition to savor the beauty of Surry County. She kept checking Richmond.com for news about what had happened, fearing the worst. And finally, when they were about five miles from her parents' place, the site posted a story about a fatal accident involving a vehicle and a freight train.

The police had not yet identified the victims, so the biggest question in Jenny's mind was still unanswered.

Had Rogers been in the van?

Or was he coordinating the operation from somewhere else?

To a certain extent, Jenny couldn't decide whether it even mattered. A man with DeGange's wealth could hire an unending supply of disposable bodies. The Praesidium could just reload and come after her again, couldn't it?

But how soon would the onslaught come? And in what form?

They were about three miles from the farm when Jenny started talking softly.

"I've been thinking about Candy Bresnahan," she said.

"Oh yeah?" Nate said, his eyes on the road ahead as he drove.

"Before she almost shot me, she said, 'This has to end.' But before that, she said something else."

"What's that?"

"'I'm tired.'"

"Huh," Nate said. "And you think that means something?"

"Maybe. The more I run it through my head, I don't think she was talking about me. You don't get tired because of something related to a stranger you've never met. You get tired because of your own stuff. I think she was referring to her personal situation."

"Talk me through it."

"Vanslow DeGange is an old man. Rogers says he's in good health, but he still won't live forever and everyone in the Praesidium understands this. Unless they find someone with the gift, how do they stay in business? As I understand it, they had been looking for a replacement for years. They just hadn't found one. And then I came along."

"Yeah, how *did* they find you, anyway?"

"Well, for starters, the way the gift apparently works is that proximity does matter. Just like all of us, DeGange is more aware of things that are closer to him, whether it's closer spatially or closer in time. He's more likely to have thoughts regarding those things. So let's assume for a moment that if Candy was in White Stone, Virginia, DeGange was too. At least some of the time."

"Sure."

"Richmond isn't that far away. He apparently became aware of me having this gift some time ago. He just didn't know who I was. But I was on his radar screen, as it were. And then, slowly, as he approached the moment we're in right now and the time beyond it, he started being able to see more and more of this tall woman, not only having the gift but doing the work of the Praesidium. And they eventually figured out that person was me."

"Really," Nate said like he didn't believe it. "So after all this, you're going to work for the Praesidium?"

"Supposedly."

Nate was quiet for a moment. "I don't mean to be selfish about it, but if that's true, it kinda sucks to be me."

"Not necessarily. Maybe Rogers wasn't lying about working out some kind of arrangement."

"So I'm relying on Rogers' veracity for my continued existence. Great," he said. "Anyhow, what does this have to do with Candy Bresnahan being tired?"

"Oh, right. I think she's actually tired of being in the organization. She's been saving the world for the better part of three decades. That has to get exhausting. When she says 'This has to end,' she's not talking about me. She's talking about the entire Praesidium. She wants Vanslow DeGange to be able to die without a replacement so she can go back to being a small-town grandma."

"Why couldn't she just leave? Rogers made it sound like working with the Praesidium was voluntary."

"Maybe it is at first, before you get in too deep," Jenny said. "But you really think they're going to let someone like Candy just walk away? Someone who knows everything about the operation? That's a huge liability. From a strictly legal standpoint, the Praesidium isn't some altruistic organization dedicated to saving human lives. It's a vast criminal conspiracy organized around committing serial murder. Every single one of them could be indicted based on having that PR brand alone. All it would take is one person who has departed telling law enforcement to keep an eye on what goes on there—one person who knows just how often the Praesidium is involved in a murder—and everyone still involved goes to jail for a long time."

"So Candy could basically never get out."

"True. Except if DeGange dies and there's no replacement. At that point, the Praesidium disbands and everyone goes their own way. Yeah, any one of them could still inform on the others. But there's no longer an ongoing operation, so the only thing you could inform about is stuff that's already happened, stuff that would get you in trouble too."

"Meaning there's an element of mutually assured destruction."

"Precisely."

They bounced along the dark, unlined country road for another quarter mile or so.

"And that brings me to the other thing I've been thinking about," she said.

"Yes?"

"I've figured out how we can get out of this. It's probably the only way out."

"What's that?"

"Vanslow DeGange has to die," she said.

"You mean we have to kill him?"

"Pretty much."

"Since it seems to be either him or me, I agree with you. There's just one problem."

"What's that?" she asked.

"We have to find him."

"Yeah."

"And we have to do it before he finds us," Nate said. "Any idea how we are going to do that?"

"None."

"Can't you just gaze into the future and figure out where he'll be at some specific moment?"

"I'm trying," Jenny said. "Believe me, I'm trying."

Everything was dark when they arrived at Seb and Deb's place.

Almost too dark.

Seb normally kept a light on over the barn out back, believing it discouraged anyone who might have a thought about busting the lock and helping themselves to his tools.

Had he just turned it off, or . . .

Nate already had them rolling up the long gravel driveway. In the gloom, Jenny could just make out the smudge of the house at the top of the small hill. It was, much like the people who lived there, solidly constructed: a two-story brick farmhouse with a porch that wrapped around the front and both sides. Jenny's great-grandfather had built it. And each generation since then had lovingly maintained it.

For a moment or two as she got closer, Jenny worried the Praesidium had gotten there first, that Seb and Deb were already dead, that her family was traipsing into an ambush.

But it didn't feel like a thought arriving from the future. It was more run-of-the-mill anxiety.

She peered into the night until she made out Seb's tall shape silhouetted against the brick, standing on the side of the porch that was nearest to the driveway.

As she got closer, she could see he was loosely carrying a rifle in one hand. And a smaller figure—Deb, of course—was keeping vigil next to him.

Seb and Deb, as always.

They got the girls inside the house—Parker to a bed, Cate into a crib—then convened at the kitchen table.

Jenny immediately recognized that Seb and Deb had switched into farmer mode (or perhaps never left it). Which meant they weren't going to let this rattle them. Whether it was a sick calf or a murderous secret society coming after their daughter, it was just another problem to tackle. They were ready for it, because they were ready for anything.

Deb had just put on a fresh pot of coffee. Seb had his rifle across his knees and kept glancing out the window. They kept the lights off inside the house, just in case.

"So when are you thinking these fellas are going to come after you?" he asked.

"No idea," Jenny said. "Maybe tonight, maybe a week from tonight. There's no telling."

"Okay, then we should probably keep watch," he said. "We'll do it in shifts. I've got some floodlights I can turn on. No one is going to be able to sneak up on this place. If you see or hear anything, raise hell."

"And then what?" Jenny asked.

"You let me worry about that," Seb said gravely. "I'll take first shift. You two look pretty tired."

"I'll take the second shift," Nate quickly volunteered.

Jenny nearly objected, then decided against it. She was already starting to recognize that her best chance to be able to sense the currents was to be well rested.

The last thing she did before turning in was to check her phone.

Richmond.com had updated its story about the train accident. There were four victims altogether.

None was named Lorton Rogers.

CHAPTER 43

NATE

A soft rain had begun falling while I slept.

By the time I jolted awake to the 3:55 a.m. cell phone alarm I had set for myself—so I wouldn't be late for my turn at watch—a fog had rolled in, as often happened in the low country that hugged either side of the James River.

When I spread apart the blinds to have a look, all I saw was this charcoal-gray mist that seemed to have smothered everything.

I walked out to the front porch to relieve Seb, who was sitting in a rocking chair, in the dark, with the hunting rifle across his knees.

"Anything to report?" I asked.

"Been using my ears more than my eyes," he said. "So far, all's quiet."

Then he added: "For now."

"Why don't you go get some rest? I got this."

He paused like he wasn't sure he believed me, then slowly rose to his feet with a grunt.

"Mind giving me the rifle?" I asked.

I felt myself straighten and stick out my chest as I asked, as if—ridiculously—I needed to affirm my masculinity before handling a firearm.

He jerked his head behind the rocking chair. "There's another one right there. I'd just as soon keep this one with me."

"Is that one . . . loaded?"

"Yeah," he said. "Ten-round magazine. It's automatic. That means it'll reload for you."

He seemed like he wanted to add more, then thought better of it. But when he reached the front door, he said, "You know which end shoots, right?"

"The pointy one," I said.

"Right," he said. "Like I said, raise hell if you hear anything."

I promised him I would. After shooing him away, I started patrolling the length of the porch, pausing now and then to listen—because staring out into the fog wasn't doing much good.

Eventually, I sat on the rocking chair, though I can't say I was ever really comfortable there. It was nerve racking, not being able to see more than ten feet beyond the porch. Vanslow DeGange himself could have been midway up the driveway with the First Infantry Division right behind him, and I felt like I wouldn't have been any the wiser.

As the time passed, the animals began waking up—a cacophony of Angus cattle bellowing and roosters sounding. There was no sunrise to speak of, just a gradual transition in the color of the mist, from dark to light gray.

I can't say the time passed quickly. But it definitely passed. By the time Seb spelled me at 8:00 a.m., some of the fog had burned off. The rain continued.

When I returned inside, everyone was awake, including the girls. Deb had already established that she was on kid duty. The old farmhouse had a half basement that Seb and Deb had finished many years earlier. It now served as a combination playroom for the girls and entertainment center for the grown-ups. It left Jenny and me alone in the kitchen to plot our next steps.

The first issue at hand was Barry Khadem, who had been desperately trying to contact Jenny and was (justifiably) out of his mind with worry. His hired bodyguards had gone incommunicado. He had driven by our place and found it locked up tight, with no one answering the door.

There was now a pile of texts, emails, and voice mails all asking where she was and whether she was okay.

We debated how to respond, mindful that while Barry worked for a law firm, he wasn't a lawyer. Any communication we had with him might, eventually, be legally discoverable by the police.

As far as we knew, Rogers had left those dead bodyguards in our dining room, with the murder weapons—covered in my fingerprints—somewhere nearby. He was keeping the threat of framing me for those murders in his back pocket, using it to prevent us from going to the police—and, perhaps, to blackmail us in ways we hadn't even imagined yet.

And there didn't seem to be a lot we could do about that at the moment. We couldn't return to our house, since Rogers would almost certainly have it under surveillance and/or have turned it into one big trap. I could imagine a horde of Praesidium henchmen surrounding the place the moment we stepped inside.

Even if we could access the place, I didn't know what we would do. Dispose of the bodies? Attempt to find and destroy the guns? Any of those types of efforts could easily backfire and make me look even more guilty—if not seal the question of my guilt entirely in the minds of law enforcement.

Eventually, we decided on a carefully worded email to Barry. Since the police would be able to roughly recreate our movements based on where our cell phones pinged, we stuck with the truth: we had decided at the last minute to spend the weekend at Jenny's parents' house in the country, having left late on Friday night; the guards were at our house when we departed, but we could not advise him on their current whereabouts; and he needn't worry about her, because she was in a safe location for the weekend.

We then got to work on the next issue, the one that was far more daunting:

Finding Vanslow DeGange.

We had one possible lead on the man's location. The driver's license for Candice Carter Bresnahan—who had been a member of the Praesidium in good standing up until she'd gone rogue—listed her address as White Stone, Virginia.

So that's where we began our search.

CHAPTER 44

JENNY

The question in Jenny's mind was not if Rogers would come for her again.

It was when.

The Praesidium had already dedicated significant energy to bringing her in. It wouldn't quit now simply because she had slipped away.

What she still couldn't figure out was why it was now willing to be so violent about it. The first time Rogers had approached her, he had laid out everything quite openly—like he was offering her a position at a competing law firm and it was her choice whether to accept.

She had considered it and declined. And while he had attempted to be persuasive—about the power she would yield, about the riches she would command—he had stopped short of coercion.

This latest effort had a very different feel to it. A more desperate feel. The Praesidium was acting like it was running out of time.

So while this was a lull, it wouldn't last long.

The next onslaught was coming much sooner.

She kept hoping another thought about the future would arrive and give her guidance about what to expect. But nothing was happening in that department.

It was almost like the harder she tried, the less likely it was to happen.

What she was left with, then, was just logic. The Praesidium had lost four men in the train accident. That may well have been the entire contingent Rogers had been dispatched with to Richmond.

Still, there would be reinforcements. The train accident was nothing more than a temporary setback.

With Nate staring intently into his laptop, she got to work doing the same with hers.

Barry Khadem had already done a fair amount of due diligence on Candice Carter Bresnahan. And Jenny similarly found that, from an investigative standpoint, Candy was a dead end.

Her post office box in White Stone, Virginia, was not.

Candy wasn't the only one who used it. Thanks to LexisNexis, Jenny was soon inundated with others who also conducted business through that post office box. There were dozens of names suddenly flashing across her screen, including those of all four victims of the train accident.

Recognizing she was about to get overwhelmed by information, Jenny opened a new spreadsheet to keep track of it.

Before very long, she had tallied twenty-seven people—including Lorton Rogers—associated with that PO box.

Were these all Praesidium members? That certainly seemed like a reasonable assumption.

She started searching those names, seeing if any of them might yield a physical address nearby. But all the other addresses associated with them were far from White Stone and the Northern Neck, probably previous addresses. Obviously, whatever rules the Praesidium had developed for its membership to hide its precise whereabouts had been successful.

Interestingly, some of the previous addresses overlapped. There were PO boxes in Colorado, California, Washington State, New York City, and New Hampshire. And those PO boxes, in turn, had other names associated with them.

Were these other locations for the Praesidium? Other homes that Vanslow DeGange owned?

But each of those PO boxes was attached to fewer names; and whereas people sometimes flowed from elsewhere to White Stone, it seemed that no one went from White Stone to somewhere else.

White Stone was the hive.

Jenny knew a little about the Northern Neck, having first visited it for long-ago high school basketball games. Like Surry County, the region was sparsely populated, consisting mostly of farms. It had abundant waterfront property, with the Rappahannock River forming its western boundary and the Chesapeake Bay defining the east. Its citizens tended to mind their own business, having either grown up in or chosen to relocate to a place where you could easily find enough land that you didn't have to see your neighbor.

It seemed like as good a place as any to base a secret organization. Because for as much as it was out of the way and quiet, it was still in the middle of the US Eastern Seaboard, a relatively short trip—especially by air or water—to cities and states that were home to tens of millions of people.

And yet—and this was now their problem—it was also huge. Lancaster County alone was more than two hundred square miles. Add the counties that shared the same peninsula, and you were looking at an area roughly the size of Rhode Island. They couldn't exactly start wandering around and knocking on doors.

At noon, Nate went to relieve Seb from watch duty. After Deb insisted they eat lunch, Seb asked for Jenny's help with "a chore"— which turned out to be setting up a series of trip wires around the property.

This would be their early-alert system.

There were three main ways to gain vehicular access to the farm. The driveway was the first and most obvious. There was also a back exit, a sort-of-road—really, just some ruts in the grass—that started behind the barn and led out to another field, which connected to another field, which connected to a road. Lastly, there was a path in the woods that wasn't wide enough for a car or truck but could be traversed by a four-wheeler or all-terrain vehicle.

At each location, they selected what they felt was the best spot to stretch a thin wire across the roadway, keeping it low so it hopefully couldn't be seen. Seb rigged it so when the wire was depressed, it would complete a circuit connected to a battery. That, in turn, would send electricity to a combination buzzer/light in the kitchen.

All the materials came from Seb's seemingly endless supply in the workshop.

Once they had the system set up and tested, Seb got a strange look on his face.

"Okay," he said. "Now that's done, there's one more thing I need to show you."

"What?" Jenny asked.

"Just come on."

Jenny followed Seb as he tromped down into the basement. He walked to the entertainment center and started shoving it away from the wall where it normally lived.

"Dad, what are you doing?"

"We always told you this was a half basement."

"Yeah. And?"

"It's not."

He went to the corner of the room, knelt, and peeled back a section of carpet, which came away easily to reveal a square piece of metal the size of a salad plate.

"This is getting weird," Jenny said.

Seb pressed down on the plate. There was a loud click, and suddenly the wall—a section of laminated-faux-wood, 1980s-style paneling that Jenny had looked at a thousand times since childhood—was gliding to the left, revealing a steel door.

"What," Jenny said, "is *that*?"

"I finished this basement when you were a baby. It was the Cold War. Your mother and I worried about being close to DC. It was a very different time."

"You built a bomb shelter under the house?"

"It's properly ventilated and lined with enough concrete to withstand a good bit of fallout. We never told you about it because at first you were just a little kid. We didn't want you to worry. After that? I don't know. The Berlin Wall had fallen. The Cold War was over. The whole thing almost seemed silly."

He shoved open the door, which swung easily on its heavy hinges, like it had recently been oiled. He turned on a light to reveal a room with two simple beds, a toilet, and shelves laden with water jugs and cardboard boxes.

"There's another button to open and close the wall right here," he said. "So you can seal yourself in. No one will know you're in there."

"Dad, why are you telling me all this?"

"Your mother and I discussed it this morning. If those buzzers go off, we want the four of you to come down here—you, Nate, and the girls. You'll be safe in here."

"While you and Mom, what, shoot it out with those guys?"

"If they start shooting, we'll call 911. We can hold them off until the authorities get here. I don't think those Praesidium fellows will want to shoot it out with the Surry County Sheriff's Office and the state police."

"But we can't call the police. Nate's fingerprints—"

"Nate isn't here, as far as we're concerned," Seb said. "Neither are you. We'll stick your truck in the barn under a cover."

"Dad, I can't have you—"

"We'll be fine," he said. "Or we won't be. Your mother and I have made up our minds. If those buzzers go off, we want you down here—got it?"

CHAPTER 45

NATE

My next shift on watch duty started unremarkably and stayed that way, at least for a time.

I was walking a loose circle around the house, rifle in hand, keeping an eye on the distant woods. The rain had stopped, leaving a low cloud cover to cast a gloomy pall over a Saturday afternoon.

Now and then, I came close enough to the house to hear Deb with the girls, who seemed to be in great spirits, what with Grandma slathering them with attention.

Seb and Jenny were busy too. Seb had dipped into his prepper-worthy stash of spare junk and created this alert system, and they were hollering back and forth to each other, a father and daughter who didn't even need full sentences most of the time. Warding off would-be attackers seemed to be a situation my father-in-law had been born to handle.

Otherwise, it was just the cows, the chickens, the goats, and me, the human being trying to ignore his lack of creature comforts. I had been up since 4:00 a.m. and was definitely feeling it. I had been wearing the same clothes since Friday morning. My feet, clad in jogging shoes ill matched to a soggy day on the farm, were soaked.

I was admittedly not as sharp as I should have been. So when I first heard this faint hum, almost like a swarm of bees, I dismissed it as, I don't know, a distant chain saw.

Except it wasn't revving up and down like a chain saw. It was more constant. And more high pitched.

Like the buzzing of a mosquito.

Or a drone.

Rogers surveilling us, getting as much information as he could about the property before he moved in with a fresh band of trouble.

It had to be, right? It certainly sounded like the whirring of tiny rotors. And it was coming from somewhere above me. What else could be causing it?

I tried to pinpoint the exact source of the noise, wanting to be able to see it and confirm my suspicions. But the humming was so diffuse—this maddening combination of everywhere and nowhere—that I couldn't say for sure where it was.

It was also entirely possible I simply couldn't see it, owing to the cloud cover. Though perhaps that was good news. If I couldn't see the drone, Rogers couldn't see us, right? Unless he had an infrared camera? Or something similar that could penetrate clouds?

Eventually, I enlisted Seb and Jenny in my drone hunt. They agreed the sound was drone-like, but they were no more successful in spotting any unidentified flying objects than I had been.

Not long after I summoned them, the sound faded into the distance, then stopped.

Taken in sum, the experience was both indefinite and unnerving.

At 4:00 p.m., when I should have been relieved, Seb was still working on his trip wire system, trying to get it just right. I volunteered to stay on watch for another four hours, feeling that was the most useful thing for me to be doing.

When Seb finally relieved me at 8:00 p.m., twilight was nearly finished. There was no moon to speak of. It would soon be a very dark night in Surry County, Virginia—the perfect time to sneak up on someone.

Jenny suggested I try to get some sleep so I could be sharp for the midnight-to-four shift, but I knew that wouldn't be possible. Rogers was coming for us. If not this night, then the next one.

I reheated some old coffee, then returned to my search for the Praesidium. With Seb insisting the aboveground floors of the house stay dark—he didn't want anything on the porch backlighting him and making him an easy target—Jenny and I retreated into the basement.

There, after a brief tour of the bomb shelter—because of course my father-in-law had a secret bomb shelter—Jenny and I went back to work.

She was still searching public documents, trying to get a physical address for a confirmed Praesidium resident. My focus was on Google Maps, specifically the satellite view. If the compound was home to that many people, in addition to DeGange himself, it would be a significant piece of property with a number of buildings. It wouldn't be something you could hide, even in an area the size of Rhode Island.

The only question was: Would I be able to spot it?

If I had one thing going for me, it was that I had most likely been there. The Praesidium's next-closest base was New York City. I was sure when I had been kidnapped, they had taken me to White Stone.

I thought of how quiet it had seemed outside that window, how it made me think I had been taken to a rural area. That description certainly fit the Northern Neck, which was now appearing in its totality on my computer screen. I zoomed in to where the satellite view gave me a 1,000-foot scale, then began working systematically through each square.

The region was bounded by jagged shoreline—formed by a series of creeks, inlets, and rivers, all of which emptied into the Chesapeake Bay.

The inland portions were a haphazard checkerboard of farms and forests. The houses were well-spaced single-family residences, most of them small.

Along the water the dwellings tended to be larger—grand waterfront homes, mansions surrounded by estates. Any number of them might have served as home to the Praesidium. Or just to a retired investment banker.

When the 1,000-foot scale yielded nothing obvious, I zoomed to the 50-foot scale, the closest Google allowed me to go.

It was slower going at this level of detail. I felt voyeuristic, like I was practically peering into people's living rooms. I saw their cars, their boats, their docks jutting into the silty water.

I could feel my attention and energy levels starting to flag. Now and then, I grabbed the skin on my thigh and gave it a pinch.

"Honey," Jenny said, after she caught me midpinch, "if you're that tired, why don't you get some sleep?"

I looked up at her briefly. She was clearly exhausted too.

"No," I said. "I just have to push through."

There may have been something about changing my field of vision for just a moment, because when I returned my attention to the screen, something winked at me. It was this perfectly round circle of white paint, set in a rectangular slab of asphalt.

A helipad. Who in Lancaster County, Virginia, needed a helipad?

It was set beside a large mansion, in a huge open area that—my first time through, at the 2,000-foot level—I had probably dismissed as a soybean field.

From this closer vantage point, I could tell it was grass. Whenever the satellite image had been taken, it had been mowed into a crosshatch pattern, like a Major League Baseball outfield.

In back of the grassy area, half-hidden in the trees, there was a series of smaller buildings—little houses, connected by paths, tastefully set at angles to increase the privacy for those inside.

It was definitely a high-density residential arrangement. But could it be, say, an upscale assisted living facility? With the helipad used for medical evacuations?

The cluster of buildings and the field occupied the entire tip of one peninsula, what looked like about two hundred acres and several thousand feet of shoreline jutting out into the Chesapeake Bay. It was halfway in between White Stone and a town called Kilmarnock, though it was entirely possible someone living there would decide the White Stone Post Office was closer.

I started studying the main structure. It was a massive thing, with rooflines going in every direction. I counted fourteen chimneys and four balconies. There were probably at least a dozen bedrooms.

Did one of those bedrooms have a Rembrandt in it? My tired heart began beating stronger in my chest as I studied the entire mansion again.

That's when I noticed, on one of the balconies, the tile had a very subtle pattern to it, formed by brown pieces that were just slightly darker than the tan pieces around them.

There was no mistaking the image being formed: a *P* and an *R* inscribed in a square.

"Jenny," I said. "I've found it."

CHAPTER 46

JENNY

There was little question in the Welker clan where Jenny had gotten her stubbornness.

It came straight from Seb. As such, Nate's revelation about the Praesidium's location was followed by a heated exchange between father and daughter.

This, however, proved short lived. Once Jenny convinced Deb of her way of thinking—that eliminating Vanslow DeGange was the only way to end this, and that it made sense to strike with haste—the quarrel was effectively over.

It was decided: Seb and Deb were staying with the girls, with the understanding that they would dive into the bunker the moment a buzzer sounded, or at any other sign of intrusion; and Jenny and Nate were headed up to the Northern Neck.

Because just as it was a dark night in Surry, it would also be dark in Lancaster.

The perfect night to sneak up on someone.

It was nearing eleven o'clock when they pulled out. Jenny had given Nate her silver-plated handgun, after refilling its ten-round magazine. She had taken one of Seb's pistols, a Colt that was older than she was but still worked great, and also a rifle, one with a scope, even if it struck her as unlikely she'd need its longer range.

This was killing an old man in his bed. It would have to be done up close.

If the thought of that gave her pause, it didn't last. From a moral standpoint, this was another one of those philosophy-class questions, the kind Rogers loved to ask. Except it was an easy one.

Would you kill a stranger who was threatening the person you loved most in the world?

Every. Time.

They had both donned black clothing, borrowing items from Seb as needed. They visited the girls because Jenny insisted, although—and Nate was firm on this—they didn't kiss them.

It went to one of the simpler doctrines of parenting survival: never wake a sleeping toddler.

Then they departed. As Nate drove, Jenny talked through their plan. From what Nate had seen in the satellite picture, the Praesidium's compound had only minimal security. The one entrance from the road had a small guard shack next to it, likely connected to a gate. The shack was built into a wall that ran along the eastern edge of the property—the side that wasn't bounded by water—to discourage trespassers.

The shoreline was protected by stone riprap and nothing else. The only enemy the Praesidium appeared to be concerned about coming from the water was erosion.

And it might have seemed counterintuitive, except not when Jenny thought it through. The Praesidium was always the instigator, the agitator, the agent of change in the lives of others. Its operations were undertaken exclusively on foreign turf. Praesidium members probably weren't even aware of the headquarters' location until they were already in deep.

Besides, nothing actually happened at the White Stone compound. It was entirely likely no one had ever attempted to take the fight to the Praesidium before.

There was, therefore, wisdom in not having any over-the-top defenses. To anyone boating by on the Chesapeake Bay, this was just another rich person's house on the water.

And that would be the weakness they would exploit.

The next issue would be getting inside. Nate was confident—perhaps too confident, Jenny thought—about the key card he had swiped, reasoning that since it belonged to Rogers it would give them access to wherever they needed to go.

Jenny hoped he was right.

Because sometimes hope was the only plan.

Once inside, they would just have to stay quiet and find DeGange before anyone else found them. Which was probably the biggest flaw in their strategy: Was it really possible to sneak up on someone who could sense the future?

But now that Jenny was starting to understand how the gift worked, she was less concerned about that. Vanslow DeGange truly could not see everything, particularly when it came to Praesidium-related actions.

He hadn't seen Candy Bresnahan going rogue and getting herself killed.

Or Jenny not killing Nate.

Or those four men dying in the train accident.

Unless . . . *had* he actually seen those things? Had DeGange, in fact, allowed them to happen because they fit into some larger scheme? One that perhaps even Rogers didn't know about?

There was no way to be sure. And, really, this led Jenny to the ultimate leap of faith she was making: that Vanslow DeGange, seer of death, would be so attuned to the wrinkles created by others he might not be able to sense the dip left by his own demise.

She ruminated on that for a while and, with Nate following the blue line on the GPS, tried to settle into the ride, relax, and will herself to have some glimpse of what was about to transpire.

She thought about the three most recent times it had happened: the woman with the orange hair, Martinique, and then the train.

In all three cases, she hadn't really been trying to see the future. She hadn't been aware of her thoughts at all. She had been hyperfocused on the moment—what Rogers was saying, or trying to get away—when, suddenly, the thought had arrived.

The currents seemed to be flowing past her all the time. So how did she make her mind grab onto them?

If Rogers was correct, and people who had this mutation were developing another sense, it was just a question of learning to pay attention to it, of becoming aware of what was always around you.

When you wanted to see something, you had to open your eyes and look at it. When you wanted to smell something, you inhaled through your nose. Touch, taste, hearing—they all had actions associated with them.

What was the action here?

She looked out into the ebony blackness of the night, at the headlights of the rare oncoming car, at the tree trunks that blurred as they passed. She purposefully chased away images of Parker and Cate, because even though she could trust Seb and Deb to keep them safe, thinking about her children still brought worry. And anxiety didn't seem to be consistent with thoughts appearing in her head.

Now and then, she gazed over at Nate, who was taking small sips of coffee to stay alert.

That didn't seem to help either.

Finally she turned her thoughts to Vanslow DeGange again. She wished she had met him at some point. Nate had described him: his large hooked nose, his curly white hair, the puffy mole above his right eyebrow.

She still couldn't properly picture the man. Whenever she thought about him, he was this big blank spot.

Just the man she had to kill.

CHAPTER 47

NATE

We crossed over the bridge that spanned the Rappahannock River, then passed through the speed trap–size town of White Stone.

Maybe a mile later, my GPS told me to turn right. This was the road that would take us toward the tip of this small peninsula that contained the Praesidium's compound at the end.

The night was dark already, and we soon entered this tunnel of trees that had me searching for something higher than high beams, if such a thing existed.

When we came out the other side, we were met by a fogbank, likely telling us we were getting closer to a cool body of water on a warm spring night. I kept driving east until we came to a fork in the road that I remembered from Google Maps. If we chose right, we would soon come to the main gate of Praesidium property.

I turned left.

"Where are you going?" Jenny asked, the first words either of us had spoken in a half hour.

"This road leads to several houses that are on a cove. I was going to find one that looked unoccupied and park there. We cross someone's backyard and we're on the beach. From there, it's a short walk to the Praesidium's place."

"Got it," she said.

We continued in silence for a quarter mile or so. The houses were low and modest until, abruptly, they weren't. To our right there rose a row of McMansions, like some unchecked invasive species. They all fronted a small cove.

"How about that one?" Jenny asked, pointing to a property with a FOR SALE sign on it.

There were no lights on. No cars in sight. No flower boxes, outdoor furniture, or other signs of current habitation. The grass was about two weeks overgrown.

"Perfect," I said, turning into the driveway.

Little in the way of tree cover shielded us from the neighbors, who might wonder why someone was real estate shopping at 12:45 on a Sunday morning. With luck, none of them were awake to notice.

I put the car in park.

"Okay," she said. "Here goes nothing."

"Wait," I said, placing my hand on her arm. "We're going to be careful, right? No cowboy stuff. At the first sign of anything amiss, we run back and hightail it out of here."

"Because there's going to be a better time to do this?" she asked. "Honey, I wouldn't say this is now or never. But since the alternative is sitting around for whatever Rogers comes up with next, I'd rather it be now."

She had a point. And since she had already slid out of her seat and was retrieving the rifle from the back of the SUV, I was assuming she didn't want to sit around and discuss matters further.

I grabbed the silver-plated pistol from the glove compartment and stuffed it in the back waistband of my pants. She was already marching across the lawn, toward the water, with long strides. The rifle was slung across her back.

It took an effort to keep up with her. She reached the edge of the lawn and plunged down to the beach, not breaking stride. Then she angled right, toward the Praesidium compound.

I did the same, and we continued in that position—her in front, me behind, which was how our marriage seemed to work best—as we walked past several more houses on our way around the cove.

The water was millpond flat. Tiny curls of waves, the largest of which was maybe three inches, licked the beach. The tide was going out, and Jenny was walking just above the waterline, where the sand was firmest and she could keep up a good clip without being bogged down by softer sand.

We surely looked odd, a pair of beachcombers out for an after-midnight stroll, but legally there was nothing anyone could do to stop us. There's an important concept in English common law, which was then adopted in US law, that the sea belongs to no man (or no person, if English common law had been a little less chauvinist). That includes the beach, up to the mean high tide mark. We were at least safe from the law there.

Whether we were also safe from other forces remained an open question.

Before long, the last of the houses were behind us. We were now skirting what I knew to be the backside of the Praesidium compound, though there was nothing to mark it as such. It was just beach, a small strip of natural grasses, and then a thick stand of loblolly pines.

There was something primordial about it, this section of shoreline that bled quickly into wilderness. I kept looking through the trees, seeing if I could glimpse one of those houses I had seen from the satellite. But between the woods and the inky darkness of night, there was nothing visible.

We rounded the edge of the cove and were now facing the Chesapeake Bay. The riprap—a pile of white and gray stones that was probably six feet high and ten feet deep—had started. Up ahead I could see where the forest ended and Vanslow DeGange's massive lawn began.

"Jenny," I whispered.

She stopped and waited for me to come closer.

"Let's climb over the rocks here," I said. "No one from the house will be able to see us."

She nodded and began scrambling across them. I followed her. We crunched through the forest for thirty yards or so until we reached its edge.

This was the point of no return. From here, it was just open grass between us and the main house, this hulking black shape. I could barely make out the rooflines, dormers, and chimneys jutting up into the dark-gray sky.

There were no lights on, inside or out. It seemed every bit as uninhabited as that FOR SALE place had been, and I wondered if we were, in fact, storming an empty mansion.

Vanslow DeGange *was* here and not in, say, California, wasn't he?

Jenny had paused behind the last thick tree between us and the clearing. I joined her there.

She was wearing her own jeans and an overlarge black sweatshirt that belonged to Seb. Her hair was up in a ponytail. I could smell the light sweat that had broken out on her. She looked incredibly alive.

This was probably not the most suitable time to be aroused by my wife or be thinking that she was gorgeous, but there it was.

"You're cute, you know that?" I whispered.

"I know it's been a while," she said. "But if you're trying to end our dry spell right now, I have to tell you, I *really* don't think this is the time."

"Come on," I said. "Where's your sense of adventure?"

She grabbed the back of my head and kissed me hard on the mouth. "Later, for sure. I happen to know a nice little bomb shelter."

"Is that thing soundproof?"

She gave me a playful whack on the ass. "Okay, let's focus. That place is huge, and we don't know where DeGange is—first floor? Second floor? When we get over there, we should split up. We'll be able to cover ground more quickly that way."

"But we only have one key card."

"I'll just have to find my own way in."

"And if either of us trips upon an old man with a mole on his forehead we—"

There was no need to complete the thought.

"Exactly," she said. "When you hear a gunshot, that's the sign to hightail it back to the car."

"How will I know you're the one doing the shooting?"

"If I'm not, it means it's coming from someone else, and you should hightail it even faster."

"Good point," I said.

Some plan.

I nodded my head toward the house, which was roughly three hundred yards away. "Okay. You ready?"

"Ready as I'll ever be."

"I think we have to stay low and crawl."

"I was thinking the same thing."

"After you," I said, gesturing toward the lawn.

"Such a gentleman."

She went down on her belly, then started slithering toward the house, commando-style. I let her get a short head start, then went after her.

This grass was short, well manicured, and slick with dew. After a few feet, I was soaked.

Nevertheless, I settled into a rhythm. It was a little bit like swimming, just ten times more arduous. Now and then, I'd lift my head to inspect our progress. The rest of the time, I kept as low a profile as I could.

Thirty yards of progress became sixty, then ninety. We were really out in the open now, passing near the helipad, which was roughly halfway between the forest and the house.

It had no helicopter on it, as had been the case in the satellite photo. The Praesidium must have kept it somewhere else. Either that, or it no longer had the aircraft.

I continued my crawl, staying alert for a warning shout, a flashlight cutting the night, something that would signal we had been spotted.

Nothing came. It remained dark and quiet. Truly, the loudest sound was our labored breathing.

Soon, I was judging the number of yards left to the house, counting backward with each stolen glimpse—seventy to go, fifty to go, and so on.

By the time we reached the semisafety of the side of the house, my arms and legs were shaking and my abdominal muscles were on fire. Jenny flung herself against a section of stone foundation and tilted her head up, straightening her windpipe so she could suck in as much air as possible.

I huddled next to her and caught my breath for a few moments as well.

We were on the north side of the house, with the bay to our east and the rest of the peninsula to the west.

From my Google-based aerial reconnaissance, I knew that the balcony with the Praesidium logo was on the south end. That was where—based on nothing more than a hunch—I thought DeGange's bedroom might be. Didn't it make sense the grand leader's balcony would be decorated with the logo that he loved enough to have branded on human beings?

I wanted this to end as quickly as possible. And maybe I even wanted to be the one to end it. I didn't relish the thought of killing a man. I just wanted to spare Jenny the nastiness.

So, when I finally stopped gasping, I tapped her on the shoulder and whispered into her ear, "I'm going around to the other end and starting on that side."

She gave me a thumbs-up.

I stood up. Now that we were next to the house, it was less vital to stay quite as low. The first-floor windows had enough elevation to them that I could walk in a hunch and still stay beneath the sight line of anyone inside.

Being mindful of the noise I was making, I quietly picked my way around the corner, then across the width of the house. The only fraught portion of the trip was a large patio that required me to go on my belly to stay beneath the brick retaining wall that fronted it.

I had just crossed that obstacle when I started to hear this rhythmic thumping coming from the sky in the distance. This was not anything like the buzzy whine of the drone I had heard earlier. It was deeper, more resonant.

A helicopter.

I looked up, peering into the underside of the clouds, hoping to be able to see something. The Doppler effect told me it was getting closer. But was it definitely coming here? Maybe it was just a coincidence—some other rich person's helicopter.

That thought abruptly ended when seemingly every light on the property came on at once.

For a moment, I was stunned, stupefied. I stood there, shielding my eyes, a dumbstruck deer in the blinding brilliance of all those headlights.

When my senses returned, I threw myself next to the house, under a window, making myself as small as I could.

But I was still terribly exposed. Between the landing lights on the helipad and the floodlights from the house, most of the yard was lit up, almost like daytime. The black clothes I was wearing were like anti-camouflage against the off-white siding of the house and the matching foundation. Anyone walking outside would easily be able to see me.

My heart was pounding almost as hard as the helicopter rotors that were fast approaching.

When I looked up this time, a dot of light had emerged from the clouds. I watched the dot grow larger until I could see the aircraft itself. It was a decent size, with a rounded prow made almost entirely of clear plastic, such that it reminded me of the eye of a housefly. If I had to guess, I'd say it sat roughly eight, in addition to the two pilots.

It came from above the water to my right. As it passed overhead, I could feel the thump of the rotors with my body. I feared that if anyone was looking down, they would easily see the man pinned against the side of the house.

The vessel hovered for a moment, its light swiveling downward to further illuminate the landing area. Then, slowly, majestically, it descended, staying perfectly level until its skids kissed the ground.

Almost immediately, the pilot cut the rotors, which began slowing but still had a lot of momentum to disperse. The door on the side of the chopper opened.

A man dressed in black tactical gear stepped out first, followed by another. They stood to the left side of the door and helped out the next passenger.

Rogers. He was wearing khakis and a blue windbreaker. No military-style garb for him.

From inside the helicopter, someone handed him something, which he then passed to one of the men next to him. I couldn't see what the package was, because of the distance involved, and because his back was shielding it. He received another item, which he handed to the other man in front of him.

Then the three of them turned and started walking toward the house.

In a nauseating instant, I saw they weren't transporting items or packages.

They were carrying children.

CHAPTER 48

JENNY

Something went blank in Jenny's mind the moment she saw her girls being toted across the lawn like so much luggage.

It was probably because of their little faces. The floodlights from the house were bright enough that Jenny had no problem making out their expressions.

The shock.

The fear.

The panic.

Cate had her mouth open and her eyes pinched. Jenny couldn't hear her younger daughter's wails over the sound of the helicopter, but the little girl was in obvious distress. She didn't know where she was or what was happening, just that it terrified her. Jenny could feel the anguish in that visceral place where parents experienced their children's pain.

Parker was, in some ways, even more difficult to look at. Her face registered something that was worse than confusion: comprehension. She was three. She *knew* this wasn't her house, and that these men were not nice, and that her mommy and daddy—who should have been with her—were nowhere around, and that she and her sister were in terrible danger.

Save me, her eyes seemed to be saying. *Someone please save me.*

Jenny didn't used to believe in maternal instincts. She'd thought it was a cultural myth, created by the patriarchy to keep women in their place.

Then she had two babies and it was like she had grown a third arm, one that was forever groping for her children. It was a need that was deeply physical, and it compelled her to hold her children, to breathe them in, to feel their skin, to nurture them in every way. Those girls might have left her womb, but they never stopped being a part of her.

As such, any thought of self-preservation or caution was gone.

Nothing mattered more than the safety of Parker and Cate—not herself, not killing Vanslow DeGange, not the safety of her husband.

And this was the moment. Once the men took the girls into the house, they would only become more difficult to rescue.

Unslinging her rifle from her back, she raised it until she had it firmly anchored against her shoulder. Jenny was a fine shot. Her father had taught her how to hunt, how to handle a firearm. She had taken down animals from a much longer distance than this.

If she fired from her current hiding spot against the house, she could probably eliminate both men before they even knew where the shots were coming from. But the moment that thought formed, so did a competing one.

The girls.

It was one thing to fell a deer from a blind in the woods of Surry County, when your heart rate was down, your arms were fresh, and there was no real pressure on the shot.

Shooting a man—while her heart was still pounding, while her body was still recovering from a three-hundred-yard crawl, while her nervous system was going haywire—was something else entirely.

Both men were carrying the girls against their bodies, so she couldn't simply aim for center mass. She would need to go for a head shot, a smaller target. Plus, she didn't know how much of a factor the turbulence from the helicopter would be. The rotor wash would push the bullet down, but by how much?

She didn't dare pull the trigger. Instead, she waited until the group was about halfway across the lawn. Then she emerged from the shadow of the house with one eye in the scope and the other on the men.

"Freeze!" she shouted. "Don't move!"

The lead man, the one with Cate, actually startled before coming to an immediate stop. The other man, who was a few steps behind with Parker, also halted his progress.

Jenny walked a few more steps toward them. She was roughly sixty feet away. It felt like the right distance—close enough that she could control the situation, not so close that they would be able to make a move on her.

"Put them down," Jenny barked. "Put them down or by God I'm planting a bullet in your forehead."

Neither man had yet made a move when Rogers shouted, "No, lift them up. Use them as shields."

The men immediately complied, holding the girls out in front. Parker was squirming ineffectually. Cate might as well have been a sack of flour.

Jenny kept her rifle up but knew she couldn't possibly use it.

"You're a monster, you know that?" she yelled.

"I'm doing what I have to do. The bomb shelter was a good thought, by the way. Too bad it had vents that lit up like Christmas trees when we looked at the house with the night vision goggles. Led us right to them."

"Go to hell."

"Your parents are fine, by the way. Or I'm sure they will be once someone finds them. There was no room to bring them on the helicopter, so we had to tie them up."

Rogers was still behind his men, keeping both them and Jenny's children between himself and the angry woman with the rifle.

"Now," he said. "Put down your gun and come inside. Your children are staying here, just like you're staying here. This is your family's new home. Where's Nate?"

"He's not here."

"I'm sure that's not true," Rogers said. "But we'll find him soon enough. Now put the gun down."

Jenny didn't move. She also didn't know how to end this stalemate.

Rogers did. He partially unzipped his windbreaker, dipped his hand inside, and brought out a pistol, which he promptly held to Parker's temple.

"No!" Jenny screamed.

In the act of bringing the gun to the child's head, Rogers had exposed himself, just slightly, enough that she could take the shot. The helicopter was still making a lot of noise, but the downdraft from the rotors was dying off quickly. From sixty feet, with a scope, she could aim just above his ear and maintain every confidence a bullet would wind up there.

She moved the rifle, centered the crosshairs on that neatly parted, gunmetal-gray coiffure, and—

Got tackled from behind, by a man she neither saw nor heard coming.

The man's shoulder plowed squarely into Jenny's back. Her arms reflexively flew outward, to break her fall, and she lost the grip on her rifle, which sailed out of her hands.

Whatever air had been in Jenny's lungs was almost entirely displaced when the man landed on top of her, and she heard herself grunt as she was driven into the wet ground.

The guy outweighed Jenny by at least seventy pounds, and she could feel the hardness of his chest and arms wrapped around her. She tried to get her legs and arms underneath her, so she could buck him off.

But another man was just behind the first. When he arrived, he sat on her legs, depriving her of whatever leverage she might have been able to gain. Jenny grunted and strained, pouring all her strength into her attempts to free herself.

All of which were futile.

Before very long, the first two assailants were joined by another pair. They had her hands cuffed behind her back and were carrying her—still thrashing uselessly—into the house.

CHAPTER 49

NATE

I watched the confrontation unfold from behind a planter at the edge of the patio, which was as close as I dared get.

It all happened so quickly. I wasn't frozen as much as I was uncertain. I couldn't hear what was being shouted back and forth, and I didn't want to throw Jenny off. She seemed to have the situation under control.

And then she didn't. When I saw the man sprinting up behind Jenny, I tried to warn her. But neither she nor anyone else could hear my shouts above the still-spinning helicopter rotors, just as she had been unable to hear that man's footsteps on the soft grass.

Then it was effectively over. Emerging from my hiding spot would only make matters worse. I was badly outgunned and outnumbered. In addition to Rogers and the two men who had already climbed out of the helicopter, two more men and two women had followed, plus a pair of pilots. There were also the two men who'd tackled Jenny. And who knew how many more people in the house.

Charging out to confront them would have been reckless, foolish, and, more than anything, pointless.

We had lost this battle.

I had to focus on the war. Nothing that had just happened changed my immediate goal:

Find Vanslow DeGange.

And kill him.

The job had gotten harder, since the Praesidium would no doubt be hunting for me. But at least for the next few minutes, I could take advantage of the diversion Jenny and my daughters were creating as everyone figured out what to do about them.

Once the last of the passengers had come in from the helicopter, I backed away from the planter and crept toward the side of the house with the Praesidium-logoed balcony.

I went up on my toes for a glimpse into a window nearest the corner of the house. It was a lovely sunroom, probably a place Praesidium members enjoyed in the wintertime.

But it didn't look like anywhere DeGange would be hanging out at this hour. I had to get to that balcony somehow.

It required only a few seconds of study before I spotted my best— and probably only—way up. Running from the ground to the second floor on the side of the house was a trellis covered in blooming growth that did not appear to be roses or anything else forbiddingly prickly.

The only question was whether it was sturdy enough to support two hundred pounds. I strode over to it and plunged my hand through about fifteen inches of greenery until I found the latticework underneath.

I gave it a quick shake. It didn't seem to be going anywhere, so I reached for a spot above my head with both hands, grabbed on, and hoisted myself up. I had to dig around with my feet to find footholds, but soon I had purchase there too.

It was not the quietest work, what with the tearing of vegetation required to find each new portion of the trellis. But there seemed to be no one outside to hear it. One foot and one hand at a time, I made short work of the climb and was soon vaulting over the banister and onto the tile balcony.

I crawled over to the side of the house and tried to look inside, but the windows were covered with vinyl. Just like the room I had been held in the first time I was here.

Then I confronted the door. Which was, of course, locked.

This was the moment when I'd discover whether that key card I'd swiped was more than just a worthless piece of plastic that the Praesidium had deactivated the moment it was discovered missing—or that had never opened certain doors to begin with.

Holding my breath, I touched the card to the small pad on the left side of the door.

I was immediately rewarded with the grinding of a mechanical lock unclenching itself.

Like that, I was inside. But, immediately, I was disappointed. The PR porch had not, as I hoped, led to Vanslow DeGange's sleeping quarters. It was the Rembrandt room.

Perhaps DeGange was in the next bedroom. Or the one after that. I would just have to keep looking until I found him.

I closed the door behind myself. Then, with barely a glimpse at the multimillion-dollar wall hangings, I crossed the room and stopped at the door that, as I'd learned during my last visit, led to the second-floor hallway. I listened for a moment.

All was quiet. I held my key card against the reader, and again it worked perfectly, disengaging the lock. Then I slowly eased the door open and peered around the edge.

The lights were on. And there was a man at the top of the stairs, at the midpoint of a long hallway.

Rogers.

He was looking down the stairs and seemed to be directing some kind of effort coming up from below, but I closed the door before I even had a chance to hear or see what he was up to.

I needed a place to hide. Quickly. I looked around at the room. In the middle was that four-poster bed. It was supported by a platform, so

I couldn't simply slide underneath it. There were also no closets to sneak into. Older houses simply didn't seem to believe in those.

My only option was the en suite bathroom. It wasn't perfect. But it would have to do.

I closed the door behind me and flicked up the light switch. The bathroom had a modern feel, having been redone within the last decade or so. There was a generous vanity with a mirror running the length of it. On the far side of the room was a large walk-in shower behind a glass door and a glass wall.

Again, there was no closet. The linens were stacked on a stand-alone wire shelf.

In other words, there was nothing to give me cover. If someone came in here, I would be spotted as soon as they turned the light on.

With that in mind, I depressed the light switch, plunging myself into darkness.

For better or worse, this was where I was going to be for a little while.

I checked the time on my phone. It was 1:22 a.m. I decided I would risk a glimpse into the hallway every twenty minutes. As soon as the second check was clear, I'd enter the hallway and try the next room down.

Not knowing where else to go, I felt around in the dark until I found the toilet, then sat on the lid. It was as good a place as any to spend the next twenty minutes.

Except it turned out I didn't get nearly that much time. There were voices coming my way. I could hear them coming down the hallway, even if I couldn't make out the words.

Then someone entered the Rembrandt room.

"Watch her head, watch her head," a man's voice said.

"It would help if she'd stop thrashing," another said.

"Stop thrashing," the first one said.

As I pulled my gun out from the waistband of my pants, I heard Jenny swear at the guy.

She was still fighting them with everything she had.

My beautifully stubborn wife.

"You're just making it harder," Rogers said with that preternatural calm I had come to recognize so well.

This must have been what Rogers was directing from the top of the stairs: the transportation of my wife into the room where he obviously liked to keep his prisoners.

Jenny replied to him with another curse, followed by some indistinct vocalizing.

"Ouch," the first one said, apropos of what, I couldn't tell.

"Just throw her on the bed and then make sure she stays there," Rogers said. "I'm going to get some more rope."

This was met with perhaps ten seconds of silence as, presumably, they tossed Jenny atop the four-poster's mattress.

"You got her?" one man asked.

"Yeah," the other said.

My wish-upon-a-star now was that they'd tie up Jenny and leave her there, unaware of just how close I was. I could untie her and—

That thought was quickly obliterated and replaced by a rush of dread when the first man declared: "All right. I gotta take a leak."

I stood and took two silent steps toward the wall in front of me, then turned and put my back against it.

Out in the Rembrandt room, the old hardwood floors groaned as the man clomped my way.

The door to the bathroom opened, letting in a sliver of light. I saw a hand groping for the light switch, then the arm and body attached to that hand.

Finally, the bathroom lit up. My visitor was wearing the black tactical gear the Praesidium seemed to favor for its operatives. He was a few inches shorter than me, though at least thirty pounds heavier, with a lot of gym muscles to weigh him down.

His head was still bent in the general direction of the switch, and as he straightened, he saw me—with the gun raised and the barrel pointed at the hairless patch between his eyebrows.

The surprise on his face was complete. His jaw opened slightly but no words came out of his mouth.

"Don't move," I said, calmly, in a normal speaking voice.

He hadn't really been moving much, but he stopped anyway. Only his eyes continued. They were darting back and forth between me and the gun I was holding, like he was trying to figure out if he could reach either. We both knew he'd have the advantage if this turned into a wrestling match.

I had no intention of letting that happen.

"Turn around," I said.

He did as he was told.

"Lace your fingers behind your head."

Again, he complied.

I grabbed the back of his shirt with one hand and, with the other, held the barrel of the gun to the soft indent at the base of his skull.

"What's your name?"

"Bobby," he said.

"Okay, Bobby. Tell your friend out there what I'm doing," I said.

"Tino, he's got a gun to my head," the guy said.

"Very good, Bobby," I said, then called a little louder: "Tino, we're about to come out. You're going to get on the other side of the room. I better not see you holding a weapon or your friend here is really not going to like it. Do you understand?"

Tino said, "Yes, sir."

"I'm going to want to see your palms facing me, and your arms out in front of you. Got it?"

"Yes, sir," he said again.

Gripping Bobby's shirt tighter, I turned him toward the door, then gathered myself close behind him, so his body would be between me and the rest of the room.

"Okay," I said. "Nice and slow now. Let's see some little baby steps."

He was a good soldier, shuffling his feet forward. Slowly, we entered the room. My eyes quickly darted to Jenny.

She was on her feet, having removed herself from the bed because Tino was now too otherwise occupied to keep her there. Her hands were still cuffed behind her. Her legs had been bound together at the ankles. Her hair was disheveled and her face was a mess of grime and grass, but she seemed to have plenty of fight in her.

Tino was in front of the open door on the far side of the room, near a narrow table and chair that had been set up in front of a mirror.

I had just steered Bobby fully out of the bathroom when Rogers came back down the hall. He was still wearing his windbreaker. He had a length of rope in one hand and a gun in the other.

Tino moved to the side to make way for Rogers to enter the room.

"Oh, Nate," he said, like he was disappointed.

"Don't move," I said.

I crouched a little lower behind Bobby, thankful for the man's width.

Rogers scowled.

"You really think I care about him?" he asked.

And then, quite casually, he lifted the gun and fired twice.

I yelped in terror and reflexively threw myself to the floor, rolling behind the bed, near Jenny's feet. She had screamed as well.

The moment I'd let go of him, Bobby had dropped like his skeleton had turned to jelly. He landed with a heavy thud. His catastrophically ruined forehead was turned so we could see it. If there was any life left in him, it was fast departing.

My face was wet with blood. Not mine. Or at least I didn't think so.

I scrambled a little closer to the bed, which was now the only cover I had.

Tino yelped, "What the—"

"Shut up," Rogers said.

Then he fired again.

Tino let out a brief howl. The next noise was his body crashing into the table on the far side of the room.

Then came the sound of footsteps. Rogers was on the move. But not in my direction. He was moving away now. He had seen my gun. And now that it was no longer trained on Bobby, Rogers knew I would likely point it at him next. He wasn't that foolhardy.

"I found him," Rogers shouted. "He's in the Rembrandt room. He just shot Bobby and Tino. I'll keep him contained in here. Get some men around the house in case he tries to go out the window. If you have a clear shot on him, take it."

It sounded like he was in the hallway, just to the side of the door.

"Okay, Nate, enough games now," Rogers said. "We're about to have you surrounded. And if you keep your gun with you, I promise someone is going to take you out. But if you put down your gun right now, I promise you won't get hurt. You, Jenny, your girls, you'll all be fine. Better than fine."

It was clearly a lie, just like so many of the other things he had said to me. I didn't bother answering him. He was probably just trying to bait me into talking so he could start shooting at the sound of my voice.

I briefly took stock of the situation. I was armed. Rogers was armed. I was hiding behind the platform bed, which wasn't exactly bulletproof if someone really started blasting away at it, but it would at least shield me somewhat from light arms fire. Rogers was behind a wall.

It was possible I could shoot him through the wall, but then what? Even if the bullets did penetrate whatever they'd made walls out of a hundred years ago, they might not have enough velocity left to kill him.

More to the point, killing Rogers would only improve my situation so much. The property still contained an untold number of Praesidium members, more than I could possibly gun down.

"Come on, Nate, think it through for a moment. You have to realize there's no escape. We've got more manpower. We've certainly got more bullets. Just surrender already," Rogers said, almost like he was reading my thoughts.

"Rogers, why are you doing this?" Jenny yelled. "I've told you, I'm never going to come work for you."

"That doesn't matter," Rogers said. "What matters is that you're staying here."

What did *that* mean?

How could it not matter?

Wasn't that what this was all about? His offer from two months ago. His attempts to get Jenny to kill me. His kidnapping of the children. Wasn't it all aimed at convincing, cajoling, or blackmailing Jenny into being part of the Praesidium?

This had to be another lie.

Though he was telling the truth about one thing: there was no escape. I was penned in. Trapped.

Unless . . .

The thought came to me suddenly. It was dangerous, for sure. And totally insane in any measurable way. Though I was suddenly convinced it would actually work.

Rogers had proven himself to be ruthless, willing to murder indiscriminately to get what he wanted.

But there was one person he absolutely wouldn't kill.

Jenny.

I looked up at her.

"I'm sorry for this," I said softly. "Just go with it."

She tilted her head at me.

Then I stood up and placed myself behind Jenny.

With the gun at her head.

"Drop your weapon, Rogers," I said. "Or I swear, I'll kill her."

"What are you talking about?" Rogers said.

"*Drop. Your damn. Gun.* All of you are going to drop your guns. And then you're going to get the girls, and then the four of us are walking out of here."

"Nate," he said calmly, "we both know you're incapable of shooting her. You've already proven that."

"You're right. I might be bluffing. You really want to find out? You and I both know you've scoured the world looking for someone with the gift and she's the only one you've been able to find. Are you really going to risk her life? I'm willing to bet you're not."

Rogers hadn't shown so much as one inch of himself from behind the door.

But suddenly, at the top of the stairs, there was a figure, an old man with a tumble of curly white hair that a bedhead had styled in various directions. He was not tall, but he stood like he was, erect and proud even after all the years and all the gravity.

It was Vanslow DeGange. Even if Rogers hadn't shown me his picture, I would have recognized him by his commanding presence.

He wore vintage, button-up pajamas that hung off his bony frame. His hands were knobby. His feet were bare. He turned down the hall and started ambling toward us, moving reasonably well for a man midway through his nineties.

Despite the recent gunfire, he seemed to be totally unheeding of his own safety. In his right hand, which hung loosely by his side, he held a gun, a silver-plated pistol, just like the one in mine.

I was sure it had also been stamped with the **WHITE CHUCK NO. 8** oval.

When he got within about thirty feet of me, I could make out the mole on his forehead. I made it my new target as I swiveled my gun away from Jenny.

But he just kept walking toward me, like being able to sense death had guaranteed him immortality.

In another few steps, he would be close enough that even I couldn't miss. I planned to put several shots into him, hoping that when the Praesidium members learned their leader was gone, they would decide to quit with all the killing.

Cut the head off the snake and the body dies, right?

I took in a deep breath, felt the hardness of the trigger, and prepared to squeeze.

Then, to my utter shock, Jenny threw herself at my arms, blurting, "No, Nate. Don't shoot him. Don't do it."

I couldn't have if I'd wanted to. Jenny's entire weight fell into me. It was all I could do to keep her from crashing onto the floor.

And, truly, I was flummoxed. Why was Jenny suddenly protecting this singular menace? Why didn't she want to finish what we'd come here to accomplish? What was going through my brilliant wife's head?

DeGange had stopped just short of the door.

"Lorton," he bellowed. "What the devil is going on here?"

CHAPTER 50

JENNY

The first emotion Jenny experienced upon seeing Vanslow DeGange was profound loathing.

This was the man who wanted her to kill her husband.

The man who seemed to have no misgivings about ordering the murder of strangers when it served his purpose.

The man who'd had her daughters kidnapped simply so he could use them as chess pieces.

And then DeGange drew closer, and she felt this uncertainty coming over her. There was no animosity coming from him. He was just this old guy, all loose skin and thinning bones, shambling along barefoot in his pajamas.

There was death surrounding him, yes; it came off him in waves as strong as anything Jenny had ever felt.

But it wasn't Nate's death.

Or her death.

Or the girls'. Or her parents'.

The nearer he drew, the more sure of this she became.

Sure enough that she hurtled herself into Nate, knocking him off balance, almost taking both of them down. This ended with Nate embracing her awkwardly, which was where they still were when DeGange reached the doorway and began surveying the scene.

Jenny still did not detect any threat in his bearing, just a cool intelligence at work. He scanned the bedroom; then his face drew into a scowl as he glanced down and to his left, toward where Rogers was hiding.

And Rogers was, as usual, the first to start talking.

"Everything is fine, Mr. DeGange," he said, a little desperately. "Just a misunderstanding with our guests here. I'll get it sorted out. You can go back to sleep."

"I'll be spending too much time sleeping soon enough, thank you very much," DeGange replied gruffly.

Jenny kept her focus on DeGange, curious as to what his next move would be. He leaned into the room and soaked up the sight of the two Praesidium men, Bobby and Tino, now lifeless.

She could almost see DeGange's mind doing the calculations. You didn't need to be a crime scene expert to tell that, contrary to what Rogers had so loudly claimed, Nate hadn't been the one to shoot them. Not from where he was standing. Not given where the bullet holes were and where the bodies had ended up.

The killing shots had clearly come from Rogers' direction.

And now DeGange's scowl was firmly fixed on his employee.

"Lorton," DeGange said. "Are you responsible for this?"

Rogers had no response.

DeGange looked back into the room. Jenny saw his gaze fall on her for the first time. He openly gawked for a moment; then his head tilted with curiosity.

"You're Jenny Welker, aren't you?" he said, like it both pleased and startled him.

Jenny noted the change in DeGange's voice now that he was addressing her. It was warm. Caring. Like he was speaking to a dear friend, even though they'd never met.

"Yes, sir," she said.

He turned toward Rogers. "What's she tied up for?"

DeGange's sharp tone had returned. So had his disapproving demeanor.

"I told you, it's just a misunderstanding," Rogers said. "She thinks I'm going to harm her husband and I keep trying to explain to her that they have nothing to fear and that they will be treated very, very well here. Everything is going to be fine."

"It doesn't look fine."

"I just need to talk some sense into them."

"You need to talk less, Lorton," DeGange said.

"Sir, this is all—"

"Shut it, Lorton," DeGange snapped, then turned back toward Jenny, a gracious smile spreading across his lined face.

"Ms. Welker, I'm Vanslow DeGange. This is my house. I wish we could be meeting under different circumstances. Strange as it sounds, I feel like I know you already. I've been seeing you in my thoughts for a long time now."

Jenny nodded. Her throat constricted slightly.

There was still death everywhere around him.

But she had finally figured out whose it was.

"I'm starting to feel the same way, sir," she said. "I just now had a thought about you."

"You saw me dying, didn't you," he said, his smile never leaving him.

There was no self-pity in his tone. At least not that Jenny could detect. He genuinely seemed to be more concerned for Jenny than he was for himself.

"Yes, sir," she said. "I'm terribly sorry."

"I'm not. It's about damn time, if you ask me. But enough about that for a moment. Can you explain what's going on here? Pretend like I don't know anything."

"I'm not sure where to start," Jenny said.

"Okay, then start with this: Are you here under some kind of duress?"

He struck Jenny as the kind of wise person who would ask a question even though he already knew the answer—just because he didn't want to make the mistake of being too sure of himself.

"Yes, sir, I am," she said.

"She's confused, Mr. DeGange," Rogers pleaded. "If you'll just please let me—"

"I said shut it, Lorton!" DeGange roared. "Now, Ms. Welker, I'm sorry. Has Lorton here been threatening you in some way?"

"Yes, sir. Rogers tried to get me to kill my husband. Then, when he failed at that, he kidnapped my children from my parents' house and—"

"Kidnapped!"

DeGange looked sharply down toward his left, where Rogers was still cowering out of Jenny's line of vision.

But she didn't need to see him to know what was going to happen next. The thought arrived in her head almost simultaneously with the wave of nausea it caused.

"Mr. DeGange, it's not like that," Rogers was mewling. "If you'll just let me—"

"No, sir, don't!" Jenny yelled.

It was too late. In one startlingly fast movement, DeGange raised the gun and fired four times in Rogers' direction.

The gunshots were deafening. The sounds echoed through the house, though they were soon replaced by a silence that, to Jenny, seemed every bit as loud.

She couldn't see where the bullets hit. She didn't really want or need to. From that distance, the first bullet would have been more than enough to put Rogers down. The final three ensured he didn't get back up.

DeGange was still focused on Rogers—or what was left of him—in a way that seemed particularly unguarded, allowing Jenny a few heartbeats of time in which to study the old man candidly. He didn't take any pleasure in killing. That was quite clear. His mouth was clenched in an odd sort of way, drawn up toward his cheeks, though not in a smile. He seemed to be struggling with something.

Then she watched a solitary tear form in DeGange's right eye and track briefly down his cheek before he wiped it away.

It struck Jenny that Vanslow DeGange had long ago made the selfless decision to dedicate himself, his talents, and his fortune to saving the lives of others.

And yet it had resulted in a long life during which he was constantly surrounded by death.

Which was probably a lot of what made him so keenly look forward to his own.

DeGange broke the silence by clearing his throat.

"I wish you didn't have to see that," he said, his voice having gone slightly hoarse. "I always have had something of a blind spot when it came to the members of my little group, particularly Lorton. I trusted him. But it's now clear to me he's been abusing that trust. He violated the oath he had taken. And there's only one punishment for people who violate the oath."

DeGange sighed noisily and tossed the pistol to the side.

"And I'm sorry this seems to have involved you and your husband to the extent it has," he said, strolling into the room. "I didn't know exactly what Lorton was up to. But I'm afraid I'm still the one to blame."

Jenny became aware of Nate tensing, still unsure of whether to allow DeGange any closer, even though the old man was now unarmed.

She reached out and gently seized Nate's wrist, lowering his gunsights until they were trained on the floor.

"It's okay, honey," she said. "We're safe now."

Nate didn't say anything. He also didn't fight her.

"I feel like I owe you both an explanation," DeGange said. "But first, let's get all this junk off you and go someplace we can chat."

At DeGange's orders, one of the men who had tackled Jenny earlier appeared with a handcuff key and unlocked her hands, while another untied her ankles.

She could already feel the places that would turn into bruises later. Her muscles were starting to stiffen. And there was only so much longer she could stave off the utter exhaustion.

But Jenny knew she had been fortunate. For all Rogers' malice, the Praesidium had not done her any lasting harm.

As DeGange arranged for "the cleanup"—as he so euphemistically put it—Jenny and Nate stole off to check on the girls.

Both were still confused and agitated. But seeing Mommy and Daddy settled them down considerably. Jenny and Nate got them properly situated for sleep, with Parker in a canopy bed that she said made her feel like a princess; and Cate, who was still in a crib at home, on a king mattress they had dragged onto the floor, lest she roll off.

Seeing them doze off, with her husband at her side, set Jenny at peace in some deep place. There was still so much uncertainty about what she would do with this gift of hers, about how it would or wouldn't evolve as she became more sensitive to it, about how she'd live with the knowledge of it.

But as long as she had Nate and the girls, she really felt like she could deal with whatever happened. There was nothing quite like almost losing them to sharpen her focus on what really mattered.

Her family. The people she loved most.

Wasn't that what life was ultimately all about?

Before too much longer, she and Nate had joined DeGange in his study. There, he invited them to take a seat.

"Are your little ones comfortable?" he asked.

"Yes, thank you," Jenny said.

He smiled amiably; then his face took on a more serious cast.

"I told you earlier I'm the one to blame, and I am," he said. "As you know, I'm dying. Well, we're all dying. It's just a question of when. But unlike everyone else, I know exactly when it's going to happen. And I'm guessing you do as well?"

Jenny did. She had watched it happen.

"This Friday," she said. "A little after two in the morning."

"That's right. Very good. I stopped taking my blood pressure medicine a while back, so this is overdue if you ask me. It looks to me like a massive stroke, which I'll suffer in my sleep. I doubt I'll feel a thing. Pretty good way to go, don't you think?"

Jenny didn't answer. For whatever DeGange's thoughts about it, she couldn't help but feel a sense of tragedy about this incredible light being snuffed out.

"Sorry," DeGange added. "That was macabre. When you get to be my age, you stop worrying so much about dying and start worrying about having a good death instead."

He shook his head, then continued: "Anyhow, I didn't want a little thing like my death to disturb anything too much, and I was trying to get my affairs in order. You see, I have no heirs."

Jenny looked at him uncertainly. "Why does that matter?"

"To decent folks like you and your husband, it probably doesn't," DeGange said. "To Lorton Rogers? It mattered a lot. Life has been pretty fair to me, as you can probably tell, and now I'm worth a good little bit of money."

He said this like he hadn't really been deserving of it, and therefore it embarrassed him. Jenny understood. She sometimes felt that way about her own salary.

"You don't have to apologize for being well off," she said.

"Well, maybe, maybe not," DeGange said. "But I certainly have other things to apologize for. I had put Lorton in charge of the day-to-day around here. I'm too old and tired most of the time to be bothered. He knew I was going to be dying soon, and I may have inadvertently created an incentive for Rogers to do exactly what he did."

"How so?" Nate asked.

"Long ago, I arranged two contingencies for when I died. In one, if my replacement had been identified—someone like your wife, who could sense the currents—the bulk of my fortune would be dedicated to creating a foundation whose mandate was to continue the work of the Praesidium, hopefully in perpetuity. My will dictated that Lorton would be the executive director of that foundation. He would have been reporting to a board of directors, of course, but he would still have had enormous authority to use my fortune as he saw fit.

"If, on the other hand, the Praesidium hadn't identified my replacement, all the money was to be given away. And not by some foundation that slowly got sucked dry. I wanted to go out with a bang. Everything you see around you and a whole lot you don't see would have been sold. All of the proceeds would have been distributed to disadvantaged Romani all around the world, folks who really needed it."

"And Rogers would have gotten nothing," Jenny said.

"I assure you, he would have been fine. Like all members of the Praesidium, he had been receiving a generous stipend. He should have had enough saved up to live comfortably for the rest of his life. Just not quite *this* comfortably. Obviously, Rogers didn't want to give that up. He wanted access to the money, the houses, the helicopters. He wanted it all to continue just as it was."

Jenny still felt confused. "But I never agreed to be the Praesidium's new leader. How would the clause have been triggered with me being held captive?"

"That's why I said this was all my fault," DeGange said. "The way the will is written, if someone who can sense the currents has taken up residence with the Praesidium at the time of my death, then the foundation is created. I should have probably figured out a more clever way to word it. I just thought that would be the most cut-and-dried way to delineate whether someone was really one of us."

Jenny finally understood Rogers' desperation—why, even when she'd told him she wasn't going to work for the Praesidium, he had persisted in his course of action.

That doesn't matter. What matters is that you're staying here.

Rogers was like a corrupted politician. Having grown addicted to the taste of his own influence—and to the trappings that came with it—he would do anything to stay in power.

"And with Rogers gone, what happens now?" Jenny asked.

"Nothing changes, actually," DeGange said. "If you would like to move here with your family and continue the work of the Praesidium, you are welcome to do so. If that's not the path you want for your life, I understand that too.

"The choice, my dear, is yours."

EPILOGUE

NATE

It was an immutable and ever-present fact of stay-at-home caregiving, one I had come to learn altogether too well:

The world could have its spasms and crises. Empires could rise, leaders could fall, the course of history could change, and it could all affect me mentally in whatever profound way it wanted to. Yet to some extent it wouldn't change my life that much. First and foremost, I still had two little girls to take care of.

And so, two days after the drama in White Stone, I was back in Richmond, catching up on dishes while the girls ate dinner, waiting for Jenny to get home.

Embracing that timeworn cliché, we were taking life one day at a time, trying not to make any firm decisions about our future just yet.

Jenny had spent most of Sunday and Monday deep in conference with Vanslow DeGange, downloading the sum of his wisdom, making the most of what little time he had left. During one of our brief conversations, I asked Jenny whether DeGange could be convinced to resume his medicine or consider some other intervention that might prolong his life.

She said he had no interest in that. He was ready to go.

Beyond that, I really hadn't seen her much. What little time she was taking away from DeGange's company, she was trying to spend with the girls.

In the meantime, other matters were slowly being settled.

The Richmond police had been notified about the murders that took place at our house. The Praesidium—which had cameras trained on both our front and back porches—had footage of the event. But the killers were now dead, victims of that tragic run-in with the train. And Lorton Rogers, the person who'd ordered the killing, was missing. Or at least that's what the authorities believed. The Praesidium had seen to it he would never be found.

So on the criminal side, there was really nothing more to worry about.

On the civil side, one of DeGange's lawyers had already reached out to the families of the slain bodyguards with a more-than-generous offer, far more than what they would have received in the cold calculations of a wrongful death suit.

Jenny and I had only briefly discussed the trauma we felt over those innocent lives lost. I sensed it wouldn't be the last time we had that conversation. Grief could be like that, I supposed. If it struck all at once, we'd probably be too incapacitated to deal with it. So it meted itself out slowly, to be dealt with in smaller—though still painful—doses over a longer time period.

The fact was, in one way or another, we would be living with the fallout of this past week for the rest of our lives.

In the shorter term, I had already begun taking care of some of the messes I had helped create. That began with calling Heather Matthews and apologizing for my bizarre visit. Without explaining the full circumstances, I told her I had been wildly wrong about a suspicion of mine. I think I at least convinced her I wasn't an ongoing threat.

Then I reached out to Buck McBride's family, eventually speaking to his brother—his real brother, not the fictional one I had made up. I told him about the conversation Buck and I had shared, then asked if he wanted to see the video the hospital had sent me. He declined.

The family was, of course, devastated by Buck's passing—particularly Buck's mother. But it was also coming around to accepting it. While cleaning out Buck's room, hospital staff had found a note in which he admitted he had been contemplating suicide for some time. He wrote he was mostly just searching for peace.

I truly hope he found it.

As for the Welker Lovejoys, we returned to our house in Richmond on Monday evening. Whoever the Praesidium had hired to clean it had done a remarkable job. There was no sign of Friday night's bloodbath.

On Tuesday morning—this morning—Jenny had gone to work at the normal time. And the girls and I had also done our usual thing: the park, the coffee shop, and the grocery store, all bracketed around the inviolable sanctity of nap time.

No one came up on my back porch to drug and kidnap me. No one tried to make me kill my wife. No one made predictions about the future—not about this Tuesday, or next Tuesday, or any other Tuesday, for that matter.

I never thought I'd be so grateful for a boring day with the girls.

Parker had just asked for more strawberries—which I was dutifully cutting for her—when I saw Jenny walk through the back gate.

As soon as she opened the door into the kitchen, the girls cheered her arrival.

She kissed them first. Then it was my turn. I shut off the sink, dried my hands, and turned toward her so I could get a hug out of the deal as well.

"You're early," I said. "How was work?"

"Busy. Super busy. But good busy."

"How so?"

"I had a meeting with Commonwealth Power and Light's chief counsel and, without divulging my source, showed her the documents Greg Grichtmeier leaked to me."

"Oh my. How'd that go?"

"She handled herself pretty well, actually. After taking a little time to digest it, she excused herself and went immediately to J. Hunter Matthews' office."

"Wow," I said.

"When she came back, she said CP and L was willing to consider admitting wrongdoing and settling."

"That's . . . incredible."

"Well, not so incredible when you think about it from her perspective. She pretty clearly wants to keep this as far from a courtroom and from the public eye as possible. I think she also has her eye on the criminal provisions in the Clean Air Act. The feds could start tossing people in jail over this, and I think she wants to keep her ass covered and her boss's ass covered if it goes that way. She swore up and down neither she nor Matthews knew the Shockoe plant was out of compliance."

"Do you believe her?"

"I believe that's her only safe position. The fact is, I handed them a scapegoat on a silver platter. Who wouldn't take advantage of that? But, being less cynical for a moment, it's certainly possible the head of the generation division had reasons for trying to keep this quiet. All I know is, the chief counsel said when she left Matthews' office, he was already making calls to see how soon the plant could be safely taken off-line."

"How about that."

"That's not all," Jenny said. "She offered to immediately establish an emergency fund for medical expenses that the plaintiffs could use while we negotiate the settlement amount."

And then Jenny got this sly grin as she continued: "I also extracted one more promise from her as a sign of good faith."

"What?"

"They have to buy Danece and Clyde Henderson's house from their landlord and then sign the deed over to the Hendersons, free and clear."

I laughed.

"Jenny Welker, I think you're dazzling, do you know that?"

"I've heard that before, yes."

She reached around and grabbed ahold of my butt, pressing our pelvises together as she kissed me again.

Then she pulled away a little and said, "I've been thinking a lot about the Praesidium, though."

"Yeah? Me too."

"You go first."

"I would," I said. "But this is not my gift."

Truly, my gifts were my girls. All three of them.

"It's still your life, though," she said. "And this family's life. I want to do what's best for everyone."

"I know you do. And I have to be honest—I'm still trying to come to terms with everything. I might spend the rest of my life doing that—and I'll thank you for not telling me just how long that life is, by the way. But without trying to dodge responsibility, this just isn't my call. The girls and I will be fine doing whatever you choose. They're young and I'm flexible. The fact is, you've been born with something incredible and it's up to you to decide what to do with it. Follow your conscience. I'll support you either way. You know I always do."

She looked up at me, searching my face to gauge whether I was committed to that line.

And I was.

"You're pretty dazzling, too, you know that?" she said.

She buried her face in my neck, and I just held her for a moment, savoring the feel of her breath on my skin.

"I just don't know," she said. "Part of me feels this . . . sense of obligation. I've been given this incredible ability, and I really should use it to help people. On the other hand, I see how dangerous it can be. Especially in someone like me who doesn't really know how to use it yet. Mr. DeGange has been teaching me some things, but . . . even if I meant to do the right thing, I might not. What if I actually make things worse?"

"You might not even know," I said. "It wouldn't be an easy life, that's for sure."

She exhaled forcefully, then declared, "If I did decide to do it, some things would change around the Praesidium, I can promise you that."

"I figured as much."

"The ends aren't going to always justify the means."

"Absolutely not."

"I guess we should just talk more later."

"Of course," I said. "Whatever you need. We'll figure it out together. Or not. This could be one of those things where there's no right answer."

I said that with all sincerity. Naturally, I wished there were some obvious choice to be made here. As much as anything, I had this child-like yearning to know how the story ended.

But the grown-up in me knew not all stories have neat endings.

Most, in fact, do not.

And it is a mark of maturity—or, perhaps, just an acquiescence to the complications of human existence—to be comfortable with that kind of ambiguity.

There was really only one thing I knew for certain: whatever happened, whether Jenny continued the Praesidium's work or not, we'd be okay as long as we had each other.

Isn't that what love really is?

She squeezed me one more time, then turned her attention back to the girls, who promptly began basking in the glow of their mother's affection.

And because a stay-at-home parent's work is seldom done, I went back to the dishes.

That's what I was still doing when the back gate opened, and Seb and Deb started walking across the path toward our deck.

Seb had a bandage around his head, the result of having fallen when the Praesidium had hit him with a tranquilizer dart. Deb was unmarked by the weekend's events. Her surrender had been a little more graceful.

They were otherwise on their way to a full recovery. It takes a lot to rattle a pair of old farmers.

"What are your parents doing here?" I asked.

"Surprise!" Jenny said. "They're taking the girls for the night."

"They are?"

She grinned at me.

"It's been too long," she said, arching an eyebrow.

I smiled back lasciviously.

"I dunno," I said. "I was sort of looking forward to the bomb shelter."

"We can cross that off the list some other time, I promise."

"Deal."

A few short, sweet minutes later, Seb and Deb had hustled the girls out of the house. And Jenny and I were treated to the rarest treasure parents of young children can be given:

We were actually alone in the house together.

Jenny pulled out her phone and tapped it a few times. I immediately recognized the first chords of the Nitty Gritty Dirt Band's magnificent acoustic rendition of "Bless the Broken Road."

"Will you dance with me?" Jenny asked, just shyly enough to be adorable about it.

"Always," I said. "And for the rest of my life."

We met in the middle of the room, our arms curling around each other, and let the music sweep us away.

ACKNOWLEDGMENTS

The author acknowledges that after reading this novel, some people might assume he has deep-seated issues with his wife, Melissa, that he felt the need to work out in prose.

He does not.

In fact, the author rather loves his wife, Melissa. And their children. More impressively, after an entire COVID lockdown, he *still likes them*. He appreciates their endless love and support. And therefore he thanks them for being the very core of his happy life.

The author also acknowledges he's got some wonderful editors, starting with Jessica Tribble Wells and Adrienne Procaccini, who did seamless work tag-teaming this novel, and Charlotte Herscher, who leaned into the developmental editing with her usual brilliance.

The author further acknowledges the rest of the team at Thomas & Mercer, including Brittany Russell, Sarah Shaw, Laura Barrett, Susan Stokes, Anna Laytham, Lindsey Bragg, and Gracie Doyle, all of whom work very hard to keep putting great books in readers' hands.

The author acknowledges Meagan Beattie, his "terrific PR gal." (That's in quotes because it's a private joke. The author would never actually refer to someone as a "PR gal," even if it's true that she's terrific.)

The author acknowledges his agent, Alice Martell, who is a force of nature, one not to be messed with under any circumstances, including book acknowledgments.

The author acknowledges David Kaiser, the Germeshausen professor of the history of science and physics at Massachusetts Institute of Technology, who first put the idea in the author's head that the laws of physics show no particular preference for the direction in which time travels.

The author acknowledges several magnanimous people (or their family members) who made donations to charities so that the author would use (or abuse) their names in these pages. Thanks to Robert "Buck" McBride, Greg and Kara Grichtmeier, and Kenneth L. Neathery Jr. for their generosity.

The author acknowledges that as a former stay-at-home parent himself, the full-time caregiving of children is one heck of a tough job. He salutes all those who take it on, whether in a private capacity or as professional day care providers.

The author acknowledges he drank too much Coke Zero during the writing, rewriting, and editing of this novel and even during the writing of these acknowledgments. He is aware he ought to cut back. He also admits he probably couldn't if he tried.

The author acknowledges the staff at Hardee's, where he wrote much of this novel (at least until the pandemic sent him packing). He looks forward to his return to the corner table someday.

The author acknowledges that in America the subject of global warming is a controversial one and that certain people may be currently pondering spiteful one-star reviews in which they accuse the author of injecting his politics into this narrative. The author would ask them to remember that recognizing the existence of global warming is *not* political. It is an observable fact that the planet is getting warmer. Saying what policy should (or shouldn't) be implemented is the political part, and the author has attempted to avoid promoting any particular opinion or viewpoint on that subject.

Also, this is just a story. So relax.

The author acknowledges he is fallible, particularly when it comes to the output of his big, fumbly fingers, and that while many conscientious editors have combed this manuscript thoroughly to ensure that no typos or grammatical errors remain, even they cannot protect the author from himself. As such, the author appreciates notes from his readers correcting his errors, so long as they're kind and understand he tried his best.

Also, the author just appreciates his readers in general. The author cherishes the opportunity to entertain them and hopes he will be able to continue doing so for many decades to come.

The author acknowledges the universe of book people who make being an author such a joy: booksellers, librarians, other authors, reviewers, bloggers, podcasters, journalists, and the like. He is thankful that they create an atmosphere in which words matter.

The author acknowledges that while these acknowledgments may have veered into the silly once or twice, that should not be taken as a sign he is insincere about them. He really is genuinely thankful to everyone acknowledged herein, and also to anyone he may have stupidly forgotten.

ABOUT THE AUTHOR

Photo © 2016 Sarah Harris

International bestselling author Brad Parks is the only writer to have won the Shamus, Nero, and Lefty Awards, three of American crime fiction's most prestigious prizes. His novels have been published in fifteen languages and have won critical acclaim across the globe, including stars from every major prepublication review outlet.

A graduate of Dartmouth College, Parks is a former journalist with the *Washington Post* and the *Star-Ledger* (Newark, New Jersey). He is now a full-time novelist living in Virginia with his wife and two school-age children. A former college a cappella singer and community theater enthusiast, Parks has been known to burst into song whenever no one was thoughtful enough to muzzle him. His favored writing haunt is a Hardee's, where good-natured staff members suffer his presence for many hours a day and where he can often be found working on his next novel.